The Loner's Heart

Anne Carrole

A Hearts of Wyoming Book

For more information on the author and her work, please visit http://www.annecarrole.com
Published by: Galley Press
Cover by: Rae Monet
Edited by: Dori Harrell (Breakout Editing)
Cover Copy created by: http://www.blurbcopy.com
Layout and formatting by www.formatting4U.com

Hearts of Wyoming series

Book 1: Loving a Cowboy
Book 2: The Maverick Meets His Match
Book 3: The Rancher's Heart
Book 4: The Loner's Heart

Acknowledgments

I'd like to thank my editor, Dori Harrell, for her patient assistance with this book and my sisters for their continued encouragement and for being horse crazy when we were young! A special thanks to my wonderful and generous readers, without whose support none of this would matter.

Chapter 1

Haylee Dennis dug her fingernails into the edge of the leather car seat as her aunt Paula drove the SUV through the large puddles left by that morning's soaking rain and down the long gravel drive of some stranger's ranch. With each lurch and bounce, the words *hire me* became a silent prayer.

"So where's the wife?" Haylee asked as outbuildings came into sight.

"As far as I know, he didn't marry the mother. He's never said a word about her either." Aunt Paula drove onto a patch of dry grass, shifted to park, and shut off the motor. "And I didn't ask. You let me do the talking. He's not the most approachable son of a gun, but deep down he's a good man. Just takes more digging to find it."

"I'll take your word for it." As long as he didn't lie, cover up, or manipulate. Those sins had recently risen to the top of her bad-guy list. "But how do you know he'll be here?"

"Men have to eat lunch. If we are going to catch him, it would be now."

Aunt Paula, dressed in her uniform of denim and chambray, hopped out of the car in one quick movement. For an older heavyset woman, she was pretty nimble.

Haylee emerged from the passenger side, her digital single-lens reflex camera hanging from the strap around her neck. She crinkled her nose at the smell of manure salting the freshly washed air. It was a ranch, after all, she reminded herself.

She noted the small white-framed house with a swing set in the side yard, the weathered barn before them, the beat-up truck parked haphazardly nearby. And the acres of grassed plains that rolled beyond to the gray shadows of distant mountains stretching to touch the thin clouds that striped the blue sky. This, not Denver, was what western living was all about.

Though the grounds looked well tended with neat fence lines and a decent layer of gravel marking the drive, none of it looked particularly prosperous.

Well, that could also mean he wasn't doing anything he shouldn't be doing. A thought that, until recently, would have never crossed her mind.

This was a real working ranch stripped of romanticism.

She snapped a few pictures, careful to get the framing right and to adjust for the bright sunlight heating the air. Stepping beside her aunt, Haylee's white sandals slipped on the muddied footpath.

"There he is." Aunt Paula pointed to a shirtless figure with his back to them in the shadow of the barn.

A tall, slender male with broad shoulders and muscled arms was dousing water on a beautiful chestnut-colored horse with a black tail and mane. He paid particular attention to the horse's legs before reaching for the faucet to stem the flow of water.

Laying down the hose, he picked up the black Stetson sitting on the fence post, angled it on his head, and turned around. Haylee's mouth went dry as the bare-chested cowboy emerged from the shadows, with dirt-spattered jeans that hugged lean thighs, boots caked with mud, and a muscled chest that he'd clearly gotten from honest work instead of a gym membership.

Lordy. This was her aunt's neighbor? The man who was supposed to hire her? The man she'd be working for? She brushed her sweaty palms down the front of her white capris.

His face, partially shadowed by the brim of his hat, was all lines and angles and handsome enough that he could have starred in an Old West movie. All that was missing was a gun at his side…at least she hoped it was missing, considering the way he was frowning. A barking border collie followed the rancher, apparently eager to round up the intruders. But one word from the man and the barking stopped. Focused on their unexpected company, bare-chested cowboy and excited dog continued toward them without breaking stride.

Haylee was sorely tempted to raise her camera and start snapping, but her future depended on making a good impression, and she was well aware that some people didn't like to have their pictures taken.

Aunt Paula waved her fleshy arm, as if he hadn't already spotted them. He pushed up the brim of his hat, and even from a distance, she could see the frown deepen on a weathered face that sported a strong jawline, slightly long nose, and narrowed eyes.

Her aunt had failed to mention that her neighbor was smoking hot.

Not that it should matter. The shock of the last few months would take a long time to wear off. And the irony was, her ex-husband hadn't cheated on her, nor was another woman involved—things that usually led to the dissolution of a marriage.

"Bet you're surprised to see me," Aunt Paula said.

In unison the man and dog stopped a few feet from Aunt Paula. The dog promptly sat down, as if he'd been given some silent signal. The hot cowboy nodded his greeting. "Mrs. Johnson." His gaze strayed to Haylee. It was direct and unsparing, as if he was sizing her up…and found her lacking.

At five foot two she was used to being overlooked and underestimated.

"This is my niece, Haylee Dennis."

Haylee's throat constricted at the sound of her maiden name. She had taken her marriage vows seriously…until she couldn't. The man she'd said those vows to was not the same man she'd divorced.

"Ma'am." The cowboy touched the brim of his hat, drawing her attention away from his chest (had she been gawking?) to a pair of intense hazel eyes flecked with gold. For some reason hazel was not an eye color she associated with a man who looked like he'd stepped out of the pages of *American Cowboy*. His eyes should have been a deep brown to go with the thick dark hair that escaped the band of his hat when he pushed it up. Or gray to go with his cool demeanor.

"We are hoping Haylee will live at our house until we sell the place, while we head out to New Mexico. There's a house come up for rent down there in a community where we have friends, and we want to grab it."

"You're selling?"

Aunt Paula had placed her house and five acres of land on the market three months ago. That it hadn't sold was likely due, in Haylee's humble opinion, to the small size of the two-bedroom cabin, the large barn in need of repair, and the homestead's remote location. A location that suited her needs at the moment.

Aunt Paula placed her hands on her hips. "I told you we were selling months ago."

His eyebrows arched, as if he couldn't quite reconcile that statement. "Sorry to see you go."

"Mr. J just can't take another Wyoming winter, what with his arthritis. It's acting up even now. Haylee needs a place to stay. We need to move." Aunt Paula glanced Haylee's way.

Haylee had been working to rebuild her freelance freight-auditing business, but with only one client, and that client brand new, she needed some sort of steady income. Though she was staying with her aunt rent-free, she still needed utilities, gas, food, and general necessities. Her personal savings was small, and she hadn't asked for anything from her ex-husband, which neither her family nor friends could understand. But how could she take Roy's money and still look herself in the mirror?

"Hope you know what you're in for." His drawl came over as more of a growl, like the dog sitting patiently at his side had spoken for him. "Winters are pretty brutal."

"I've spent several years in Denver already." And she was originally from Chicago, where winters weren't exactly mild.

"Uh-huh," he said and shifted his gaze back to her aunt.

Haylee's stomach dipped. This wasn't going to work. Haylee would only have two options: move in with her friend in Cheyenne, though she was likely allergic to Jenna's cat, or move back to her parents' home in Chicago, the thought of which caused an ache in the pit of her stomach.

"Mr. J has her all fixed up. Had the generator repaired. She'll be fine." Aunt Paula positively beamed. "And we are hoping the place will sell long before winter."

"What can I help you ladies with today?" He nodded toward Haylee. "That camera around your neck for something?"

"Just a hobby. I'm taking pictures of Aunt Paula's place and the surrounding area to put in an album for her." Haylee knew how quickly things could change, and she thought her aunt would appreciate a memory book of the way things had been when she lived on Cottonwood Road.

"Is Delanie here?" Aunt Paula looked around as if the child would pop out of thin air.

"She's at school."

"Summer's coming though. Have you thought about what you're going to do now that her sitter, Camille, is gone?"

"Her preschool has a camp program. It's a half-hour drive but…" His voice trailed off.

"We'll, that's why we're here."

He didn't say anything, just stared at Paula, with an expression of someone waiting for the dentist to pull his bad tooth.

"Haylee is looking for part-time work. Thought she'd be able to care for Delanie after school, like

Camille did. She's developing her own business. Something on the internet, but right now she's looking to pick up some extra money until it gets off the ground. And she'd be right down the road."

The gaze he swung to Haylee froze her in place, as if a blast of arctic air had enveloped her. She heard her heartbeat in her ears as she waited for his response. First one beat, then another…and another.

He crossed his arms over his bare chest. "Her preschool is working out fine."

The balloon of hope she'd filled with her aunt's optimism, and which had been slowly leaking air since she'd arrived at the Martin ranch, popped.

What was that western saying? No sense beating a dead horse.

"That's great that she enjoys school. It was very nice meeting you." Haylee turned on her heel to leave, but her foot stuck in the mud, and she wobbled. Before she knew it, her butt met the damp hard surface of the ground. Mud splattered on her white capri pants, her navy top, her hair, her bare legs and arms, and the camera. Startled from her fall, she sat there in a puddle of mud.

Her aunt's laughter filled the air as Haylee felt a wet tongue on her cheek and looked into a pair of dark sympathetic doggie eyes. A chuckle bubbled in her throat looking for an escape route. Life had been so hard lately that being covered in mud seemed as good a reason as any to let go. So she sat, petted the soft coat of her new fur friend, and let laughter consume her. So much for making a good impression.

But her laughter ceased when strong hands reached under her arms and suddenly she was lifted up and onto her mud-covered feet as if she was nothing more than a bag of feathers. She turned to face her gallant knight.

Trace's grin was broad, and his hazel eyes sparkled in the sun's golden light, as if he was actually seeing her, Haylee Dennis, instead of some generic version of irritation. His features, seemingly carved from rock a minute ago, had softened with his smile. An unwelcome twinge occurred near her heart.

"You okay?" he asked, his grin still wide.

"Fine. My ego is a little bruised though."

His mouth crooked up, and for that split second, Haylee felt a connection has he held her gaze.

Her aunt bustled over. "You know that drive to and from camp is killing you. Haylee could help there. And who watches Delanie when you get back? Taking her out in the pastures with you may be all right in June, but not when you have to harvest hay or move the herd." Apparently Aunt Paula was not going to let a positive moment go to waste.

He broke the connection, turned his attention from Haylee to her aunt. "Delanie enjoys spending time around the ranch."

"So you can't use any help, Trace Martin?" Aunt Paula demanded.

He shifted his weight from one foot to another. His serious countenance had returned, but he didn't utter an answer.

"Thank you for your time," Haylee cut in. Any more and her aunt would sound like she was begging.

"Sorry." His look was sympathetic.

Haylee didn't need sympathy—she needed a job. One with enough flexibility to allow her to build her client list, and this had seemed perfect. Considering how much Haylee loved children, if she could get paid to chauffeur Delanie to and from school and watch the child for the few hours after camp, it would have been ideal. Haylee would have most of the morning and afternoon to work on developing her business, and Trace would have someone to watch his daughter when he was still busy with the ranch. Alas, it was not to be.

Even though he didn't know her, it was clear he didn't like something about her and wasn't interested enough to find out more.

While Aunt Paula said goodbye, Haylee patted the head of the dog. At least he seemed to like her. Nothing more to say, she turned, this time with more care, and headed for her aunt's SUV, brushing what dirt she could off her body and clothes.

"We just need to work on him, is all," Aunt Paula said as she put the SUV in gear and headed back down the gravel drive. "Men like him take a little time to get used to an idea."

"I think his no was pretty final. Men like him also don't change their minds." The mud that remained was beginning to dry on her skin, making her feel even more uncomfortable, if that was possible. "You understand, Aunt, that I don't have a choice. I have to go where I can find work, as much as it pains me."

"Roy seemed like a decent guy. I can't believe he left you with nothing or that the courts wouldn't make him give you something. What kind of lawyer did you have?"

Her aunt didn't know how mistaken she was about Roy. "I didn't ask for anything. We were only married two years." And she hoped that period would be just a footnote in her life and never become the headline.

"What can we do?"

"Jenna is taking me to a rodeo tomorrow. I'll see if taking my allergy pills makes any difference with her cat. If I can handle it, I'll ask her if I can move in with her in Cheyenne, and then I can periodically check on your place." She'd try anything if it meant she didn't have to move back in with her parents in Chicago, but having her allergies not kick up would be a miracle. And though Jenna would help her without question, moving in with Jenna without paying her full share of rent would be a difficult pill to swallow. At least with her aunt, Haylee would have been taking care of the place in lieu of rent.

But Aunt Paula shook her head. "I just wouldn't feel comfortable leaving our place unattended with so much of our stuff still there. The agent said furnished places sell better, and we need any edge we can get. We just won't go to New Mexico, is all. I'll call first thing on Monday and tell them that we can't rent the place."

Failure never got easier.

Trace watched from the classroom doorway as his daughter, Delanie, lifted her small pink backpack out of a blue cubby against the far wall, decorated with lots of indecipherable kids' paintings and scrawls. The smell of disinfectant permeated the air as two teachers wiped down the tables. Other mothers, and a few probable grandmothers, were retrieving their kids. The women slipped by him, the only male, with a furtive glance and no acknowledgment. He preferred it that way.

What had Paula Johnson been thinking, showing up like that? The last time someone had surprised him, it had been Delanie's mother on his doorstep with a four-year-old child with his eyes and hair color, declaring he had to parent the child, or she'd be sent to foster care. He'd taken one look at the tyke, who'd seemed as scared as he'd felt, and his stone-cold heart had melted.

And today, right before Paula's surprise visit, he'd learned he could be facing a custody battle, when he thought everything had been settled. Life sure threw curve balls, and today he'd been pitched a humdinger. Surely, though, he had right on his side.

"Are we going riding when we get home?" Delanie looked up at him, her hazel eyes brimming with excitement.

Good thing his daughter had taken to ranch life like a pig to mud. Delanie was thriving on the ranch, and he was pretty sure that was the sole reason she tolerated his presence. He'd gotten Moose, a sweet, energetic border collie, largely for her, although the dog had turned out to be a first-class herder. He'd also bought a T-ball set, a swing set, and recently, a two-wheeler bike with training wheels. So far, she wasn't a natural at riding it, but didn't all kids learn eventually?

"Have to see about the herd when we get back." The morning storm meant he hadn't had time to complete his check on damaged fencing or riled-up cattle.

Trace glanced at his phone. No calls from Corey, the kid he'd hired on for the summer. That was a good sign.

"Can't we ride Buck?" Buck, the calm older horse he'd recently added to his remuda, was destined to be Delanie's in the near future.

"Not this time. Too difficult for the horse in this

mud. Probably take the pickup." He plucked the backpack from her outstretched hand and tried to ignore her pout. "You have fun today?"

She shrugged. "It was okay. Melinda cried a lot."

Apparently Melinda was prone to crying.

"Sometimes people just feel sad, Delanie." He'd learned that the hard way. The less people knew what you were feeling, the less power they had over you. But he guessed it was different when you were five years old. Because then, presumably, people would be there to help you. Presumably.

"No. She just wants attention."

That too. "Let's give her the benefit of the doubt."

"What's that mean?"

"Let's assume she had a reason to cry that was heartfelt."

"She didn't."

"You cry." Like every time her mother called.

"That's different."

Now his baby looked mad. He'd said the wrong thing. Sometimes raising Delanie was like walking on eggshells. Not that he would trade a minute of it. But it was hard. Especially for someone like him.

"Let's go. Daylight's a wastin'." A change of subject and scenery might save him.

She moved through the hallway and out the door on fast feet.

There might be something to having someone help with Delanie again. Camille, the former housekeeper, had been an older, grandmotherly type who had the right combination of concern and discipline, and Delanie had liked her. During calving season, Camille had cared for Delanie so he didn't have to take the child in all sorts of weather to see things that were bound to cause a lot of questions. When the woman had said she couldn't work for him because her drive out to his ranch was too long during bad weather, it had been tough…tough on Delanie. Loss was something the child felt deeply. Considering her circumstances, that was understandable.

And that was why he hadn't entertained the prospect of a woman looking for a short-term assignment. And the fact Haylee Dennis seemed around his age, had crazy curly blond hair, big blue eyes, and nice curves in a cute little package didn't help matters. The last thing he needed was to be distracted by a woman who wore white pants and sandals to a cattle ranch. Having someone as pretty as Haylee Dennis around would be real torture for a man who had been living like a monk for the last year—real torture.

He threw the backpack into the backseat of the truck, settled Delanie into her car seat, set the sippy cup of water he'd brought with him into the cup holder, and closed the rear truck door. Climbing into the driver's seat, he adjusted his sunglasses and started the engine. It roared to life despite being over ten years old. Paid to be handy with engines.

He drove onto the highway and dialed up some country music, placing the volume on low. If things went according to plan, Delanie would be snoozing on the half-hour trip back and ready to head out after he gave her a snack at home.

Life had finally settled into a routine, though he had to admit, it would be nice if he didn't have to pick her up every day. The hour-plus round trip put a serious dent in his time running the ranch, and the ranch wasn't on the firmest footing.

Still, he didn't even know if Haylee Dennis had experience with kids. The fact Moose had liked her didn't count. The fact he had liked her, especially after she'd fallen in the mud and laughed it off, counted more against her than for her. And what was she doing way out here when she was clearly a city girl, from her open-toed sandals to her pale skin?

Something didn't add up.

He checked his rearview mirror. Delanie's head had rolled to one side, her eyes closed. Yup, they had settled into a routine, and he didn't need anyone to fiddle with it. Even if the woman seemed desperate for the job. Especially if the woman seemed desperate for the job.

He spent the half-hour ride contemplating the list of things he still needed to complete before he could call it a day. As he drove down the potholed gravel driveway, a look in his rearview mirror revealed Delanie was stirring. He was happy not to have to wake her out of a deep sleep. Some milk with pudding left over from last night's dessert would make for a quick snack.

As he got closer to the house, the sight of Corey sitting on top of one of Trace's horses, waiting for him, started his stomach churning. That only meant one thing…and it wasn't good.

An hour later he was mending the gate a bull had butted off its hinges during the storm. Delanie groaned from the seat of the pickup about how hungry she was.

He was fooling himself about having a routine. He was a rancher. There was no routine.

Chapter 2

Haylee knocked on the door of her friend's apartment located on the outskirts of Cheyenne and listened for footsteps. Jenna Thompson's apartment was on the second floor of the two-story building and accessible through an open stairway without much to block it from Wyoming's winter cold and wind. Right then the dry summer breeze felt good, and Haylee had full view of the busy two-lane street that bordered the front of the building. It was a better situation than the crowded skyscrapers and noise of Chicago or Denver, but definitely not as picturesque as her aunt's cozy cabin nestled among the cottonwoods.

The door opened, and Jenna stood there holding a tabby-colored cat. With long black hair, a tanned complexion, and a willowy body clothed in a jean skirt, cowgirl boots, and a sleeveless blouse, Jenna, who hailed from Wyoming, looked every bit the cowgirl Haylee wasn't.

The cat took one look at Haylee and hissed.

Not a good start.

"Mimi, be good," Jenna cooed to the cat that looked like she was interested in anything but being good. Jenna waved Haylee in. "She just gets stressed when she first encounters people. Best to give her some time to get to know you before you pet her. She's got trust issues."

Haylee could relate. She stepped into the apartment and looked around. She hadn't been in Jenna's new apartment nor met the newest addition, Mimi, but she recognized several pieces of cottage-type furniture that Jenna had in their old college apartment in Denver. A television was planted on the painted-white bookcase on the near wall that still housed accounting textbooks. Across on the far wall was a familiar red sofa, Jenna's favorite color, with various shapes of white pillows resting on it. The floors were builder-beige wall-to-wall carpet, and the walls were painted off-white. The room housed both the living area, small kitchenette to the left side, and dining table separating the two. It looked large enough for two people to share.

"I remember these." Haylee pointed to two white painted stools that had their legs shortened and were covered by a white board to serve as a coffee table.

"I'm the queen of repurposing." Jenna set Mimi down, and the cat ran toward the hallway that Haylee guessed led toward the bedrooms.

At least if the cat was not in the same room, Haylee's allergy medicine might have a fighting chance. Hopefully, it was just her imagination, but her eyes felt itchy.

"Want some coffee before we head out to the rodeo?"

Haylee nodded. "And to use your bathroom. It was a bit of a haul from my aunt's."

Jenna pointed down the hall. "First door to your left. The room across from it is the spare room."

Haylee scurried to the bathroom and, when she was finished using it, glanced into the spare room. It was a decent size with a full bed and more of the painted furniture Jenna favored. The rose-covered quilt on the bed and fake roses in a small vase on the nightstand that looked like it had once been a magazine rack in another life, gave the room a decidedly feminine charm.

She rubbed her eyes. The cat probably claimed this as its room, by the way Haylee was tearing up. She feared the option of moving in with Jenna was going to be sneezed right off the table.

She found Jenna in the kitchen area of the open room, pouring coffee into ceramic cups. The kitchen side had a large window where light streamed in, making it bright and airy despite the dark cabinets and granite counters. "We'll have our coffee in the living room. Are you hungry? I've got some donuts left over from work yesterday."

Haylee shook her head, grabbed her cup of black coffee, and followed Jenna into the living area. The couch was as comfortable as Haylee remembered, and she sank back against the pillows. "So tell me about the rodeo."

Jenna had convinced Haylee to go to the rodeo with a free ticket, since Jenna's boyfriend had bowed out a few days ago. With its crop of real cowboys, Haylee thought the rodeo would provide good photography material, not that she would do anything with it. Photography was a hobby, a passionate hobby that would remain just a hobby since it didn't pay the bills.

"Not much to tell. There's pretty much a rodeo somewhere in Wyoming every weekend in the summer. You'll see."

Haylee sighed. "I don't think Wyoming is going to work out."

"Why not? You've got a rent-free place."

"Turns out my aunt's neighbor doesn't think he needs help with his daughter. She's going to a preschool."

"And the cowboy can't be persuaded?"

Haylee shook her head. "Not to mention that I fell in the mud, flat on my butt, in front of him. Not the best first impression." But he had picked her up and set her to rights. She could still feel the strength of his hands under her arms.

"Were you wearing those?" Jenna nodded toward Haylee's flip-flops.

She'd dressed in shorts and a T-shirt, and flip-flops had seemed the comfortable option.

"White sandals. Just as bad."

"Isn't the audit thing working out?"

"Takes time. The market has changed in two years. My old clients moved on." But time was something she didn't have. If she was going to stay at her aunt's, she needed to earn money immediately.

"It's been tough since the divorce, huh?"

She still felt the bruises in her heart. "It doesn't feel good to have failed at marriage." It felt rock-bottom bad, especially given the reasons. How could she have been so wrong about Roy's character? The question still haunted her. Because if she was wrong about him, how could she trust her judgment about anyone?

Jenna raised the cup of coffee to her lips, and her eyebrows arched as she looked over the rim at Haylee. "Failed is a strong word. More like a mistake. You made a mistake. He wasn't the man you thought he was. It happens."

Haylee hadn't confided the details of her reason for breaking up with Roy, other than to say she'd found out some things that made her realize they did not share the same values…and never would. Jenna hadn't asked for the particulars, and Haylee hadn't revealed any.

"But why didn't I see it?" The black coffee tasted strong and flavorful, just the way she liked it. Too bad her nose was too clogged to smell its fragrance.

"Do you want me to be sympathetic or honest?"

"Honest, of course." Haylee braced herself. Honesty might prove brutal, but she was all about the truth these days.

"You were playing it safe with Roy. He was older, mature, settled."

And he had checked all the boxes. Responsible, hardworking, smart, and, yes, financially secure. Too bad at the time she hadn't thought to add "had integrity".

"I thought I loved him."

"Honestly I always thought he was more smitten with you than you were with him. It seemed once he'd declared himself, you tried too hard to fit into his world."

Because once you're chosen, someone can always un-choose you if you don't try hard enough. Which, ironically, was exactly what Roy did when she gave him an ultimatum.

"Maybe."

"I think a lot of it goes back to…you know."

Haylee took a deep breath. "Being adopted?" It wasn't a subject she talked about much.

"And your parents having Livvy."

After giving up trying to get pregnant, her parents

had adopted her as a baby, and then three years later had been blessed with the birth of their own flesh-and-blood daughter.

"They never treated me any different."

But once Haylee had grown into adolescence and realized what being adopted meant, she had *felt* different. Had felt she had to be perfect, had to be good, or she would get sent back. Only she didn't know where back was, her birth mother having died a few years after Haylee was born, and she had no clue about her biological father, which actually made the prospect of disappointing her parents scarier.

Jenna set down her coffee cup and stared at Haylee with an unsparing eye. "You do look for stability and security in a man. You've never liked risks or surprises or drama."

And look what she got.

"You make me sound as if I was in love with boring." Haylee's throat felt tight as she swallowed a gulp of coffee. Guess the allergy medicine wasn't working.

"For reasons only you know, you seemed to gravitate to boring. Look who you picked as your best friend in college." Jenna chuckled. "I'm about as boring as they come."

"That's not why we became best friends, but after the drama with my roommate freshman year, I was grateful to room with someone who wasn't a bundle of emotional angst." Her freshman roommate had always been in tears about something, whether it was her boyfriend forgetting her coffee or a professor making a negative remark on a paper or Haylee not spending enough time with her.

"So maybe, like you chose me for your roommate, you should do the choosing next time rather than wait to be chosen. And maybe you should apply that to your work as well. Maybe look at doing something else, something you really love instead of settling for the familiar."

There was no doubt Haylee should spend some time doing an autopsy on what went wrong with her marriage and analyze the choices she'd made, but it wasn't going to be today. This was likely her last weekend in Wyoming, and she was determined to enjoy herself.

"Can we peel back the onion on my choices in men and work another day? My eyes are itching, and my throat is closing."

"Your allergy medicine isn't working?"

Haylee shook her head. "Not yet anyway."

Just then Mimi sauntered into the room with her tail held high and made a beeline for Haylee. Before Haylee could react, Mimi was brushing her furry body against Haylee's bare leg. Haylee stifled a sneeze. "I'm ready to head out to the rodeo." It might be her last and only chance to experience one.

* * *

The phone rang, and the acid in Trace's stomach rose to his throat, as it did every Saturday morning around this time. He took a deep breath as Delanie dashed into the kitchen as if cued.

The look of excited anticipation in her eyes grabbed him like the jaws of a crocodile—and just as painful.

"It's Mommy," she squealed, jumping up and down like an animated exclamation point.

Yeah, he knew. He fished his cell phone out of his jeans pocket, swiped the screen without looking at the caller ID, and held it to his ear. "Hello, Doreen."

"Delanie there?"

The raspy female voice had become all too familiar. And yeah, he didn't want to speak to her either. Not after the underhanded way she'd handled the custody issue. No heads-up. No by-the-way. Just a surprise court document to let him know that she'd turned his world upside down again.

Trace held the phone out to Delanie, whose unbridled eagerness to speak to the woman who didn't deserve the child ate at his soul. He pulled out a chair from the kitchen table and settled down to listen to the one-way conversation, alert for any clues about what Doreen or Delanie might be thinking.

The custody evaluator appointed by the court had been interviewing everyone Trace knew, from his brother and sister-in-law, Ty and Mandy, to the child psychologist who had worked with Delanie, to Delanie's preschool teachers. He'd also had to pay for the services of a special court psychologist to provide her input to the court evaluator, all of which his lawyer had informed him was standard in custody cases. And now there would be more rigmarole because Delanie's mother had decided, without a word to him, she wanted visitation rights.

And yet almost a year ago she'd begged him to take Delanie, not that it had required much begging. He hoped the custody evaluator wouldn't be swayed by the mere fact that Doreen was Delanie's mother. He might have some baggage, but Doreen had a friggin' truckload.

"Yes, Mommy," Delanie said as she slowly paced back and forth in front of the kitchen counter, like a miniature guard on duty. "I still like school.

"I have a new friend. She lives far away. Her name is Lauren."

Why hadn't he known that?

"Daddy has been fine."

He resented that her mother had to ask about him every time she called. He wasn't the one who had neglected his child. Well, at least since he first learned he had a child. If he had known earlier, he would have been involved from the start.

"Have you learned your lesson yet?" Delanie asked in the voice of a guileless child.

His insides burned like he swallowed lye soap.

"I want you to come home, Mommy. I *need* you to come home," Delanie pleaded as tears trickled down her face. "Don't go, Mommy. Please…"

Delanie's full-throttled cry meant the line had gone dead. She slammed his phone into his hand and ran out of the room.

Trace followed, stood at the entrance to her small bedroom, and watched as she laid on her twin bed with the princess coverlet she'd begged him to buy, her face buried into her pillow, sobs filling the air. Another's cries clawed at layers of memories, trying to surface. Trace maintained his focus on the child before him in hopes of keeping those memories where they belonged…buried.

"Delanie." He called her name using his softest voice. "Are you okay?"

Her face still buried into the pillow, she shook her little head.

"Can I do anything?" He knew the answer, but he had to ask. Every time he had to ask.

"I want my mommy," she mumbled into the pillow. "I don't want you. I want my mommy."

And there it was. The knife that hollowed out his heart and made his insides raw.

"Did you forget we're going to the rodeo today?" He'd learned to plan something for Saturdays.

Her sobs had become gasps for air. "Will we see Aunt Mandy?"

"Yup. And Uncle Ty."

Delanie raised her head. "I forgot." She sniffled. "Will Uncle Tuck be there?"

"I imagine so." His sister-in-law's stock company was putting on the rodeo, but whether her brother would be in the lineup wasn't a sure thing."

Her small hand wiped her tear-stained cheek. "I can wear my cowgirl boots."

* * *

As they stood at a vendor booth at the local rodeo on the beautiful early June day, Haylee plopped a putty-colored felt hat with gold beads studding its black band onto her head. "What about this one?"

Haylee was astonished at the mass of people at the local rodeo. From the jammed parking lot that was really just a field, to the bustling walkway that encircled the cinder-block outdoor arena, there were people everywhere, mostly wearing cowboy hats or baseball caps with heavy equipment logos. Women sported shorts and boots, the men in jeans despite the warmer weather. The grilling scents of burgers and hot dogs from the nearby food tent wafted through the air. She was definitely in cowboy country.

Jenna stared at Haylee, crooked her mouth into a thoughtful pose, and nodded. "That looks authentic enough."

Haylee laughed. "And not like I'm trying too hard?"

"You should look the part, at least."

"Right now I can't afford anything extra, much less a cowgirl hat I'm never going to wear again." She set the hat back on the table, hesitating just a second to imagine wearing it. Haylee had lathered on the suntan lotion, and a sun hat dangled from the back of her neck. She'd have to forgo looking the part considering the cost of the cowgirl version. "I don't know what I am going to do." But she feared she knew exactly what she would have to do.

"Move in with me."

"And your cat? I'll be miserable sneezing myself to oblivion." Not to mention the itchy eyes, constricted throat, and stuffed nose she'd experienced despite her allergy pill. "As sweet as it is for you to offer, it's clear I'll have to go back to Chicago and live with my parents."

And admit she'd failed…a word that was anathema at her house. To the Dennis family, people who failed just hadn't worked hard enough. Of course, when her father had spectacularly failed, it was due to other people, no matter that the family finances had been sent into a tailspin her parents had yet to fully recover from. Clearly Hugh and Elle Dennis had one set of standards for others and another for themselves, but you couldn't tell them that.

Her mother and father would welcome her home. Mom would be sure Haylee's room was in good order, she'd serve Haylee's favorite foods, and her father would get up every morning to make her breakfast before she started whatever job she could find. And of course, she'd have to listen to her sister Livvy's lectures on healthy eating every time she took a bite of food. At the age of twenty-six, going home a divorced woman, divorced from a man her father had pronounced "perfect" for her, was not an enticing prospect.

Jenna sighed. "And the cowboy has the only job near your aunt?"

"My aunt's place is so far out I'd have to drive close to an hour round trip to find anything decent…even a crossing guard position. And that kind of drive would just eat away at the time I need to build my client base." Haylee absently picked up a leather belt. It was finely tooled with a large silver buckle and would look great with a pair of jeans. She set it back on the table. "It was too perfect to be true. I mean, I don't need to earn a lot, just enough to buy food until I can get some money flowing from paid clients. Unfortunately, clients tend to want you to do the work *before* they pay you for it."

"Yeah, they are peculiar like that." Jenna smiled. "There's some cheaper tourist-type hats over there." She pointed to a table where the merchandise was scattered haphazardly.

"I doubt I can afford them either. I'll just have to keep with what I have."

* * *

"But I have to go. Now." Trace's daughter peered up at him with rounded eyes and lips pursed in a familiar pout.

People jostled past them as they stopped in the middle of the Saturday crowd swarming the vendor tables and food tent before the start of the regional rodeo on a picture-perfect, if hot, day. Looked like it had drawn the usual crop of local wranglers, ranchers, and a few urban cowboys from nearby Cheyenne. These days he was drawn more to rodeos that included Ferris wheels and merry-go-rounds to amuse his daughter, but seeing her aunt and uncle would have to suffice for this one.

"Can't you wait until I find Aunt Mandy?" This was the moment he always dreaded when out with his daughter. The bathroom moment.

At her young age, he didn't feel comfortable letting her in the public restroom alone. He'd tried once to take her into the men's room with him when the urinals weren't occupied, but his luck hadn't held when they'd exited the stall. Angry looks from the two men were one thing—answering his daughter's questions about standing up when urinating was a totally different thing.

So he was usually left with tagging some young mother and asking her if she would look after his child. And since asking for help had never come easy, it was always a grin-and-bear-it moment.

Delanie shook her head, her hands on small hips.

"I really have to go."

Trace looked around for someone to ask. His gaze snagged on curly blond hair at a five-and-dime vendor table. What were the chances?

Today she wore shorts, a stretchy tank top that revealed more than it concealed, a flimsy hat dangling off the back of her neck, and flip-flops, of all things, on her feet. Her camera hung from a strap between her two fine breasts.

Hadn't she learned her lesson about wearing sandals? Looked like she was planning to top off her outfit with a touristy cowgirl hat that wouldn't be worth anything in Wyoming weather.

Tapping her to take Delanie to the ladies' room seemed a ballsy move considering he'd told her he wouldn't hire her to look after his daughter. But after yesterday when he'd had to put the ranch's needs above Delanie's, he been reconsidering that stance. Maybe this was a sign.

He felt the tug on his jeans and looked down.

"I really have to go, Daddy. Take me in with you."

Grabbing Delanie's hand, he hurried toward the vendor's stall, wondering how he was going to broach the subject, when Haylee turned.

Her arched eyebrows and open mouth affirmed she had spotted him. She set the cheap hat back on the vendor's table and pasted a smile on her face as he wove between the crowd, careful that Delanie would not get bumped.

"Ma'am," he said when he stood in front of her. "Didn't expect to find you here." Maybe that wasn't the best thing to lead with, but the way Delanie was dancing around, he didn't have time to consider.

"Trace Martin." She said his name with similar surprise. Her gaze immediately shifted to Delanie. "And this must be your daughter. Hi, Delanie. I'm Haylee, and this is my friend Jenna."

Delanie buried her neck in her shoulders.

"Pleased to meet you, Jenna." He tipped the brim of his hat with his fingers. "Miss Haylee," he said, addressing his daughter but nodding in Haylee's direction, "is Mrs. Johnson's niece."

"I have to go to the bathroom," Delanie announced.

Trace felt the heat rise up from his neck collar as Haylee looked to him for answers.

Nothing to do but ask. "I'd be much obliged if you could take her. I don't feel comfortable taking her into the men's room, and she's too young to go by herself."

Her blue eyes widened, but she nodded. "I'd be happy to take her." She looked around. "I just don't remember where I saw a restroom."

"The arena ladies' room was back there, near the food tent." Jenna pointed to where they had just been. "I'll come with you."

Haylee reached out, and Delanie tucked her small hand trustingly in Haylee's. "Where will we meet you?"

"I'll be waiting right here. And thanks." He'd averted another crisis, and that was all that mattered, right?

The bathroom was where Jenna had said, and Delanie was an independent little girl and able to take care of herself, though Haylee recited her own mother's standard warning not to touch anything, the bathroom being an all-too-typical example of a crowded venue's standard on cleanliness. While Delanie was in the stall, Haylee whispered Trace's identity as Aunt Paula's neighbor to Jenna.

"One word. Hot," Jenna said. "And it took some guts on his part to ask you."

Before Haylee could comment, Delanie exited the stall, and Haylee supervised hand washing. Everything taken care of, they were soon walking back through the crowd to meet up with Delanie's father.

"This is my first rodeo. Is this your first one, Delanie?" Haylee asked, trying to make conversation.

Delanie shook her head. "No. I've been to lots. My aunt Mandy and uncle Ty own rodeos."

Haylee frowned. "Do they now?" She'd never heard of owning a rodeo, but maybe that was how it worked.

"They have lots of horses and bulls. But you can't ride them unless you are a special rider. My uncle Tucker—he's not really my uncle, but that's what I'm supposed to call him—he rides horses. He's riding today. And Shane's daddy is riding too."

Whoever Shane was.

"Well, it seems rodeo is a family affair. Does your daddy ride?" That would definitely be worth the price of admission.

"He rides horses at the ranch. Not in the rodeo. I don't want him to. You can get a boo-boo in the rodeo. Aunt Mandy is always worried Uncle Tuck is going to get hurt."

"Well, I imagine that happens. And I guess it's a good thing your daddy doesn't rodeo."

Delanie nodded. "I can't afford to lose anyone else."

Had her mother died? Aunt Paula said she didn't know much about the mother, only that Trace wasn't married to her. Surely she would have mentioned if the woman had died.

Trace came into sight. He was leaning up against the hat stall's post, and not for the first time, her pulse ticked up. It was just physical chemistry, she reminded herself. Nothing more.

His facial expression relaxed as he spotted them.

It was hard to raise a child alone. So why was he reluctant to hire help? Or, more specifically, her?

Trace watched as his daughter walked toward him, hand in hand with Paula Johnson's curly-headed niece. They wove seamlessly through the crowd of weekend cowboys and cowgirls. Trace hated the mob of people who came out on a weekend to get their "western" on. Made him feel like a penned bull longing for pasture. Looked like Delanie was comfortable with the woman. But he'd have to see more, a lot more, before he'd consider hiring her. Was he considering hiring her?

Or was he just considering her?

There was no denying Haylee was a pretty woman, albeit in an unconventional way. Though small, a lot of shapely leg was showing out of those jean shorts. She had a body like those gymnasts he'd seen on TV in the Olympics—petite but with long legs. Except Haylee had a nice pair of breasts pushing out her top. Yup, she might be tiny, but she had curves in all the right places. Not that it mattered. Much.

He was in her debt. Especially after he'd turned her down for a job and probably alienated his only neighbor, a good woman, in the process. Least he could do was offer up a bite to eat.

"Thanks again," Trace said as the trio approached. "Since there is some time before the rodeo starts, I was wondering if you two ladies would like to join Delanie and me for some eats over at the food court. My treat, by way of saying thanks."

"Yippee," Delanie exclaimed.

"Fine with me," Jenna answered.

Jenna was taller than Haylee, though that wasn't saying much, and the opposite in coloring.

Haylee bit her lip, seemed to be considering. Even if his heart sped up while he waited for the answer, it was no big deal if she turned him down. "Okay," she finally said. "But I insist on paying for my meal. All we did was take Delanie to the bathroom."

"Providing relief to both her and me." Trace wasn't lying about that.

Chapter 3

Under the food tent, Haylee and Jenna settled onto their bench seats across the picnic table from Trace and Delanie. After wrangling over the payment for the food, Trace won out, as he knew the people working the cash register. Propelled by the large fans cooling the area, the tantalizing smells of cooked beef, Mexican spices, and french fries mingled in the air. Haylee dug into her pulled-pork sandwich and listened to the cacophony of diners' voices while she watched Trace place a napkin on his daughter's lap, arm muscles flexing under his black T-shirt.

It was hard to pinpoint his age. His taut and muscled body moved with the flexibility of a young man. But his tanned, weathered face and the weariness she saw in his eyes made him seem older, if not wiser.

The man, who had been so closed mouthed yesterday was now smiling and chuckling as he watched his little girl slather mustard on her hot dog like the child was creating art, messy as it was. He slid another napkin to his daughter, anticipating a mouth painted yellow. This obviously wasn't his first rodeo, so to speak.

And yet, the two didn't seem totally comfortable.

Maybe it was the way Delanie insisted she wipe her mouth instead of her father. Or the fact the little girl had set her small hat between her father and herself. Neither act in and of itself should have garnered notice. Yet…

"So Delanie said something about her aunt and uncle owning the rodeo?" Jenna said, dusting her slice of pizza with red pepper.

As Trace had just taken a big bite of a burger, Delanie provided a one-syllable answer.

"Yup."

Trace's Adam's apple bobbed as he swallowed. He had a nice neck. Thick and tanned.

"My sister-in-law and brother own Prescott Rodeo Company, which supplies this rodeo with livestock, but they don't actually own the rodeo. They have some of the best buckin' stock in the country though. Mandy's maiden name is Prescott. She's the granddaughter of the company's late founder, J. M. Prescott."

"Wow, a woman in the rodeo business." That was a unique and interesting field for a woman. Well, really for anyone.

"You haven't met Mandy. She's as tough as they come. Has to be to stay married to my brother."

Interesting comment.

"And she said a family member is entered in the rodeo but that you don't compete?" Haylee was curious.

He looked at Delanie, whose mouth, once again, was smeared yellow. "Wipe your face, sweet pea," he said, sliding another napkin toward her.

Haylee fished a packet out of her pocket. "Can I wipe your face with this?" She held up a moist towelette. She never went anywhere without them.

Delanie nodded. Haylee leaned over the table and gently wiped away the mustard from the youngster's mouth.

"What do you say?" Trace instructed when Haylee was done.

"Thank you, Miss Haylee." Sitting there with a clean face, Delanie looked like a little angel.

Haylee would have enjoyed taking care of the child.

She glanced at Trace, met his gaze. A tingly sensation sped through her body, from her ears to her belly to her toes.

"The family member would be Tucker, Mandy's brother," he said, clearing his throat. "Doesn't want anything to do with the business end of things. Just wants to ride. Have to admire someone who goes after what he wants and the world be damned."

"But you don't compete, do you?" Jenna asked, having polished off the slice of pizza.

He shifted his attention to her friend. "No, ma'am. Only at ranch rodeos, and then only in events that keep me on the back of a horse."

"Ranch rodeos? There are different types of rodeos?" Haylee had so much to learn. The wide-open spaces, living-large mentality, and appreciation of the great outdoors was so different from her experience in cities with mostly asphalt or concrete under her feet. Even the move to the suburbs when she was in middle school hadn't provided more than a postage stamp for a yard. It was a different world, and she would never get to experience it now.

"Yes, ma'am." Trace looked past her this time, like he was searching the tent for someone. "Ranch rodeos have cowboys from different ranches compete in events that reflect their real work. For instance, no one rides bulls on a ranch. Or wrestles a steer. Now team roping and tie-down roping are more like what you do on a ranch. And I've only broken a horse once in all the time I've been ranching."

"You broke a horse, Daddy?" Delanie said, her voice wavering.

"No, honey. Not like that." Trace had turned his attention back to his daughter. "When you say you broke a horse, all it means is that you trained it to allow you to ride it. You know, like breaking them of their bad habits."

"Like Mommy is being broke of her bad habits?"

So the mother wasn't dead.

The cowboy shifted in his seat, and his brow furrowed. "Something like that. If you're finished with your hot dog, we'll go find Aunt Mandy and Uncle Ty and get our seats."

With that, a very pretty and very pregnant woman around Haylee's age placed her hand on Trace's shoulder.

"No need to go looking. We're here. Or at least I'm here."

Trace looked up, and a smile broke out over his previously frowning face. "Howdy, Mandy."

She nodded as Delanie squealed her delight. In another second, Delanie had flung herself out of her seat and into her aunt's arms.

"Careful, sweet pea. There's a baby in there," Trace cautioned.

Delanie rubbed her cheek against Mandy's ballooning stomach. "Sorry, baby. I forgot," she whispered.

"It's okay, sweetie," Mandy said, patting Delanie on the head. "Maybe it will encourage her or him to come out." Mandy shifted her gaze to take in Haylee and Jenna. "I didn't know you were bringing anyone. I can scramble up some more seats for you."

"We didn't come together."

Mandy's eyebrows arched.

"Mandy Martin, this is Haylee Dennis and her friend…Jenna, is it? I'm sorry I didn't get a last name."

"Jenna Thompson."

"Pleased to meet you both," Mandy said. "I can wrangle you all some seats close to the action if you'd like."

Though Mandy's eagerness to oblige was sweet, it would be a tad awkward considering Trace hadn't hired her.

"We have our seats, thank you," Haylee said.

"Haylee's never been to a rodeo," Jenna interjected. "I think it would be great for her to be closer if it isn't a bother. Our seats are in the nosebleed section."

Haylee glanced at Jenna, giving her a *what are you thinking* look. Jenna shrugged.

"No problem," Mandy said. "We get more than enough courtesy seats. I might join you, at least for saddle bronc riding. Can't stay on my feet for too long anymore."

"When are you due?" Jenna asked.

"In a few weeks. Now I know how Libby felt when she was at my wedding," she said, addressing Trace.

"Everyone seems to be having kids these days," Trace acknowledged.

"One way or another." Mandy patted Trace's back. "If you wait here, I'll just slip over to the trailer out back and get two more seat tickets. You want to take a walk with me, Delanie?" Mandy held out her hand.

With the quickness of a rabbit spotting a carrot, Delanie jumped out of her seat and grabbed Mandy's hand. The two were off before Haylee could get the "thank you" out of her mouth.

Trace stared at her from under the brim of his hat, and his gaze swept from the top of her hatless head to her chest, and back again, pulling heat with it until a fire settled at the base of her neck as if he'd just planted a kiss there.

Like it or not, it seemed Haylee was going to be spending more time in rugged cowboy country. She just hoped she was up for it.

Chapter 4

How he ended up in the front row of the VIP section of the arena sitting next to Paula Johnson's pretty little niece was beyond him, but there Trace was, watching the bareback riding while explaining to her and her friend what a *mark out* was. With the flimsy straw hat on her head and flip-flops on her feet, Haylee Dennis looked as out of place as a pony at the racetrack. Her gasp as a rider hit the ground had him wondering if she'd ever seen a rodeo before. In the next breath, she was clapping as another cowboy made the buzzer, even though he got a score of seventy-four. But she had apparently found plenty to photograph, if the clicking of her camera was any indication.

Delanie was engrossed in finishing off the ice cream cone he'd bought her after she'd done her best imitation of a puppy dog to plead with him. Delanie's remark about her mother and bad habits had gotten to him, and he was in a mood to indulge her.

By the time the saddle bronc riding started, Mandy had joined them like she'd promised, squeezing her bulky body into the seat next to Delanie.

"I brought Delanie some caramel popcorn." Mandy handed the bag to her niece but not before taking a handful for herself. "I'm eating for two, and one of us is very hungry," she said in response to his raised eyebrows.

"Are you still planning to stay home with the baby through September?" he asked. Mandy was as hands-on as you could get, and Trace was laying odds she wouldn't be able to keep away from the circuit when her livestock were performing.

"Yes," Mandy mumbled through a mouthful of popcorn as she offered some to the others. They declined. "Believe it or not, Tucker is going to step in to help Ty. I never thought I'd see the day, but I guess he's afraid his new niece or nephew is going to be knee deep in manure if he doesn't." She tossed her wavy brown hair as she laughed. "Your brother, of course, doesn't believe he needs any help. Guess he thinks I don't do anything worthwhile."

Her tone was teasing, but Trace bet they'd had a few words over it.

"That sounds like Ty." His younger brother was never one to give much credit where credit was due. Took after their late father. Although Trace guessed he was the same way, though he'd been trying to be more mindful since Delanie's arrival.

"That's Tucker," Mandy squealed as a lanky blond-haired cowboy was getting set on a penned bronc. "That's Uncle Tuck, Delanie."

Delanie, long finished with the chocolate cone, a splotch of which decorated her pink shirt, stood and nudged herself between Mandy's legs.

Feeling the pinch in his heart, Trace kept his focus on the arena. Delanie could have climbed onto his lap if she wanted to see better. But though things had improved tenfold from when she'd shown up on his doorstep, there seemed to always be an undercurrent that rippled through his relationship with his daughter. And if he was truthful, rippled through most of his relationships.

"Is that your brother, Mandy?" Jenna asked, leaning forward to get a closer look.

"That's him," she said.

"He's kind of cute." Jenna's smile was wide.

"He thinks so too," Mandy quipped.

The gate opened, and Tucker flew out on the back of a stout bucking horse named Miss Begotten. The sound of a camera clicking filled the air.

"Nice mark out," Trace said as the clock counted down the eight seconds.

The buzzer sounded, and Tuck was still on. The pick-up men pulled alongside the bronc, Tucker swung onto one of them and, when he dismounted, the crowd roared. He waved his hat in Mandy and Delanie's direction and blew a kiss.

Mandy leaned over Trace, her shoulder knocking into his shoulder, to address Haylee. "I'd be real appreciative of a copy of any of those pictures you took. I think Tucker would too."

"I'd be happy to send them to you."

Mandy searched her pocket and pulled out a business card. "You can send them to that email address."

Tucker's score flashed on the screen. An eighty-two.

"Tucker's gotten pretty good over this last year," Trace allowed.

"Well, he's been riding enough." Mandy settled back in her seat. "And Chance has been coaching him."

Chance Cochran was married to a friend of Mandy's and was a star bronc rider who had been to the Finals National Rodeo more than once.

"Chance is here, isn't he?" Trace asked.

"Yes indeedy. He's got a family to feed."

He felt Haylee's hand on his forearm. Warmth seeped through him like a paper towel soaking up water. He turned and was caught in the sight of a tantalizing set of blue eyes. He'd obviously been too long without a woman for a mere touch of a stranger to cause so much havoc.

"Why wasn't his score higher?" she asked.

Trace cleared his throat, hoping to get back some equilibrium. "Saddle bronc is one of the harder skills to master because it's all technique. You start with a mark out like in bareback riding, holding your feet at the horse's withers until the first buck. Then you and the horse become one, with your feet moving in motion with each buck of the horse. Tuck did a good job, but he bobbled some at the end of the ride when the horse went a little wild."

"I'll have to pay attention, because I thought his ride was wonderful," Haylee said.

Hopefully, she wasn't going to get enamored with rodeo riders, who were generally known as the playboys of the West. And why he should care, he didn't know.

Trace found himself sneaking glances at Haylee as the riders paraded their skills, watched as she toyed with her hair during the eight-second count and bit her lip at the end of the ride. He wondered if her hair was as soft as it looked and what those shiny lips of hers tasted like. Yeah, he'd been too long without a woman.

Finally Chance Cochran's name was called. The crowd clapped. Chance was a favorite on the circuit and a moneymaker.

"If you want to see a good ride, my bet is on Chance to show you how it's done."

Still standing between Mandy's legs, Delanie clapped her excitement. Haylee started clicking her camera.

The gate opened, and Chance didn't disappoint. He was pure art in motion as the fringes of his chaps waved in the air and his legs moved in perfect time with a horse that was bucking high and hard. It was a sight to behold.

When the buzzer sounded, Chance jumped off the horse as if it were the easiest thing in the world, but anyone who had ridden a bronc knew it wasn't.

"That was amazing." Haylee was clapping so hard, her hat had fallen to dangle at the back of her neck.

Well, at least Chance was married.

The score flashed up on the screen. An eighty-nine, seven points more than Tuck's and well deserved.

"Why didn't he get a hundred? Seems everyone thinks it was a great ride." Haylee's pretty eyes were wide with concern.

"Highest score in saddle bronc riding was a ninety-three, I think, given to Billy Etbauer back in 2003 or 2004. Trust me—Chance is thrilled with an eighty-nine."

That wrapped up saddle bronc riding, with Chance winning the event. Mandy patted Delanie's back. "I have to get back to work, sweetie. I want to show some things to Tucker while he's here. Get him ready. You want to come with me and say hi to Tuck?"

Delanie nodded, her smile wide, filling her face, crinkling her eyes. He was fortunate to have his sister-in-law in their lives. How his brother had gotten so lucky was still a mystery.

"Don't forget about those pictures," Mandy said, addressing Haylee before training her gaze on Trace. "And you can come get Delanie later and say hi to your brother." She looked at Trace as if it was more command than suggestion.

Trace gave an obligatory nod. There would be no getting around seeing his brother. Not that there was still bad blood between them. Delanie, with an assist from Mandy, had helped to paper over hard feelings from long ago, and Trace was still in Ty's debt, literally. But Ty was a force to be reckoned with, and sometimes Trace just didn't feel like reckoning.

"I'm going to get a beer. Anyone want anything?" Jenna said, rising.

Haylee asked for a beer. Trace passed. He had a bottle of water and water or coffee was all he allowed himself these days.

As Mandy, with Delanie in tow, and Jenna departed down different aisles, Trace found himself alone with Haylee. The sun, bright and hot, beat down on him. Moisture beaded on his brow, the back of his neck, under his arms.

He glanced Haylee's way. She was smiling at him. Like she was expecting him to say something. Heck.

"You enjoying the rodeo?"

She nodded.

He ran through possible conversation topics. The weather was supposed to be a tried and true topic, but what was there to say about a picture-perfect day? Something they had in common? He came up empty. Except…

"How come your aunt and uncle didn't come? I know they like a good rodeo."

"They're still tying up loose ends and hoping to find a solution." The curly ends of her hair were swirling around her pale face in the breeze. She should really put her hat on if she was going to protect all that creamy-white skin.

"I thought you were the solution."

Haylee cocked her head as she bit her bottom lip, turning it a rosy pink. "I was. But without work, I can't stay out there. I need to find a steady-paying job while I build up my business."

Trace shifted in his seat. Much as he could use the help, there was still the problem of Haylee being a temporary solution, which would force Delanie to face another person leaving. That was the key issue. Along with the fact she was too damn attractive for his own good.

He hadn't replied to her comment. Haylee hoped she hadn't sounded peevish. If he didn't need someone, he didn't need someone. And if she just happened to be the someone he didn't need, well, it was his loss.

Just then the crowd erupted in applause as a tie-down roper scored a time of 6.7 seconds.

Haylee snuck a glance at Trace. His legs were

spread apart, barely fitting into the space between the rows, and he was staring out into the arena, his profile strong, angular. With sunglasses on and his cowboy hat, his picture would look perfect on a poster advertising the rodeo if they wanted to attract more women.

Maybe it was for the best that Trace didn't think he needed anyone, didn't need her. When Aunt Paula had told her that the neighboring rancher was interested in childcare for his five-year-old daughter, she had imagined someone older and much less attractive.

His appeal was simple biology, nothing more. He was a good-looking man. A little too quiet for her taste, maybe, but definitely hot.

"You have much experience working with children?" He clasped his hands between his spread-apart legs and leaned forward like he needed a better look at what was going on in the arena.

"Look—don't go making a job where there is no need. I'm not a charity case. I have skills. Just means I have to move closer to the action, is all." She wasn't desperate, though at times these last few months she'd felt desperate. "But yes, I was a camp counselor from high school through my college years, for young ones at a day camp and then for older children at sleepover camp. Not to mention years of babysitting." And practically raising her younger sister while her mother and father worked to give them a decent life after the recession blew everything to bits. "And I am Red Cross certified." Something her camp counseling days required and she'd continued.

She was also a financial analyst with a BA degree in accounting, but that would probably be even less impressive to him.

"So what is the business you're starting? Photography?" He pushed his sunglasses up his nose.

"No." Although if she could have made a living as a photographer, nothing would have made her happier. "It's kind of a niche business. I'm a freight auditor for small and midsized businesses, to find savings in their shipping bills. The industry is notorious for billing mistakes, from weight discrepancies to routing errors. I get a percentage of the savings I find." Sounded boring…and had been until it wasn't.

He glanced her way with a *what the hell kind of job is that* look.

"Went to college in Colorado, where I did an internship at a company that provides that service to Fortune 500 companies. They weren't interested in any corporation that didn't have at least a million in transportation costs. I figured there were plenty of smaller companies that could benefit, and while I was still in school, I started developing a clientele."

"You don't look like you've been out of school too long. What happened that you have to start over?"

That was the million-dollar, or two, question.

"The short answer is, I got married."

"He didn't want you to work?"

She'd give Trace props for sounding irritated at such an idea.

"Actually, I ended up working for Hauser Trucking, his company." Her ex-husband owned one of the businesses she'd audited for her clients, but Trace didn't need to know that or anything about Roy Hauser. Because too many questions could lead to complicated answers.

"Didn't work out, huh?"

That was an understatement. "Neither the marriage nor the job." It was still painful to admit. Not the divorce, but the fact she'd been duped. On all fronts. "My former clients found someone else in the interim, so I have to start over." Not to mention the market appeared to have changed in those two years, and now her competition included do-it-yourself software.

She was still hopeful it would work out. But getting started, building credibility, and praying nothing Roy had done would be discovered and take down her business reputation were the things that kept her up at night.

"So you like working with numbers?"

"It pays the bills."

"Seems what you do for hours on end should do more than pay bills." He removed his white cowboy hat and ran his fingers through a head of thick brown hair.

She had an urge to do the same. Luckily, he quickly placed his hat back where it belonged.

"Like ranching?"

"Hard to make money at it. People who do it, do it because they love it. No other reason makes sense."

She admired that. "If I did what I loved, I would be a photographer. All my electives in college were in graphic arts and photography. But you have to have a lot of luck, enormous talent, determination, and a lot of money to hold you over until success comes. I'm lacking all of those things." Hard to admit, but the truth. And after the events of the last few months, she was all about the truth.

He didn't say anything for a long time, letting the announcer and applause fill the silence.

Haylee lifted her camera and shot more pictures of the cowboys performing in the arena. She was tempted to swing her camera in Trace's direction and see if she could capture him on film. It would certainly be an interesting memento. For her aunt, of course.

But just as she'd screwed up the courage and trained the camera on him, he turned his head toward her and removed his sunglasses.

"What do you like to photograph?"

She was startled by the question. Not because she didn't have an answer, but that he would care enough to ask.

She lowered her camera to see if he was interested or just being polite and found herself mesmerized by a pair of hazel eyes with gold flecks that glistened in the sun. She suddenly felt thirstier than a cactus waiting to bloom. Where was Jenna with that beer?

"I tend to gravitate toward scenes that tell a story. An old barn against a stark sky, a car with dents, a row of similar houses but with one that looks out of place. And faces. I love to photograph faces. Not conventionally pretty faces. But faces that reveal a history." Like his.

"You sound pretty excited when you talk about photography. Not when you talk about accounting." His mouth grabbed the contours of a water bottle, his Adams apple bobbing as he swallowed. Full lips, firm jaw. He was probably a great kisser.

"It all comes back to paying the bills." She shrugged, hoping she could shrug off the image of being wrapped in his arms that had popped into her head uninvited.

"You're not originally from around here, are you?"

"I'm from Chicago. My parents still live there, so now I will probably end up living with them until I get established again. Doesn't say much for a woman of twenty-six." No need to massage the truth. It wasn't like she was ever going to see this guy again or had any chance of being kissed by those lips.

"You like the city?"

She thought for a moment. She wanted to be honest with him, and herself. "I did when I lived there. I didn't know anything else. But really, the landscape of the West speaks to me. I have so many photographs of great places and all within a short drive of where I lived in Denver. It's amazing how many stories I find out here."

The announcer's voice boomed the score. Haylee checked the arena. She'd been so engrossed in conversation she hadn't been paying attention.

"What is this event?" She raised her camera, looked through the viewfinder, and started snapping.

"Team roping. More like what you do on a ranch."

"Do you rope?" she asked in between contestants. With his long limbs and large hands, she bet he could do anything…including entertain a woman.

"I wouldn't be able to ranch if I didn't. Though some people don't ride horses anymore, or do things the traditional way, that's not me. I like my horse, my rope, my spurs."

"Do you wear chaps?" With nothing else?

"When I work the range."

"I'd love to photograph you in action before I go. If you'd be willing." It was worth a shot. Not the chaps-with-nothing-else scenario, of course. She wasn't a pervert. Just a red-blooded American woman with an overactive imagination.

"As long as they don't appear on Facebook or something. I'm not one for the public eye."

Now why didn't that surprise her? "Once my aunt Paula moves, I won't have any reason to come back here. Until Uncle Archie's arthritis got so bad, they really liked Wyoming. I just don't want her to forget it, so I'm putting together an album for her." She didn't want him to think *she* wanted the pictures of him. She wasn't a stalker or anything. Besides, photos of a working cowboy would really tell a story.

"You ever visit when you were younger? I know your aunt and uncle only moved here a little over ten years ago. Not that we were close, but I don't remember ever seeing kids around their place."

"Once when I was in high school and looking at colleges. Their house was always too small for guests. My sister and I used sleeping bags in the front room. We thought it was a great adventure. I think that is when I fell in love with the West and decided to go to school out here." A fateful decision with unforeseen consequences.

"Are you the younger or older sister?"

"Older."

"I'm the older brother."

"We are the responsible ones."

"I know we are supposed to be."

And life didn't always turn out the way it was supposed to. Not that anyone would describe her sister as responsible. But right now, no one would use that adjective to describe her either.

With that, Jenna appeared at the end of the aisle

and handed Haylee a cup of beer before sliding into her seat.

"What did I miss?" Jenna asked.

"Cowboys." Haylee took a sip of her drink. Its yeasty flavor was welcomed.

Jenna laughed. "There were tons, and very friendly ones, in line for beer."

"Gotta watch out for rodeo cowboys," Trace said, shooting an unexpected smile in their direction that made Haylee's heart stutter.

He really could be a heartbreaker if he smiled more. Made her wonder why he didn't.

"A rodeo cowboy is the quintessential rambling man," he continued.

"Being from Wyoming, I'm well aware," Jenna said.

"Cowgirl, are you?" Trace slid his sunglasses into place and looked in Jenna's direction.

Jenna would be more his type. Tall, willowy, and western. Haylee felt the uncomfortable tug of jealousy.

Get a grip, Haylee Dennis. He was a lone-wolf cowboy she had nothing in common with and would likely never see again. He'd asked her about her experience with children, which had sparked hope, but then changed the subject and moved on. For whatever reasons, and there were probably many, he'd scoped her out and decided to pass…on all fronts.

"Not really. Parents work in the energy sector. Dad's an engineer. I'm working for an energy company too, as an accountant."

"That how you two met?"

Haylee nodded. "Jenna and I were in a lot of classes together. A lot of boring classes," she added for Trace's benefit.

There was that boyish grin of his again. Yeah, he had to stop doing that, because she wasn't sure how long a heart could palpitate before she'd have to worry something was wrong.

"You make my case, Haylee. You should try doing what you love."

"Easier said than done." Haylee tucked a strand of unruly hair behind her ear and looped it around her finger. "So about taking photos of you." What did she have to lose?

"Tomorrow. Around ten thirty, Delanie and I will be heading out to check on the herd. But wear boots and, with your pale skin, something to keep the sun off you. Something sturdy."

The boots would have to be fashion boots, and the sun hat was all she had. "Around ten thirty then. Thanks."

He touched the brim of his hat and shifted his gaze back to the arena.

Had she done a foolish thing…again?

Chapter 5

"So that's the cowboy who wouldn't hire you?" Jenna let out a low whistle as Haylee maneuvered her compact car into a line of vehicles doing a slow crawl out of the rodeo parking lot.

"He doesn't need help."

"He does seem a devoted father, and the little girl is a sweetie. So are you going to photograph him?"

Jenna sounded more eager than Haylee was. Not that she regretted the photography opportunity, just the fact she'd be spending time with a man who'd sparked something in her she hadn't felt in a long time, the same man she'd failed to impress enough to hire her. Not the best combination for building self-esteem.

"Seems I am."

"He's really hot. Bet he's interested in more than your photographs."

"You've had too many beers." She'd enjoyed talking with him, maybe too much. Looking back, she realized she'd talked about herself more than he had about himself. She couldn't remember the last time that had happened with a man. And certainly not with Roy, when everything had to revolve around him.

She wished she had learned more about Trace. All she had were impressions. Impressions that he was a devoted father, liked going it alone, wasn't all that impressed by her. But as for facts, she didn't even know how old he was, much less the thing that she was most curious about...what had happened to Delanie's mother.

Jenna propped her feet on the door to the glove compartment. "I'm sober enough to know what I saw. Don't tell me you aren't interested."

"The only thing I am interested in is finding work." That was the only thing she should be interested in.

"Oh my God, have you seen your face?" Jenna asked.

Haylee cringed. She'd been afraid to look, but she had felt the heat in her skin since she'd slid into the car. She craned her neck to look in the rearview mirror. Her face was the color of a salmon. "I guess the lotion didn't work as well as I hoped." And she'd been so distracted by Trace she'd forgotten to put her sun hat back on.

"Does it hurt?"

Haylee shook her head. "Not yet, but no doubt I won't get much sleep tonight. And I am photographing Trace tomorrow morning."

Jenna shrugged. "Well, it was nice of him to agree, and it was nice of him to take us to lunch. Seems like a good guy and a good dad."

Haylee had to agree in the *good dad* department. It was heartwarming to see this hunk of a cowboy so attentive to the needs of his daughter. But it had nothing to do with her.

"Too soon." Too soon to think about getting back in the dating game, and maybe it would never be the right time.

Trace walked in search of the trailer that served as the mobile office of Prescott Rodeo Company, mentally kicking himself as the scents of horses, hay, steers, and manure permeated the area by the arena where the livestock were penned. He should have offered Haylee the job. Truth was, his daughter needed more care than his ranch allowed him to provide. So what if she was temporary. So what if she was an attractive woman. He should be able to deal with both.

His brother came into sight, propped against the trailer's side, talking to a rodeo hand. Fact was, Ty looked like he was more hand than boss in his faded jeans, chambray shirt, and Stetson. Seeing Ty now, no one would have guessed he'd recently been a corporate lawyer for a land development firm.

The brothers shared the same coloring, except Ty's eyes were gray, like their father's, and Trace's were hazel, like their mother's. They also shared the same stubborn streak, which had caused not a little trouble between them. But that was in the past, and he owed Ty—big time.

As Ty caught sight of him, a smile graced his brother's face. Was a spell when neither of them smiled much. Hadn't been much to smile about. But since Ty had married Mandy and found out he was going to be a father, his brother was smiling more often than not.

Nothing like a good woman to bring out the best in a man. Not that he would know.

"Hey there, big brother. Delanie's out with Tucker, riding around on one of the parade horses," Ty called, moving away from the cowboy with a signal that he was done.

Coming within reach, Trace shook his brother's hand.

"You enjoy the rodeo?" Ty asked.

"Sure." Although with Haylee beside him, he hadn't been able to concentrate on the action in the arena.

"Heard you had some company. Mandy came back here all excited."

"About what?"

"The women you were with."

"Daddy."

Saved from responding, Trace turned around to see Delanie running toward him, hair flying and Tucker not far behind.

"I got to ride one of the horses with Tucker. And see Shane's daddy, though Shane isn't here. He still needs his naps. And a nice man was teaching me how to twirl the rope, though I wasn't very good."

The words came out all in a tumble as Delanie drew up almost breathless from running.

"Sounds like fun." Trace looked up to catch Tucker's attention and nodded. "Thanks."

"I always have fun with Delanie," Tucker said. "Can't wait for another little one to be added to the family."

Trace liked Tucker. With his laid-back ways, Tucker Prescott was easy to be around.

"I'm going to see if Mandy has anything more she needs to show me," Tucker said with a sigh. "Seems I'm going to be hanging up my spurs for a while." With that, he sauntered up the steps and into the mobile office.

"Where's Miss Haylee? And Miss Jenna?"

Delanie asked, looking around as if she thought they were hiding somewhere.

"They headed home."

"I wanted to say goodbye." Her lips pursed in a pout.

"You'll see Miss Haylee tomorrow, as a matter of fact. She's coming to take some pictures." Meaning he'd be spending the evening cleaning up the place so it didn't look like he a needed a housekeeper.

"Of me?"

"Maybe." He wasn't sure exactly what Haylee wanted to photograph.

Ty arched an eyebrow. His brother was never one to let something go. "Is Miss Haylee the blonde? Hear she's a pretty little thing."

Trace would ignore that. No sense commenting and adding fuel to the fire.

"We can take her out and show her the ranch. I'd let her ride Buck," Delanie offered.

Trace had to chuckle at his daughter's exuberance. At moments like these, no one would suspect all the turmoil she'd experienced in her young life. Turmoil he was committed to avoiding going forward, if the courts would only agree. "We'll probably have to take the pickup. I'm not sure she can ride a horse."

"I can give her some pointers." Delanie was full of confidence.

Ty slapped Trace on the back. "Maybe you can give your dad some pointers on women, Delanie. I have a feeling he could use some."

Haylee trudged up the dirt path from her car toward the barn, snapping pictures as she went. She'd worn shorts and a T-shirt with a pair of black leather booties, and her sun hat was hanging off the back of her neck. She was sure she looked like the perfect example of a city slicker, especially with her red-toned skin. She'd slathered on aloe lotion as soon as she'd gotten home yesterday, and it had taken the sting out, but she still looked like a salmon.

Didn't matter. She was here to take photos.

There was much to like, photography-wise, at the Martin ranch. The small house set on the plains with the gray mountains in the background. The barns with patches of wood in various stages of weathering signaled the many repairs that had been made over the years. The faded vinyl-sided shed. A bay horse and a tan horse grazing undisturbed in the corral, their black tails switching away the ever-present flies.

Something about the setting spoke to her. Maybe it was the peacefulness, or the beauty of nature's green plains, blue skies, and taupe-colored mountains that reflected the dappled sunlight from the eastern sky, or the smell of fresh earth, or the fact that in such a place it was easy to imagine the first settlers making this land their own. Whatever it was, Haylee felt like she belonged. Which was just crazy since, it appeared, she was destined for a city, and Trace had already told her there was no job.

Her aunt had gotten excited when Haylee mentioned she would be photographing Trace, thinking, erroneously, that he'd also reconsidered hiring Haylee. He hadn't, and it wasn't like he had invited her—more like she had ambushed him.

Regardless, at least her aunt would have pictures not only of her house and yard but of her neighbor's, by which to remember Cottonwood Road. And that was why Haylee was doing it.

Not that any potential buyers had been by that weekend, and no one was scheduled. It appeared a five-acre parcel was harder to sell than a large ranch that could be developed or a smaller suburban lot that had neighbors nearby, or so the real estate agent claimed. Someone who had a few horses, so the outbuildings would be a plus, not a minus, enjoyed privacy, and wanted to live on the land had to be out there. Except for the horses, that was Haylee, at least at the moment. And if she had the money, horses would have been on her list.

She didn't know how to ride, but she'd love to learn. The photos she could take from the back of a horse were bound to be spectacular. How many times had she been driving and come upon a perfect scene, but pulling off the road was not an option, so she'd had to pass it by? On horseback, there would be nothing to hinder her from taking the perfect picture. And she loved horses, at least the few she'd been around. Something majestic yet personal about a horse.

How hard could riding a horse be? She'd taken one lesson, when she was in middle school, at a friend's riding academy, but the cost of regular lessons wasn't something her parents could afford at the time.

Maybe Trace would give her a lesson. She'd probably swoon and fall right off the horse if he was sitting behind her. Strong arms enclosing her. Her back against his chest.

She gave a mental shake. She had to stop thinking about that man. He wanted nothing to do with her. And that was for the best. Recently divorced, she was so not ready. He was a country boy. She was a city girl. And she would be leaving tomorrow.

She stopped at the entrance to the barn and peered into the darkness. Stalls lined the walls, a concrete floor stretched between the rows, and dust motes danced in the light from the window on the opposite wall. Didn't look like anyone was in the barn. Yet the pickup was in the yard. Hadn't he said they'd ride out at ten thirty? So where was he?

Her pulse skittered as she turned around to go back to the car. He was striding up the path, the dog clipping his heels. He wasn't wearing a hat, so his full head of thick dark hair was now visible. He was handsomer without a cowboy hat than with one.

What must have been a surprised look on her face caused him to chuckle. "Hope I didn't scare you. Saw you looking around." He glanced back at the house. "We're just back from church, and Delanie is inside using the bathroom, and I'm having a cup of coffee before we head out. Like some?"

"That would be great." She wasn't sure if the thought of riding a horse or the thought of Trace was making her nervous, but regardless, she needed something to calm the rapid beating of her heart.

The dog sat at her feet like he was awaiting her command. She bent down and petted him, his coat shiny and soft. "What's his name?"

"Moose."

Interesting name for a dog.

"You got some color yesterday," he said.

Well, at least her blush wouldn't be noticeable. "A little too much sun."

"See you brought that hat and are wearing boots, although those aren't exactly what I had in mind."

"It's all I have with me," she said as she straightened

"They'll do, I suppose."

"You don't have your chaps on." She'd been picturing him in chaps, and not over his jeans either.

He grimaced. "Another day maybe. Too hot today."

He turned on his heel, and she followed him and the dog back to the house. He held the screen door, and she stepped past a wall with hooks holding a kid's cowgirl hat, several cowboy hats in neutral colors, and assorted jackets. Trace led her into a small kitchen with an oversized wood table and just one row of cabinets above a counter that also contained the sink, gas stove, and dishwasher. She breathed in the comforting scent of coffee wafting from the coffeemaker taking up most of the remaining counter space.

The compact kitchen looked like it had been updated not too long ago. The cabinets didn't appear to be wood, the counter was laminate made to look like granite, and the vinyl flooring was trying hard to look like tile. It was clean and neat though, and that was all that should matter. Haylee could have cooked in that kitchen, if he'd hired her. But if cleanliness was any measure, Trace was doing okay by himself as a single father. Guess he'd been right that he didn't need any help. Too bad.

"How do you like your coffee?" he asked, taking the pot in one hand while he reached for a cup from the stand on the counter.

"Black." She needed her caffeine unadulterated.

"Woman after my own heart."

She thought she saw a blush of red in his cheeks as he looked away.

"You're here!" Delanie rushed through the

doorway, ran right into Haylee's knees, and threw her arms around Haylee's legs with a squeeze.

"So good to see you again, Delanie." And Haylee meant it. They would have had fun together.

"Do you want to take my picture?" Delanie looked up at Haylee, eyes shining with the excitement of a youngster for anything new.

"I would love to. Maybe we can get one with you by the horses." It would be a nice shot.

"Daddy said you can't ride, so we are taking the pickup to see the ranch."

"Oh." She looked at Trace for confirmation and tried not to show her disappointment. She'd hope to get pictures of him on a horse, working cattle, or whatever they called it.

"Wasn't sure you knew how to ride." He handed her a cup of coffee. The aroma alone was comforting.

"I don't. But I'd love to learn some day." A sip of the coffee confirmed that it was strong and tasted heavenly. Something to be said for a man who could make a good cup of java.

"It would take more than a day—believe me."

If she were to stay in cowboy country, she'd enjoy spending time learning from Trace. But she wasn't staying. And he wasn't offering.

"I would like some pictures of you on a horse though. You know, the whole cowboy thing."

He held the cup to his firm lips and took a sip as he studied her before answering, as if debating the merits of compliance. "When we come back, I'll saddle up Archer."

Delanie released her grip on Haylee's legs. "No, Buck. So I can ride too."

He chuckled. “Or Buck.” He tousled his daughter’s hair, and she had the satisfied look of someone who had gotten her way.

“Interesting name for a horse. Is that how he got his name, he bucks?” Why would Trace ride a bucking horse with his daughter?

“Maybe you should get on him and find out.” There was a smirk on his face, as if he was daring her.

He didn’t know whom he was daring.

“I’m game.”

His eyebrows arched. “You’re on then.”

If this was her last day on Cottonwood Road, Haylee was determined to make the most of it.

Chapter 6

"Do you want to see some of the pictures?"

Trace turned his attention to Haylee, who was sitting in the front seat of his pickup. It was odd to see her there, to see a woman in his truck, a pretty woman at that. He pulled to a stop next to the barn and wondered what she thought of his dented truck with fabric torn seats and enough dust on its exterior to choke a chimney sweep.

"Sure."

The whole time he'd been in the pickup, he'd been hit with whiffs of her perfume, some sort of vanilla-tinged scent that had him thinking about homemade pies and sitting by a fire.

He was curious to see what she had found so interesting among the sparse trees, grassy plains, and rocky canyons. She lifted the strap from her neck, still pink from sunburn, and handed him the camera. Staring into the viewer, he ran through several pictures of his herd, the expressions of his cows and steers ranging from curious to annoyed, the mountain range whose peaks seemed to touch the clouds, the creek that looked like a ribbon of blue trickling through the range, and of Delanie. He paused at one where Delanie looked like a sprite dancing in prairie grass.

The woman had an eye for a good picture. So much so, he'd have to ask her to send him a copy of some of them, especially those that included his daughter. He hadn't thought to take many pictures of Delanie, usually leaving that to Mandy and Mandy's mother. Having some of Delanie at the ranch that would someday be hers would be special.

Haylee leaned over, bringing that vanilla scent with her, to see what had caused him to pause. His heart beat faster, as if he was on high alert or something.

"She's a natural for the camera," Haylee said. "The ones she took are at the end."

He breathed deep, filling his senses with her fragrance. If he bent his head just a little, his lips would touch her hair, which looked like threads of curled gold silk. Made him itch to run his fingers through it, to feel its texture.

In a heartbeat she shifted back to her own side of the cab.

Her change of position did little to relieve temptation.

"Look at my pictures, Daddy."

His daughter seemed taken with Haylee, especially since Haylee had allowed Delanie to snap a few pictures with the expensive camera. He'd warned her off, but Haylee (and Delanie) insisted. Luckily, nothing bad had happened, and Delanie seemed thrilled with her pictures of the dog.

He swiped the screen, and there was a picture of Moose looking at the camera with what appeared to be a doggie frown. Seemed Moose didn't like his picture taken any more than Trace did. The next few were of Moose in various stages of sniffing the ground.

"Nice pictures, sweet pea." Finished, he held out the camera to Haylee. "Would it be too much to ask you to send me a few of these?"

She grabbed the camera, and her fingers brushed over his like a hot stick. As if the friction had caused a spark, something deep inside him ignited, burning through him like a wildfire through brush.

She stared at him, her blue eyes wide, her hand on the door handle, her head cocked, and her lips pursed. Lips that needed to be kissed. By him.

"I can send all of them," she finally said, turning her focus to the door handle.

"Thanks." He opened his door. The truck had gotten way too warm.

Back at the barn, he saddled up Buck for the next round of shots, giving him a moment to think about the tiny dynamo who kept on clicking as Delanie led Haylee around the barn, explaining which horse matched which stall, pointing out where the saddles were kept, and instructing Haylee on the need to curry the horses after a ride. All things he had shown his daughter. Nice to know she'd been listening.

He also heard Delanie telling Haylee not to be afraid of riding. That her daddy knew everything about horses and was a great teacher. He hoped he'd live up to that endorsement.

He adjusted the saddle's stirrups and tried not to glance at Haylee in high-heeled black boots, shorts that showed off her slender legs, a tight T-shirt stretched across her chest, and a flimsy hat that hadn't been worth much when the wind whipped through the canyons. Those black high-heeled boots had him thinking about slow dancing. They certainly weren't cowgirl worthy, more fashion than practical, and probably worse than sneakers. That was a city girl for you.

His attraction to her, physical as it might be, was a good reason not to hire her. It would be much less risk to his equilibrium for sure. But what about Delanie? What about her needs?

"You want the lesson first or the pictures?" he asked, cinching up the saddle as the two sidled over.

"Pictures, because I'll get to ride," Delanie answered.

"I asked Haylee, and she gets to decide. She's the guest, right?" Teaching his daughter manners was a full-time job at this age.

"I vote pictures too." Haylee stroked Delanie's hair in female solidarity.

"It's you and me, kid." Trace led the horse out into the attached corral, and Moose, Delanie, and Haylee followed to the clip-clop of the horse's hooves.

The sun was bright at the moment, though the sky was dotted with high white clouds. Barn smells filled the air in the heat of the late-morning sun. Moose wandered to the far side of the fence in search of new scents, and Trace secured Buck's reins to a fence post as Delanie ran over. Trace picked her up and placed her on the saddle, checking to be sure his daughter was secure before he swung up onto the horse.

"Soon I'm going to ride Buck on my own, right, Daddy?" Delanie looked over her shoulder at him.

"Soon, sweet pea."

"I noticed Delanie had a cowgirl hat in the house. Would you mind wearing it, Delanie, if I ran and got it?" Haylee asked.

Delanie assented, and Trace watched as Haylee jogged back to the house, holding her camera in one hand so it wouldn't bump. Her hat hung off her back, her curly blond hair flew, her tight butt bounced, and he found himself admiring her form…when he shouldn't be doing any such thing.

"I like Miss Haylee, Daddy," Delanie said, cutting into his thoughts.

"She's a nice lady." Too nice to just look at.

"I wish she was staying."

"You do?" Why did he fear that?

"She could come over, and you and I could have playdates with her."

His idea of a playdate wasn't going to be his daughter's, and that was the problem. "I think it would be more like when Miss Camille came."

Delanie's mouth pulled in. "I wish Miss Camille hadn't left."

So much loss for one so young. "It's not working having me doing ranch stuff with you?"

Delanie shrugged her shoulders, but her pout was still there, making him feel guilty as hell.

"Miss Haylee wouldn't be able to stay for long though. Probably just for the summer."

Delanie shrugged again, but this time she wore a small smile on her face. "Better than nothing."

He looked toward the house. Haylee was jogging back, hat in hand, breasts jiggling. She might not have been raised in the country, but she had a natural athleticism about her. She scrambled through the fence rails and was breathing hard by the time she handed up the hat to Delanie. Other reasons for breathing hard crowded his mind.

"What do you say?" Trace prompted, needing to shake off those images.

"Thank you, Miss Haylee."

"Now you two look perfect," Haylee said as Trace adjusted Delanie's hat so his chest wouldn't cause it to go askew.

Buck shifted his weight, impatient to get moving.

"How do you want us?" he asked.

"Just like that for a second or two."

The clicks of the camera came in rapid succession.

"Now turn the horse and walk toward me," she directed.

More clicks. He felt a little foolish, as if he were some model faking it, but Delanie was enjoying the attention, smiling and waving for the camera.

"Now turn him and walk the horse away from me. I'll take some shots from the back with the mountains in the distance. If you could lean just a bit to the right, Trace, I think I can frame it so I can catch the back of Delanie's hat too."

He headed toward the far fence at a walk. More clicks of the camera.

"Okay, come back, and I'd like to take separate pictures of each of you on the horse."

Why the heck was she taking all of these pictures? Surely Paula only needed one picture of him and Delanie to remember them by. But he wasn't going to spoil the fun as long as Delanie was enjoying it.

After he headed back to the beat of camera shots, he dismounted, leaving Delanie on the horse by herself.

Haylee stepped close to him, too close. So close he caught a whiff of vanilla. That perfume, he feared, would cause him to forever associate the scent of fresh pastries with her.

"Is there a way we can safely make this look like she's riding by herself?" she whispered in his ear, scrambling his insides.

Damn. He wondered what she would think if she knew the havoc she was causing inside him. He needed to get a grip if he was really going to hire her. "I think she'd enjoy that picture."

Handing Haylee the reins to hold, he strode over to another post and lifted a rope with a clip. "Lead line," he said, holding it up before he clipped it on the bridle.

"Great. I can brush that out, and it will look like she's alone up there." Haylee handed Delanie the reins.

"Hold them like I showed you," Trace said.

Haylee clicked away, and he had to admit the smile on Delanie's face was worth the fuss.

"Now can your daddy have his turn?" Haylee asked.

"Don't you have enough pictures yet?" Awkward didn't begin to describe this posing business.

"Not any of you doing cowboy things."

"Cowboy things?"

"Galloping around the corral."

"More like a canter in this space."

"Whatever it's called, but yes, something with action." She twirled a strand of hair around her finger and bit her lip. She looked too damn cute with her eyes wide and her rosebud mouth in a *please* expression. Nice lips, full and pink and kissable.

Delanie tugged on his sleeve. "Yes, Daddy. Then I can have a picture of you."

Did Delanie actually say that? It was the first time she'd asked for a picture of him, though she had one of her mother on her dresser.

"Can't say no to that cute face."

He lifted Delanie off the horse and set her on the ground. "Now stay here with Miss Haylee, Delanie." He turned to Haylee. "I know you'll be taking pictures, but if you could just be mindful of where she is…"

"I'll stay put, Daddy." Delanie's five-year-old promises were like cotton candy, sweet to the taste but disappearing in a second.

"I'll be mindful," Haylee said. Her upper lip tucked under her lower one, as if she was thinking on something. "Just stand there a second with the mountains in the background without the horse."

More clicks. If his brother saw any of these pictures, Trace would be in for a ribbing for sure.

"Now with the horse."

Trace stepped next to the animal. Buck looked at him as if to say *can't you stop this?* Trace knew just how he felt.

"Okay, you can mount up."

Trace swung up onto the horse. The clicks started.

"How about I trot out to the far fence, then come in a little faster? Will that be enough?" He hoped so.

"That would be super. Thank you."

The shutter kept clicking as he turned the horse toward the back fence. Moose moseyed along, finished with his investigations. When Trace reached the far end, he turned the horse around. Delanie was standing dutifully by Haylee.

He nudged Buck, and the horse broke into a loping canter toward the duo. The camera was lifted to Haylee's eye, and then Delanie started running toward him.

He pulled on the reins just as Haylee leaped forward and tackled Delanie. Both of them stumbled to the ground, camera and all.

"Delanie, I told you to stay there," he shouted as he dismounted Buck, photo shoot officially over. Moose ran ahead to check on the duo as the two sat on the pasture ground, laughing. Children didn't listen. But he had to say, Haylee showed good protective instincts. He only hoped her camera survived the tumble. He strode over as the two were untangling from each other.

Delanie bounced up, appearing to be fine except for the splotches that decorated her like someone had dabbed a paintbrush in mud and flung it in her direction. "I thought Moose was getting too close to Buck's hooves."

"Moose knows how to behave around horses," he continued. "You were the one who risked getting hurt, not Moose. You need to listen to me, Delanie."

Trace bent down, and for the second time since he'd met Haylee, he reached under her arms and lifted her onto her feet. She weighed next to nothing, but touching her, however innocent, sent a warm zing through him. Not so much, though, that he didn't notice her wince.

"Something hurts?" God he hoped not.

She looked down at her dirt-covered knee. A scrape was oozing blood. "Just that."

"We've got to get that cleaned out before we do anything else," he said. Infections were all too easy.

Delanie leaned over to check out the cut. "You have a boo-boo, Miss Haylee."

"Seems I do. How about you, Delanie? Are you okay?"

He appreciated her concern for his kid.

"Nothing hurts on me," his daughter confirmed.

"What do you have to say about causing a ruckus, Delanie?"

His daughter looked down at the ground. "I'm sorry, Miss Haylee."

Haylee rubbed Delanie's head. "It's nothing, Delanie. A little antiseptic spray and I'll be fine."

"The camera?" He held his breath as she checked the lens.

Then she aimed the camera and snapped his picture. "Doesn't seem to be any problems."

He thanked his lucky stars because he sure didn't have money lying around to replace it. He wasn't sure, but he figured with the size of the lens and the make of the camera, it would have been a sizeable outlay.

After tying up Buck, he herded the crew back to the house and, in the kitchen, settled Haylee in a hard-backed chair while he rounded up bandage strips, antiseptic, and cotton balls. Coming back into the kitchen, Delanie was holding her stuffed dog in one hand while she patted Haylee's knee with the other and told Haylee that her daddy would fix her up.

Smiling to himself, he knelt down before Haylee and tried not to be distracted by the pair of fine, creamy-white legs that were eye level.

"I can do that," she said.

Yeah, she could, but he wanted to.

He dabbed on the antiseptic and saw her flinch as

he applied it. It wasn't too bad of a scrape, but enough that he needed to clean it out.

"These boots of yours are a step up from sneakers, but you need real boots if you're serious about riding. Your feet are so small you could probably fit into Delanie's boots."

He dabbed around the scrape

"I'm not going to be here after today, and I'll have you know I'm an adult size five."

She was leaving that soon?

"And besides, it's nothing."

He liked that she was willing to shrug it off, but infections were a serious thing. "Best to clean it out."

Smooth skin and the desire to kiss his way up her curvy leg made concentration difficult…but added to the enjoyment. Not to mention that baby-blue eyes and pink lips were a dangerous combination. He took his time dabbing at the cut, holding her leg in his other hand, skimming his thumb across her silky skin.

For a moment, he let his imagination run, and it ran right to having those legs wrapped around his waist and her breasts on the same plane as his mouth.

"Does it hurt?" Delanie asked.

"Not much." Haylee bit her lip.

"Always stings me." Delanie leaned closer to the scrape. "But only for a little bit. Then I don't notice it."

He gave himself a mental shake, dabbed a dry cotton ball over the cut, and applied the bandage strip. "Good as new."

Standing up, he reached out his hand. "You still up for a riding lesson?"

"Absolutely. I may never get another chance." She took hold of his hand, her fingers fitting snugly in his palm. Unfortunately, his pulse kicked up at her touch. He hoped to hell she couldn't tell.

She rose off the chair, stood there in those crazy high-heeled boots. She barely came up to his shoulders. He fought the urge to tug her closer, to pick her up and squeeze her to him, to see where things went. Only he was certain things would go nowhere but down the drain.

He wasn't relationship material. Hadn't he screwed up one of the most important relationships in his life? Wasn't the fear he'd screw up with his daughter driving him crazy now?

How bad would he screw up a romantic relationship? He didn't understand women and wasn't the kind of guy women fell for anyway. Besides, what could he offer a woman, any woman? He was a loner, didn't have much money, and came with way too much baggage, most of it tattered. Any decent woman who learned about his past would go running to the hills like a horse fleeing fire. He'd avoided anything more than momentary flings with women he'd never see again because failure was certain to be the outcome of anything more. And if he failed with a woman now, it could hurt the one person whose affection he could not risk losing, Delanie.

So why would he torture himself with being around a smart, self-assured, college-educated woman like Haylee, especially when a man who had his own trucking company hadn't fit the bill?

What he and Delanie needed was another grandmotherly type like Camille, not a pretty young city woman with beckoning blue eyes and temptingly kissable lips who was only looking for a temporary gig.

Delanie held out her stuffed dog to Haylee. "You can hug Buddy. It will make you feel better."

Haylee took the stuffed dog and gave it a squeeze, making his daughter smile.

Despite everything though, shouldn't he do what was best for his baby girl?

* * *

Was it normal to be turned on by the mere touch of a man? Haylee stood in the pasture, waiting for Trace to adjust the saddle stirrups on the horse he called Buck. How did a man who worked with his hands have such a gentle touch, like a soft whisper, against her sensitive skin?

With his reserved manner, quiet patience, and introverted ways, he was the kind of man who made a woman want to get close and dig under his protective layers to find out what really made him tick. He was an enigma, and that made him attractively intriguing.

Only she wasn't ready for that kind of serious romance. A fling maybe. But he was a father, had a daughter to consider, and she'd never been the kind of girl who could do casual. But Trace Martin made her wish she was.

Trace stepped back from the horse, lead rope in hand. "It's your turn."

Now that the moment of truth was here, her heart was racing. She felt light headed. And an image of her falling off the horse blasted into her head.

"So are you going to tell me how Buck got his name before I get on?"

"Maybe." He chuckled.

Delanie had been ordered to sit on the fence in a tone that brooked no argument, and she gave none. Moose kept her company, also banished by the same tone of voice.

"Seriously. He seems nice enough but…" She brushed the soft, short fur of the horse's neck. Buck turned his face toward her and nudged her side, as if saying he liked her touch.

"It's his color. It's called buckskin." His eyes sparkled, as if he was enjoying the joke.

And of course she should have known that, considering the pretty taupe color and black mane and tail that marked the horse.

She squared her shoulders, took a deep breath and, with her heart still hammering against her rib cage, tried to slide her foot into the stirrup, but it was too high for her short body. One more area where height was a problem.

"Here." His hands made a cradle as he crouched lower. "Put your good knee in here, and when I lift you up, swing your other leg over the saddle."

He stood so close she could see those gold flecks in his hazel eyes, so close she could feel the heat coming off his body, so close she could reach out and touch him.

"Hopefully, not clear to the other side though. I've met the ground today once already."

The corner of his mouth crooked up. "Trust me."

As appealingly innocent as he looked, trust was something she was plumb out of these days, but she placed her knee in firm hands, grabbed the horn, and he lifted her as if the weight was of no consequence. She landed square on the saddle, her legs spread wide and her feet dangling above the stirrups.

"You are a tiny thing," he said in a tone of resignation that made her feel even smaller as he adjusted the stirrups again. His hand clasped her boot at the ankle, giving her a start as he guided her foot into position.

"That scrape feel okay?"

She nodded. The only thing making her uncomfortable was her attraction to him. As a working cowboy with muscles to spare, he came across as tough and capable. But his reticence to say nothing more than necessary, as if he didn't want anyone to get too close, to know too much about him, suggested he had a story, and it wasn't likely to be a very pretty one.

Without a word, he strode over to the other side and repeated the process of adjusting the stirrups. His head bent over his task, a stray lock of hair escaped from under the hatband and brushed across his forehead. She could see perspiration forming on the back of his strong neck—tanned, not burned, from the sun. He guided her left foot into the adjusted stirrup with the same gentle touch.

As she tried out her new position, he grabbed the back of the saddle.

"Now me." His arm brushed her thigh, and he swung up onto the rump of the horse.

Before she could process, strong arms wrapped around her and grabbed the reins, locking her in his embrace, pushing her against his warm body. His heat seeped through her, beads of sweat prickled the back of her neck.

Had she known that was going to be part of the lesson, she'd have asked for it sooner.

He held up the reins. "Take these in your left hand."

She grabbed them as his breath tickled her cheek. His firm chest supported her back, and his strong arms swiped her sides to rest his hands on his thighs. She was in heaven. It had been so long since she'd been this close to a man, her senses were in overload causing her to feel lightheaded and unsettlingly limp.

"Scootch back against the cantle."

His words were a soft breeze in her ear.

"The what?"

"Back of the saddle."

If he kept whispering in her ear, she wasn't going to be able to concentrate on riding. Because sitting in front of him, she was aware of every shift of his thighs, the heat from his chest, the brush of his face against her hat. Surrounded by a sea of Trace Martin testosterone, all her senses focused on him, not his explanation of how to rein a horse. And of course, the instructions were opposite of the English way of riding, so any little bit she could remember from her one lesson at her childhood friend's riding academy was useless. Great.

"Now use your heels to gently nudge him into a walk."

His breath brushed her earlobe. Haylee forced herself to concentrate.

"Remember, cross over the rein in the direction you want the horse to turn."

She followed his directions, and lo and behold, the horse started to walk. Of course, she couldn't tell whether it was her command or Trace had done something, but the important thing was the horse was in motion.

Her body rocked against his firm chest as the

buckskin moved, and she had to consciously resist grabbing the saddle horn for balance.

"Okay, rein him to the right."

Trace's voice was low and soothing, and she wasn't sure if that was for the benefit of the horse or her. She did as he said, and the horse turned.

She wished someone could have taken a picture. Instead, she'd have to rely on mere memory, but she was pretty sure all she would remember was the feel of Trace behind her.

"Shouldn't you be holding the reins?" *And wrapping your arms around me again?*

"You're doing fine. I'm here if you need me. Buck is the calmest horse I have. I actually bought him from your aunt a while back when Delanie came to live with me. Figured he'd be the right temperament for her, and he's not a bad herding horse either. Not my best cutting horse, but he can move cattle, and he isn't spooked by an ornery bull."

"So much to think about when you run a ranch."

"That is an understatement."

She was aware of him shifting his weight, of his chest grazing her back. Of his warm breath on her neck.

"Turn the horse again to the right."

She moved the reins, and the horse responded. They faced Delanie again. The little girl sat on the fence with her elbows on her knees and her head in her hands.

"Delanie looks bored. We don't have to continue…"

"She'll wait. Moose is as good at herding children as cattle, and she knows it."

She laughed. "Who would have thought."

As she walked the horse around the corral, she tried to relax, but the man sitting behind made that difficult. He was just a man, she reminded herself. But her pulse raced, her palms were sweaty, and she was aware of the brush of his body against her back, the brush of his legs against her thighs, the brush of his arms against her shoulder. If this was how she now reacted to a good-looking man, the fact he didn't want to hire her was probably a blessing.

Buck was a gentleman, calm and steady like his owner, but when Trace asked if she'd had enough, she nodded.

No sense pushing fate, for either the horse or the man.

"Guide him to the fence post."

Whether she was guiding him or the horse was simply walking in that direction was hard to discern, but as they approached the fence, Trace's rough hand covered her left one, and he tugged gently on the reins. The horse stopped. His hand lingered over hers for a moment, and she was hemmed in by man, soft fabric, and horse.

"You never want to pull hard on a horse's mouth if you can avoid it. Slow and gentle and with tenderness."

Her insides quivered. Was he talking about horses or something else?

Trace slid off Buck, freeing her for a second, before he rested his hand on her thigh. "You want to try dismounting?"

Haylee checked the long distance to the ground. "Is there another way?"

"Sure is." He held up his hands.

She took a deep breath. Talk about up close and personal.

Leaning over, she rested her hands upon firm shoulders, and allowed herself to be gathered into a solid pair of arms. She slid down his body like he was a pole and she was a dancer. The scent of soap, combined with fresh earth, tickled her nostrils and his warm body heated hers as his breath puffed against her forehead.

It was easy to imagine being embraced by him, kissed by him.

She looked up. Like an intimate caress, his gaze perused her face, her lips, her throat causing her pulse to jump with each stop.

What would it feel like if he kissed her?

He stepped back as if he'd heard her thoughts…and wasn't interested.

"I've been reconsidering," he said, sliding his hands into his pockets. "If you haven't made other plans yet and are still interested, I'd like to hire you to watch Delanie. And if you can cook dinner too, that would be a plus. You'd get an hourly wage and gas money, of course, so you can pick up Delanie after school or camp." He named a modest sum. "It would be three until six, sometimes six thirty if that isn't a problem, Monday through Friday, including holidays if they fall on those days and you can spare the time. Cattle don't take a day off, unfortunately. Is it a deal?"

Chapter 7

Haylee started work on Monday, despite sore thighs from her short riding lesson. By Wednesday Haylee's aunt and uncle were headed for New Mexico, and by that cloudy Friday she was able to master the small kitchen enough to attempt a Julia Child pork recipe with all the trimmings while Delanie sat at the kitchen table, engrossed in making clay models of foods. So far there was a pizza in yellow clay with little red clay spots on it, a long white clay log that Haylee guessed was bread, and a brown clay cake with pink squiggles on it. Not a vegetable to be found.

And then there was the cowboy taking a shower in the bathroom down the hall. Trace had come in from the range covered in dust and announced he was showering before dinner. Try as she might, the image of Trace that first day, drenched in water, his chest bare, played on a loop in her mind as she basted the meat and then closed the oven door. Yeah, she had a serious case of lust that had only intensified each day she'd worked for him.

So far she seemed to have scored well in the meal department, making dishes like beef stew, baked ziti, and meatloaf from Trace's surprisingly well-stocked freezer and pantry. She didn't figure Trace for a foodie, so she'd ditched her beef pappardelle, salmon cindy, and similar recipes, though there was probably a chicken fricassee and ham cassoulet in his future.

Roy had enjoyed cooking as much as she did. But Roy's interest in recipes was not a match for the quiet sparkle that appeared in Trace's eyes as he sniffed the air for a hint of the menu. Considering he had been the one who had to prepare meals after a hard day out in the elements, she was sure even scrapple would have been appreciated as long as he didn't have to make it.

"I'm hungry, Haylee." Delanie looked up from clay pie she'd just assembled.

"Your father will be right out. Want some milk and a piece of homemade bread to tide you over?" Haylee set the oven on warm now that the dish was ready.

Delanie nodded. The child was, gratefully, not a fussy eater. In fact, she had attacked every meal with gusto, but the little girl was still rail thin, like Haylee had been at that age.

As Haylee finished pouring Delanie some milk, Trace appeared in the doorway, dressed in black work-out pants and a white T-shirt stretched over his chest, revealing a nice set of biceps bursting out of the shirtsleeves. His hair was damp, and a few beads of water adorned his forehead. He hadn't shaved, as evident from the five o'clock shadow that graced his jaw.

The man was a western Adonis, but she'd known some pretty good-looking men, and none had caused her heart to palpitate, her palms to sweat, and her stomach to feel like someone had taken an eggbeater to it. The odd thing about Trace was that he didn't seem aware he was a walking calendar model.

She pulled the pan from the oven, set it on top of the stove, and retrieved a floral platter from one of the cabinets.

If it was just a physical attraction, would she be looking out the window a dozen times while making dinner, hoping to catch a glimpse of him, or feel shy and awkward when in his presence?

Moving the pork to the platter, she reached for the carving knife that was shoved into a slit in a block of wood. Trace was by her side in an instant.

"I'll cut." He carefully removed the knife from her hand, as if she'd been ready to commit a lethal act. With a nod in her direction, he began to carve the meat in precise, even slices.

Truth was, he intrigued her. She had a ton of questions. Did he grow up on this ranch? Were his parents alive? Where was Delanie's mother? Did he have a woman in his life? But his reluctance to engage in conversation beyond a day's pleasantries, as well as the fact none of it was her business, had kept her curiosity in check.

When he finished slicing the pork, Haylee set the platter on the table, and Trace slid into his usual spot.

Still, it would be nice if he could engage in some conversation beyond the one-syllable responses he gave to any attempts to engage him.

"Smells good," he said as she dished out a sizeable portion of meat, potatoes, and vegetables for him.

It was his usual comment, but she still felt a twinge of satisfaction as she placed the dish before him and set to placing a smaller portion of the same on Delanie's plate. Delanie had shoved her clay food aside, eager for the real deal.

Having served everyone, Haylee grabbed a seat at the table. Trace had been insistent she eat dinner with them rather than go home to the cabin to eat by herself, for which she was grateful. She hadn't been prepared for the isolation of working from home and in the "hinterlands," no less, where she didn't see a car, much less a person for most of the time.

"Everyone have a good day?" she asked, digging into her own plate and savoring the taste of the seasoned pork. Living so far from people, and only speaking with a five-year-old, precocious as she was, Haylee wasn't ready to give up hope she could get Trace talking.

"Fine," Trace said. He hadn't even lifted his head to look at her but concentrated on his meal like he was waiting for it to come to life.

"We're going to start camp next week." Delanie filled in the silence as they ate, describing the main difference between preschool and camp—a wading pool for warm days.

As Delanie chattered on about who was staying for the camp and who wasn't, Haylee stole a glance in Trace's direction looking for clues as to whether he liked the meal. His stoic expression revealed nothing. Only a second helping convinced her he enjoyed the dish.

Finished talking, Delanie scooped up the last of her food leaving a clean plate. Patting her tummy, she asked if she could go outside to the swing set.

"Take Moose with you," Trace said, pointing his fork at the dog that rested near the kitchen door.

As the door slammed shut, Haylee rose to clear off the table.

"I'll get that." Trace stood, his tall body crowding

her in the cramped space as he grabbed plates off the table. "Thanks for the meal."

"I can do it." The man was paying her, after all, and giving her free dinner, which had she not eaten with him, her meals would have consisted of a lot of mac and cheese—ironic for a woman who prided herself on her cooking.

He glanced back at her over his shoulder. "You cooked. I clean up. That's the deal around here."

The muscles on his back flexed as he bent to load the dishwasher. "Besides, I want to talk with you."

Had she done something wrong? She paged through her memory and came up empty, but she braced herself for bad news. He'd been reluctant to hire her. Maybe now he was having second thoughts. And what would that mean for her aunt and uncle? For her? She had that uncomfortable feeling in her stomach, as if she had eaten too much of a rich dessert.

After turning on the dishwasher, he strode to the screen door and leaned against the doorjamb so he had a clear view of the swing set.

"Have I annoyed you in some way?" She bit her lip and waited.

He glanced in her direction. "Why do you say that?"

"You barely spare a word for me." Did that sound needy?

He cocked his head and gave her his full attention. "Is there something particular *you* want to talk about?" He looked truly puzzled.

"I'd like to know something about what you do out there." She nodded toward the back door.

He looked bemused. "I work."

"At what?" Conversation with Trace was like pulling a tree stump out of hard ground.

"Today I baled hay, but the baler had a bent tooth. Part has to be sent for." He ran his hands through his hair, as if her questions were confusing him.

Only this was the most conversation she'd had with an adult all week.

"How much hay do you need to bale?"

He crossed his arms over his chest, as if he was trying to decide if he was annoyed or amused by her questions.

"It's a crap shoot. I try for the middle ground, which usually means that if it's a bad winter, I'll need a lot and have to supplement by buying at sky-high prices and likely lose money. If it's a mild winter, I'll have to sell some dirt cheap."

"I bet I could come up with a calculation to provide you with the optimum amount to plant that would maximize your return and minimize your loss. I'm a pretty good financial analyst."

"Uh-huh." He didn't seem impressed. "You make out a grocery list for next week?" His focus shifted outside.

Her shoulders slumped. She couldn't even convince Trace to give her a chance, even though she'd no intention of charging him. Pretty much how her week had gone.

At least he was talking about next week. That sick feeling in her stomach eased some.

"I left it on the counter." She was planning on pot roast and maybe that ham cassoulet.

"Everything going okay?"

She nodded.

"I was wondering, if you wouldn't mind, and only when you are taking care of Delanie of course, of allowing me to track your location on my phone. If you were to break down or something, well, you are on some pretty isolated roads, and you don't know the area yet."

"Sure." She hadn't thought of it, but it sounded like a good idea.

"You can track me as well. Cell service is spotty out on the range, but you'd have an idea in case I didn't come in or something."

"Sounds like a plan."

"I'm not much for technology, but sometimes it comes in handy." Crossing his bare feet, he rooted in his pocket for something. The loose fabric of his work-out pants fluttered against his thighs. "Here." He pulled out a white envelope and held it out to her.

When Haylee reached for it, his roughened fingers touched hers, and she felt that unsettling tingle again. She needed to keep it together just a little while longer. Just until she was out the door and in her own car.

She peeked at the bills it contained, smiled, and tucked it into her back pocket. Now she'd be able to put some food back in her own refrigerator.

"Thank you."

"See you Monday?" he asked, as if in need of reassurance. "We can get in another riding lesson in the evening if you'd like."

"Monday for a lesson would be great." She'd been afraid to ask about another lesson, afraid he'd wonder if her interest was more in him than riding. And truthfully, after a week seeing him every day, breaking bread with him at night, watching the sweet way he interacted with his daughter, she wasn't sure which it was.

He nodded at her sneakers, which she had found much better than sandals for running after a five-year-old. "Did you get boots yet?"

"Just have my booties." Though she hated using them for riding, and the slender heels clearly weren't suitable for the task.

He shook his head. "I guess those will have to do."

"See you Monday," she said as she grabbed her purse. Now she could relax, have a glass of wine, watch one of the shows she'd recorded, knowing she had money in her pocket and a job to come back to.

"And, Haylee," he said as she brushed past him. "You don't annoy me in the least."

"I think I'm attracted to my boss," Haylee said, sipping her margarita in the lounge of the Cattleman's Club. It was Saturday and she'd driven up to Cheyenne to see Jenna and spend the evening. An hour into her visit, her itching eyes had driven them out of the apartment, any thought of staying over vanquished. And now that Jenna's boyfriend, Kent, had shown up, Haylee was definitely a third wheel who would head home in a bit.

Kent had offered to get them both another drink from the bar. Jenna had accepted, and Haylee, aware she'd be driving, had passed. Considering the area around the bar was at least four deep, Haylee expected he would be a while.

She was surprised to find any club scene in

Cheyenne, but the Cattleman's Club was hopping, and cowboy hats were, apparently, de rigueur. The black tables gleamed under the light from a single candle, and the dim lighting above kept the large space from feeling cavernous. The dance floor was packed, and the music was country. She'd already done a few line dances, so she was happy to take a break.

"Well, who wouldn't be, but what happened to 'it's too soon' and 'I'm not ready.'" Jenna grabbed a fistful of the complimentary popcorn sitting on the table.

"Still true. But I'm having a hard time fighting biology. Brain says one thing. Body something totally different. It's just that the man looks so fine." Or maybe it was how good he was with his daughter. Or how considerate he'd been, asking her to eat with them. Or…how needy she'd felt lately. "You know he's teaching me how to ride."

"Oh, riding lessons. Nice personal time." Jenna eyed Haylee like she was sizing her up. "Question is, how does he feel about you? If he's not feeling anything, then you have nothing to worry about. It will be like desiring a hot actor, like Ryan Reynolds. Nice to look at. Great to think about. But never going to happen."

Haylee sighed. "Only I don't see Ryan Reynolds in the flesh every day, now do I? This cowboy is unbelievably hard to read, so I don't think I would know if he did like me. And it would actually be pretty much of a disaster if he did."

"Maybe you are just feeling vulnerable. You are all alone out there, living like a hermit."

Haylee took a swig of the remnants of her drink. "Maybe that's it. But it doesn't change the fact that I can't seem to help myself even though I know it is bad on so many levels. He's my boss. He's got his own issues." Because there was something he wasn't saying about Delanie's mother. Haylee refused to believe the woman just abandoned such a sweet child. "And I'm still raw from getting a divorce from the man I pledged to love in sickness and in health, for richer or poorer, till death do us part." But the vows hadn't said anything about criminal behavior.

"Maybe it's just rebound stuff going on," Jenna said over the din of the music and chatter.

Haylee shook her head. "It's been a year since Roy and I started down the divorce path, so I don't think it's rebound." It was something more. "I've never been this preoccupied with anyone. I can barely have a thought without him being in it." She'd never had trouble concentrating when she'd been dating Roy.

"What's the worst that can happen if he's interested?"

"Ah, I could lose my job when we break up, as we most certainly will since we have nothing in common, not to mention I'll be moving on after the sale of my aunt's place." She could not let mere physical attraction ruin a good thing, even if it was a temporary good thing.

"So then don't pursue anything."

"Easier said than done. There is something about him…a lot about him I like. It's not just a physical attraction. I just can't put my finger on what it is."

Jenna raised her eyebrows. "Maybe on a subconscious level, you realize he's the one. Because, honey, sometimes love just hits you over the head."

"Totally not. He is so not my type."

Jenna leaned forward. "You mean the damn-the-torpedoes, success-at-all-cost type? The financially secure, never-worry-about-money type? And where has that gotten you?"

"I'm not as shallow as you make out." At least she hoped she wasn't. "There's a lot I liked about Roy beyond his business acumen." Which was seriously flawed, it turned out.

"Uh-huh." Jenna's tone couldn't have been more dismissive. "I have never met anyone more afraid of becoming one of those—what did you call them?—bag ladies, than you."

"No one wants to be homeless." That wasn't an irrational fear.

"But most people with a college degree and some smarts don't worry about it all the time like you do."

Maybe some of her fear stemmed from feeling alone in the world, despite the good intentions of her parents and sister. It was a feeling she'd never been able to shake. But she wasn't crazy just because she worried about losing everything, because look what had just happened to her. Not to mention, her parents had almost lost their house in the Great Recession debacle on Wall Street, her father being a commodities trader. Her mother had gone back to work in real estate, and Haylee had readily taken over after-school care of her sister. And for a fee, the care of several other children on the block, and spent most of her weekends babysitting. She still remembered the dread she felt every time she heard her parents argue about money. There was nothing out of the ordinary about wanting to be on firm financial footing.

"Financial security is a worthwhile goal, as any of our finance professors would tell you."

Jenna raised her glass to her lips. "That's why you went into finance, isn't it? You were hoping to find out the secret to becoming wealthy."

"Finance provides a good career path. If I can't make a go of my own business, there are plenty of corporations where I can get a job, especially in Denver. I won't go jobless." And hopefully, not homeless. "I'm a hard worker. I've got skills."

"Yes, you do, and I admire that you are trying to start your own business, don't get me wrong. But business is one thing. Judging a potential husband only on his ability to provide for you financially is…well, it isn't enough. Maybe that's what your subconscious is trying to tell you."

"In any event, I'm not interested in a potential husband…financially or otherwise."

On the hour ride home that night, Jenna's words swirled in Haylee's mind. Was she already feeling something for the cowboy on some subconscious level, like Jenna said? Or was she just feeling a biological attraction to the first man who paid her a modicum of attention after a failed marriage? And was she resisting those feelings because, by the look of things, Trace wasn't exactly swimming in money? Was she that shallow?

The safest path was to bury her feelings. She hoped her heart was listening.

* * *

Trace sat atop Archer and watched as Corey, the young high school kid who worked for him, rode along the outskirts of the herd on one of Trace's horses, a rope in hand. The teen had picked up roping like he'd been born to it, and now that school was finally out, Trace tried to spend time each day letting the kid practice.

His phone vibrated, and he looked at the caller ID. "Got to take this," Trace called "Check out that fence in the far pasture for me?"

As Corey headed off, Trace hit the accept button and braced for bad news.

"Hello, Dan." Nothing good came of a lawyer calling midday. "What's up?"

"I made sure to tell the court evaluator that you had someone to look after Delanie now. She wants to interview her. This week. That okay?"

Trace heaved a sigh. "Guess it will have to be. I haven't really talked to Haylee about the custody suit." Or about Delanie's mother.

"Well, I expect now might be a good time. I'm asking you one more time to reconsider settling this thing without the court. All she wants is to visit her kid, Trace."

"You know where Delanie will have to visit her? The worst that will happen is what Doreen is asking, so I don't see the benefit of settling anything."

"Not true. The judge could also determine that you shouldn't have permanent custody."

Those words pierced Trace's thick skin like none other. "Is that likely?"

"When you let one person decide things, you are always taking a chance. He's not too thrilled that you two haven't worked it out. And you do have some baggage. Just think about it. There's lots of kids who see their parents there."

But how many had been left by their mother with a virtual stranger? Had been neglected by that mother? Had been exposed to things no child should be exposed to? Her mother had abandoned her just like Trace's mother had him and Ty under different circumstances. Delanie was young, much younger than he had been, and therefore the child might be able to forget her mother if she wasn't seeing her all the time. Then again, it had almost been a year, and his daughter still had a picture of her mother on the dresser and waited for those phone calls like she was waiting for Santa.

"I'll think about it."

Sitting on the comfortable plaid sofa in the living area of her aunt's cabin that Monday after lunch, Haylee hit the Print button and listened for the sound of the printer located on the table near the kitchen. Though the cabin was small, the large open area that housed the kitchen, dining table, and living room made it feel spacious, and with the stone fireplace that must be a treasure in the winter, it also felt homey. Surely someone would find it appealing.

Haylee just had to see a hard copy of the email notifying her of her first photography sale. Only twenty dollars, but these days, every little bit counted because in the last week she'd only added one additional account to her freight-auditing business. Apparently, in the two years since she had left the marketplace, software had improved and there were a lot more auditors offering their services to the small customer.

She plugged in the URL for her bank account and scanned the account activity. Yup, the funds had landed. Switching back to her email, an unfamiliar name snagged her attention. The subject line: *More photographs?*

She didn't usually open emails from people she didn't know, but she clicked on this one and read the simple request: *Did she have any pictures of cowboys?* The sender went on to say she had purchased a landscape picture of Haylee's for the background of a book cover and wondered if the photographer had any photos of a cowboy to license.

Haylee typed the sender's name into the search screen, and a website popped up with lots of book covers with titles like *His Lonely Heart* and *The Cowboy Comes Home*. From her own knowledge of graphic design, Haylee could tell the covers were well done. And something she would love to do herself if she could pay bills doing it.

She sat back, tapped her finger against her chin. Of course she had pictures of cowboys. Lots of them from the rodeo, but she didn't have a release from any of those cowboys, which was why she hadn't posted them on the website that licensed photographs. The only cowboy she knew that she could get a release from was Trace.

As long as they don't appear on Facebook or something. I'm not one for the public eye.

She doubted he'd be interested, but she could at least ask.

Her cell phone rang. She glanced at the caller ID and steeled herself as she hit the button.

"Hello, Livvy." She hadn't heard from her younger sister, Olivia, since she'd made the decision to stay in Wyoming.

"How's it going in cowboy country?" Her sister's voice sounded cheerily forced.

"Good." As long as she didn't need money.

"I thought I would come for a visit."

Haylee's mind grappled for an excuse. She wasn't ready for her sister. She loved her, but it was no secret they were two different people who couldn't spend twenty-four hours together without getting on each other's nerves.

"You know I'm working every day. I can't really show you around."

"Don't you get the weekend off?"

"Sort of." Of course she did.

"Good. I'll be coming this weekend."

No asking if it was okay. Or if Haylee had other plans. She didn't. But the presumption irritated her nonetheless.

"Do I have to pick you up?"

"I'm flying into Denver, and yes."

"You sure you want to spend money on airfare?" As a yoga instructor, Olivia didn't earn much, which was a constant source of irritation to her parents, who had paid for a decent college education for their two daughters. She supposed her parents felt both of their children had let them down.

"Mom's paying for it. She's sending me to check on you."

Haylee closed her eyes and silently counted to ten. "Great. What day are you coming in? I have to work on Friday until 6:30."

"I'm taking that cheap airline, and they aren't scheduled to get in until 7:30, but since they are always late, no probs. Besides, I can wait."

Apparently her sister had booked the flights without talking to Haylee first, but that was Livvy. She did what she wanted and just assumed it would all work out. Sometimes it did. Often it didn't.

"Fine."

"Line up some hot cowboys, would you? Aunt Paula says you work for one, and I can't wait to meet him. See you soon."

The line went dead.

Haylee gritted her back molars. The one thing she would not do was introduce her sister to Trace Martin.

Chapter 8

Trace retrieved the cardboard box from his pickup and waited for Haylee and Delanie to step outside after dinner. The conversation with his lawyer had been playing on a loop in his mind all day, and he was dog tired. But he'd promised Haylee a riding lesson that Monday, and the early summer evening, when it stayed light so late, was the perfect time for it. Besides, he had a little surprise for her and was amazed at his eagerness to give it to her, though he wasn't sure how she'd receive it. He was just showing his appreciation for all the home-cooked meals. Nothing more.

There was no denying that he thought about her…a lot. But he was wise enough to know that was a recipe for disaster. To start with, sophisticated city girls like Haylee were out of his league. A guy with his past didn't attract sane, reasonable women. Add to that the fact they had nothing in common except she loved to cook and he loved to eat. And then there was his abysmal track record with women specifically, and most people in general. Not to mention she was here only temporarily and the caregiver for his daughter, which was working out too well for him to screw it up for a one-night stand. There was enough drama in his life. He didn't have the bandwidth for any more, much less drama he created.

He waited by the pickup as Haylee walked hand in hand with Delanie up the path toward the barn and pastures. In those short black boots, a sleeveless top, and jean shorts, her curly hair wisping around her smiling face, no flimsy hat in sight, Haylee reminded him of why he shouldn't have hired her. Too cute for his own good.

But tonight he had to talk to Haylee about the court-appointed evaluator's interview and tell her things he wasn't exactly proud of. Haylee would undoubtedly be shocked. He'd gotten the distinct impression she'd been sheltered from the worst of life and too sweet, too happy, and too trusting to understand life's underbelly.

From the moment he would confess, she'd think differently about him. She'd understand what a loser he'd been and probably still was. She'd know the ugly in his life. She'd learn his weakness. She'd be glad her stint was temporary and never look at him in a good light again.

Not that there was any possibility with someone like Haylee, but he'd be closing the door on the fantasy.

His hand tightened around the box. His child was all that mattered, all that should matter.

"What's that, Daddy? For me?" Delanie asked, breaking away from Haylee at a run.

"No, sweet pea, it's for Haylee. I bought it at the store when you were getting sneakers." Delanie was at a stage where she seemed to need new sneakers every few months.

Disappointment marked his little girl's face.

"What is it?" Delanie stood before him, her focus on the package. "Can I open it?"

"It's for Haylee to open."

Delanie turned toward Haylee, who was coming behind her. "Can I open the present, Haylee?"

Haylee frowned. "That's for me?" She looked more annoyed than curious. Maybe he had done the wrong thing. No surprise there. Story of his life.

He handed the box to Haylee. "Let Haylee open it."

"You can help me, Delanie." Haylee held the box out, and Delanie opened the lid.

He heard his heart beat in his ears as Haylee's mouth formed a perfect O and her eyebrows arched. "Are these for me?" She placed the box on the ground and pulled out a plain brown barn boot. "And a size five. How did you know?"

"You mentioned your size the other day."

"And you remembered?" She hopped around, trying to pull off her black boot.

He opened the truck's door. "Sit in here. It'll be easier."

Carrying the box, she hopped over and plunked herself onto the driver's seat. Two nicely shaped legs dangled out of the cab. He knelt down.

That urge to kiss his way up her leg surfaced. He tamped it down. Not the time. Not the place. Not the person.

"What are you doing?" she asked.

He grabbed her unzipped bootie at her ankle. "Pulling these off you." His fingers brushed creamy skin as he pulled on the zipper and slipped the boot off. For a little thing, she had the nicest legs. He unzipped the other boot and pulled it off. She wiggled ten dainty toes painted blood red. Toes he could imagine sucking one by one and then licking his way up her leg.

He looked up, and his gaze snagged on her sweet smile. A surge of electricity zinged through him like lightning following a wire. Yeah, this could get hazardous. He rose.

Her toes disappeared into one boot, and then she tugged on the other and stood up. "They fit. How much do I owe you?"

That hurt. "Nothing. It's a gift. In appreciation for the meals you're cooking us."

She looked up at him. "You paid me for that already."

"I may have paid you to make us dinner. I didn't expect those dinners to be lip-smacking good."

"Really, I can't…"

He placed his finger on her warm, moist lips, and his whole body shuddered like he'd stuck his finger in a socket. She stared up at him with a look that made him want to wrap his arms around her and kiss her until those sweet painted toes of hers curled, circumstances being otherwise. But circumstances weren't otherwise. "Consider it a favor. Not sure my insurance would cover you getting your foot trampled. Those things you call boots are cute enough, but they won't save your toes. These barn boots may look plain, but your pretty little feet are safe."

"When you put it like that…" She looped a strand of curly hair around her finger. "Guess all I can say is thank you."

That smile of hers sent a funny feeling in the vicinity of his heart. She was temptation wrapped up in a sunny blond package of pure sweetness. And lord knew he had a sweet tooth. "I've never had cowgirl boots before. They're so comfortable."

She wrapped her old boots in the box and laid it on the seat, closing the truck door. "I'll get these later."

However attracted he was to her, he'd just be pining after something he could never have. He'd had his fill of that in other areas of his life. He didn't need to add to it.

He felt a tug on his shirt.

"Daddy, let's saddle up. You promised to take me on Archer."

"So I did."

He held out his hands, and Delanie grabbed one and Haylee the other, Delanie's hand cold, Haylee's warm and soft. The trio walked up the path together.

This was what some men had. A good woman, a kid or two, and a ranch to call home. He may have two of the three, but he knew he wasn't cut out to have it all.

Haylee only half listened to Trace's instructions on cinching the saddle as Buck stood patiently in the pasture. The rest of her mind mulled over the fact he'd bought her a pair of barn boots that fit her. It was so…considerate. Her heart had skipped a beat when she'd looked up at him and he'd looked like…well, he'd looked like he wanted to kiss her. And crazy thing was, she would have let him.

Maybe not so crazy, since she'd confessed she

was falling for the guy. And his thoughtful gift only made the attraction stronger.

Not that a practical gift for safety reasons was a declaration of romantic interest. She was reading too much into things, likely because she was lonely, like Jenna had said.

There had been many things she'd loved about being married and sharing her life with someone, especially in that first year, before she'd known what was really going on. She'd loved cooking for a man who prided himself on his gourmet taste. She'd liked the comfortable evenings together watching TV or entertaining their mutual friends. She'd enjoyed waking up to someone who had professed his love for her. She'd liked belonging somewhere and to someone. And she'd loved working alongside him to make their business successful. Until she realized that the man she did those things with was not the man she'd thought he was.

That experience should prevent her from being attracted to a guy she knew nothing about. A man so closed mouth she couldn't tell if he liked her food, much less her.

"Today you can ride by yourself," he said, coming around behind her.

She hoped the disappointment didn't show on her face. She'd been looking forward to the torture of up close and personal.

He held out cradled hands, and she placed her knee in their warm embrace. She was lifted onto the saddle in one movement and swung her other leg over Buck.

"Boots feel okay?" he asked as he grasped her leather-protected ankle and tugged to make sure her foot was securely in the stirrup.

"Great. It was very thoughtful. A girl could fall for a guy like you."

She instantly regretted her slip of the tongue as Trace's head jerked back liked she'd slapped him. *She* could fall for a guy like him, but she hadn't meant to admit it.

"Don't." He turned and walked toward Delanie.

Trace watched Haylee out of the corner of his eye as they rode their horses in tandem into open pasture. The tall grasses swished against the legs of the horses. They wouldn't do anything more than a walk today. He had Delanie with him, for one thing. And an inexperienced rider, for another.

Archer threw his head up, anxious to let loose. Yeah, he knew just how his horse felt.

He hadn't expected being around Haylee on a regular basis to cause so many restless nights and fantasy dreams. There was something about that woman keeping Trace's attention, and he wished he knew what it was so he could get over it.

Coming in every day to the scent of home cooking and a woman in his kitchen, *this* woman in his kitchen, had him hankering after something that had always been out of his reach…a permanent relationship that included hearth, home, family. Considering his own upbringing and his troubled past, he knew his life was about as far from a Currier and Ives picture as a man's could be, but that didn't make him want it any less.

Knowing his brother, Ty, had that picture only added to his frustration. Somehow, Ty had been able to break out of the shackles of broken dreams and shattered emotions and find happiness with a woman who was the perfect match for Trace's stubborn, arrogant, and driven brother.

But Trace knew there was no one for him. No one wanted a broken-down recovering alcoholic who preferred living like a hermit to having a social life, didn't understand people, much less women, was struggling to make ends meet, and was just plain rotten husband material.

And the sheltered city girl with curly hair, simmering blue eyes, a sense of humor, strong spirit, and a way with kids, not to mention the skills of a gourmet chef, wasn't the one for him.

Didn't make him want her any less though.

So while he shouldn't have treated her comment about falling for a guy like him as if it were a declaration rather than a throwaway compliment, he'd panicked. Because when he told her the truth about himself, she'd be thanking her lucky stars she hadn't fallen for someone like him.

"How far are we riding?" she asked, her body bouncing as Buck moved into a trot.

Archer was eager to follow, but Trace held him steady.

"Far as you feel comfortable." Bouncing like that, it wasn't likely to be long. Not that he wasn't enjoying the motion of her breasts and body, but she'd be plenty sore the next day.

"Give a slight tug on your reins to slow Buck down to a walk. And slide back against the cantle. You won't bounce so much."

Yeah, he was in trouble. He'd known it when he'd first seen her. Knew it when he hired her. But he'd been arrogant, thinking he could control his attraction.

Buck, now slightly ahead, responded to her tug and settled back into a walk.

"Be careful you don't squeeze your legs. He'll take that as a command you want to go faster."

Now he had a nice view of a firm backside in stretched-tight shorts.

"Are we going out to the herd," she called from ahead.

Not likely. "Take us a full hour to reach the summer pastures. You'd have to come in the morning for that if you want to get there by horse."

"I'd like to bring my camera again if I did."

He'd like to run his fingers through the ringlets of blond hair tumbling along her shoulders. He bet it was as soft as her skin.

"Daddy, I just saw a rabbit." Delanie held on to the horn and leaned over. "But he ran away."

Just the reminder he needed that he wasn't in any position to think about Haylee that way. She wasn't for him. He wasn't for her. He had enough on his plate. No sense asking for trouble by taking on something he knew would fail.

Up ahead, Buck swung to the side, nostrils flaring, and backed up, prancing around like he was going to take off.

"Hold on, baby girl," Trace said and wrapped his free arm around his daughter as he urged Archer to catch up to Buck.

Haylee was holding on to the horn with one hand as she tugged on the reins with the other. Buck stopped, but his nostrils still flared.

Reaching Buck, Trace angled Archer near enough so he could reach the reins if he had to, but Haylee seemed to have the situation under control.

"You okay?"

She nodded, but her face was white, and she had a death grip on the saddle horn.

"You did really well, cowgirl." Trace meant that sincerely.

"Why did he do that?"

Trace glanced past Buck and spotted the cause of the commotion. A coyote stood in the middle of the field, staring out at them, not moving a muscle.

"Damn coyotes. They're getting bolder and bolder."

"Daddy, you said a bad word."

"My apologies, sweet pea." He tried not to swear around his child, but sometimes it just tumbled out.

"He's not bothering anyone." Delanie defended her newfound friend.

"He'd bother Moose if we had taken him with us. Coyotes may look like dogs, Delanie, but they are wild, and they'll go after a dog or a calf or a chicken if they get the chance. That's why Buck was dancing. He doesn't like them any more than I do."

"Bad Coyote."

Yeah, his child's loyalties were easily changed at this age. And that was what scared him.

He'd have to come back alone and find the predator. Out in the wild, coyotes were looking for one thing…prey to kill. Trace waved his hat, and the coyote, as if on cue, took off in the opposite direction.

He jammed the hat back on his head and turned his attention to Haylee.

"You want to head back?"

Haylee's chest rose as she took a deep breath. "No." She squared her shoulders. "I did do pretty well, didn't I?"

"You handled it just fine." Except for gripping the horn.

"You get many of them out here?"

"More than I'd like." One was more than he liked. "Most of the time they go after rabbits, skunks…or your aunt's chickens when she had them." He smiled. He knew Paula Johnson had shot a coyote or two in her day, but he didn't think it was the time to mention it or the rifle he always carried on the back of his horse. "But I've lost more than one calf to coyotes." And they'd cleaned a carcass down to the bones. "We also get a bear now and then and, closer to the mountains, a mountain lion on occasion."

She nudged Buck into a walk. "Maybe you and Archer should lead the way."

An hour later as they rode back to the barn, Haylee tried to concentrate on the waving grasses, the rolling taupe-colored hills in the distance, and the stream that cut a blue path through the flat pastures, but she was fighting biology, and as she stared at Trace sitting high in the saddle, biology was winning.

She wasn't worried about Buck, surprisingly. The horse's nervousness had scared her at the time, but he'd behaved quite well by letting her know something dangerous was ahead yet not sending her flying off his back. Now that she understood why, she felt safe on Buck. She trusted the horse.

And that was how Trace made her feel…safe, secure. But, after what she'd gone through with Roy, she knew better than to trust those feelings.

They reached the pastures by the barn, and she watched Trace flick open the corral gate and ride through. She, or rather Buck, followed. The ride was over, and she would be heading home in the waning light of day. To an empty house. In the middle of nowhere.

She'd wanted this. And in some respects it suited her needs. Kept her from bumping into Roy. Kept her from knowing what he was up to. It also kept her isolated. And alone.

Cowboy that he was, Trace dismounted Archer in one smooth motion and then set Delanie on the ground before tying his horse to the post. "Nudge Buck over here, and I'll tie him up and get you down."

No need to nudge Buck. He was already heading for the fence post.

"I have to go to the bathroom," Delanie said. And she took off toward the house like a bullet.

"Hurry back out as soon as you're done," Trace called after her as he secured Buck to the other fence post.

He wandered around to her side and held up his arms. "I've got you."

Yeah, she was afraid he did, and without even trying.

She leaned toward him, rested her hands on his firm shoulders, and he gathered her to him as if she wasn't anything more than a small bale of hay. She scraped against his warm body as she slid down the front of him, down his muscled chest, past his tight abdomen, past his groin, until her new boots hit the ground.

His hands held tight to her waist, and she looked up into eyes filled with exactly what she was feeling. It was going to happen. Days of craving his touch, and it was going to happen. She tightened her arms around his neck, brushed her fingers along the smooth skin where his hair feathered his collar, and stared up at him with a dare in her eyes. Or pleading. She wasn't sure which.

He lowered his face to within an inch of hers. "You've been driving me crazy since you fell in the mud. With your blond curls, your sweet ways, and those shorts that expose all that leg. I shouldn't be thinking about you like this."

Hazel eyes bored into her, making it hard to breathe. "If it's not now, it will likely be never."

She nodded, giving him silent permission. His lips swept across hers like a soaking rain across dry fields, and his rough hand cupped her cheek, holding her mouth in place as he took what she was offering.

She urged him on, running her hand across his jawline, stubbled with a five o'clock shadow. His tongue rimmed her lips, and she opened her mouth so he could slip inside. She felt him shudder as she rubbed against his firm body and the prominent bulge in his jeans. Raw power surged through her, and a moan slid up her throat and into his mouth. His lips created a heat that danced along her arms, circled her chest, and plunged down her abdomen to settle between her thighs.

She leaned into him as his fingers splayed through her hair, holding her head as he kissed her hard and long before his hands brushed the side of her neck, traveled to her shoulders, and then cupped her breast. His tongue danced with hers, his thumb found her nipple beneath her clothes, and like a switch, she rose up on her toes, prepared to let biology take over.

The slam of the kitchen door filled the air. He stopped, stiffened, stepped back. Electricity arced between them.

"I..."

"Me too," she gasped.

Chapter 9

Haylee sat on the worn couch in Trace's living room and marveled at how wonderful she felt. She'd turned off the overhead light and, instead, lighted the small lamp on the table, which gave a warmer, more intimate glow. Having finally kissed Trace, it was as if a giant pressure valve had been turned to release. She didn't know where this would take her, but at the moment, she didn't care. He had asked her to stay until he put Delanie to bed. She'd happily complied.

There was no putting the genie back in the bottle, and she, for one, was happy it was freed.

They would just have to be careful around Delanie. She didn't want the little girl to get confused about what was going on. But that didn't mean they shouldn't explore the relationship. For the first time since things had gone south with Roy, she felt like a desirable woman again, young, giddy, and infatuated.

She looked around the living area, and it was as if she was seeing it with new eyes. Eyes that wanted to know more about the man who occupied the home, had grown up in the house, and was now raising his daughter there. Her gaze snagged on a pretty platter set on an easel atop the cabinet that held the television. She rose to examine it more closely.

It was an odd pattern, with colors of gold, ruby, and forest green woven in something that looked both Victorian and Asian, against a white background.

"That was my mother's, and probably her mother's before her," Trace said.

Her heart jumped in her chest at the sound of his voice. She turned around to face him. "It's lovely. And unusual."

"Don't know what happened to the rest of the plates. Probably sold them when times were tough. But that platter always had pride of place in our house." He thrust his hands into the pockets of his jeans. "All I really kept of my mother's. Reminds me of…well, better times when we were a family." He shrugged, clearly uncomfortable with the subject for reasons Haylee would have liked to explore, but not tonight. "Delanie always wants me to use it, but I told her I'm keeping it safe to pass down to her."

He turned and strode into the kitchen.

"Coffee?" he asked as he flicked on the lamp near the table.

She followed. "Too late for me." Though she probably wouldn't be able to sleep anyway.

Haylee settled into the slat-backed chair she'd come to think of as hers. Her purse was on the table where she'd left it. He'd kissed her like a man in command, overwhelming her senses, making her weak in the knees and desperate for more. She was anxious to know what came next.

He poured out a cup from the pot left over from dinner and set it in the microwave. She waited for him to turn around, but he didn't until the microwave had beeped and he had removed the coffee.

He sat down across from her and extended out his legs. The glow from the small lamp barely illuminated his face, leaving much in shadows. But she could see he was tired…and worried.

"I'm sorry I took advantage."

"You didn't take advantage." She'd wanted it as much as he did.

He frowned. "It was an impulse thing. I haven't…well, it's been a while, and…you were there. And you are an attractive woman."

He'd kissed her because she was convenient? Her insides ached just like when her sister had kicked her in the stomach one day for no apparent reason when they were young.

"It won't happen again. I promise." He held up his hand as if taking an oath.

She wanted it to happen again. And again. But apparently it hadn't been as mind blowing for him as for her. Guess he'd been disappointed…or dissatisfied or any of those "dis" words—like disaster.

"Just say you're still okay watching Delanie."

All he wanted from her was sitter service. She'd been a momentary temptation, and now he was over it. Too bad she wasn't. Anger filled her like steam from a boiling pot of water, but she took a deep breath and nodded. She wasn't about to let him see the steam escape. She still needed the job.

"It was just one little kiss." She hoped she sounded nonchalant and not aggrieved. She picked up her purse.

"There are some things I have to explain before you leave tonight."

He'd done enough explaining, thank you very

much, because apparently everything he'd said to her before that kiss had been a lie. He'd just been in some sort of lust overload that had scrambled his brain. Too bad he hadn't realized it before he'd scrambled hers.

"I really think I should go." And figure out what had gone wrong. Why had she so badly misread his intentions? Just like she had misread Roy's character. She should know better than to trust a man, or, it appeared, herself.

He placed his hand on her arm. He wasn't holding her firmly, just resting his hand there, but it was enough of a gesture to keep her seated.

"You know I'm going for permanent custody of Delanie, but I don't think you know all the reasons why. I'd like to explain them now and ask a favor."

Now he wanted a favor? She clamped her lips together, wondering whether she should just tell him to go to hell. But his eyes had darkened with—pain? Pleading? Sorrow?—and she nodded.

He released her arm from his warm grip and leaned back in the chair. "I knew Delanie's mother for only a week. It was some week, but then I wasn't exactly clearheaded at the time. I picked her up in a bar because…" Trace took a huge gulp of coffee this time and focused on the white door of the refrigerator. "Back then I was drunk most of the time."

His gaze swung back, holding her in place, searching for her reaction. She tried to remain expressionless, hanging on to two words—*back then.* She wasn't one to judge, but truth was she was surprised. Maybe she shouldn't have been, because come to think of it, she hadn't seen a can of beer or a bottle of wine or any liquor anywhere in the kitchen.

"It's a long story, but right after that, I got some sense kicked into me, literally. Got help and got sober. That was almost six years ago. However, once an alcoholic, always an alcoholic, but now I'm a recovering one."

Way more complicated than she'd imagined. But why was he telling her this now? After he'd kissed her and told her he didn't want to kiss her ever again?

"I didn't know about Delanie." His fingers drummed on the table, providing a strange backbeat to his story. "I never thought to check up on that woman. She was a barfly, and I didn't go to bars anymore. She knew my name, knew I had a ranch, but never bothered to contact me. Until about a year ago. There was a knock on my door, and when I opened it, there was Doreen holding the hand of a little female four-year-old version of me. Same hair color. Same eyes."

He stopped drumming his fingers, looked down at his cup as he took another gulp of coffee, and shifted his legs under the table. "I thought Doreen wanted some money, and based on what I saw, I was going to give her some, though as you might have noticed, I'm not exactly swimming in cash."

Trace's bent head and the monotone way he recited the facts of his life made him difficult to read, but Haylee kept her eyes trained on him, looking for clues.

"But Doreen didn't want cash. She wanted me to take care of Delanie." Trace paused and lifted his head. The pain in his eyes was unmistakable, and Haylee had to mentally restrain herself from reaching for him. "Doreen had gotten into way more than alcohol in the intervening years. She was using hard drugs, had started dealing to make money for her and Delanie, had gotten caught, and was being sentenced to jail time. I can only imagine…"

Haylee felt the floor shift under her chair as he closed his eyes for a moment.

Delanie's mother was in prison, and he'd chosen this awkward moment to tell her?

She hadn't a clue what to say or do.

"Anyway." Trace had opened his eyes, keeping them focused on the coffee cup on the table. "None of Doreen's relatives would have anything to do with her, and she had no one to care for Delanie. I was the only hope of keeping her child, our child, out of foster care. I had a DNA test done, not because I doubted the obvious but to allow me to claim her and obtain temporary custody, and then I filed for permanent custody."

"That was a wonderful thing you did." She wondered how many men, alone, would have so readily taken in a child and turned his world upside down.

He rested his elbows on his knees and finally raised his gaze to meet hers. The raw emotion she saw in his eyes seeped into her bones like a February chill.

"But I was a stranger to her. A man she didn't know. With the help of Mandy and Ty, I was able to get counseling for both her and me. I don't go in for that sort of thing, but I was desperate."

How many men would have subjected themselves to that for the sake of his child? Roy hadn't even wanted to go for marriage counseling. "It appears to have worked."

His shoulders sagged like he was carrying a huge

boulder. “Some. She’s still…well, let’s just say it’s a work in progress.” The drawn lines of his face testified to the difficulty of that admission.

“But you don’t have permanent custody yet?” No wonder he often looked worried. The thought of Delanie in foster care made her stomach curdle like sour milk.

“Not yet. There’s been a new wrinkle. When I filed, I filed for sole legal custody. Doreen left her on my doorstep and, except for her regular phone calls to Delanie, never said another word about it. Never has asked to see Delanie, and I’ve never offered. Prison is no place for a five-year-old, and it’s been hard enough explaining to Delanie where her mother is without using the term.”

Haylee had thought the mother had abandoned her child to go study somewhere. Some women just weren’t maternal. And some women, even those in prison, were. “Never seeing the child you love would be difficult.” A thought about her birth mother breezed through her mind, but she resisted letting it land.

Trace shook his head. “She’d made the choice to become a criminal knowing what could happen to her.”

Just like Roy had made a choice…and her birth mother had made a choice. Both had given Haylee up.

Trace continued. “She can’t have joint physical custody, of course, but she has petitioned the court for visitation rights. Which means I would have to haul Delanie over to Lusk and walk that child into a prison so she could see her mother.”

“Children do see their parents in prison.” And women saw their husbands, only she’d chosen not to wait around to be one of them.

"Not Delanie. Not if I can prevent it. Her mother abandoned her. Her mother neglected her. It will be hard now, but time will make it easier."

Given her own past, Haylee doubted that, but she didn't voice that doubt. He was in no mood to hear it.

A recovering alcoholic. A child whose mother was in prison. It was a lot to take in. But it didn't change the way she felt about Delanie. Only about Trace.

He'd taken in a child he hadn't known, had gotten help for them both, and had done everything he could to keep her. In her eyes it only made him more attractive. Because, from all accounts, her own biological mother had readily given her up.

"You've clearly got a lot on your plate." More than she had ever imagined.

He wiped a hand across his brow. "I wouldn't have told you all of this now, today, if it wasn't that the court has appointed an evaluator to interview everyone connected with me or Doreen for a report that will be given to the judge to make a decision in this case. On whether I get custody and she gets visitation rights. I can't imagine the court siding with Doreen, but apparently I'm in the minority, or so my lawyer tells me. There's also a chance they won't see me as fit for legal custody, even if I am her father, so this court evaluator's report is important. Now that you're taking care of Delanie, she wants to interview you. Sometime this week. I have to get back to them tomorrow with a date and time. I'd try to schedule it during your work time. I'd come in and care for Delanie then."

"Of course. Whatever I can do." She couldn't imagine that the court would deny Trace custody. Despite what he'd told her about his past, it was the present that should count, and he was a good father, a very good father.

"I'm not sure what the court is looking for, but my lawyer tells me hiring you has made my case stronger."

And the stakes were enormous. Delanie's fate lay in the balance.

"I'm glad I can be of help."

He peeked at her from under lowered brows. "She'll likely ask how long you'll be staying."

She would have to be honest. "It all depends on how long it takes to sell the property. And I have no control over that."

"I figured you'd say that." He rose, his expression grim as shadows played across his face. "I can tell the evaluator you'll be interviewed?"

Haylee nodded. She'd been through a tornado of emotions with snippets of information coming at her in all directions. She needed to go home, lick her wounds, and think about everything that had happened, that had been said, and if she could, she needed to put that genie of feelings for Trace back in the bottle. His life was far more complicated than she'd imagined. She should feel relieved that she'd dodged a bullet. She didn't.

"Thanks," he said as he turned his back on her and put his empty cup in the kitchen sink.

Haylee pushed out her chair, grabbed her purse, and pasted on a smile as she stood. "No problem."

Long after Haylee had left and Delanie had fallen asleep, Trace sat at the small desk crowbarred into the spare bedroom, staring at the detailed cost breakdown on the computer screen in hopes of finding somewhere to save money so he could actually turn a profit. Instead, his mind replayed kissing Haylee like it was a scene out of *Groundhog Day*.

The taste of her, the fresh scent of vanilla, the softness of her lips, the feel of her trim body against his. He'd kissed Haylee because he'd wanted to since the first time he saw her, sitting in mud, but it was like opening a Pandora's box of feelings he had buried for so long he forgot he was capable of them.

He hadn't been with a woman he actually cared about since before his father had died. And that had been Judi Barnes, who had left Wyoming to make her fortune in California and ended up marrying a guy in real estate, if he remembered correctly. Someone had told him she had two kids already. She'd been a crazy girl, willing to do anything on a dare and far too wild for him to handle at the time, but she'd been a lot of fun. Shortly after his father had died, they'd broken up because she wanted him to go with her to California and he wouldn't leave the ranch.

With the two most important people in his life at the time leaving, he'd taken to drinking and neglecting the one thing he'd sacrificed for, the ranch. Then he'd taken to carousing as well as drinking and neglecting the ranch. And then he'd picked up Doreen. Shortly after that, his brother had found him, beaten the crap out of him, and shoved him into rehab, paid up the mortgage, and dared Trace to stay sober.

It was a tough time but a hard lesson Trace needed to learn. And he did learn it. In a few months it would be six years he'd been sober. He knew he was a tough-minded son of a gun if he wanted to do something. Trouble was, after his father had died and given how his mother had died, he hadn't wanted to do anything but wallow in self-doubt, made worse by comparing himself to a younger brother who had done everything right…and was still doing everything right.

Once sober, Trace had realized his ranch was all that mattered, and he'd done all he could to build it back. He'd made progress. The year beef prices went through the roof, he put money into the house and outbuildings. Then the drought came, and he had to build back the herd. After Delanie was part of the equation, he'd swallowed his pride and accepted money from Ty and cattle from Mandy in order to sustain the ranch, provide Delanie with the care and counseling she needed, and hire a lawyer so he could gain permanent custody of his child.

His self-imposed ban from bars, the isolation of where he lived, and the arrival of a daughter made it hard to meet women beyond a momentary fling. And then this curly-haired angel had shown up, and he'd fallen all over himself just to be near her. Just to get a smile from her. Like some high school kid with a crush.

He wasn't a relationship kind of guy. Knew more about horses than women, and had no business kissing that one. It was the path to a lot of troubles he didn't need. An impulsive moment, and he was no longer an impulsive guy.

But he didn't regret the kiss, just telling her that it wouldn't happen again. Because he wanted it to happen again…if his life was different. If she wasn't temporary. If he was relationship material. If he could offer her something more than a broken-down cowboy. If…if…if…

Tomorrow he'd have to face her knowing she knew the truth. Knowing he'd lost her respect.

He should join one of those online forums and find an independent, low-maintenance woman who didn't mind getting her hands dirty, enjoyed ranch work, liked kids, could cook, and would be in it for the long term, and forget about a curly-haired city girl who wore sandals to a ranch, laughed when she fell on her butt, and kissed like a goddamn goddess.

Yeah, good luck with that.

Chapter 10

Haylee's mind churned like a food processor chopping carrots as she drove home from Delanie's school. Delanie took her nap in the car seat as Haylee steered down carless byways and past wide-open prairies dotted by oil rigs and propeller-type windmills. She felt such tenderness for the child asleep in the backseat that she wanted to make the upheaval in the little one's life disappear. If cooking good meals, playing, and caring could do it even for a little while, she'd try.

But what had kept her up most of the night was a recovering alcoholic with a child, a mortgage, and a past. Not to mention he was a none-too-prosperous rancher at Mother Nature's mercy. She couldn't have conjured up a worse prospect for a relationship if she'd tried.

On the other hand, he'd told her some hard truths about himself. Hadn't lied or glossed over them or made any excuses. Once sober, he'd lived a decent life, and when confronted with an extraordinary obligation, he'd moved heaven and earth to assure Delanie had a home with him. A private man, he'd gone to counseling, endured the investigations of a court-appointed evaluator, and confided the worst of himself to Haylee, a virtual stranger. He'd done everything he could to gain legal custody of his child.

What wasn't to admire about a man like that?

And that man had kissed her. A kiss that had made her feel like a woman again. A desired woman. In that moment she had felt like she was floating in a hot-air balloon, like she was no longer the woman who had been in a failed marriage to a man she no longer trusted. For a moment, she'd been embarking on a new relationship with a man who wanted her. But it was only for a moment, and then he'd popped her balloon.

It was difficult to deny the truth, try as she might. She had feelings for Trace. Her heart was in deep trouble, and her head couldn't seem to do anything about it.

And she would see this man regularly for the next few months. Because even though her head couldn't change her feelings, her practical side wouldn't let her give up the only reasonable economic solution—a rent-free home and ready cash—to her current predicament.

Not that her finances had improved much. She didn't earn a commission check until the client booked the savings from the audit, so she was at least two months away from seeing any money.

She'd had some decent interest in her photographs though. In fact, the cover designer who had asked about cowboys had also asked if she had any graphics background because the designer was looking for someone to handle a few simple projects. Ironic that while her own heart was bruised, she'd be creating covers for romance novels. Guess she was a glutton for punishment.

Not to mention she still had to ask Trace if he'd sign a release so she could sell his photos. As she drove the car down the gravel drive, her emotions warred. On the one hand, she wanted to see him if just to be near him. On the other hand, she was still raw from his rejection.

Maybe Trace would be out with the herd, although there would be no avoiding him when they ate dinner. She could tell him she was taking her dinner home to eat, but then he might think she cared more about that kiss than she wanted him to know.

Parking the car on dry grass, she glanced toward the barn, as she did every day, and her heart skittered a beat as Trace ambled out of the shadows, Moose by his side. He wore his cowboy hat, jeans, and a white T-shirt stretched across pure muscle. Her pulse skipped into double time.

She cut the engine, and as if cued, Delanie stirred. Within a minute, Haylee had unhooked Delanie from the car seat. The child scrambled out as if she hadn't just been sleeping, and met her father on the path as Haylee extracted the child's backpack from the car, along with the little present she had for Delanie.

"Lauren wants me to come to her house next week for a playdate. Can I?" Delanie clung to her father's knees.

Trace looked at Haylee for an explanation.

"Her mom was there when I picked Delanie up, and she asked."

"What day?"

Haylee shrugged. "She didn't say, but I got her number so you could call her."

"Please, Daddy." Delanie jumped up and down like her feet were glued to a pogo stick.

"Is it okay with you?" He directed his question to Haylee. "It would mean you wouldn't be watching her that day."

She depended on the money she made caring for Delanie, but how could she deny the little girl a fun time with her friend?

"It's fine. Plenty to keep me busy." She wished.

"You want to call and arrange it? That way you could help decide the right day." He shrugged. "Maybe we could spend some time on riding lessons then."

Haylee didn't comment, but that would be a really bad idea. No more riding lessons. No more close and personal time. Obviously the man could shrug off a kiss, her kiss, like it was nothing more than an annoying fly. She couldn't.

"Thank you, Daddy." Delanie beamed as Haylee handed her the backpack.

"Go in the house, sweet pea. I set out some of those cookies you two baked the other day." Trace glanced at Haylee, his expression serious. "I have some things to talk over with Miss Haylee."

Trace watched Delanie run to the house, Moose at her heels, and waited until the screen door slammed. Haylee stood to his side, ramrod straight. She was back to wearing sneakers, and her jean shorts continued to show a lot of leg. Her pink T-shirt was covered by her folded arms, as if she was hugging herself, a purse dangling from her shoulder and her other hand clutching a small paper bag. She looked as irritated as a dog that couldn't find its bone.

She was likely still mad at him for kissing her. Not any madder than he was at himself for giving in to temptation like that. He'd had enough life lessons about giving in to temptation.

Best to forget that kiss. Besides, no woman would be interested in a man with his baggage, baggage he'd laid out in detail. Baggage that would cause any woman to run in the opposite direction, especially a college-educated good girl from a loving family, like Haylee. A woman who could have any man wrapped around her finger—except maybe the brainless twit who had divorced her.

His first priority was Delanie, and he would put up with anything, even a woman who made his blood run hot and conjured up all kinds of hearth-and-home fantasies, if it helped his daughter.

"What?" She sounded as annoyed as she looked.

"I got the word from the court evaluator. She'll be out this Friday around four o'clock, right when you get home with Delanie. I'll be here to take care of Delanie until you're finished."

Her mouth drooped. "My sister is coming for the weekend, and I have to pick her up from the airport that evening." She nibbled at her bottom lip.

He had to stop looking at her lips.

"I was hoping to leave a little early, like right after I cooked dinner," she continued.

"You can still do that. And if you run into a time crunch, don't worry about dinner. I can always rustle up an omelet for Delanie and me. I can still cook. Just glad I don't have to."

"That's very nice of you." Her mouth softened, and her stance relaxed as she twirled a strand of curls around her finger.

"Feel free to bring your sister around." He was

still curious about Haylee. He'd told her all, well almost all, his secrets. He knew little of hers and doubted she had any. She'd been raised in the bubble of a functional family. What secrets could she have?

"I don't think we'll have time. But she did ask to go someplace where there would be cowboys. I was thinking of taking her to a rodeo if there was one around."

He pushed up the brim of his hat. Funny that she wanted to go to rodeos all of a sudden. "There will be one just over the border in Colorado next weekend. Delanie and I are going on Saturday if you'd care to join us." At least he'd get to meet her sister and maybe find out a little more about the domestic goddess working for him. Not that he should be interested.

She bit her lip before answering, as if thinking about it. A gust of wind fluttered a wisp of hair across her lips. Slender fingers brushed it away.

Now that he'd tasted her, it was going to be a living hell seeing her every day. But it was a hell he'd made, and he would deal with it.

"Can't. Other plans for Saturday. I was interested in Sunday. Something to do before we have to head back to the airport."

Guess she wasn't keen on him meeting her sister.

"I can see about getting tickets for you from Ty and Mandy. They're running the thing. That's one reason we're going." The other was to provide something for Delanie to look forward to after a call from her mother. He didn't trust that Doreen wouldn't mention her desire to see Delanie, and then he'd have hell to pay for sure.

"Thanks. Now I have a favor to ask you."

She cocked out a hip, and he wondered what he was in for. If she asked him to kiss her, he'd be real troubled to say no, seeing how damn cute she was when annoyed. But that, he was sure, would never happen.

"Shoot."

"You know those pictures I took of you the other day, the ones for Aunt Paula?"

He nodded. "You didn't put them up on social media, did you?"

"No. But I did put up some pictures of the scenery around here, and someone licensed one of those for a book cover. She also asked if I had any photos of cowboys. The only cowboy I know well enough to ask for a release is you. But if you don't want to do it, I'll understand."

"I don't want to do it." Never in a million years would he be on some book cover. Never.

She pursed her lips, looked like she was going to say something, but instead started walking toward the house. She'd said she'd understand. Apparently not.

He followed, watching the motion of her hips, the wiggle of her backside, and the curve of her legs in motion. Yeah. He was big into torturing himself.

Delanie was already on her second cookie, and Trace went right to the paper-decorated refrigerator to get her some milk. Since Haylee had come, he could barely see the white of the fridge, as it was covered in so many of Delanie's coloring masterpieces held on by assorted magnets—many from bars he'd once frequented, a few from ranch supply stores, and one from her preschool. Perusing them was like a walk through his past.

"Delanie," Haylee said, setting down her purse. "I have something for you. Something you asked for."

As Trace turned around, Haylee held out the paper bag.

Delanie tore into the bag. "Look, Daddy. It's us!" Delanie shoved the picture in his face.

There it was, a silver-framed picture of the two of them on horseback, Delanie all smiles, he not so much. But Haylee had captured something in that picture. Even a cynic like him could see Delanie's excitement at being on the horse and his cautious protectiveness as her father. Haylee Dennis was a damn good photographer, he'd give her that. And a lot more.

"I'm putting it on my dresser." Delanie shot out of the room, and her footsteps could be heard down the hall.

Trace felt a lump in his throat at his daughter's enthusiasm. For a picture of him. "Thanks."

"My pleasure."

For the first time that day, she didn't sound defensive.

If only she could be interested in a beaten down cowboy with baggage.

* * *

The week whizzed by, probably because Haylee wasn't anxious for Friday to come and the sibling gods were being perverse. One more day and her sister would be here, she thought as she scanned the yard for a sign of Delanie. They were playing hide-and-seek before she had to start the grill. Hamburgers were on the menu tonight, by popular request. Made her wonder if the pair were a bit tired of her cookbook recipes.

There weren't many places to hide around the house. She'd checked behind the overgrown honeysuckle, old lilac, and elderberry shrubs with no luck.

She headed toward the barn. It would be a while before Trace got back, so no fear of running into him. These days, Haylee only saw Trace at dinnertime, and she'd honed her rapid-eating skills so she was out before he finished. The less time she spent in the company of temptation, the better off she would surely be.

If they talked at all, it was about Delanie. Haylee had set up the playdate for the following week, to coincide with an interview for a job at the company where she'd once been an intern—a job her bank account would need if things didn't work out with her business venture or if her aunt's place sold quickly. The freight-auditing market had apparently moved on without her. And though there hadn't been much activity yet at her aunt's place, the real estate agent recently reminded Haylee that it only took one buyer who fell in love with the place and when that happened, things were likely to move fast.

Haylee needed a contingency plan because the last thing she wanted was to find herself penniless *and* homeless.

She ambled past the corrals, where Buck and two other horses were grazing, and into the barn. The smell of hay and manure filled her nostrils as she wandered past the empty stalls. A shadow of movement caught her eye in the tack room. Thinking it was Delanie, she sidled over.

"Miss Haylee." Corey's head popped into the opening.

"Corey, it's you."

"Just getting ready to head home. Got to work tonight at the grocery store."

Haylee had met the young man just the other day. He worked weekends and after school during the school year, but being it was now summer, he had transitioned to working during the day.

"Did you see Delanie anywhere? We're playing hide-and-seek, and I'm not having any luck finding her."

Corey wiped a hand across his brow. It had yet to cool down from the heat of the day, and the barn was even hotter. "No, ma'am. I've been back about fifteen minutes, currying Buck and putting the tack away. I ain't seen anyone come in here. Want me to help you look?"

"It's nice of you to offer, but you have to get on your way. She promised she wouldn't go far. I'm sure I'll find her."

Haylee turned and headed out into the bright sunlight. Where else to look? She was trying hard not to worry, but Delanie was her responsibility, and even though this was just a game, not finding the child concerned Haylee. Her nerves felt like an elastic band that had been stretched too far, ready to break.

She'd become very fond of Delanie in the short time she'd been Delanie's caregiver. Very fond. And ever since she'd learned the truth about Delanie's mother, protective as well. The child was in for a rough future. Even with a strong father figure like Trace, Haylee knew there would always be a hole in Delanie's heart, something missing, something longed for.

And the girl had no idea that some stranger was going to make decisions for her that would affect the rest of her life…and ultimately her happiness. The court evaluator's visit had been ever-present in Haylee's thoughts these last few days.

She hurried back down the path toward the house and called out the child's name. "I give up, Delanie," she said in a loud, clear voice as she neared the house. "You win this one."

There really wasn't anywhere else to hide. Haylee checked her watch. Enough time had passed to call it quits. She shouted again, tamping down the frantic feeling bubbling up inside of her. "I give up, Delanie."

Then she heard it. The faint sound of giggling coming from near the house, but not in the house. But then sounds could be deceiving. She opened the back door and listened. More giggling, but definitely not from inside the house.

She stepped nearer the slanted, paint-chipped wood doors that likely covered an old cellar. The giggling sounded louder. Haylee picked up one of the doors, heavier than it appeared.

There sat a pleased-looking Delanie at the top of the steps leading to a dark dirt-floor that looked like something out of a B horror flick and way too spooky to explore.

"I win!" Delanie announced as she leaped out into the yard.

"Yes, you certainly did win." Relief filled Haylee like a surge of gas flooding an engine. "And you are covered in filth." Haylee brushed the child's shorts, and a cloud of dust billowed out. "Promise me you won't hide down there again." Haylee peered into the dark abyss as she lowered the door. "Heaven knows what's down there. Doesn't look like anyone's been in there for years." Haylee shivered. She'd always hated horror movies.

"I didn't go down the steps."

Haylee smiled as she wrapped her arms around the youngster and gave a squeeze. "Well, that's a good thing. But look at how dirty you got just from sitting on those steps." Haylee released her grip. "Let's go and wash you up."

"Can I have some more of those brownies you brought?"

Haylee always tried to have a snack when Delanie got home, and today's treat was homemade brownies. But Delanie had already eaten two small squares.

"Too close to dinner now. But I'll help you practice riding the bike."

Delanie shot out of Haylee's arms and ran to the back door. "Deal."

Tomorrow was the interview with the court evaluator. The knot in her stomach tightened.

Chapter 11

"You ready for this?" Trace askcd, leaning against the counter, his arms crossed over his chest. He was dressed in his cowboy attire, and he wore a black cowboy hat that he hadn't bothered to take off when he entered the house. She had just gotten home from picking up Delanie from summer camp, and the child was in her bedroom changing into an outfit more suitable for a ride on Buck.

"I think so." Haylee had spent a restless night, her mind churning through possible questions and answers.

"She's going to ask you about me. What kind of person you think I am." His gaze was so intense it felt like his eyes were boring holes into her.

"I think you are a great father to Delanie."

He raised his chin and looked at her with skepticism. "Really? Nice to hear. I hope the court feels the same way."

"Me too."

Footsteps rang out from the hallway, and within a second Delanie had breezed into the kitchen.

"We'll be out in the corral if you need us."

"Don't you want to say hi?"

"We've met. Best leave her to her business." He cast a glance in Delanie's direction.

"Right." Haylee was on her own. Just as the pair exited out the back door, the front door bell rang. She took a deep breath as she passed through the living room and noted that everything was clean and tidy and a plate of her cookies was on the coffee table. She'd tried to straighten up yesterday, but it was clear that Trace had spent a good part of the day getting the place to look just so.

She glanced at the china platter on top of the television cabinet. Maybe Trace's mother was watching over her son and granddaughter, because at that moment, Haylee wanted all the help she could get.

When she pulled the door open, a grandmotherly sort of woman greeted her. "I'm Dr. Graham. Haylee Dennis, I suppose?" She shot out a hand from the arm weighed down by a large black tote.

Haylee nodded and shook the woman's slender hand. Dr. Graham's hair was in a salt-and-pepper bun, and spectacles balanced on a thin nose. She wore sensible shoes and a light-gray pantsuit that might have been in style a decade earlier.

"Won't you come in," Haylee said, needlessly, because the woman was already halfway inside the house.

"Is this where we will be meeting?" Dr. Graham asked, glancing around the room.

Haylee wondered if it measured up.

"Yes. Can I get you some coffee? Tea?"

Dr. Graham reached inside her tote and pulled out a bottle. "I have water, thank you."

Haylee invited her to sit down. Dr. Graham chose the sofa. Haylee sat across from her in the green chair. "Some home-baked cookies?" Haylee picked up the plate.

Dr. Graham shook her head. Haylee's stomach certainly didn't feel up for any, but she wished she had brought in some water. Her tongue felt like sawdust had been sprinkled on it.

"So how long have you worked here, Ms. Dennis?" Dr. Graham adjusted herself on the couch and pulled a laptop from the tote. Balancing it on her knees, she opened it up and started clicking.

"Just a few weeks."

Dr. Graham raised her head and peered at her from over the top of her glasses. "Only a few weeks? Is this just for the summer then?"

Already she'd felt like she was failing. "Possibly." Haylee went on to explain about house sitting and needing to earn some money while she got her business up and running.

Dr. Graham typed into her computer. "So you're an accountant, not a nanny?" The disdain in her voice was palpable. "Do you have any experience with children, or is this just something that is convenient?"

The interview was off to a rocky start. Haylee explained about her jobs as a babysitter and camp counselor and tried to discern from Dr. Graham's stoic expression whether any of it made a difference. "I truly care about Delanie, Dr. Graham. She's a wonderful child who, as you know, has been through a lot. She is thriving now that she is settled at the ranch with her father."

"Is that your *expert* opinion, Miss Dennis?"

"That's my opinion as her caregiver."

Dr. Graham adjusted her glasses. "As her caregiver then, how would you characterize Mr. Martin's relationship with the child?"

"They seem like a typical father and daughter. Loving and respectful."

"And how would you describe Mr. Martin's parenting style?"

"Patient but firm."

"Do you have examples?"

Haylee's mind went blank, and the clicking of the keys stopped. The incident with Moose in the corral passed through her head, and she related how Trace made Delanie sit in a time-out after disobeying his order to stay where she was. Only as the woman's keyboard clicked away did Haylee wonder if the woman might object to Delanie even being in the pasture. The back of her neck was suddenly damp, and she wished, again, that she had a glass of water.

"You mentioned before that Delanie was thriving. What has made you draw that conclusion, Miss Dennis?"

"She's a very happy child. After all she's been through, her change in circumstances, she seems to have adjusted wonderfully, from what I can tell."

"If you could be more specific, dear, it would be helpful." Dr. Graham's tone seemed a bit condescending.

"She enjoys running around the ranch. She loves when he takes her riding. She loves her dog. She loves her father." *Think Haylee, think.* "When I pick her up at preschool, she's eager to come home. She runs to greet her father. She's excited to tell him about her day, and he's excited to hear about it. She draws pictures for him. She wanted a photograph of him and her for her dresser, so I took one, had it framed, and gave it to her. You should have seen her face light up—she was so excited."

Dr. Graham's fingers never left the keyboard. Haylee breathed a quick sigh of relief.

Dr. Graham asked Haylee's opinion on the preschool, if Delanie had friends, and what the child's interests were.

"And how would you describe Delanie relative to other children her age?"

"She's bright and energetic…and happy. I know she gets annoyed with a girl in her class that apparently cries a lot. I haven't watched her all that long, but so far, she hasn't had any temper tantrums or crying bouts."

Dr. Graham straightened. "Now I am going to ask you some very personal questions about Mr. Martin." Dr. Graham's eyes narrowed like a hawk looking down at its prey. "I assume you know your employer's past and that of the child. These are important questions, and they have to not only be asked, but answered truthfully. A child's fate is at stake, and the court takes its role in this matter very seriously."

Haylee nodded, bunched her hands into fists, and pressed them into the chair cushion on each side of her for support.

"Have you ever seen Mr. Martin take an alcoholic beverage or ever wondered if he was inebriated?"

"No."

"Has Mr. Martin ever acted inappropriately toward you?"

Haylee hoped the memory of his kiss hadn't flushed her cheeks. "No." She'd wanted him to kiss her.

"Has Delanie ever talked about her mother or mentioned a desire to see her?"

"Yes, she has talked about her, but no, she has never mentioned to me a desire to see her."

"Do you have any insight into her feelings about her mother?"

"No." She only knew what Trace had told her.

"Is there anything more you would like to add?"

"Only that Trace is a wonderful father. He has changed his whole world around for his little girl, and he has done it gladly out of love."

Dr. Graham closed her computer without typing in Haylee's response, as if her conclusions didn't matter. Haylee felt she'd been more interrogated than interviewed.

Dr. Graham tucked the computer into her tote, grabbed the water bottle, and rose. "The court's responsibility is what is best for the child. Good day, Ms. Dennis." The woman shoved out her hand. Haylee shook it.

She walked Dr. Graham to the front door and showed her out without a clue as to whether her answers had hurt or helped Trace's cause, but the hollow feeling in her stomach said the former. She checked her watch. It was time to leave, but she hadn't made dinner.

She heard the slam of the back door. As he entered the room, there was a frown on Trace's face and worry in his eyes. His whole life, his happiness, was dependent on the opinion of one person.

"I saw the car leave. I left Delanie on the swing set for the moment." He dug his hands into his pockets. "How'd it go?"

"I don't know how it went." Haylee rubbed her hands together as if she could conjure up the answer. "She was very hard to read."

"What did she ask?" He stood there looking so vulnerable, so desperate. She resisted the strong urge to hug him, tell him it was going to be okay. He wouldn't appreciate it, and she wasn't sure it was true.

"A lot about me. And if I thought you were a good father. I told her the truth. That you are a great father."

His strained expression eased some. "A great father?"

"You are, you know. She's a lucky little girl to have found you."

Trace shook his head. "I'm the lucky one. She's giving me something to live for, to work for, to care about."

"And the fact that you feel that way instead of burdened is…" Pressure in her chest increased. "Remarkable. And a testament to your character."

He looked down at the floor. "Character? After what I told you?"

"Yes."

He raised his head and held her gaze for a long heartbeat before turning to go to the kitchen. "I'll take care of supper. You go and fetch your sister."

Haylee looked around the bustling baggage claim area and checked her phone for the time. Livvy should be arriving any moment, and that thought had her insides jumping. She loved her sister. She just didn't love being with her sister.

The whole trip to the airport she'd tried to push the court evaluator's interview out of her mind, but she kept replaying the questions and hoping her answers would sound better in her head. They hadn't. Like Trace, she'd have to wait and see. It had to be excruciating for him, and he was bearing it stoically and alone. Her heart pinched. At least she had Livvy's visit to distract her.

It would just be two days and then she would send her sister back home. Assuming eight hours of sleep, Haylee had thirty-two waking hours to fill. Tonight they would head to some hot spots in Denver, tomorrow was a visit to Jenna in Cheyenne, and Sunday was a rodeo in northern Colorado before ferrying Livvy back to the airport. Haylee took a deep breath. That should keep her sister busy and away from Trace's ranch. One look at Trace and Livvy would be weaving stories to their parents, who still hadn't come to terms with Haylee's divorce from the "perfect man."

Haylee checked her watch again as the luggage carousel alarm sounded and bags of assorted shapes, sizes, and colors slid out of the chute. People rimmed the edge of the conveyor belt—families, businesswomen in suits, single men in cowboy hats. Where was Livvy? Haylee hoped she wouldn't have to pay for more than an hour of parking in the short-term lot.

"I'm here."

Haylee whirled around. There stood her sister, arms outstretched, dressed in skinny jeans, high-heeled sandals, and a strappy pink top with rhinestones everywhere. Unlike Haylee, Livvy's hair was straight and a darker shade of blond, courtesy of a bottle. She'd pulled it back in a ballerina bun, and spangly earrings dangled from her lobes. The outfit screamed city girl, and why not? That was who Livvy was. Her sister loved the bar scene, the hustle and bustle, and the fact that within such a large populace it was easy to find her tribe of free-spirited, yoga-loving, meditation-practicing, health-food-crazy friends who also had no money.

A hug and then Livvy stood back and examined Haylee.

"You don't look emaciated. Guess country living is agreeing with you."

It was true that during the last few months of her marriage, Haylee had lost at least ten pounds, and on a short frame, it had showed. But her appetite had definitely improved, and having a job where she had to cook a decent dinner surely helped.

"And you look as good as ever," Haylee said. She meant it. Livvy had always had a slender figure and flexible limbs. The better to teach yoga.

"It's all about eating healthy. You are what you eat."

Haylee had listened to too many of Livvy's lectures on the evils of high fructose corn syrup and carbohydrates. She needed to change the subject. "We should look for your bag." Haylee motioned to the moving carousel.

"This is all I have." Livvy twirled around to showcase an overstuffed backpack hanging off her back. "I fit everything in here so I wouldn't have to pay. This airline charges even for carry-on. Imagine."

Well, no fear that Livvy would stay too long at least.

"Car is this way." Haylee moved toward the double doors leading outside, Livvy following.

"Are we heading back to the ranch?" Livvy asked as they stepped out into the warm night air and headed across the driving lanes to the parking garage.

"I thought you'd like to enjoy a little bit of

Denver first, and believe me, Aunt Paula's place is not a ranch."

"But you are going to show me the ranch where you work before I leave. I just love horses and cowboys," Livvy said. "You know, giddyup and all that."

It was going to be a long weekend.

Chapter 12

Not only did Livvy dance up a storm until midnight, but Haylee had to navigate the long drive home along Route 25 while Livvy dozed in the passenger seat.

Of course, Livvy slept late the next morning. Once she was up, they headed out to Jenna's the moment they polished off the egg-and-bacon sandwiches that had been a favorite growing up. Keeping Livvy occupied was Haylee's prime objective. An occupied Livvy wouldn't ask questions Haylee didn't want to answer, and there would be no time to scope out the rancher down the road and give Livvy more fodder to pass on to their parents.

Jenna suggested visiting a nearby ghost town, but a downpour forced a change of plans, so they went shopping, Livvy insisting she wanted a pair of authentic western boots and hat. They finally found the boots, at a price tag that had Haylee wondering how much Trace had spent on her boots. Even the cheapest, plainest boots cost over a hundred dollars. Of course, Livvy bought a bright-blue touristy pair with lots of detail that cost twice that amount, but no hat. How her sister could afford such a luxury on a yoga instructor's pay, Haylee didn't question, though she wanted to. Toward evening, they ambled over to the Cattleman's Club, got a great table because of the early hour, and waited for the bar to pack out with enough men in cowboy hats to keep Livvy entertained. Who knew her baby sister was so good at line dancing?

By Sunday morning, Haylee was dragging, but the promise of a rodeo over the border in Colorado had Livvy chomping at the bit. As they moved through the vendor stalls that rimmed the arena in the sizeable Colorado town, Haylee looked for the hat vendor she had seen at the other rodeo. Now that both sisters sported the boots, which Haylee had paired with her jean skirt and Livvy with a pair of cut-offs that showed off her stunning legs, they both needed a hat to complete the look. It would pinch a little in Haylee's pocketbook, but she actually had a little spending money from the sale of the photos, and since Trace had gotten tickets for her through Mandy, this rodeo excursion wasn't costing her more than food and gas.

"What do you think of this one?" Livvy said, modeling a gray hat with turquoise stones studding the band. Haylee had to admit her little sister looked good in it, and it went with Livvy's crazy blue boots.

"Get it if you can afford it."

"Take my picture in it."

Haylee raised the camera hanging around her neck and snapped a few photos as people streamed by. It was a noisy crowd, but most people tried to avoid photo-bombing the pictures.

Livvy checked out the images on the screen and nodded. "Sold."

Haylee picked through the hats sprawled on the

counter. This wasn't the same vendor, but maybe they had something she'd like just as much. She pulled out a tan hat with a dark-brown leather band and plopped it onto her head.

"How about this for me?"

Livvy squinted at her. "With those boots and that hat, you look like one of them."

Haylee wanted to ask who "them" was, but she let it slide. Time was too short to point out to the city girl that she was in "their" state, not the other way around.

"So you haven't said much about the little girl you take care of. Sort of odd that's what you're doing now, isn't it?" Livvy fished some money out of her bag.

Haylee sighed, hoping she wasn't in for a mom-supplied lecture. "I need some money until I can get my sales numbers up. Works out perfectly while I take care of Aunt Paula's place for her."

"Out in the boonies. But you always did like kids. I'm surprised taking care of me all those years didn't scar you."

"You were a brat. Delanie is sweet. Five is a wonderful age." Livvy was ten by the time Haylee had to watch her so their mom could go back to work. A spoiled ten at that.

"Where's the mom?"

"Not in the picture." Short and to the point.

Livvy shrugged. "Well, if it's working for you."

Livvy went to pay, and Haylee breathed a sigh of relief that she had gotten off without revealing more. She checked the price tag on the hat. A little more than she wanted to pay, but not absurd. And the felt fabric seemed sturdy enough that Trace wouldn't be teasing her about it.

She'd tried to keep thoughts of Trace at bay, but that had become a futile exercise. She could still see him standing in the doorway, looking worried, scared, and filled with doubts after the court evaluator had left. And then there was the kiss to replay again and again. No relief there.

Haylee joined Livvy to pay for her tan hat and motioned to the food stands. "It's going to start. Let's grab some beers and find our seats."

Ten minutes later they walked down the aisle to their courtesy seats near the bucking chutes, when a warm flush consumed Haylee. Sitting in their row was a tall cowboy and his daughter. What were they doing there? Trace had said he was coming on Saturday. Had he purposely changed the day to meet her sister?

Nothing to do but move forward and hope Livvy didn't embarrass Haylee or herself.

"Who's that?" Livvy said in her ear. "He's banging."

"Aunt Paula's neighbor. His brother got us these tickets."

"The one you work for? I'm feeling a hot flash coming on." Livvy waved a hand, fanning herself, and Haylee felt her sister's elbow in her side.

"No wonder you didn't want me to meet him. You wanted him all to yourself."

"Just behave. He's not in the market." At least not for her.

Haylee pasted on a smile as she reached the seat row. "Hey."

Trace was facing away from her toward Delanie, but at the sound of her voice, he turned. His eyebrows rose as he took in Livvy.

"Surprised to see us?" he said in that low drawl of his.

Just hearing his voice sent a pleasurable shiver through her. "Well, yes. You were coming yesterday."

Within a heartbeat, Livvy had slid past her and was, to Haylee's horror, settling down next to Trace.

"I'm Olivia, by the way. Haylee's sister. You can call me Livvy." She reached out her hand in greeting.

Trace took a moment to assess the woman before shaking her hand. With that Livvy leaned over Trace so that she was mere inches from his body. "And you must be Delanie."

"Hi." Delanie looked at Livvy and then at Haylee and then back at Livvy. "You don't look like sisters."

Haylee scooted next to Livvy. "It's because she's got straight hair."

"She's taller than you."

"By only an inch or two." Leave it to a child to be so perceptive. Most people didn't notice, or at least comment. "Livvy, this is Trace Martin and his daughter, Delanie." She figured she should do a formal introduction even if Livvy had taken the lead.

"So this is what has been keeping you so occupied you don't have time to call." Livvy batted her eyelashes at Trace like the flirt she was. "She didn't even offer to take me to see your ranch, and I've never been to a ranch."

That flush consumed Haylee again.

"Any time you want to come see it, you're welcome."

Did Livvy actually place her hand on his arm?

"That's so kind of you, but shouldn't you ask your missus first?"

Trace glanced at Haylee before answering. "I'm not married."

Livvy turned back to Haylee with narrowed eyes. "Difficult situation then, raising a young child. But I'm sure Haylee is helping you out."

"She's been great."

"I just bet she has been." Livvy settled back in her seat. "So tell me—what are we going to see in this arena? I know nothing about rodeo."

"Seems to run in the family," Trace said. Then he patted Livvy's hand and began to explain.

Haylee raised her camera and started shooting the opening parade. It would be a long three hours.

Haylee really had no reason to be irritated with her sister. Livvy had been an enthusiastic audience, and she peppered Trace with questions about each event, and for his part, he seemed happy enough to educate her. Still, Haylee had insisted Livvy accompany her to the bathroom when she needed to escort Delanie. No way was she leaving her sister alone with Trace.

Though why she was jealous when Livvy lived hundreds of miles away, and was really just being friendly, she didn't examine too closely.

Tucker hadn't performed in this rodeo, but Chance Cochran had, and finally the bull riding was coming up, the last event of the afternoon.

"Is Lonnie in this one, Daddy?"

"He is." Trace turned toward them. "He's a friend of Chance Cochran's, and they often travel together."

"Riding bulls seems so dangerous. Why would anyone do it?" Livvy asked.

"Got me. Fans seems to love it, though."

"But they get hurt a lot." Delanie put her hands over her eyes. "I don't like to watch."

"We can go, sweet pea," Trace said.

Delanie shook her head. "No. I want to see Lonnie. I told him I would cheer for him."

"How about I watch and tell you what is going on?"

Delanie nodded.

The event began, and it was a wild one, with cowboys being tossed to and fro by angry bulls. Most, gratefully, wore helmets to prevent head injuries, but at least one had his leg stomped on.

Lonnie was finally up.

Delanie uncovered her eyes and stared at the pen where the rider was getting set. "I can't look," she said, putting her hands back over her eyes as the gate opened. "Tell me when it's over, Daddy."

Eight seconds and the buzzer sounded. "He made it, honey."

Delanie clapped and shouted his name. Lonnie took his helmet off and nodded to the stands where they sat.

"He's cute," Livvy said. "Can we meet him?"

"Sure," Trace said.

"I'm not certain we have time." Haylee brushed back her hair, which had been blown into tangles by the ever-present breeze. She knew there was time—she just wanted to get out of there.

"I think we do," Livvy said firmly, giving her sister a *don't mess with me* look. "It would be fun to meet a real bull rider. You can bring your camera and take a picture."

"Maybe you can get a release from him," Trace

said as he rose. "We can head to the locker area now and catch him. Riders usually don't let any moss grow on them before they head to another rodeo."

"This is so exciting." Livvy certainly sounded excited as they shuffled out of the row into the already crowded aisle. "What did he mean about a release?" Livvy whispered in Haylee's ear.

Haylee shrugged, intent on ignoring the question.

Her parents had discouraged her from pursuing photography. No money in it, they had said. Haylee didn't want to add fuel to the fire. There would surely be enough questions from her mother after Livvy reported back about Haylee's employer.

Trace led them through the crowd and down some steps to the locker room entrance. "You three stay put, and I'll see if he's still here." He disappeared inside the long cement-block hallway.

One cowboy was exiting and gave them both the once-over before moving on. Probably thought they were rodeo groupies.

"Wait until I tell my girlfriends. They are going to be pea-green with envy."

Haylee held Delanie's hand. "I didn't know you liked cowboys."

"Neither did I until I came out here. And now I can't wait to come back."

Great.

A few seconds later Trace emerged with a cowboy about two inches shorter. He had his cowboy hat covering most of his brown hair, except for a lock that fell over his forehead. The man had changed into clean jeans and a plaid shirt. His gaze fell on Livvy…and stayed there.

"Lonnie, these ladies here are some new fans of yours. Haylee Dennis and her sister, Olivia."

"Livvy, please." Livvy stepped forward and held out her hand. Lonnie shook it, his focus never straying.

"You stayed on," Delanie piped up.

Finally Lonnie looked at someone other than Livvy. "I did, pumpkin. Must have been because you were cheering me on." His forefinger swiped her nose.

"Would you mind taking a picture with me?" Livvy asked.

Lonnie's smile was wide as he opened up his arm for Livvy to step into. Haylee raised her camera and clicked. They did make a cute couple.

"If you and Chance are staying around, we could grab something to eat. Maybe the ladies could join us," Trace said.

Thankfully, Lonnie shook his head. "Heading out to another rodeo in the southern part of the state and have to make it there by eight tonight."

"Isn't that far?" Livvy hadn't moved from his side.

"That's why we have to leave now." He pushed his hat back. "But I'm real sorry that's the case. I would have loved to show you around, darling. Next time." He winked.

"I'm just visiting. But I think I'll be back."

"Follow me on my Facebook page. Lonnie Kasin."

"I'll do that." Livvy stepped out of his embrace. Haylee had never seen her sister's cheeks so red.

* * *

"And why didn't you ever mention that cowboys were so…spectacular?" Livvy said as Haylee pulled her car into the departure lane of the terminal.

"They are men, like every other."

"Hardly. These guys are so…rugged. And such daredevils. And yet they have the nicest manners." She sighed. "I've never been called *ma'am* so much in my life."

"Not all cowboys rodeo. Some just work hard in all kinds of weather to make a decent living." Like Trace, and to her, that was just as heroic.

"I'm coming back. Even if I have to pay for the trip myself," Livvy said, her hand on the door handle.

"You are always welcome." And Haylee meant it. Even though she had been on pins and needles most of her sister's visit, she'd had a surprisingly good time. "What are you going to tell Mom and Dad?"

"What I've already texted them. That you are happy, enjoying life, and they shouldn't worry about you."

"Thank you."

"It's true, so you didn't have to keep us on a breakneck schedule just to avoid talking to me about what's going on in our life."

Haylee swallowed. "I'm sorry. It's just…"

"I don't understand what went wrong between you and Roy, and it may be none of my business. But as your sister—for we are sisters, Haylee—I just want to know you are happy with your decision and moving on…and you are." Livvy spread her arms. "Hug?"

Haylee wrapped her arms around her sister. She might not be happy, but she was moving on. She just wished she knew in what direction.

Chapter 13

Several days later Trace sat in the neat and spacious office of his lawyer, trying to extinguish the burn of anger that filled him. Though he had paid the fees for a court psychologist and anything else the court evaluator needed for the damn report, apparently he wasn't allowed to see the document. Only hear about the contents from his lawyer. A lawyer who could afford leather chairs, plush carpets, and a ton of books on built-in bookshelves. The law office was nicer than Trace's house.

"So let me get this straight. The court evaluator recommended that Doreen be given visitation rights." Trace drummed his fingers on the armrest.

"That's right." Dan sat behind his big mahogany desk and looked over the rim of his glasses. Dan looked more like a slick corporate lawyer than one who did family law. He wore suits with button-down shirts, shiny patterned ties, and expensive-looking shoes. In his thirties, his desktop sported a picture of a full-figured young woman and two smiley-faced little boys.

"So I should take a five-year-old to a prison? And even the psychologist agreed with that?" Didn't anyone care about the harm it could cause a child to see her mother in jail? For more than a decade, he'd be taking his daughter to a barred and barb-wired institution with guards who wore guns to see a woman who didn't deserve the label of mother.

"According to the report, your daughter wants to see her mother."

It was like someone had her fist around his heart and was squeezing the blood out of it. Delanie had often said she wished her mother was at the ranch. She'd never asked him to take her to her mother. "And if we go to court?"

Dan tapped his pen on the manila folder that contained the report. "The judge is going to listen to the court evaluator and the psychologist we paid to weigh in on this. That means he is going to grant that right to Doreen, if you go to trial or if you don't go to trial. The judge isn't going to ignore the professionals. Settle and save yourself aggravation and money."

And it wasn't even Trace's money. It was Ty's.

"And be aware." Dan waved his pen in Trace's direction. "If you decide to go to trial, Delanie will undoubtedly have to take the stand, and Doreen's lawyer is going to ask your daughter a ton of questions about how well you are taking care of her and if she's happy."

"Does the report say she's not?" Sweat trickled down his back despite air conditioning blowing out of a ceiling vent.

"The report says she wants to see her mother. And that Delanie thinks you don't want her to. That's not going to sit well with the judge." His lawyer leaned forward. "The report also states that Delanie doesn't like having to go out on the range with you, especially when the weather is bad."

Trace closed his eyes. He'd been trying so hard, and it didn't seem to matter. Delanie wanted her mother. Not him.

Dan continued. "You've solved that by getting a caregiver, but the report noted that the caregiver had been noncommittal with regard to how long she would stay."

"I'll find another sitter when the time comes." He hoped he sounded more confident than he felt.

"But Doreen's lawyer is going to see that and make that woman take the stand, and if she says this is just a temporary gig, well, who knows what the judge will think of that."

"The court doesn't care that Doreen is incarcerated. Or that I'm doing the best I can, which is a helluva lot better than Doreen did when she had the chance."

"You've all of that in your favor, as well as the fact you are the biological father. But the courts don't like to come between a mother and her child. Lots of children visit their parents in jail, unfortunately. And it's not like you've been a Boy Scout in the past either. We go to trial to try to contest visitation rights, and your past is going to come up, likely with your daughter sitting in the courtroom."

Felt like a grenade had just exploded in his insides.

"What do you advise then?"

"That we offer Doreen visitation rights in return for uncontested custody, and avoid going to court. You can offer her once a month, which I think the judge will view as reasonable given the distance."

"You think she'll take it?"

"One thing the report noted was that Doreen took a long time to petition the court for visitation rights. I imagine Doreen's legal services lawyer is telling her right now that the judge isn't going to look too favorably on that. Plus, Doreen is going to have to take the stand too. And I don't know how she would feel about her history coming out in front of her daughter. I'm pretty sure Doreen's legal services lawyer, who no doubt has a full plate already, is going to pressure Doreen to take whatever deal you offer."

"Like you are pressuring me?"

Dan smiled. "Hey, a parent who drags out a custody suit is like the gift that keeps on giving to us lawyers. So if I thought you'd win on the visitation rights, I'd be pushing for it. "

"Can I think about it?" He needed time to process.

"Don't take too long. We have some leverage at the moment because I'm betting Doreen's lawyer doesn't want to go before a judge any more than the judge wants to see us in court."

Trace stepped into his kitchen, and Moose greeted him, tail wagging. The dog, and maybe Archer, were the only two living things that seemed to care about him. What did that say? Trace toed off his boots and left them by the door before turning around.

"Your timing is perfect," Haylee said as she opened the oven.

The smell of something wonderful filled his senses.

"Just heard from the peanut gallery that she's hungry."

Haylee wore shorts and a sleeveless top that showed off her creamy pale skin which she seemed to have kept from getting burned again. It was hot today, and by the whirring sound coming from the living room, Haylee had apparently cranked up the window air conditioner. He couldn't blame her. With the oven going, it was warm in the cramped kitchen.

Why couldn't he have a normal home life? A good woman like Haylee to come home to. A daughter who loved him. Seemed he was destined to be alone. Even Delanie apparently preferred a drug-addled mother to a father who worked hard, tried to be there for her, and adored her. There must be something wrong with him that the people he cared about couldn't find room in their hearts for him. From his mother to Delanie and now to Haylee.

"Me too." He headed to the sink and washed his hands, then threw water on his face and dried it with a paper towel. "What smells so good?"

"I made a casserole with ham, sausage, and beans."

He sniffed the air. "Smells better than that."

If they were married, he'd lean over and kiss her, wrap his arms around her, and give her a bear hug. Because he could use a hug right about then.

Married? When had that thought crept into his mind…his heart? Having Haylee around had not only made him wish for something more, it had made him wish for her. And that was the path to heartache.

"It's a French recipe, so there are some different seasonings, is all. I think you'll both like it." With potholders covering her delicate hands, she lifted the steaming dish out of the oven and set it on another potholder on the table.

"Delanie, it's time to eat," he called. "Where is she?"

"She's washing her hands."

"Everything go okay today?"

"Fine. And with you?"

He nodded. He'd told Haylee where he'd be that afternoon, but he didn't want to talk about it. What would he say? His daughter wanted her mother and wasn't happy with him? He didn't think he could get those words out over the lump in his throat.

He opted to change the subject. "Your sister seemed nice. I think there may be something there with that bull rider. Lonnie's a good sort."

Haylee crinkled her nose. "A bull rider? So not her type. She's a yoga-loving, health-nut city girl. But I kind of miss her now that she's gone."

"Siblings are like that. A pain in the butt when they are around. A hole in your heart when they aren't."

Delanie was in the doorway before he could take another breath and dashed to her seat without a greeting. Trace pulled out Haylee's chair before sitting in his.

He looked across at his daughter, dressed in her little polo shirt and denim shorts, eagerly watching Haylee dish out some casserole, and wondered what he had to do to get this child to love him. To want to be with him rather than just putting up with him.

"Blow on it before you take a mouthful. It's been in the warmer, so it's likely to be a little on the hot side," Haylee cautioned Delanie.

Haylee scooped out a portion for him, and Trace let the scent of meat and spices roll over him. There was something to be said for a good meal. Delanie was already shoveling hers into her mouth despite the warning. Trace took a bite. Hot and tasty. The woman sure could cook.

He'd bet she was good at a lot of things, but he had too much on his mind to let it wander down that dead end.

"Tomorrow I'm going to Lauren's, right, Daddy?" Delanie said, looking eager for her playdate.

"I believe that's right." He looked at Haylee for confirmation, and she nodded.

Trace debated whether he should bring anything up to Delanie and finally decided he had to find out the truth, however painful and despite Haylee's presence. "Last time you talked to your mother, Delanie, did she say she wanted to see you?"

Delanie shook her head, keeping her eyes focused on her meal. "But I want to see her."

"You've said you wanted her to come here, but you never said you wanted to visit her. Do you want to visit her?"

Delanie nodded as if she was afraid to speak. He guessed he should have been asking these questions all along. If that was what the kid wanted and the psychologist didn't think it would harm her, should he really deny her? Besides, did he really know what was best for her on an emotional level? Hell, he'd buried his emotions when he'd buried his mother, and look where it had gotten him. Nowhere.

"I'll look into it. Not promising anything, but… I'll see."

The smile that lit his child's face broke off another piece of his heart.

Haylee had felt like a voyeur watching a family through a window. There had been real pain in Trace's tone when he spoke of Delanie's mother. Delanie had eaten silently during the rest of the meal, and when it was over, sprinted into the living room to watch the half hour of television she was allotted at night. Haylee began to clean off the table.

"I've told you before that you don't have to do the cleaning up." Trace rose from the table, and she was aware he was behind her as she set the lid on the casserole.

"You're nice enough to invite me to eat dinner with you each night…"

"A meal you cook. Of course you're invited to eat with us."

"A meal you pay me to cook. But I am grateful. It sure beats eating by myself."

Trace picked up the plates from the table as Haylee put the leftover casserole away in the refrigerator. Most days she'd scurry out as fast as she finished dinner, but today, after he'd stepped through the door looking as lost as a dog someone had abandoned, her heart wouldn't let her.

At least there was enough for dinner tomorrow, and it helped that Trace was amenable to leftovers. Some men who paid for their meals to be cooked wouldn't be.

"Eating by myself was my life up until…well, up until Delanie." He rubbed his chin while he peeked in the living room, as if assuring himself that Delanie was settled. "I could use a woman's perspective if you have a minute."

She hoped the surprise his words caused didn't

play on her face. She didn't say anything as he methodically stacked the plates. She'd learned that when it came to talking, Trace needed time and space.

When he bent to load the silverware into the dishwasher, she found herself admiring his fine butt and strong thighs, not that she should be looking, mind you.

"If I'm not keeping you from something?" he said, turning around. Had he caught her staring?

She shook her head. All that was waiting for her at home was a pile of bills to wade through. If the company she was interviewing with tomorrow would just come through for the future so she would know she had a job when Aunt Paula's house finally sold, she could relax a bit.

He motioned for her to sit down at the now cleared table and followed suit, his hands clasped before him.

Every grimace line in his face showed his internal struggle at confiding in her.

"I saw the lawyer today." His voice was low, almost a whisper, as if sharing a secret.

She nodded, afraid to make a response that might spook him.

"He thinks…" Trace stopped in midsentence and drew a deep breath. "He thinks I should settle with Doreen over visitation."

He looked at her as if he expected some sort of reaction, but she schooled her expression and simply nodded again. She had no expertise in this area, but she did feel some sympathy for the mother.

"Instead of taking it to trial, he wants me to offer visitation rights, which he sees as a slam dunk for her based on that court evaluator's recommendations. He says I'd have to testify if we go to trial, and lots of things…" He wiped his brow with his sleeve. "Well, things might come up that wouldn't be good for Delanie to hear."

His jaw had clenched, and he looked like he was wound tighter than an old watch.

She chose her words carefully. "But you still want to contest it?"

He glanced back at the doorway to the living room before answering. "Taking a child to a prison to see a convicted criminal? Only, you heard Delanie. She wants to visit her mother, but she has no idea what that means."

Haylee could see both sides, but if she were Delanie, she knew she would feel the same way as the child did. Her own biological mother had died before Haylee knew to ask. "At what age do you think she would be aware her mother was in prison? Or someone in her classroom wouldn't search her mother's name on the internet out of curiosity? Delanie does talk about her mother being away, learning her lesson, which, by the way, I think is an admirable way of presenting it."

"I don't know what age, but I guess it is going to happen." Trace leaned back. "But what will she think if she sees guards with guns and her mother behind bars?"

"I think prisons nowadays are better prepared for family visitors. There may not be bars in the visitor area, and the guards are probably going to look like policemen to her. You said the courts were likely to grant visitation rights. Why fight it?"

He rubbed his hands over his face, as if trying to wash away a memory.

"I'm not even sure Delanie wants to be with me."

The catch in his throat reverberated through Haylee with earthquake force. "You are wrong, Trace. Delanie loves you. She loves the ranch."

He shook his head. "She loves her mother. She tolerates me because she has to."

As if it were a reflex, she reached out, touched his solid firm arm, and was gratified he didn't pull away. "She talks about you all the time. All the things you can do. Ride a horse, herd cattle, fix trucks, and work hard. She put the picture of the two of you on her dresser."

"Yeah, next to the one of her mother and her."

"She sees what we all see, a hardworking man who cares."

From under lowered eyebrows, Trace stared at her a long time without saying anything, his head bowed, his hands clasped between spread knees. "She doesn't like going out on the range with me. She told the lawyer that."

Doubt could be so corrosive.

"She's five. Playing house, tag, or hide-and-seek is far more in her wheelhouse than riding around in a pickup truck while you tend to your work. Besides, I'm here now so she doesn't have to."

He raised his head, and she saw the torment reflected in his sad eyes.

"For how long though, Haylee? When your aunt and uncle's house is sold, you'll be moving on."

Considering the next day she was interviewing for a job in Denver at her old company, she couldn't refute what he said.

"You'll find someone else."

He looked at her with part skepticism, part scrutiny.

"She was thrown to a man she didn't know and didn't trust. And didn't love." He shook his head. "And I don't think any of that has changed. She never seems comfortable with me."

Haylee had noticed that hugs were infrequent, a kiss on the cheek never witnessed. "Have you talked to her about it?"

He grimaced. "She's five. I'd probably scare her to death talking about it."

Haylee was pretty sure it would scare Trace more than Delanie. "I'd try it. Find out what's holding her back from showing her affection, because she clearly does love you, Trace. I'm not a psychologist, but even I can see that."

"I'm not a loveable guy, if you haven't noticed."

He was definitely loveable, and that was part of her problem. "Ask her. Something may be holding her back from expressing it, but I know it's there."

He rose. "Kept you long enough. Thanks for the pep talk."

"It wasn't a pep talk. It's my sincere opinion."

He nodded, but it was clear that Trace wasn't listening, didn't want to hear, wouldn't risk it.

Having set the kitchen to rights, Trace entered the living room only to find Delanie bouncing a ball off the wall. The china platter that had belonged to his mother rattled on the top of the cabinet. Most memories of his mother were tinged with dark shadows. This platter represented happier times.

"No balls in the house, Delanie. I've told you that

before." The din of the air conditioner had masked the sound of play.

Delanie stopped. "Sorry," she said, her eyes wide, as if she was expecting repercussions. And why that should be when he'd never touched her when she misbehaved, he didn't know, but like a splinter that couldn't be removed, it chafed him.

He stepped over to turn the air-conditioner unit off. By now the plains would have cooled down enough that an open window would suffice. And save him money.

At bedtime, he sat on Delanie's bed, Moose by the door, as she knelt to say her prayers, feeling worse than before he'd talked to Haylee. Because Haylee had given him hope, and the more hope he held, the greater would be the fall when nothing materialized.

Finished, Delanie rose, and instead of scrambling into bed under the princess coverlet, she stood before him, her sweet face serious. God, he loved this child, despite everything.

"Thank you for answering my prayers, Daddy."

"Answering your prayers?"

"I've been praying every night that you would take me to see Mommy. Every night."

He'd only said he'd look into it, but his daughter had taken it as a commitment. "You never said anything about visiting your mom."

"I didn't want to make you mad."

"Why would you think that would make me mad?"

"Every time I say something about Mommy, you look mad. I know you don't like her for making you take me…"

"Whoa, sweet pea. Is that what you've been thinking? Your mother didn't force me to take you. I wanted you." With all his sorry heart.

Delanie bit her lip and stared at him with wide eyes. How could she have gotten that impression when he'd done everything he could think of to make her happy?

"You never said." She hugged her stuffed dog closer.

Everything except that, apparently.

"I guess I'm not so good with words." He held her small face gently between his two hands. "So let me say this to you so there is no doubt. I want you with me. If I had found out about you sooner, I would have been in your life. I never intend to leave you."

"Why are you so mad at Mommy then?"

He dropped his hands from her face. How did he explain something so complicated to a child without saying bad things about her mother? This was why relationships blew up on him. He just wasn't good with words…or feelings.

But he looked into those serious hazel eyes and knew he'd have to take a stab at it. "If I am angry with your mother it's… I didn't even know about you until that day. I missed a lot about you as a result. And…well, I think she could have been a better mother to you, is all."

"Mommy loves me. She tells me so every time she calls."

And there it was. A simple truth.

"Do you believe I love you, baby girl?"

She didn't answer right away, just bowed her head, as if afraid to tell him the truth. The knife buried deeper into his soul.

When she raised her head, she said, “I try to be good so you won’t send me away. I forgot about the ball in the house.”

Trace felt the blood drain out of him. Without the court’s approval for custody, he couldn’t even reassure her that he’d never send her away. “Delanie, I am doing everything I can to assure you are with me always. Because I love you, honey. I may not say it much, but I do. Not sure what I can do to make you believe it though.”

For the first time since Delanie had come to live with him, she climbed onto his lap and wrapped her arms around his neck. “You’re taking me to see Mommy.”

Chapter 14

At exactly six o'clock, Trace pulled into the paved driveway and past the manicured lawn of the large house that was in the subdivision of five-acre lots residing behind stone pillars off the county highway, a commuter suburb of Cheyenne only forty minutes from the city. The houses were large, brick faced, and three-car garaged. Different world than the ranch.

He'd called the lawyer and told him to go ahead and agree to give Doreen visitation rights in return for uncontested custody. He still didn't feel comfortable, but it was what Delanie wanted and the report endorsed. He'd deal with it like he'd dealt with everything else, one step at a time.

One of those large swing sets with a wooden fort and colorful slide was visible in the back as he parked the truck. No children played on it though.

He walked along the sidewalk, past foundation plantings that were still small, testifying to the young age of the development, and up to the massive ruddy-brown door. The bell chimed like church bells, and he heard hard footsteps. The door opened, and a woman not much older than he was opened the door. She had chin-length blond hair and a slender body clothed in a T-shirt and yoga pants. She looked like a college-cheerleader-turned-mom. Probably had married the star athlete, and they'd settled down to a storybook life. For some people, life just worked out.

"Mr. Martin," she acknowledged and stuck out her hand. "Melissa Leonard. Come in."

He shook the woman's hand and stepped into a two-story foyer with light from the setting sun streaming in the high windows, illuminating the hardwood floors and catching on the silver-framed mirror and dainty secretary desk, where a Bible sat.

"Delanie ready?" He was hungrier than a bear after hibernation and anxious to get home and have some of Haylee's leftover casserole.

"They are down in the basement, playing. I'll call her up in a moment. Come on back to the kitchen. I've some home-baked cookies that the girls had for a snack, if you'd like."

Trace looked down at his dusty boots. "No, ma'am. I'll pass, if you don't mind. I'd like to get going. We've still got a half-hour ride ahead of us."

She nodded but didn't move. Instead she looked at him, wrung her hands, and coughed.

"Something wrong, ma'am? Something with Delanie?" Anxiety pushed up his blood pressure.

"No. Delanie is fine." Her eyes darted to what he thought might be the basement door. "Mr. Martin…"

"You can call me Trace."

Her lips had flatlined, and a frown was on her face. "Trace, I don't know how to ask this, but, well, I hope you understand that as a mother, I really have to ask."

Trace shoved his hands into his pockets and waited, uncertain where the conversation was going.

"I thought the woman who picked Delanie up was

Delanie's mother, but Delanie told me that she is her sitter."

Trace felt warmth flood through him.

"Is Delanie's mother…is she in prison?"

Why he hadn't been prepared for such a question, he didn't know. He should have been. But it had never crossed his mind that anyone would find out about Delanie's mother so soon. His mind grappled for answers, but there was only one he could give. The honest one. "Delanie's mother was convicted of a crime and is serving time. But Delanie is not aware of the circumstances, and I would appreciate it if you didn't mention it in her presence."

The shock on the woman's face was quickly replaced by pursed lips and a deep-set frown.

Trace had to know. "What made you ask?"

"Your daughter said her mother was away learning her lesson. I asked if she was at school, and Delanie said it was a place you went when you did bad things. So of course I asked the child her mother's name and checked on the internet. I wanted confirmation from you that I had the right woman." She lifted up her chin and straightened her spine as if preparing for a fight. "Under the circumstances, I'm sure you understand why, beyond seeing each other in camp, which I can't prevent, I will not be encouraging Lauren's friendship with your daughter."

It was like someone had shot him with a high-powered stun gun, stopping his heart.

"I don't see why. Delanie is an innocent child, and I am sure she didn't give you any problems while she was here. I'm her father and a respectable rancher in these parts. My family has been ranching our land since homesteader days. Long before you arrived here, I imagine."

Melissa clasped her hands tightly in front of her. "She was well behaved but…I can't risk Lauren associating with…criminals. Or children of criminals."

Trace glanced at the Bible sitting on the secretary. "Are you a Christian, Melissa?"

"Yes."

"Doesn't the Bible teach not to judge lest ye be judged, or forgiveness, or anything related to being kind to others?"

"I don't appreciate the attack, Mr. Martin. As a mother it is my duty to protect my child. And while I might be forgiving in my heart, I will not take risks with my child."

He wasn't going to win a war of words with the woman. "Just get my daughter, please, and we'll be out of here."

She turned on her heel. "I won't mention it to the other mothers. I'll leave it to them to do their own due diligence."

She made it sound like she was doing him a favor. He'd like to be able to tell her to shout it to the world, but Melissa Leonard was a stark reminder that the world was an unforgiving place, even when it concerned an innocent five-year-old child.

It took only a minute for Melissa to call Delanie up and for Delanie to gather her stuff.

"See you at school," Delanie said cheerily as she hugged her little friend and skipped out the door. He followed and heard the door slam behind them.

Trace hadn't said goodbye or taken another look at Melissa Leonard.

"Did you have fun?" Trace forced himself to sound casual and not let anger into his voice.

"Yup. We played house. Lauren was the mom, and I was the dad. I wanted to be the mom, but Lauren wanted to be the mom, so I let her."

"You're a good kid, Delanie." That he could say with feeling.

"Can we invite Lauren over to our house? She wants to see Moose, and I told her you would give her a ride on Buck."

How many times would disappointment be played out in her young life once people found out? He'd been so consumed with getting custody that he hadn't anticipated any of this, and he should have.

"We'll see, Delanie. Depends on Lauren's mom, I guess." How did he keep his daughter from these slights, from the hurts that would only get worse as she grew older?

Life wasn't fair, for sure. If Delanie was going to be put through hell by contemptible people, at least he'd be there for her.

Monday of the following week was the Fourth of July, and Haylee had gone to the ranch early since Delanie did not have camp.

Haylee had arrived that morning armed with books from the town library and a list of items for a scavenger hunt outside so they could enjoy the warm weather. Trace had also hooked up a sprinkler, and Delanie and Moose had fun running under the fanning water. After Haylee read *Angelina Ballerina*, Delanie wanted to dress up like a ballerina, and Haylee had set about fixing Delanie's hair in a bun as Delanie sat at her little-girl vanity table in her princess-themed bedroom.

Haylee had spent much of the prior week feeling guilty for having gone on an interview for a freight auditor job with her old company. The firm seemed interested and had even asked when she'd be able to start if they offered her a job. She'd been vague, talking of months, not weeks.

She had tried not to read anything more into it than a perfunctory question asked of any candidate. Truth was, it was becoming more and more obvious each day that time was running out on her business experiment. If the company offered her a job, she feared her bank account would force her to take it, regardless of timing, regardless of her aunt's needs…or her own desire.

"Would you rather be a cowgirl or a ballerina?" Haylee asked, trying to make conversation and distract from her own fears. Amazing that Delanie was the only person she spoke with lately. Trace's one-word responses could hardly be called talking.

Delanie put her finger to her cheek and cocked her head. "I want to dance in the pasture grass so I can be both."

A diplomat in the making. "You like living on the ranch then?"

Delanie nodded. "I hated where I lived before. It smelled bad. And Mommy wouldn't let me outside because she never felt good. Daddy's taking me to see her."

Haylee hadn't expected to get into issues about the child's mother, but Delanie's news was welcome. And brought back some of Haylee's own yearnings during childhood. Yearnings to meet her birth mother and the grandparents so willing to give her up, yearnings to know where she had come from, yearnings she had tucked away a long time ago. "You like living here with your father though."

"I'm never leaving. I'm never going to be bad so I have to leave."

Haylee wrapped her arms around Delanie and squeezed the slender little body close to hers. "You have nothing to worry about, Delanie."

"I want to see what I look like in Daddy's mirror." Delanie broke free of Haylee's embrace and rushed out of the room, headed down the hall.

Haylee followed, feeling a little apprehensive about stepping into Trace's private space. In the few weeks she'd been there, she had managed to avoid checking out his room. It was at the end of the hall across from another bedroom, and Haylee really had no reason to go down that way.

She peeked into one bedroom. A twin bed with a plaid coverlet sat on the far wall, while on the near wall was a small student-sized desk, which held a computer, its top scattered with papers. Next to it was a three-drawer dresser that had file folders on top of it. Other than the Denver Bronco pennant above the bed, the faded curtains at the window, and a current calendar above the desk, there was nothing on the walls. The room was clearly Trace's office now.

She switched her focus to the other bedroom. There was Delanie, dancing on a king-sized bed with a large wooden headboard and covered in a Native American-style blanket. Across from it was an oak dresser with a mirror reflecting Delanie's image.

"You need to get off the bed, Delanie. You could fall and hurt yourself."

Delanie looked back at her with skepticism. "I do this all the time. Daddy lets me."

Haylee didn't doubt that was true. "But I'm responsible for your safety at the moment, and I don't feel comfortable with you jumping on the bed. You can jump all you want once your dad gets home if it's okay with him."

Delanie shook her head, but she jumped down from the bed, landing safely on the braided rug that covered the oak floor.

Haylee scanned the room, looking for clues about Trace. The space was devoid of clutter, unlike the office next door. The bed was made, there were no clothes strewn about the floor, and nothing sat on his dresser but a brush and a picture of Delanie. It was one of the photos Haylee had taken of Delanie dancing in prairie grass.

She felt a pinch near her heart. He'd liked her work enough to frame it, though the frame was a worn brass one that looked like it had seen better days. Made her wonder what picture had been in that frame before.

She heard the back door slam, and suddenly felt like a voyeur. Trace had said that he and Delanie would be heading to town for the Fourth of July carnival, so Haylee didn't have to worry about dinner, and it appeared he had come in early to keep that promise.

Gratefully, Delanie was off in a flash to greet him. Haylee exited and made it to Delanie's room just as Trace crossed into the hallway from the living room.

Delanie rushed to greet him. "See my hair, Daddy? Do you like it?"

He bent down on his haunches, ran splayed fingers through his hair, and stared at his little girl with such tenderness it made Haylee ache inside. He looked dusty and tired, but he gave his daughter a big smile. "You look beautiful, sweet pea."

Delanie leaned over and planted a wet kiss on her father's cheek.

Something had decidedly shifted for the good in their relationship.

"You ready to head out to town?" he said as he rose. "You are welcome to join us, Miss Haylee. I'm just going to take a quick shower, and we'll head out."

"Come…come." Delanie danced in the narrow hallway. "They have fireworks and rides."

It was tempting. Living where she was, it was easy to feel isolated. But it would mean spending casual time with Trace, and she wasn't sure that was a good thing, considering.

"Can't beat fireworks and rides, can you?" Trace asked. "It's fun as long as you don't mind crowds and hot dogs." He cocked his head, and the smile on his face broadened, sending waves of tingles rippling through her like a stone skipping through water.

"I love crowds and hot dogs," she heard herself say.

The crowd was small, at least in comparison to Denver and Chicago crowds. The hot dogs, however, were yummy. All beef, of course, and lathered in sauerkraut and mustard, just the way Haylee liked them.

The carnival had taken over the town's playground

for the weekend, and the sounds of laughter and children mingled with the smell of popcorn. They walked among the vendors, games of chance, and smattering of rides, Delanie between them, holding on to each of their hands. To the casual passerby, the three of them undoubtedly looked like a family. Like they belonged together.

Family life. Simple pleasures. The kind of life she'd once pictured with Roy. But once they were married, Roy had gotten skittish about the idea of a baby…and then she'd found out why.

"I want to go on that," Delanie said, pointing to the merry-go-round.

"On that? You can ride real horses at home," Trace said, clearly puzzled by his daughter's request.

Delanie stuck her lip out. "Not like that."

Trace heaved a sigh, handed the operator the requisite amount of tickets, and settled Delanie on a big black horse among the flood of children and their parents doing the same.

He stepped off just before the carousel started, and stood with Haylee, arms crossed and a grin on his face, watching his child as the carousel turned.

"Amazing she finds that exciting," he said, huffing out a breath.

He was dressed in his cowboy gear clearly meant for town—fresh jeans, pressed plaid shirt, white hat, and polished black boots. And more than one passing woman had given him the once-over, despite Haylee standing next to him. Maybe they didn't look like they really belonged together. Or maybe those women just didn't care if he was with someone.

"It's different, is all."

"Guess different has its attractions." He looked in

her direction, his gaze pointed. "You up for trying something different?"

Her heart did a little skittered beat. "Sure," she said, wondering what he was thinking.

He nodded in the direction of a gathering a few feet away. "Mechanical bull?"

"Riding? Me?"

"You can select your speed."

Though she enjoyed amusement rides and was a little curious as to what it would be like riding a bull, after seeing all those riders get tossed off a real bull, it didn't hold much appeal. "I don't think so."

"Not a risk-taker, are you?"

He'd pegged her correctly. And for some reason, it irritated her. "I'll try if you will?"

His eyebrows arched. "Deal."

As she stood waiting in line for her turn, holding Delanie's hand, the mechanical bull seemed more imposing and intimidating than when she'd watched the real thing at the rodeo. But then she hadn't been expecting to get on the creature. At least there was plenty of bouncy type padding around the thing so when people got tossed, they landed softly.

There were a fair number of women who tried, though most looked a little inebriated. None of them stayed on. Of the men who rode, a few made it to the end.

Dusk was settling, and the lights had gone on. Maybe she'd be saved from her turn by the fireworks display.

Trace was up, and Haylee squeezed Delanie's hand as he mounted. He curled his long legs against the sides of the steel beast and nodded. It lurched into motion in spasms of tossing and turning. Trace's grin was from ear to ear, and when he yee-hawed, the crowd roared. He looked pretty commanding waving his hand in the air and whooping it up, even if it was a mechanical bull. Against her will, her heart expanded. She had it bad, and there was nothing she could do about it.

When his ride ended, Trace was still on. Only then did Haylee remember it was her turn next.

Normally she loved amusement rides, but this, as Trace had said, was something different. Hadn't she come to Wyoming for something different? Didn't Jenna say she needed to take more risks?

As Trace dismounted, he leaned over, said something to the operator, and then joined her.

"You don't have to if you don't want to," he whispered in her ear, his breath sending pleasurable spikes through her.

She squared her shoulders. "I'm going."

She stepped onto the squishy, inflated flooring, grabbed onto the bull, and hauled herself onto its back. The body of the beast was wide, and her legs, unlike Trace's, barely fit around. She heard Delanie's voice call her name in encouragement. She raised her hand like she'd seen the bull riders do, clutched the fabric of the bull with her other hand, and nodded.

The bull tossed and turned, but the motion wasn't spastic, like Trace's ride had been, but more rolling. All the same, she felt herself slipping as it raised and whirled. One good turn and she was bouncing on the landing pad. Still, she had tried it and survived. In fact, she'd enjoyed it. But it made her admire those bull riders all the more.

She jumped up, waved to Delanie, and made her way off.

"You asked him to slow it down, didn't you?" Haylee confronted Trace.

The corner of his mouth lifted up in a good-natured smirk.

"Couldn't risk you getting injured. You looked like a real cowgirl up there."

He winked, and a funny feeling zinged through her and lodged in her belly, as if something had arced between them, connecting them.

"I want to go on the tilt-a-whirl," Delanie said, tugging on her father's belt, breaking the tension.

It was just a few steps to the ride. They stood together, she and Trace, watching Delanie fly by. He was so close she could smell the fresh scent of his soap. She turned toward him, ready to tell him how much she was enjoying herself, when his cell phone rang.

His fished the phone out of his pocket and frowned as he checked the screen. "That's Mandy. I've got to take this," he said by way of apology as he put the phone to his ear.

"She's what?" Trace exclaimed. "So all is forgiven?… Isn't that near your due date?… I guess Delanie can be the flower girl…" He thumbed up the brim of his hat. "Would you have time to get her a dress?… It's nice of her to include a guest for me, but… Hope my brother isn't working you too hard… You take care. Rest a little, will you? I don't want my niece or nephew coming into the world exhausted."

With that he tucked the phone in the back pocket of his jeans. "My sister-in-law," Trace said. "She's so close to her due date I thought maybe the baby was coming."

"But it's not?"

"No." The ride had ended, and Trace strode over to get Delanie off. As the pair sauntered back, Delanie flush with excitement, Trace continued. "We have another wedding to attend though. Friend of Mandy's is getting married in just about two weeks." He glanced in Delanie's direction. "Cat wants you to be a flower girl, Delanie."

Delanie jumped and clasped her hands together. "I want to be a flower girl." Her smile was wide, her announcement firm.

"Two weeks seems kind of sudden, no?" Haylee could have bit her tongue when she said that. It really wasn't any of her business. She'd taken a year to put her wedding together, and look how that had turned out.

"Long story, but the short version is the bride-to-be is marrying a neighboring rancher, and since their families never got along, I think they are afraid their relatives will screw things up if they give them too much time." He glanced at the crowd that was moving in one direction. "Looks like the fireworks are about to start. We should head over."

"Sounds like Delanie wants to go to the wedding." Haylee stepped into line with Trace and checked to be sure Delanie was holding her father's hand. She didn't want to lose the child in the crowd.

"I do," the little girl confirmed.

"She was flower girl at Mandy and my brother's wedding. Looked cute as a button too."

Talk of weddings brought back distinct memories, memories she'd rather not think about.

"Will Mandy have had the baby by then?"

"She's due two days later. But Cat McKenna has been friends with my sister-in-law since they were kids. Nothing but going into labor would keep her from this wedding, I think."

Haylee wondered who Trace would take as a guest…not that she should care.

The fireworks were a spectacle of light and color, the ride back quiet. Everyone, including Haylee was tired. As they passed her house on the way to pick up her car at Trace's place, she noted that there was a light on in the cabin.

She didn't remember leaving a light on.

It was dark when Haylee pulled into her own driveway, though the lamp she'd mistakenly left on served as a beacon. Why she had put on a light when she'd departed in daylight, she didn't know, but she mentally chastised herself for wasting good money.

The evening had made her grateful for simple pleasures…and Trace. She had to get over him because there could be a buyer any day, and she'd leave Cottonwood Road for good.

There was nothing in this isolated part of Wyoming for her. At least nothing that wanted her. But she would certainly miss Delanie. And her father.

Getting out of the car, the buzz and clicking of cicadas filled the air like a percussion symphony. The bright stars lit the sky, but there was only a sliver of a moon. Haylee mentally traced the Big and Little Dippers before climbing up the front steps. Tracing constellations was not something she could do in Chicago or Denver since those cities were so artificially lit up at night, you couldn't see all the stars.

Out here, it looked like a million fireflies had been thrown into the sky. There was something to be said for living in the country.

She turned her key in the lock and opened the front door.

Her scream filled the silent night.

Chapter 15

"I am sorry, darling. I didn't mean to scare you."

Roy sat on her sofa, can of beer in one hand, remote control in the other, though the TV had been turned off, looking at her as if she were the intruder instead of the other way around.

Haylee clutched her stomach and waited for her heart to slow before she chanced her voice. Dressed in jeans, a short-sleeve plaid shirt, and a day's growth of stubble on his face, Roy looked a might too comfortable on her aunt's two-cushion country-style couch. He hadn't bothered to take off the green baseball cap with a tractor company logo that covered his closely cropped brown hair.

"What are you doing here?" And how did he know where to find her? She hadn't been hiding from him exactly, but she hadn't told him where she was living either. She'd given Roy her parents' address if he needed to get in touch with her, since until a few weeks ago, she hadn't been certain where she would be living.

She'd seen no reason to let him know where she was. Yet here he sat in the open space that housed the living room, dining area, and kitchen. A shiver crawled up her spine and, like a spider looking for a home, settled at the base of her neck.

"Came for a visit." He'd spread his arms across the back of sofa, one leg crossed over the other knee, as if it were natural for him to be there taking up space. "And a favor."

It was the favor she was afraid of.

She stood by the door, not inclined to step in, as if she needed to be by the exit just in case. She wasn't afraid of Roy…not afraid for any physical reason. He'd never raised a hand to her, and she never expected he would. But there were other reasons not to trust him.

"What's that?"

"Come sit down. We haven't seen each other for what, over six months?" He patted a spot on the sofa.

"There's a reason for that. It's called divorce." Recovered from her fright, she let anger fill her. "How did you get in here anyway?"

"Shouldn't leave your back door open, darling." His lips had curved into a self-satisfied smile. "Anyone could walk in. Especially out here."

Had she left the back door open? She'd gone out to hang some hand-washed items on the clothesline and, in her rush to get to Trace's house, probably hadn't checked that the door was locked before she'd left. Great.

No longer feeling off balance, she strode past him into the kitchen area and flung her purse, stuffed with library books, on the counter that formed a U-shape with a peninsula. She needed wine if she was going to continue this conversation. Thankfully, there was still some Pinot Grigio left from when her sister had visited. Opening the refrigerator door, she noted Roy had stuffed a six-pack, now missing two cans, onto the shelves of the fridge. Meaning, for some reason, he was planning to spend time at her house.

She poured herself a glass of wine, strode over to where Roy sat, and plopped down in her uncle's faux-leather recliner. "I'm asking again. What are you really doing here, Roy? What is this favor you want?"

She took a gulp of wine to calm her jumbled insides. She could only imagine what he wanted, and it wasn't anything good.

"Where does someone go to have fun around here on the Fourth of July?"

If he was trying to ignore her question, it must be something really bad. "Why are you here unannounced?"

He leaned forward as he took a sip of beer. "I actually knocked when I didn't see your car, because I wondered if your aunt and uncle were here. Where are they, by the way? You didn't murder them or something?"

He actually thought he was funny. "I'm house sitting."

"Convenient. Except for being stuck in the middle of nowhere."

"What is the favor?"

"I drove one of my rigs here."

She hadn't seen any vehicle, much less a semi, parked by the house. Even in the dark, she would have noticed that.

"I parked it behind that nice big barn you have back there."

"Is it filled with…"

He nodded. “Precious cargo. Problem is, someone has tipped off law enforcement. One of the drivers got pulled over. Not one of my rigs. Another rig. I was told they are on the hunt for others. I just need to park it here overnight, and by morning there will be another cab here with different plates. I’ll change out the cab and be on my way. Simple.”

Only it would mean she was aiding and abetting criminal activity.

“No. I want no part of what you are into. You made your choice.”

With his tight lips and clenched jaw, he reminded her of a bulldog chomping down on a bone. “*You* don’t have a choice. The rig is behind your barn. I’ll be leaving in the morning. That’s it.”

Tears sprang to the back of her eyes, but she’d be damned if she’d let them fall in front of Roy. She was done crying over him and his choices.

“I have options, Roy. I could call the police.” Except she didn’t even know who that would be out their way.

He didn’t even flinch at the suggestion. “And implicate yourself? Don’t talk crazy.”

He was right. She’d had plenty of opportunity to turn him in. She hadn’t.

“You came here knowing you would put me in danger.”

“You are not in danger. No one knows I’m here.”

“The guy who is delivering the cab knows.”

“He’s not going to talk.”

“Is he one of them?”

“No. I told him I broke down, and he’s helping me out.”

"So you are involving another innocent soul in this mess."

Roy leaned forward, his expression serious. "I don't have any other options. If I get caught, I'll go to jail."

"Walk away, Roy. I begged you to walk away. Give them the rigs and walk away."

"And I told you, that is insanity. Those rigs are worth a lot of money."

"We could have used the money we'd saved for the house. With that you would have been able to put a down payment on a new rig. We could have started over."

"I have two now and am still paying off one of them. I'd still owe on it if I turned it over to them."

They'd had this same argument for months.

"What is your freedom worth?" And what was she worth? Apparently not two rigs.

"It's just overnight. I'll sleep in the truck. We'll be out of your hair before you know what is happening. And as far as you're concerned, there is nothing in that rig except watermelons. Nothing."

She wished that were true. She gulped down the remainder of her wine. "How did you find me?"

"Your sister posted pictures of herself at a rodeo with some cowboy. Said she'd been visiting her sister in Wyoming and had a good time. She also said how cute her aunt's place was. When this situation arose, I remembered the big barn on your aunt's place. Perfect for hiding a truck. Took me a bit to find it. Had to go from memory, but I got here. Truckers do pay attention to roads."

She felt ill, like she just swallowed spoiled milk and was about to wretch any moment. There was nothing she could do about him being there. Rising, she placed a comforting hand on her stomach.

"Just promise me you'll never bother me again. Promise me." She'd left him so she wouldn't be involved. But tonight had slammed home the truth. She would always be involved because she knew. She knew what he was doing.

He smiled, showing a perfect set of white teeth. "I promise."

"Now go back to your rig. And leave first thing in the morning."

He stood. Roy wasn't much taller than she was. They had once made a cute couple. She had once convinced herself that she loved him. But she shouldn't have had to convince herself. She knew that now. A tall cowboy had taught her.

"Thanks. I mean it, Haylee. You've saved my butt."

"Question is, Roy, when are you going to save your own?"

Around seven in the morning, the roar of truck engines woke Haylee after a restless night. She looked out the window in time to see one of Roy's cabs, without a trailer, bump down the driveway. Behind it came a semi with a cab Haylee didn't recognize.

Roy had been true to his word…this time. But she didn't trust him. And she didn't want to see him again. Ever.

* * *

Stepping into the kitchen, Trace spied the Crock-Pot on the counter and sniffed the air filled with the scent of cooked beef and some spice he couldn't name.

He resisted the temptation to step over and lift the lid, knowing from his own experience that doing so could add at least another thirty minutes to the cooking time.

Leaving his boots and hat by the back door, he entered the living room. Things were so much neater now that Haylee was around. Though he didn't expect her to clean, she always left the place neat and wasn't above taking the vacuum for a spin if she could spare the time between tending to Delanie and cooking dinner.

He'd been lucky with Haylee. If she weren't so damn attractive, all would be good. Instead he was left with a yearning, like he used to have for alcohol, and likely just as bad for him. No good could come of it, but that didn't stop those feelings from surfacing.

He heard voices down the hallway leading to the bedrooms, went to investigate, and found them in Delanie's room. Only his little girl didn't look so little. She sat in front of her toy vanity staring at herself in the mirror while Haylee placed bobby pins in the bun that sat on the back of Delanie's head. His daughter was dressed in a princess costume, looking way too cute.

Hearing him, Haylee looked up, her blue eyes wide with interest, her blond curls spiraling around her pretty face. Staring down at her, he felt like someone was dangling his heart from a bungee cord.

"Daddy!" Delanie rushed out of her child-size vanity seat and straight into his knees.

She wrapped her arms around his legs and looked up at him with puppy-dog eyes. He knew that look. She wanted something.

Haylee rose from her position on the floor.

"Sorry. I didn't hear you come in."

"Nothing to be sorry about." He looked down at Delanie's upturned face. "You look mighty pretty, honey. Playing dress up?"

She nodded. "Miss Haylee wouldn't let me try on my new dress though. I told her I wanted to show you what I look like in it."

"You like your dress?"

Today Mandy had picked Delanie up from camp after lunch and taken her shopping for a flower-girl dress and dropped Delanie back at the ranch before Haylee's shift started.

Delanie nodded. "Do you like my hair? It's ballerina hair."

"It looks right cute." But it made her look older, too old.

"Miss Haylee is going to fix it this way for the wedding."

He frowned. "Is she now? Well, that wedding is on a Saturday, and Miss Haylee doesn't come here on Saturdays."

Haylee looked down at her hands. "I can come over."

"I told her you needed a date."

Trace felt heat rise, like someone had dropped a hot towel down his shirt. "I thought you were my date, Delanie."

Delanie shook her head. "Jake is my date. Aunt Mandy said he's ring bearer, and since I'm flower girl, we are each other's date. So you need your own."

"I don't need a date." He hadn't brought a date to his brother's wedding. In fact, he bet people would be shocked if he showed up with a woman. And what the hell did that say about him? "I'm sure Miss Haylee has plans for that weekend."

"Is that next weekend?"

He nodded and prayed she was busy. Showing up with Haylee would be fanning Mandy's *time to settle down with a good woman* optimism.

"I'm not busy. There's only been a few house viewings since Aunt Paula left, so the real estate broker is having an open house. Not sure it will do much good way out here though."

She looked up at him with those wide, luminous eyes of hers, and he felt a hot yank in his groin.

"If you don't want to take me, I can still come over and fix Delanie's hair. But could I at least hang out here until the open house is done?"

Oh hell. "Why don't you just come to the wedding?" Relatives be damned. It was none of their business anyway.

She smiled at him. A wide, full-of-promise smile with lips that brought back smoking memories of the kiss they'd shared. "Dress?"

He slipped his hands into his pockets. "Or pants. I don't think the bride cares."

She giggled, her soft, sweet laugh rippling through him. "No, I mean is it fancy dress, casual, cocktail?"

As if he would know. "Country, I guess. They are holding it at their ranch."

"Sounds interesting. What time should I be here?"

"It's an hour-and-a-half ride, so we should leave by twelve thirty. Wedding is at three, but I want to allow plenty of time."

"I'll be here around noon to fix Delanie's hair."

"Daddy has a date." Delanie repeated the line in a singsongy voice.

Sweat broke out on the back of his neck. Now he'd gone and done it.

Haylee sat in the front seat of the pickup next to Trace, feeling unsettled as they sped along the highway past flat plains and grassy prairies toward the wedding destination. It wasn't Trace's lack of reaction when he saw her that morning that concerned her. It was why she'd spent money she didn't really have to find the right dress, a strapless sky-blue sundress with a handkerchief hemline that fell just above midcalf, and new strappy high-heeled sandals because, unlike with Roy, she didn't have to worry about appearing taller where Trace was concerned. She'd put her unruly hair in an upsweep and applied more makeup than usual, and for what? Trace had opened the door and abruptly turned away, heading toward the kitchen, leaving a dressed and excited five-year-old to drag Haylee to the child's bedroom.

Made Haylee wonder why she'd been so eager to go anyway? It had solved a problem for her, but so would a trip to Jenna's and a movie—and it would have cost her a lot less than her new dress and shoes.

What had she expected? He'd given every indication she wasn't for him. From laughing at her city-girl boots, to teasing her about her lack of riding skills, to his apology for kissing her, to being totally unaffected when she'd "dressed to kill," he couldn't be any clearer.

His disinterest really did her a favor by keeping

her from any misguided romantic notions. She wasn't right for him, and he couldn't be right for her.

Maybe someone would offer for the house, and she'd be done tormenting herself. The thought made her unaccountably sad rather than relieved.

"So who is likely to be at this wedding?" she asked.

Delanie, looking adorable in her pink dress and her hair in a bun with a pretty ribbon cascading down her back, was tucked in the car seat playing games on Trace's phone.

"People you don't know." Not helpful.

"Which is why I'm asking." At least if she had some names and knew a little about someone, it would make for easier conversation.

"You've met Mandy. And my brother will be there."

She wondered if he was as handsome as Trace. "Will those saddle bronc riders be attending? And Lonnie, the bull rider?" Her sister had apparently friended him on Facebook. Haylee would like to take his temperature with regard to his interest, or noninterest, in her sister. Livvy was still her *little* sister, even if she was a grown woman in her twenties.

"Chance Cochran's wife is friends with Mandy and Cat, so they'll be there. Tucker, Mandy's brother, has known Cat all his life, so he's going. Not sure Lonnie knows Cat."

"It's unusual for a woman to run a ranch as much as it is to run a rodeo, no?"

"These days, ranchers come in both sexes. Isn't unusual to see both husband and wife running things together. But there are always lean times in ranching, so sometimes the husband has a town job, so the wife runs the ranch. Sometimes the wife can find town work easier, so the husband runs the ranch. Sometimes the ranch is owned by a rodeo cowboy, and since he's on the road most of the year, the wife does the day to day. Regardless, ranching is almost always a family affair."

"Did you inherit the ranch, or is it jointly owned with your brother?" She'd been curious as to why one brother ran it and the other brother did something totally different.

"I inherited it. At the time, Ty wanted nothing to do with ranching. He had bigger fields to plow. But things took a turn for the worst when I was…not paying attention. Ty signed for the mortgage on the place when it needed an infusion of cash, so I guess, in reality, he owns it with me."

There was bitterness in his tone that didn't square with the gesture of a brother helping out a brother. "You'd said before that the bride and groom had been feuding neighbors?"

"They were feuding neighbors until…well, until things worked out a few weeks ago. Land and water rights can bring out the worst in people."

"Did you ever have any trouble with the former owners of Aunt Paula's property, considering it sits on the edge of your land?"

"No, because your aunt and uncle were the first ones to ever own that piece of property other than us."

"That property was yours?" Given where it was located, that did make sense. "The house looks like it dates back to the nineteenth century. Who lived there before?"

"That cabin was built by my ancestors at the turn of the last century. My grandparents built the house I live in now when they got married. My great-grandparents had passed by the time I came along, and after some improvements, my parents moved into the cabin and lived there until Ty was born, and then we switched houses with my grandparents. My grandparents lived there until they passed. Eventually, my father needed money, so he carved out a parcel with the cabin on it and sold it to your aunt and uncle."

"I had no idea. How do you feel about my aunt and uncle selling it?"

"Wish I could buy it, but I can't, so I don't feel anything about it."

As if feelings could just be denied. But his tone brooked no further discussion, and certainly not about feelings.

Mandy settled back in her seat. For several miles she watched the flat plains of Wyoming speed by. To get anywhere it took a lot driving. To see anyone it took a lot of time. That's what rural meant.

"Must be difficult maintaining friendships when people are so far away, although social media has certainly made it easier."

"One, I don't do social media. Two, these aren't my friends. They are Mandy's friends. At one time, Mandy got it in her head that Cat, the bride, and I should be a couple because we have kids the same age and were both single."

Well, that was news to chew on. "What happened?"

He turned toward her, his eyes narrowed. "Obviously nothing."

"Why?" None of her business, but she was curious.

"As I've told you, I don't do relationships."

"Committed bachelor are you?" It would explain a lot.

"By necessity."

That sounded like a warning. One Haylee knew she needed to heed. If only her heart would listen.

Chapter 16

As they drove up the winding driveway lined with trees, Haylee decided Pleasant Valley Ranch was aptly named, nestled as it was into verdant rolling hills. Behind the single row of trees, corrals framed the gravel road, and a neatly trimmed lawn provided the setting for a large white Victorian house with a sizeable front porch. The vintage nature of the structure attested to the age of the ranch, most probably homesteaded. To the side of the house, a huge tent ruffled in the ever-present Wyoming breeze, which kept the temperature in the comfortable seventy-degree range despite it being midsummer.

There was no doubt this ranch was prosperous, considering the large, well-tended barns in the distance surrounded by new-wood railed fencing, with several horses grazing lazily in the pastures. It was picture perfect, and Haylee was determined to take a few pictures before it got dark.

"I want to play with Jake," Delanie announced from the backseat.

"That's Cat's son from a previous…relationship," Trace said by way of explanation.

Trace stopped the pickup next to a bunch of cars

and trucks parked on the grass on the side of the driveway opposite the house. By the limited number of vehicles, they were early.

"You'll have to wait until after the wedding," Trace said, addressing Delanie. "Jake's the ring bearer, so I'm sure Cat doesn't want him messing up his suit before the ceremony."

"We can play something that won't get us messy. And we can keep out of you guys' hair." Delanie had become quite the negotiator.

"We'll see what his mother says." Trace exited the car and strode around to their side and, being the gentleman he was, opened the passenger doors for Delanie and Haylee.

Dressed in a jet-black suit, pressed white shirt, and polished leather cowboy boots—which must have been for special occasions, because there wasn't a hint of a scuff on them—and a white Stetson crowning his head, he looked as delicious as a piece of vanilla cake wrapped in dark-chocolate icing with whipped cream on top. And just as bad for her.

"Come on, girls." Trace held out a hand for each to grab. She slipped the camera strap over her head and slid her hand into his firm one. Walking to the house, Haylee felt as anxious as an invading soldier, unsure what awaited her.

"Doesn't look like anyone is at the tent yet, so we'll stop in at the house. We have an hour to spare," Trace said.

"I have to use the bathroom, Daddy."

Trace chuckled. "Could've guessed that."

As they climbed the steps to the porch, the front door swung open. A very pregnant Mandy Martin stood there in a blue empire-waist cocktail dress that flowed over her burgeoning belly, a pair of fancy brown leather boots on her feet.

Trace dropped Haylee's hand like it was a hot iron.

"You made it with time to spare." Mandy's greeting was said with certainty, as if she knew Trace wouldn't keep the wedding party waiting. "And so happy to see you again, Haylee."

"Where's Jake?" Delanie asked as Mandy bent her pregnant body to give Delanie a peck on the cheek. "And the bathroom."

"Jake's upstairs getting dressed. Scoot on up there, bathroom's to the right. Cat will be happy to know you've arrived."

As Delanie whizzed past them and up the grand wooden staircase, Mandy folded her arms across her chest, resting them on her baby bump. "Cat has been on pins and needles all morning."

"Because of us?" Trace sounded flummoxed.

"No, because of the two mothers. Seems the feud is only at the cease-fire stage, and any moment Cat is afraid that a verbal grenade is going to be thrown."

Trace shook his head. "That's women. Can't let a good thing alone."

Mandy gently punched her brother-in-law's arm. "Seems there are men of that bent as well. Your brother is talking rodeo with Chance and Tucker in the parlor," she said. "It would be a good time to introduce Haylee to them before it gets too crazy. Not that there will be that many guests. Just fifty or so friends and neighbors, with a few relatives, particularly on Cody's side, mixed in."

"Lead the way."

Trace's warm hand branded her back as they moved down the hallway trimmed with oak wainscoting.

"By the way, Haylee, thanks again for those pictures of Tucker," Mandy said. "I'm having one of them framed and giving it to him as a sort of consolation prize for having to pick up the slack with the business."

"I'm glad you found one to your liking."

"They were fantastic. I had a hard time choosing."

Proud of that compliment, she hoped to do the same as a gift for the bride and groom.

They entered an arched doorway on their right and walked into a living room with large windows and comfortable furniture at odds with the formality of the room's carved wood trim and hanging chandelier. Three handsome-as-sin men turned in her direction, and breath left her.

It was clear which one was Trace's brother. They had the same color hair, same lean build, though Ty might have been an inch taller. The one who looked the youngest of the bunch with his blond hair, the bluest eyes, and a smirk on his face she recognized as Tucker from the rodeo. And the guy around her age with brown hair and gray eyes was probably Chance.

She looked back at Trace. None of those men, good looking as they were, held a candle to the cowboy standing behind her. Still, it was a lot of testosterone to step into.

"Haylee, this is my husband and Trace's brother, Ty."

Trace straightened as if on guard as his brother stepped forward.

"Please to meet you. Especially if my brother brought you."

She shook Ty's outstretched hand. His grasp was strong and warm, and the smile gracing his face seemed sincere. "And don't believe anything Trace may have told you about me."

"What makes you think I'd spend my time talking about you?" Trace seemed irritated.

"You're right, bro. No sense destroying the mood when you've got such a pretty woman in hand."

Mandy stepped closer. "And that's about the extent of my husband's charm, I'm afraid. And this here cowboy is my brother, Tucker. You saw him ride the other day."

"Did I stay on?" Tucker asked as he shook her hand.

"Yes, I believe you did."

Tucker gave a short nod. "Good deal. I've been known to get bucked off now and again."

Mandy snorted. "Mostly now and again."

"And this here fellow is my good friend Libby's husband, Chance Cochran. He's also a saddle bronc rider, but he's actually been to the FNR, meaning he's good at it."

"I saw you ride the other day too."

Chance grinned. "And I don't have to ask if I stayed on because I'm sure I did."

"Cocky bastard," Tucker muttered good naturedly.

"Keep riding Prescott stock and you'll get there," Chance said.

It was clear the banter was between two people who liked each other.

"So, Haylee, how did you meet my brother?" Ty raised a beer bottle to his lips.

"I'm living next door, well, a mile down the road actually."

"At the Johnsons?"

"Haylee is Paula Johnson's niece," Trace explained. "The Johnsons have taken off for New Mexico and are looking to sell the place, so Haylee is keeping an eye on things until they do."

"Selling Grandpa's place, huh?" Ty didn't look too pleased. "How much are they asking?"

"Too much." Trace gave his brother a cease-and-desist look, but it made Haylee wonder if Ty might be interested in purchasing it—and wouldn't that be a perfect solution.

Only, that would mean she'd have to move on faster than she'd planned. Or wanted to.

"You're from around here, Haylee?" Tucker asked.

"I've lived in this area…well, mostly Denver since college, but I hail from Chicago. City born and bred."

Ty let out a whistle. "A city girl."

"I think I was born with a western heart though."

"That's a tribute to the West, ma'am," Chance chimed in.

"I'm going to head up to see how the bride is doing." Mandy turned toward the door. "Text me when Cody gets here. Would you like to come with me, Haylee? I can introduce you to Cat and Libby and my mom. She's keeping an eye on baby Shane, who's been a good boy and taking a nap."

Haylee nodded, happy to be included.

"Let me know if your mom needs relief, Mandy. I can take over," Chance said.

"Would you check on Delanie while you are up there?" Trace looked concerned. "Let me know if you need me."

Climbing up the wide, wood-paneled staircase, Haylee was eager to meet the women in Trace's orbit, especially the bride whom he hadn't quite clicked with.

Not that she was jealous or anything. Just curious as to what type of woman didn't suit Trace.

"So she's your girlfriend? Mandy said you were bringing the girl from the rodeo. Didn't know she was living next door."

Ty's self-satisfied smirk was sure as hell annoying.

Trace glanced over his shoulder to make sure Haylee was out of earshot. "She's helping me out, watching Delanie after camp. Her coming was more Delanie's idea than mine. So no, she's not my girlfriend. We aren't dating."

"She's pretty enough that you should be."

"Cute little thing." Tucker weighed in. "Shame to have it go to waste."

"She's Delanie's caregiver. End of story."

"She seems nice," Tucker said, wiping his hair from his eyes.

The boy needed a trim.

"If you're not interested, I might give her a whirl."

"No, you won't." As Tucker's eyebrows raised, Trace realized that had come out stronger than he'd intended. “I’m not having some romance screw up a good situation.” Which was his main concern, his only concern. “I finally have someone to look after Delanie again, and considering all the things that have been going wrong, I’m not going to lose Haylee because some yahoo breaks her heart.”

“Who said I was going to break her heart? Just talking about dancing.”

“I know you rodeo boys, Tucker. Giving you fair warning.” Best Tucker heed it.

Tucker’s easy smile was back in place. “Just trying to rile you, Trace.” He raised his hands. “I’ll be nothing but a gentleman. Promise.”

He wasn’t riled. “Didn’t any of your rodeo ladies care to accompany you tonight?”

Tucker shrugged. “Too busy with rodeo, I guess.” He didn’t seem happy about it.

Trace looked around the room, ready to change the subject. “Where are they keeping the cold drinks?” His throat was parched.

“There’s some in the kitchen fridge. Outside bar won’t be open until after the ceremony,” Ty said.

“I’m ready for another beer, so I’ll get it for you. Soda or water?” Tucker offered.

“Water would be fine.”

“Pace yourself, Tucker,” Ty warned. “We have to get up early tomorrow and head out to that Colorado rodeo. Harold’s running things today so we can attend this here shindig, but now that you are taking over for Mandy, there’s no sleeping in.”

With that, Tucker disappeared down the hall in search of drinks.

Chance set his empty bottle on the mahogany side

table near the overstuffed sofa. "I'm going to head upstairs to see what's up with Shane and if Libby needs a hand. Let me know when the groom arrives. That was some bachelor party last night. We missed you, Trace."

Chance disappeared out the doorway.

Trace glanced at his brother. "Sounds like you all had a good time last night."

"Cody had an old-fashion campout. We sat around the fire, swapped stories, and got drunk as all get-out. Then we piled into our sleeping bags and slept it off."

"Not quite the Las Vegas extravaganzas you were probably used to in your old days."

Ty raised his eyebrows. "Truth was, brother, I never got invited to a bachelor party in my old days. Mainly because I didn't have anyone I could call a friend. And I don't think I would have enjoyed a Las Vegas party as much as I enjoyed last night. Turns out, Cody is a good guy. As are his brother, Jace, and his cousin Michael. Mandy did offer to look after Delanie so you could go."

Trace tended to avoid those types of affairs. No sense tempting the devil.

"Didn't seem practical." Ty knew his reasons, and it galled him that his brother preferred to overlook them. "And then I'd have to fetch Haylee anyway."

"I was sincere when I said that Haylee seems nice."

"Your point?"

"Maybe you should consider dating her. I haven't seen you with a woman since I've come back. Mandy thought you and Cat might be an item."

"Cat is marrying the man she's been interested in for a long time. The idea of Cat and me was Mandy's fantasy and hers alone." Trace was well aware of what he was missing in his life. He saw it every time he was with Mandy and Ty. But that was the hand he'd been dealt, the hand he was playing. And besides, he wasn't Haylee Dennis's type, and she wasn't his. Case closed. "Dating anyone is not in the cards. Not when I've got a full plate as it is."

"How is the custody suit going?"

"Not good. Seems Doreen has had a late awakening of her maternal instincts and is applying to the court for visitation rights."

"You're kidding. She expects you to haul Delanie to Lusk, to that godforsaken place?"

"Exactly. My lawyer says she's going to get what she wants because that court-appointed psychologist thinks it's a good idea." He let his scowl convey his opinion. "Seems the court doesn't like to interfere with a mother's rights, even a bad mother like Doreen."

"So you're not going to fight it?"

"It would mean going to court if I did, and I've got some baggage too."

Melissa Leonard's behavior had convinced Trace that there would be no "forgetting" by Delanie about her mother. People like the Leonards would be on the vanguard of reminding Delanie. Better the child sees her mother and knows the reality of it than to be shamed by other people.

Trace patted his brother on the back. "Whatever you need, I'm here for you. Delanie deserves the best chance we can give her."

As much as Ty could irritate Trace, he knew his

brother was there for him. Even when Trace had been at his worst, at his lowest, his brother literally kicked sense into him…sense he needed. There was something to be said about blood being thicker than water.

Tucker stepped into the room, bottles in hand.

"Drink up, guys! The groom just arrived."

Chapter 17

Upstairs, it was humming with activity as Haylee followed Mandy into one of the bedrooms.

There in front of a large, full-length pedestal mirror was the bride, her back to Haylee, dressed in a simple but flattering shimmering-white A-line gown. Another woman was with her, with chin-length auburn hair and a slim figure in a cocktail-length blue dress with a swinging fifties-style skirt, fixing the bride's headpiece.

The bride turned around as Mandy and Haylee entered, and Haylee was confronted with the face of a beautiful woman. Cat McKenna, tall and willowy, with her shiny brown hair pulled into a beautiful upsweep, her gorgeous smoky-brown eyes, and high blushed cheekbones, looked like a magazine advertisement for the perfect bride.

Haylee suddenly felt small and plain.

"You look beautiful," Mandy told her friend. "We'll be quick, but I've got someone for you to meet. Cat McKenna, this is Haylee Dennis. She's Trace's guest for the wedding."

Cat's eyes rounded. "Is she now? Well welcome, Haylee. I'm so happy to meet you." She reached out her slender hand with nails painted a luscious red.

Haylee shook the bride's hand. "Thank you. I'm honored to be part of your special day."

"And this is one of my good friends and bridesmaid, Cyndi Lynn Logan."

Haylee nodded to Cyndi Lynn. So many attractive women.

"I just hope it's not too special," Cat said.

Cat and Mandy exchanged glances, but Haylee hadn't a clue why a bride didn't want her day to be too special.

"Have you seen Delanie?" Haylee asked. "She rushed up here before, and I just want to make sure she doesn't get into anything before the ceremony."

"Spoken like a mom. Do you have children, Haylee?" Cat asked.

"No. But I take care of Delanie after camp, so I guess I feel like a mom sometimes."

Cat's eyebrows raised as she glanced in Mandy's direction.

"I believe Delanie is in the bedroom with Shane and your mom, Mandy. Delanie just loves baby Shane."

"He's awake?" Mandy asked.

"Yeah. Great timing, right? Libby's feeding him. Looks like we'll have to squeeze the ceremony in between Shane's mealtime," Cat said with a laugh.

"I'll show you where Delanie is," Mandy offered as she glanced toward the window. "By the way, Cody and Jace just pulled up."

"I know. I texted him to check in at the kitchen and make sure our two mothers are still speaking. You know that's been the only stress of pulling this wedding off…worrying about whether our mamas are going to come to blows."

"And?"

"So far, they've been keeping it peaceful."

"Are you really worried?" Mandy moved toward the doorway where Haylee was standing.

"Only anxious to become Mrs. Taylor. Then I don't care who is feuding!"

"Spoken like a woman in love."

"Good luck," Haylee said before following Mandy out of the room and down the hall to another bedroom.

There, sitting in a comfortable-looking rocker next to a brass bed, was a pretty young woman cradling her baby and its bottle. Behind the chair stood Chance.

Her heart pinched. The scene was a lovely family portrait. It was what she had hoped to have with Roy and now might never have with anyone.

If Haylee dared take her camera out of its case, she would have loved to snap a few photos. But she didn't know these people, and it seemed too intimate a moment to intrude upon. Plus, they had an audience. Delanie stood to the side next to a young boy about her age, and behind them was an attractive older woman with blond hair, cut chin length into a smart pageboy. All except the baby turned their attention to Haylee.

"Everyone, this is Haylee, a friend of Trace's," Mandy said, her voice respectfully soft. "We just came up to check on things. Haylee, this is Libby and her baby, Shane; my mother, Sheila; Cat's son, Jake; and you met Chance downstairs."

Delanie put her finger to her lips. "Shhh. The baby just woke up." She looked positively mesmerized by the sight.

Haylee was happy to see that Delanie's bow and ribbon were still in her hair.

"Pleased to meet you," Libby said. "As you see, I have my hands full at the moment."

"What a lovely baby boy," Haylee said. The mother beamed.

"So nice to meet any friend of Trace's." Sheila reached out her hand, and Haylee grasped it for a quick shake.

"Hi," the little boy chirped. He seemed too entranced by the sight of baby Shane to pay Haylee much notice.

"Cody has arrived, and Cat's almost ready to begin," Mandy said.

"Cat's mom is giving the bride away?" Libby asked.

Mandy nodded.

Sheila patted Libby on the shoulder. "If you and Chance can handle things, Libby, I'll go down and see if the mother of the bride and the mother of the groom need any help."

"Can I do anything?" Haylee would have appreciated something to do.

"No, dear," Sheila said as she headed for the hallway. "But I'll look forward to getting better acquainted at the reception."

The wedding was a simple yet dignified affair. The local minister performed the ceremony in a grove of trees near the house. The mothers of the bride and groom were both teary eyed, and not an inappropriate word was uttered by either of them. The party commenced directly afterward, with a local country band providing music under the large tent. Tables were set with white linen cloths, buckets of pink and yellow flowers served as a centerpieces, and horseshoes with ribbons held down the cloth napkin at each place setting. Haylee started snapping pictures.

"Are you going to do this all night?" Trace asked as he led the way to their table.

"I thought I would give my pictures to the bride and groom. It usually takes forever for the wedding photographer to deliver photos."

"I wouldn't know." Trace pulled out her chair.

They were at the same table as Mandy, Ty, Tucker, Sheila, and Delanie. Trace had positioned himself between Haylee and Delanie and across from his brother and Mandy. Sheila sat next to Haylee, Tucker next to Delanie.

Haylee eyed the bar. Did she dare drink when Trace couldn't? She wasn't sure what the right protocol was.

"So, Haylee, tell me how you ended up at the Johnsons," Sheila said as soon as Haylee's butt hit the chair.

For the next ten minutes Sheila peppered Haylee with questions from how she liked living in rural Wyoming to how she liked being a nanny to what her father did for a living. Had Haylee wondering if she was being sized up and if she had passed. Too bad it was all for naught on Sheila's part. Trace didn't want anything to do with her in the romantic department.

Attending a wedding with a man who saw you as nothing more than a caretaker for his child wasn't the best idea for a recent divorcée. What had she been thinking, asking to go along to a wedding?

She supposed her curiosity had gotten the best of her, but listening to toasts about two people who loved each other, seeing their happy faces, and remembering her own wedding and the hope and promise she had felt was a particular kind of torture.

As was sitting next to an attractive man who couldn't care less. Seemed she was a glutton for punishment.

As Trace talked to Tucker about bulls and breeding, and Delanie had wandered over to the head table where Jake sat with Cat and Cody, Haylee excused herself to Sheila and slipped over to the bar to order a glass of white wine.

At the bar, she surveyed the scene as the band rocked out to "Craving You." Appropriate.

How could she feel so alone in a crowded room? Memories of her own wedding flooded her thoughts. There were more people in attendance when she had tied the knot, many she didn't know because they were business contacts of her father. And she had felt just as alone. Like a performer in a play about someone else's life.

Unfortunately, that "play" had turned into her life, and Roy finding her at her aunt's place had brought home the fact she would never be free from his mistakes. A shiver went through her and she said a silent prayer that there would be no more unannounced, uninvited visits by her ex-husband.

On the floor, there were a few young women dancing in sparkly short dresses, some with boots, others with high heels. But there were plenty of cowboy hats, many of them standing on the sidelines. As she scanned the room, she noted a familiar face…and he noted her. Within a second, Lonnie Kasin had wandered over.

Dressed in a suit and tie, cowboy hat on his head, boots on his feet, he looked rather handsome. The man cleaned up nice.

"Haylee, is it?" Lonnie asked in a western drawl.

"Yes. Lonnie, right?" She hadn't forgotten him.

"Is Livvy here?" He sounded both confused and hopeful.

"No. Livvy doesn't really know anyone out here. She was just here on a visit."

He nodded. "I thought she would have said if she was coming my way. I don't really know anyone either, except Chance and Libby. But I was in the area and…well, you know how it is in the West. Doors are always open."

"Is that how it is?" She wouldn't know.

"Yes, ma'am. Livvy coming out anytime soon? We've been keeping up with each other on Facebook, but she hasn't said anything about another trip."

How did she break it to him? Livvy was a lot of talk, not always action. "I wouldn't get your hopes up. She's pretty much a city girl." Like Haylee.

"There's many a city girl that's found their heart in the country. Tell her I said hi, will you?"

She nodded. Lonnie lifted his hat and turned his attention to the bar.

One meeting and Livvy had captured the man's attention. Weeks and Haylee had been ignored. Wrong man. Wrong woman.

Haylee took a sip of wine. She'd head back to the table and grab her camera. At least she'd have something to occupy her.

Trace watched as Haylee wove around the tables on her way back from the bar, wineglass in hand. He took a gulp of water.

She looked gob-smacking gorgeous in a pretty blue strapless dress that hugged her curves on top and then billowed out as she walked, showing off a pair of seriously spectacular legs accented by a wicked pair of high heels. He wondered if she'd be able to dance in those things, not that he would ask her or anything.

When he'd opened the door to his house and saw her standing there, the sight of her had knocked the wind clear out of him. He'd had to turn heel and walk away so he didn't do something stupid, like reach for her, which he was sure would have been unwelcome. Since he'd told her about himself and Delanie's mother, she'd been cooler to him than an ice cube. And he couldn't blame her.

He'd no doubt shocked Haylee with his confession about what a mess his life had been and still was. She'd probably never been involved with anyone like him. She surely didn't know anyone doing jail time. And if she knew all of it, well, it only got worse from there. Not to mention, she'd already had a marriage that didn't work out. Taking on someone like him would be too big a risk for a woman with a fine education and big plans, who was only out in his neck of the woods as a favor to her aunt. She'd probably been piling up the clients and was sorry she was spending her time working for him. But the fact she was wonderful with his kid and a terrific cook made it all the more difficult for his head to ignore what his heart wanted.

He'd done the right thing telling her about himself, because after that kiss, things could have gotten hot in a hurry. And if he'd gotten in any deeper, he'd have set them both up for failure. Knowing what he had to confess, he'd made it easy on her by telling her he wouldn't do it again. Saved her from having to give him the boot when she heard his story.

Just like the lines in the song that was playing said, it didn't stop him wanting her. In every way. He wondered if she'd be interested in keeping it casual. Which considering his track record with relationships, was all it could be. And if he wanted more, well, shouldn't he be satisfied with what he could get?

The reality was she was leaving, he was staying. She was city, he was country. She had a career, he had a living. He was a poor choice for spinning dreams of happily ever after, something that, before she'd walked into his life, he'd never even thought about. And for good reason.

But a fling. If that kiss was any indication, and, he reminded himself, it was just one kiss, she might be okay with that. He could do casual. He'd been the king of casual before Delanie had entered his life, and he'd traded the title for the life of a friggin' monk.

Messy, what with her caring for Delanie. But if they were discreet, if she was interested…a lot of ifs.

Delanie had pulled Jake onto the dance floor, and the two were performing something akin to an Irish jig without the complicated steps. Ty and Mandy were trying a two-step, leaving space for Mandy's large belly. Tucker, who had threatened to ask Haylee to dance if Trace didn't, had corralled one of the ladies who had come without a date. Sheila was helping the two mothers set out the buffet. Trace sat alone at the table. So what else was new?

As Haylee reached the table, Trace couldn't but wonder if Haylee might agree to a dance. Before Tucker or someone else asked her.

"I would have gotten you a drink," he said. Or anything else she wanted.

She took a sip of wine before she set the glass on the table. "No problem. I thought I'd take some pictures." She scooped up the camera, looked into the viewer, and began snapping.

Trace's fingers tapped out the music as the song switched to "Drinking Problem." He listened to the lyrics. Sounded like him a few years ago. The band couldn't have chosen a more fitting song about his sorry life if they'd tried. If they played "In Case You Didn't Know," he was going to have a talk with that band. And why was he even going down that path?

Out of the corner of his eye, he saw Tucker coming in their direction—alone.

"Don't suppose you like to dance?"

The clicking stopped, and she lowered the camera from her face. "You asking?" She looked defiant, as if daring him.

Tucker was closing in. No way was Tucker going to slow dance with Haylee.

"Yeah." He rose, held out his hand, and felt a ring against his palm. He noted it when she'd arrived that morning. Noted it was an opal, not a diamond. "Show me what you've got."

Haylee breathed in the scent of man and clean linen as they rocked to the slow beat of a song about drinking. She'd tried to take a step back and put some distance between her and the man who scrambled her senses, but the dance floor was crowded, and his large hand against her back held her close so her breasts brushed his torso with each step. She rested her hands on his firm shoulders, and her fingertips touched the soft flesh of his neck. The heat from his hard body warmed her skin even through his shirt and her satiny dress. Trace moved with a slow sensuality that had her heart thudding in time with the beat.

She'd felt sheepish that she had slipped out on him to go to the bar, but she was pretty sure asking a recovering alcoholic to fetch a drink wasn't appropriate.

"Glad you can dance in those shoes."

His breath whispered against her forehead, creating all kinds of havoc.

"I should have worn my boots." She would have fit in better.

He nuzzled her hair. "Naw. Those are fantasy shoes."

"Whose fantasy?"

"Mine."

Haylee's heart pounded hard against her chest, no longer in time with the slow beat of the music. She looked up at him in hopes of gauging his meaning, but his stoic expression as he met her gaze revealed nothing.

He hadn't said *she* was his fantasy. Only her shoes. Was it wrong for her to want to be his fantasy? Even if it was for just a month, a week, a night?

The song ended, and the dance floor emptied as the band notified the crowd that the buffet was open, but Trace held on to her a moment more before stepping back. Had she imagined his hesitation?

Light from the overhead chandelier cut across half his face. "I have to find Delanie and make sure she eats something." He turned and walked away, leaving her alone on the dance floor, more confused than ever.

The buffet was a spread of homemade delights, courtesy, she was told, of the mothers of the bride and groom. Apparently a little rivalry was going on over the pot roast, as there were two versions of that dish.

Haylee went through the buffet line first and offered to watch Delanie while Trace fetched food. After settling a reluctant Delanie in her chair, Trace came back with plates for both his daughter and himself, his being piled much higher with food. All through dinner, Trace turned his attention to Delanie. Haylee tried to make small talk with Sheila when Sheila wasn't bopping up to help with baby Shane, the buffet table, or to talk with some friend she hadn't seen in a while.

A sense of isolation draped over Haylee like a throw hiding a stain, and she headed to the bar for another glass of wine. Propping her back against the hard rim of the counter, she took a sip and watched as people danced their hearts out. What was she doing at a wedding with a happy couple when her own life was so empty?

Everyone seemed to have someone to care for but her.

The music started up again, and the table emptied out. Delanie had made a beeline for Jake, Mandy and Ty took to the floor, and Tucker had asked his mother to dance. That left just Trace. He looked over at Haylee standing at the bar, looking lost, as if she didn't want to be there. With him.

Holding Haylee on the dance floor had him wanting to hold her in other ways, and he wasn't sure he should put himself through that misery again. And then he'd made that comment about her shoes. It had sort of slipped out, and once out, he couldn't take it back.

She'd gone silent after that, and he was pretty sure he'd scared her.

He tried not to stare as she wove her way back to the table, but it was hard to take his eyes off all that sass wrapped up in blue. He was ready to ask her to dance as she approached, when she set down her glass of wine and picked up her camera, ready to slip the strap over her head.

"So are you going to take pictures all night?" he said.

"Keeping busy."

He had ideas about how to keep her busy.

Picking up her wineglass, she drained it in one long sip. That was her second glass of wine. Not that he was counting. Not that it should matter.

What the hell. "You up for some more dancing?"

She looked at him square in the face, her eyes scrunched, her lips pursed. "Sure."

"You know any country dances?"

"I've line danced, if that's what you mean."

"Put down that camera then." He rose and held out his hand. "And just follow my lead."

Haylee was a natural, her steps graceful and rhythmic. Had him wondering what other things they'd be good at together.

And he shouldn't be wondering. Especially in the middle of a wedding with family gawking at their every move. As if his dancing with a woman was a curiosity. Mandy and Ty were the worst of the bunch. Every time he looked over at his sister-in-law, she had a shit-eating grin on her face the size of Montana. Ty just smirked.

After the third song, Haylee was breathing hard, reminding him of other reasons for breathing hard.

"Want to sit the next one out?"

The little ringlets of hair at the back of her neck, where he'd like to plant a kiss, were damp, and the indent at the base of her throat was shiny.

She gazed up at him as if trying to figure him out. Good luck with that.

"I could use a glass of wine. Would you like something?"

"I'll get you the wine. And me some water."

"I can get it." Her expression had turned serious.

"I'm not going to be tempted just touching the glass, Haylee." He wasn't that weak. "If this custody petition hasn't had me reaching for the bottle, nothing will. What kind?"

He asked the bartender for a Pinot Grigio and a bottle of water. That was what was wrong with telling people you were an alcoholic. They thought you were going to fall off the wagon any minute. He guessed he couldn't blame them. There were times, even now, when he thought about having a drink. But the little girl dancing on the edge of the floor in her pink dress and flowered ribbons wouldn't let him.

Haylee's lack of faith, though, cut deep. It reminded him of just how remote his chances were now that she knew. Yet there was a small ember of hope that burned inside of him, hope that she was different, that she saw a good man underneath it all, that she saw the man he wanted to be, was trying to be.

He looked for Haylee in the crowd, ignored the pointed glances at the glass in his hand, and found her outside the tent, leaning against one of the fence posts, looking over an empty pasture. The sun was setting, and it had already started to cool down. Goose bumps had erupted on her creamy-white skin.

He handed her the glass. "Want my jacket?"

"Oh, no, I couldn't. I have a sweater in your car."

"I'll get that for you later. Take my jacket now. I'm not cold at all." Nope, he was running hotter than an overheated engine.

He shed his jacket and lifted it onto her bare, elegant shoulders.

What the hell. He wrapped his arms around her, expecting her to stiffen and step away. But she didn't. Instead her hand covered his hands and pressed them against her warm chest.

"I enjoyed dancing with you." She looked over her shoulder at him as she took a sip of wine.

If he leaned down just a bit, he could kiss her. But he wasn't going to make that mistake again.

Likely she was just cold and appreciated the body heat.

"You're a pretty good dancer. For a city girl."

The top of her bun tickled his chin.

She pressed into him, torturing him with her closeness. Yeah, this kind of torture he could endure all night.

"You're a pretty good dancer…for a cowboy."

She took two large gulps of her wine, almost finishing it. He could smell the citrusy scent. Good thing he'd been a whiskey and beer man back in the day, so he wasn't tempted. Not by the wine anyway.

"It's beautiful at dusk out here. In the city, you barely notice dusk, what with all the streetlights. Here it's like the day is mellowing out, relaxing, taking a deep breath."

Did he risk giving her a squeeze? Making a play? Getting rejected? "Starting to like the country now, are you?"

She twisted in his arms, and suddenly her firm breasts were pressed to his chest. "Some things about the country I like very much." Her voice was soft, lyrical, and doing crazy things to his insides.

He bent his head so he could look straight into her eyes. "Like what?"

She wrapped her arms around his neck, dangling the now empty wineglass against his back.

"Like you." She breathed those two words so they puffed along his collar bone.

"Like me? After everything I told you about me? Have you been drinking too much, Haylee Dennis?" Because her declarations were too important to be merely alcohol fueled.

"Only enough to give me courage to ask you why you don't want to kiss me again."

Holding her against him, feeling her hot little body against his, he hadn't a clue. But she looked at him like she expected an answer. He'd give her the honest one.

"I figured I have too much baggage for any woman, much less someone like you. Didn't want you to feel…obligated."

She shook her head, and a tendril of hair slipped

out of the bun. "Obligated? I felt relieved, released, ready for whatever you wanted to throw at me."

A whiff of alcohol scented the air. "You sure this isn't the wine talking?"

"I could walk a straight line right now, except I don't want to step out of your arms, Trace Martin. I want to do something entirely different."

Her arms tightened around his neck, pressuring him to bend his head until his lips were close to hers. Very close. Dangerously close.

"Honey, this time you have to make the move."

Her mouth covered his, and heat moved through his body like a furnace had just exploded. She deepened the kiss, and he hung on as she devoured his mouth, her tongue tangoing with his. She tasted like citrus and wine, and he wanted more. His hands traveled to the back of her shoulders, and he stroked the soft, bare skin with his calloused fingertips. He wanted to unzip her dress, slide his hand down her spine, and cup her sweet little butt in his hands. He wanted to test the weight of each of her breasts. He wanted to thumb her hard nipples. He wanted her.

She let out a sweet moan as she bumped against his erection. His hands pressed against her soft ass, holding her in place, letting her feel just how much he wanted her.

Everything about Haylee was better than he'd imagined. The softness of her skin, the silkiness of her hair, the passionate way she kissed, the feel of her tight little body slammed against his, everything.

Pure, unadulterated lust pounded through him as the kiss got hotter, wetter, wilder. Her tongue dueled and danced with his. Her hands stroked his back. Her body rocked him. He was a prisoner of his desire for her, and he couldn't have cared less.

And then she broke the kiss, gulped for air. He seized the moment to skim his lips down her cool neck until he found the base of her throat. There he sucked a kiss and breathed in the vanilla scent of her neck. Chaos enveloped him. His insides were rioting, his body was hardening, and he was ready for more. But he had to know… Raising his head along with his hopes, he looked into her baby-blue eyes. She was tousled and mauled, and the smile on her face said she'd enjoyed it. But still he had to ask.

"You sure you want to start something, Haylee?" Doubt drummed through him with a frenetic beat. "We are from two different worlds. You'll be leaving soon."

"I'm here now. And I don't think our worlds are so very different." She buried her face in his shoulder. "I don't want to regret not finding out."

This time he initiated the kiss, and he wasn't letting her up for air anytime soon.

For the rest of the evening, Haylee was dancing on air. At some point as they were making out, Haylee thought someone had spied them, though she wasn't sure who, and she had nudged Trace that they should go inside because Delanie might get worried if she didn't see them on the dance floor.

To her relief though, no one had seemed to notice that they had slipped away, least of all Delanie, who was still bopping to the beat with her favorite partner.

Trace pulled her onto the dance floor, tugged her close, and together they swayed to the music, their bodies in perfect motion. She could breathe in his scent, feel his heat, and the long, hard bulge pressed against her abdomen. They'd made out like teenagers at a high school dance, and she felt just as giddy and infatuated as if she were sixteen.

He wanted her. And he had thought she wouldn't want him. Tonight she'd done her best to let him know how much she wanted him. She'd kissed him like her very life depended on sucking him dry. And she intended to stay wrapped in his solid, warm embrace as long as she could.

But all good things had to come to an end, and it was clear that by ten o'clock, Delanie was ready for bed. They sat at the table with Mandy and Ty, Delanie curled across two chairs. Haylee had gathered up her camera and purse, ready to leave, when Mandy leaned over and whispered in Trace's ear.

"Are you sure?" he said

"We love having Delanie. And I'm going to be sitting at home anyway since your brother has banned me from going to rodeos until well after the baby has arrived."

"Won't she just get in your way? You've got to rest."

"The pregnant lady has a need for some company. And there is no better company for a pregnant lady than her five-year-old niece to spoil."

"You're due any day."

"Just keep your phone on in case I need you. Especially given that Ty will be heading off bright and early tomorrow morning because someone knowledgeable has to help Harold, at least for the rodeo's last day. So I'll be happy for her company.

And look at her." Mandy motioned to the slumped form on the chairs. "She'll be out before Ty gets the car in gear."

"I want to go with Aunt Mandy," Delanie piped up, opening her eyes.

"Okay. Aunt Mandy keeps clothes for you at her place, so you're all set. I'll come by and get you after lunch." He turned to face Mandy. "And that will give me an excuse to check on you."

Mandy bent over and kissed Trace's cheek. "As if you need an excuse."

"Come on, peanut," Ty said as he scooped Delanie up in his arms. The child laid her head on Ty's shoulder. "Say good night to your daddy."

Trace rose and kissed Delanie's cheek. "Good night, sweet pea."

Mandy and Ty said their goodbyes and then made their way out through the smattering of guests still celebrating.

"Looks like it will just be us heading home," Trace said as he watched the trio leave.

Haylee's stomach fluttered.

Chapter 18

Trace took the keys from Haylee's hand and unlocked the door to the cabin, the cicadas providing their familiar chirping serenade. Haylee's moonlit bare shoulders seemed to glow in the shadows of the night, and he had an urge to turn a degree, bend down, and scoop her into his arms. Instead he turned the doorknob and pushed open the door.

He still wasn't sure if it was the alcohol or Haylee that had been behind all the kissing, and since she'd slept most of the way home, her true feelings remained in doubt. And he wasn't one to take a chance. Not on this.

This was something different. He'd taken plenty of women home back in the day. He'd bedded his fair share. But this was a woman he cared about beyond a night's pleasure. This was a woman who made him ache for things he hadn't known he wanted, like a wife to come home to, a friend to confide in, a lover to hold.

And yet he also knew that whatever "this" could be, it would be temporary.

On the drive home, he'd reconciled himself to that. If he couldn't have it all, he'd be satisfied with a piece. Delanie was gift enough. Things were working out with his daughter. She'd been happier since he'd told her that they'd get to see her mother as soon as the paperwork was done. She'd even told her mother that morning that she'd be seeing her in a little while. From what he could tell of the one-sided conversation, Doreen had gotten emotional in a good way.

Delanie was all he should expect in life.

It was pitch dark inside, so he reached in and flicked on the light switch, aware that Haylee had not moved. Instead she was staring at him, her face upturned.

"You should always leave a light on." She lived alone in this isolated area, a mile down the road from him.

She blinked, as if his voice had awoken her from a dream. "Guess the agent turned them all off, but I don't usually leave a light on." She stretched her neck to see inside the door, as if she expected one of the prospective buyers to still be inside. "Would you like to come in? I can put some coffee on, and I still have some of that banana bread I made yesterday."

Tempting. All of it.

"I go in there, no telling what might happen." His restraint had been sorely tested all evening. And he wasn't sure a cold shower would take care of it.

She rested her small hand on his shoulder. "Take a risk, Mr. Martin."

That was all the encouragement he needed. "Like this?" His arm encircled her waist as he lowered his mouth. He kissed her hard and hot so she'd know what she was in for. This time, he wasn't apologizing. This time he wasn't taking anything back.

She tasted like wine, felt like a soft pillow he wanted to sink into. She fed him kisses, he fed them back. Seconds ticked away, minutes passed. In the end, she would know she was kissed by a man who wanted her.

When he'd finished ravishing her mouth, he took a step back. "Still want me to come in?"

She reached for his hand. "Yes."

His heart pounded against his chest. This was the moment when all things good were still possible and he hadn't done anything yet to screw it up. This could be the moment when his life could change for the better…or the worst.

Trace stepped through the threshold, and the past grabbed him with the intensity of a mountain lion on the hunt as he scanned the interior of the cabin. He hadn't been in the place since the Johnsons had moved in. It had definitely changed since he'd been a young boy of four and from when his grandparents had lived there.

Stripped of walls, one large space opened up to both a living room and kitchen with a large wooden dining table separating the two. Gone was the braided rug where he'd steered his Matchbox cars, pretending the braids were roads. A Navajo knockoff had taken its place. Straight-hanging green drapes now enshrined the windows instead of the delicate lace curtains his mother and grandmother had favored, ones that he had to admit always seemed out of place in the all-wood structure.

The kitchen had been redone too. The knotty-pine cabinets his mother seemed to always be wiping down had been replaced by sleek white ones that didn't look like they'd met a tree, much less been one. The white stove where his mother and grandmother had baked pies and cookies was now a shiny stainless-steel model with a gigantic metal hood overhead. The candlestick chandelier that hung over the dining table had morphed into three ceiling pot lights.

And it didn't smell like he remembered. The wood scent was still there, faintly, but no hint of Murphy's Soap or fresh-baked cookies. Instead it was coffee and vanilla and Haylee. If he didn't know it had been his family's cabin, he'd have thought he was in the wrong place. At least the river-rock fireplace was still there, but the wooden log mantel with its bumps and dents that his grandfather had hewn by hand had been replaced by a large wooden rectangle with perfectly straight lines. He wished he'd known about the changes so he could have salvaged some things, but the renovations had been done during the time he was indulging his alcohol-fueled activities, and he wouldn't have appreciated those mementos from his childhood back then. He would now.

"Look familiar?" Haylee asked.

"No."

Haylee whirled around, the edges of her dress lifting with the motion and revealing her shapely legs. She wrapped her hands around his neck, and he felt the curves of her body against his as he looked down at lips that begged to be kissed.

"I know they did some renovations when they first moved in."

"A lot of renovations." Like changing the whole character of the house.

She cocked her head. "You don't like it?" She sounded surprised.

"Just not my house anymore." Or his grandparents'. "Takes some getting used to." The last thing he wanted to do tonight was take a trip down memory lane. What he wanted was standing before him looking like a fantasy woman…his fantasy.

She fed him kisses as they shuffled in tandem toward the bedroom. It was a tangle of hands grasping, jacket and tie flying, and lips kissing. Haylee heard the keys drop from Trace's hand, ringing as they hit the wood floor somewhere between the living room carpet and the bedroom. Only then did Trace pause in the hall to toe off his boots. But as soon as the boots were off, he clasped her in strong arms, pressed his lips to hers, and they started in again. It was like a storm had blown through her tangling her insides, a cacophony of lightning flashes and rolling thunder, of fierce wind and pounding rain. Haylee's pulse raced, her hands were sweaty, and her mind whirled.

If it could just be sex, it wouldn't matter. But every day her feelings had marched closer to the brink of sure disaster that was her heart's cliff. And she was jumping off.

His warm mouth pressed against her neck, and he crushed her body against his as he pulled her into the bedroom with an urgency that swept her with him. When his legs encountered the bed, he sank onto it, tugging her on top of him.

She felt wild and free and desperate for him. His fingers were in her hair, pulling out the pins so it fell to her shoulders. He raked his hands through the tangled strands and then slid his palms down the side of her neck. Strong fingers grazed her bare back until they encountered the zipper. In one movement, her dress was unzipped, and it slipped from her body, aided by a pair of strong, rough hands and her kicking feet.

She hadn't worn a bra since one had been woven into the dress. He cupped her tender breasts, and roughened thumbs flicked her taut nipples. His hard penis, protected by his denims, shoved against the fabric of her bikini underpants. Warmth pooled between her legs.

She wanted him.

"I've been thinking of getting you out of that dress since you stood at my door."

"What took you so long?"

His mouth covered hers, and the kiss that had started out sweet turned hot and urgent. His hand found her thigh and stroked her from her knee to her groin, caressing her through her bikini underwear. When his hot tongue slipped into her mouth, it pulled forth a passionate, sizzling response that sent a torch of raw lust burning through her, a desire so hot it felt like flames were licking her insides. She shoved her hand between the buttons of his shirt to touch his damp, heated skin. A moan rose up from his throat as he lifted her butt and tugged her up over his body until his hot mouth latched on to the pink tip of her breast. The suction pulled a guttural moan of pure ecstasy from deep inside of her.

"I want you, Haylee." He breathed the confession into her ear, making the air hot and moist.

She wanted him.

She shouldn't want him. She shouldn't want any man. Not with a vulnerable heart, shredded self-esteem, and a track record of bad judgments.

His mouth found hers again, and this time she opened her lips in anticipation. His tongue swept in to duel with hers, his lips eating off her lipstick, the stubble of his five o'clock shadow abrading her skin.

He tasted like sex, all-consuming sex. His scent, masculine, fresh, and woodsy, overwhelmed her senses, and she breathed him in like she was suffocating and he was her oxygen. When he shifted her onto her back, she opened her eyes. He was staring at her with laser intensity, burning into her skin like he was branding her.

His eyes never leaving her, he fingered the buttons on his dress shirt while she pulled the shirttails out of his pants. When the last button opened, Haylee pulled the shirt off his arms and ran her fingers across his bare, hard abdomen, up his naked chest, her fingers touching everywhere she could.

"You are fine, Trace Martin."

A small groan emanated from his throat, and he pressed his erection into her underwear.

She pushed down on the waistband of his pants, felt his knuckles against her stomach, and heard the satisfying sound of unzipping.

As cool air swept across her breast, she feared he had left along with his pants, and she turned to find him. His hand held a condom as he kicked his pants off the bed. The half-light that flowed into the bedroom from the living area highlighted the white of his underwear and the prominent bulge it covered.

"I've wanted you since the first time I saw you." His voice was low and sensual, his eyes hooded with lust.

He had? Because tonight was her first inkling that

her feelings might not be unrequited. It must be the sex talking. The same pheromones that were muddling her brain.

He shed his underwear, freeing his thick, firm erection, and rolled the condom down his shaft. The man was built in more ways than one.

"It's been a hell of night of foreplay. You ready?"

"So ready. Been ready."

He slid alongside her, caressed her breast, and pulled a nipple into his hot mouth. Tension, sharp, clear, and oh so pleasant, spiked from her toes to her scalp. Her hands grasped the sides of his face, and she held him there as pressure from the delicious suction increased, making her mindless to anything but him as his fingers played her through her undies. Finally, he slid her panties down, and she kicked them away.

His finger swept against her slickness and heat spiked through her. "You are so wet, honey."

And so ready. "Inside. Please. Now." It was hard to speak coherent words with a body ready to detonate.

And then he was there again, his naked body stretched over her, his penis hard, long, and reaching toward her. He spread her legs, looped her knees over his arms. "You are so beautiful."

She closed her eyes, and he fed her hungry kisses as the head of his hard, hot erection pressed into her slickness. He thrust hard and deep, stretching her as he penetrated. He growled with the intensity of a big cat, clutched her behind, and pushed again. That storm was back, whirring like a tornado, lifting her up, turning her inside out.

He withdrew and then pressed into her farther. "You like it hard, easy, slow, fast? Tell me."

She opened her eyes. Trace's long body was towering over hers, wrapping her in a cocoon of flesh and sex.

"However you want to give it to me." Despite being married for two years, she hadn't had enough experience to have a preference. But she knew she wanted this. Wanted him. Wanted to be part of him. Wanted to give herself to him.

He began to move slowly, tenderly, so every part of her body focused on the increasing tension his movements created. She wrapped her legs tighter around his waist and moved in time with the rhythm he set, letting it build. Soon his breath came harder, faster, in time with his movements, as he drove her toward the padded headboard. The rhythm increased, the beat becoming more urgent. His abdomen against her abdomen, his chest against her breasts. And then he was hammering into her farther, deeper, faster, flesh slapping flesh. Tension coiled tighter. Her back arched, and her fingers dug into his shoulders, trying to hold on…until she couldn't. The orgasm was heart pounding, body clenching, and more intense than anything she had experienced as wave upon wave thundered through her. He held her tight against his hot, hard body as her muscles contracted until a growl tore from his throat, and he drove into her again. His muscles stiffened, and her name escaped from his lips as she felt his release deep inside of her.

He remained embedded within, holding her close, as if he was afraid she would slip away. She wasn't going anywhere. Instead she listened to his strong heartbeat, and it was a long time before either of them spoke.

Lying with him she felt secure, content. She

could have stayed like that all night, but he eventually pushed up on his elbows, his head hanging down, and looked at her as if he didn't believe she was there. His lips grazed her forehead as he withdrew. Without a word, he got up and headed out of the room, undoubtedly to the only bathroom in the house.

She'd done it. Broken her vow to herself. Even as her mind raced to invent excuses, her heart was clear. She was falling for this man. Lock, stock, and barrel.

She listened for the flush of the toilet and then the padding of feet on hardwood.

Illuminated from the light in the living room, Trace, tall, naked, and muscled, looked like a god returning to his lair. Haylee felt the squeeze in her heart. This man wasn't her man. She wasn't his woman. They were two beings passing in the night, making the best of the hand they'd been dealt.

He slid into bed, sidled up next to her, and wrapped his strong arms around her. His body draped her in a sauna of heat. It had been a while since she had felt protected and loved by a man. She wasn't foolish enough to think Trace loved her, but no one had gone through the motions in a very long time.

"Penny for your thoughts," she said.

He actually smiled. "My thoughts would be worth a lot more than a penny. And not appropriate for consumption." He nuzzled the side of her neck and rested his hand on her abdomen.

"Are you sorry?"

"Sorry? Hardly." He seemed truly confused by her question.

"No regrets, I mean." If he took it all back like last time, she'd likely scream in his ear.

"You have regrets?"

"Absolutely not." Not ones she wanted to share.

"Good." He settled back against the pillow. He stroked her arm, and even though they'd just made love, she felt the sensation clear to her toes.

"You want some coffee or something?"

"Had my dessert." Those strokes along her arm got longer.

She wanted to ask him, where did they go from there? What were his intentions? Were they a couple now? Was there a future? She knew the answer to the last question was no. But she wondered if he did too.

"This used to be my room," he said.

"Really? I took the spare room because if my aunt and uncle come back, it wouldn't feel right taking their room. I like this room, even though it's small." And probably why they had to move when Trace's mother got pregnant with his brother.

Trace sat up and reached over to turn on the lamp on the bed stand. The glow seemed harsh, and her eyes had to adjust.

He got up, padded over to the closet, and ran his hand down the doorjamb. "Still there."

"What?" She propped herself up on her elbow, admiring his firm butt, his long limbs, and the muscles that outlined his back like the lines of a coloring book picture.

And this man had just made love to her. She hoped it wasn't just sex. That there was a stronger element to it beyond mere convenience, even if they would be going their separate ways.

"The notch made on my fourth birthday, and on my third and second. Charting my height. My dad made those notches. I think I might have been smaller than Delanie at that age." He looked over at her, his smile wide.

"Well, you wouldn't have been smaller than me. I was always the runt."

He walked back to bed, his half-erect penis waving against his legs. He slid under the covers, tugged her closer, and she was once again caught in his solid, secure embrace.

"You are a beautiful woman, Haylee. From your head to your pretty little toes, inside and out."

She brushed her hand along his cheek. "Thank you."

His kiss was demanding, and she was happy to oblige.

* * *

Trace wasn't sure if it was the smell of coffee or the humming that woke him up. He glanced at the time. After eight o'clock. He never slept that late. Or felt so rested. He closed his eyes again. Of course, he'd never made love twice in one night. He usually left after the first round and headed home. And since Delanie had come into his life, he hadn't even had a first round.

Deprivation, he guessed, could cause all sorts of unusual sensations. Like contentment. Or happiness. Or…he wouldn't go there.

This thing with Haylee, whatever it was, was just temporary. She would be moving on when the cabin sold. He would be staying put. Wasn't that the rationale he used to convince himself that a fling with her would be okay? Not that his body needed much convincing. But his mind sure had.

He looked over at the small wicker bed stand, and the sparkle of a ring caught his eye, a ring he'd noted on her finger from the night before. He fingered the opal ring and tried to fit it on his pinky, but it didn't get past his knuckle.

He put it back on the stand, sank back against the pillow, and closed his eyes. What was he thinking? Hell, it had been one roll in the hay—well, two, if anyone was counting. Not even a relationship yet. Because if it was anything more than a fling, he'd ruin it as sure as the sun rose.

This way there was no pressure. No commitment. No anything. Sounded perfect. So why didn't it feel perfect?

"Hey, sleepyhead."

He opened his eyes. There she stood in nothing but a T-shirt and a pair of panties, looking cute as a kitten and tempting as a rib-eye steak.

"Something smells good." And something looked even better.

"Coffee with pancakes and sausage."

Imagine waking up to her every morning.

Not in the cards for old Trace. Wife, hearth, and family were a reality for some men. He wasn't one of them. Hell, he wouldn't have Delanie if it wasn't for circumstances beyond his control. Because if he had a hand in something, well, it wouldn't turn out like this.

He sat up in bed and ran his fingers through his hair. "Tempting." And he didn't just mean the meal.

"I hope so. It's in the warmer, so you can take your shower first if you want." She turned on her heel and disappeared through the doorway.

Now he just had to figure out how not to mess this up for the short time she'd be around.

Haylee watched Trace scarf down his breakfast. He had put on his dress pants after the shower, but he hadn't worn his shirt, and she was treated to the sight of his muscled chest as a lock of damp hair fell over his brow. It had been nice waking up to a man. Waking up to this man.

Making love had been intense and all encompassing. The first time had been hot and heavy. The second, slower and intimate. And though she hated to compare, sex with Trace had been far more satisfying than with Roy, who had tended to get it on and get it over. And that about summed up the difference between the two men.

Trace looked up. Feeling her cheeks flush, Haylee shoved a forkful of pancakes into her mouth.

"I have to go check on the livestock, then pick up Delanie." It sounded like an apology.

"Can I help?" She hadn't much to do that day except post some more pictures on that licensing site.

He chuckled, low and gravely. "I think you need a few more riding lessons before I put you in with the herd." He drained his coffee cup.

"More?" she said.

"I'd love some more. Oh, you mean coffee."

He winked, causing a yearning deep inside of her. Lord, she was in trouble.

"So how do you want to work this?"

"Work what?" She held her breath.

"Us? How do you want to work this?"

Well, at least he was talking about *us*.

"You didn't think this was a one-night stand? Did I read something wrong?" He frowned. "Have I screwed up already? I told you I was terrible at relationships."

"No, you haven't read anything wrong." She set her fork down, anxious to reassure him. "I suppose it's best not to confuse Delanie."

His frown disappeared, and he sat back in his chair. "We'll have to be discreet."

"We'll work it out." She didn't want reality to break through the wonderful cocoon of intimacy and warmth that surrounded her. There would be plenty of time to figure things out. But she was curious about one thing. "Why do you always say you are not good at relationships?"

Some woman must have badly burned him in the past. As far as Haylee could tell, he was thoughtful, considerate, and caring. What more could a woman ask for?

He shrugged. "I'm not a very good father. Or brother. Or son, at least to my mother."

She begged to differ. "You are a wonderful father. As for your brother, well, I don't have the best relationship with my sister either. And I'm the one with the failed marriage. If anyone isn't good at relationships, it would be me." She twirled a strand of her hair and wondered what had happened to make the man with such soulful hazel eyes so hard on himself.

"Your mother didn't commit suicide."

Haylee felt breath leave her, like someone had sucked all the air out of the room. And yet his tone had been matter of fact, devoid of emotion. "Your mother committed suicide?" She couldn't imagine what that felt like. "How old were you?"

"Fourteen. She took too many pills, and before Dad could get her to a hospital, she died." He leaned forward, clasping his hands between his knees. His tone had been flat, as if he were talking about taking a trip to the grocery store. "I've always wondered if I'd done more, understood more about her depression. If I'd been in the house that day instead of out riding, maybe I could have saved her."

Haylee blinked back tears. No wonder the man had issues. "I am truly sorry. That must have been devastating for you and your brother. And for your father."

He shifted, straightened, and fingered the handle of the empty coffee cup. "Ty didn't realize she'd committed suicide for a number of years. He thought she was just sick since she kept to her room a lot. My dad didn't talk about it. He just ignored that she'd died by her own hand. Took me a number of years and a few detours down alcoholic alleys before I came to grips with it. As I said, not very good at the relationship thing."

Haylee reached across and touched his warm hand. "I don't think what your mother did says anything about you. Depression can make people do terrible things."

He pulled his arm away. Tucked it under the table. "They say that when someone commits suicide, they take the pain they are feeling and transfer it to those closest to them. I think that is what happened to my father."

And maybe Trace? "What did your father die of?"

"Heart attack. But I wouldn't have been surprised if the coroner had written *broken heart*. He was never the same after that." Trace's gaze scanned the cabin. "This house held my earliest memories of her…when she was still happy. I'm glad your aunt made changes. Time to move on."

She realized he was changing the subject, and she was going to let him. "What's different about the cabin now?"

"Your aunt and uncle updated the kitchen and opened it up to the living room. Looks roomier in here now. Those granite counters look real nice too. At least I can still find the bathroom."

His phone jangled in his pocket. He frowned as he looked at the caller ID. "It's Mandy's mother."

Chapter 19

Sophie Grace Martin took her time coming into the world, but, as her father explained later, that was because she was waiting for her daddy to arrive. Flying his private plane, Ty made it a full fifteen minutes before the blessed event occurred at 3:05 p.m., and Trace was amazed at how easily his strapping younger brother turned to mush at the sight of the little doll, all pink and wrinkled, who was trying out her lungs.

It also served as a stark reminder that he had not been there at Delanie's birth. Or to hear her first cries, experience her first smile, or catch the first time his daughter realized she had hands.

Haylee had insisted on accompanying Trace to the hospital so she could watch Delanie and free up Trace and Mandy's mother to assist Mandy until Ty arrived. As he stepped into the waiting room to announce the birth, he was greeted with the sight of Haylee and Delanie, wrapped up in each other's arms, napping on the stiff hospital-issue bench. It brought a lump to his throat. If only he could have the real deal with Haylee, but it wasn't in the cards. He needed to remember that, say it to himself every time he was with her, keep himself from getting in deeper than he already was. But one thing he could not do after last night—give her up for what little time they'd have together.

"Hey," he said, gently touching Haylee's shoulder.

Blue eyes opened, looked at him without recognition, and then widened. Delanie stirred.

"The baby," she said in the softest voice.

"A little girl. Seven pounds ten ounces."

"Can I see? I want to see." Delanie could go from sleep to awake in the space of a heartbeat.

"Mandy said you both can come in." Between puffs of breath, Mandy had let Trace know she was satisfied her little plan had worked and that Trace had been with Haylee when he got the call. He'd never hear the end of it, he guessed.

Hadn't been the time or place to bring Mandy back to reality and let her know that whatever was going on between him and Haylee was at best fleeting, and probably more about convenience than any real feelings. At least on Haylee's end.

Delanie popped off the seat and was pulling him in the direction of the hallway. Haylee hadn't moved.

"It's a family thing. I'll wait here."

"She asked for you. I think she'll be offended if you don't see the baby."

He didn't have to ask her twice. The trio sauntered down the hallway as if they were a family, doing a family thing. They weren't, but from the looks of the nurses and attendants they passed, everyone thought they were.

As they entered the antiseptic-smelling room, Ty was holding little Sophie in his arms, looking down at his child with a mixture of pride and awe, while Sheila fussed over Mandy, making sure her daughter was comfortable. Delanie didn't sprint over to the baby but hung back, as if instinctively aware that birth was a magical, God-created miracle to behold. Trace took advantage of the moment to get her to the hand sanitizer.

Ty looked up, his smile broad and welcoming. "Isn't she beautiful? Just like her mother. She passed all the tests. She's perfect."

Trace had never heard his brother so effusive.

But Ty was right—little Sophie was perfect, just like Trace imagined Delanie had been. Something deep in his heart ached, but he tamped it down. Now was not the time to wallow in his own failings. Now was a time to celebrate one of life's blessed events.

"Come here, Delanie. Meet your cousin Sophie," Ty said.

Delanie looked up at Trace, as if needing reassurance.

"It's okay, sweet pea."

The look on his daughter's face as she gently touched the pink blanket that cuddled Sophie made Trace want, more than ever, to give Delanie a real family with brothers and sisters, with a mother who would care about her.

He glanced at Haylee. She stood by Sheila, helping arrange Mandy's pillows for comfort.

"Could you take a picture?" Mandy said, addressing Haylee.

Haylee fumbled in her purse, whipped out her phone, and began taking pictures of Ty, Sophie, and Delanie.

Ty brought Sophie to Mandy and rested the child in Mandy's arms.

"Let me get a picture of the new family," Haylee said. "Of all times to forget my good camera." But she snapped away none the less.

"With my mom," Mandy directed.

More pictures.

"Now with Trace."

Trace frowned. He'd never held a baby. "I don't think…"

"Indulge this new mother. I want Sophie to know you were here. And according to the baby books, I'm supposed to start nursing her within the first hour, so it is now or never."

Trace took the child in his arms, aware of the fragility of the precious being entrusted to him. The baby looked up at him. Blinked. Her rosebud mouth rounded. He was mesmerized and only faintly aware of Haylee taking pictures. He tried to imagine what it would have been like if this had been Delanie, but he couldn't.

"You have to give her back," Ty said.

How long had he been holding the child? He looked down at Delanie. Her eyes were wide, her mouth open like she was captivated by the scene.

Trace gently nestled the baby back into her father's arms, a father who clearly was already wrapped around Sophie's tiny finger. He knew how easily that could happen.

"We'll leave now. Let you all get some rest," Trace said.

"I want to stay, Daddy. I want to stay with Sophie."

"I have to get back to the ranch, honey. I called Corey in, but he can only do so much. Besides, you have camp tomorrow, and Mandy and Sophie need their rest. You want the baby to get a good start in this world." Had Delanie had a good start?

Delanie hung her head. More than anything at that moment, he wanted to hold his daughter, feel her little arms around his neck.

"Can I pick you up, Delanie? Get a hug?" He held his breath.

She reached out her arms, and he swung her up. She wrapped her arms around his neck. He breathed in the scent of Delanie's shampoo and looked over at Haylee, who was saying her goodbyes and promising to send pictures.

He was lucky to have Delanie in his life, and he shouldn't reach for more.

The next day, Haylee found herself checking the pastures that led out to the herd, looking for Trace to come in for supper. The chicken breasts she would barbeque had been marinated, the vegetables skewered, and the garden salad tossed. The air was hot, the breeze warm, and the flies buzzing. Delanie was playing on the swing with a baby doll whose new name was Sophie.

She glanced at her watch. It was already six o'clock, and there was no Trace in sight.

Yesterday had been an eventful day, and Haylee was still processing her feelings. Making love with Trace had been a giant release of pent-up lust...and something more.

When she saw him holding the baby in his arms, the mixture of wonder and vulnerability in his eyes, she knew what that something was, because that moment had touched her heart, had touched her soul. She'd captured that moment in one of her photos as well.

As for Trace, he wasn't any easier to read than before their intimate encounter. He'd been quiet on the way home, which she'd chalked up to fatigue. And when he hadn't asked her to come over early for a little of that afternoon delight, she reasoned that he had a lot to do having been off the ranch for two days. If she could just see him, she could better gauge what he was feeling.

Who was she kidding? Gauging how Trace felt was for a psychic, not a mere mortal.

She shaded her eyes against the setting sun. The faint lines of a horse and rider were visible. She plopped the chicken onto the grill and listened to the satisfying sizzle.

She must have glanced over her shoulder a hundred times as she grilled. Finally he sauntered out of the barn, Moose on his heels, his long legs in a leisurely gait, as if he had all the time in the world to get to her. She plunged a fork into the largest breast. Clear juices bubbled out.

She busied herself transferring the meat and skewered vegetables onto the flowered platter. Haylee had set the table in the house because she refused to share her meal with flies, but she waited. Waited as Delanie ran over to her father. Waited as she waved the flies away.

He lifted his head…and winked in her direction.

That was all she needed. She nodded, surprised at the shyness that enveloped her as she turned and entered the house. She suddenly felt very hungry.

Trace, Delanie, and the dog flooded into the kitchen, Moose heading straight for the bowl of kibbles Haylee had set out for him by the back door.

"Wash up, sweet pea," Trace said as he headed to the kitchen sink to do just that. Delanie wandered off to the bathroom.

As soon as Delanie was out of the room, Trace dried his hands and reached for her, wrapping his arm around her waist.

"Sorry I was so late coming in tonight. Lots to do," he whispered in her ear.

Desire spiked through her like a sugar rush from a horde of delicious chocolate.

"I missed you," she confessed.

He brushed his lips across hers in a tender, sweet kiss, causing her pulse to leap and her heart to skip a beat.

Running footsteps pounded in the hallway. He stepped back. "After dinner and I put Delanie to bed?"

She nodded. She would wait for as long as it took if it meant she could have more time with Trace…and wasn't that pitiful proof of where her heart was?

Dinner was a quiet affair, shared with Delanie's doll, Sophie, who had to have her own seat at the table.

Haylee offered to clean up after dinner so Trace could spend some time reading to Delanie before he sent her off to bed, since it was closing in on eight o'clock, Delanie's bedtime.

Being in the kitchen of Trace's mom took on new meaning after what she had learned. The pretty flowered plates she loaded into the dishwasher were undoubtedly chosen by a wife and mother who had, at one time, liked cheery patterns. The silverware with embossed curlicues, the hand-embroidered table runner with threads of blue, yellow, and pink, and the trivet with two children playing were hard to reconcile with a woman so miserable she had taken her own life and left behind two sons and a husband who undoubtedly loved her.

If it confused Haylee, how could Trace make sense of it?

And continuing to live in a house where his mother's essence was contained in so many objects that he had to contend with every day had to be more than difficult. And now he was trying to raise his own daughter here, trying to give her a loving home while dealing with the child's incarcerated mother. It was a lot on one plate. Despite Trace's many burdens, he faced every day determined to do the right thing as he saw fit.

She started the dishwasher, wiped down the wood table that Trace's father had made for his wife and that had outlasted both their lives, and wondered what kind of emotional legacy Trace's parents had left him. Her own past had had a positive outcome. It could have been much different, which made her all the more grateful for her parents. But she still had issues.

She tucked the sponge back in its spot under the sink. Her feelings for Trace were growing in leaps and bounds, and she doubted there was anything she could do to stop it.

"Hey." At the sound of his voice, she looked up. Trace filled the doorway, his hand on the doorjamb, his expression hopeful. "Want to step out on the front porch? We can leave the screen door open just in case."

The air was crisp and cooler as the plains heat

died down. He indicated the two-seater rocker, and she settled next to him, absorbing the warmth of his body as he wrapped an arm around her shoulders and crossed one long leg over the other knee.

"This is nice," she said, enjoying the intimacy of the moment.

"Really? I didn't have a chance to shower. I must smell like Archer."

"You smell like man, not horse."

He smiled and kissed the tip of her nose. It was a simple but sweet gesture that captured her heart more than any lust-filled kiss.

She wanted this. A simple life. With a good man. With him.

"A lot to do today?" she asked, resting her hand on his warm thigh, enjoying the small intimacy.

"I'm bone tired. Baling hay today. Had a text from Mandy. Mother and child are doing well. She'll probably be home tonight or tomorrow."

He stroked her arm, and a pleasant shiver ran through her. She rested her head on his shoulder. This felt right, comforting and peaceful.

"So soon?" The male cicadas were in full chorus, and they filled the air with their chanting.

"No pampering for a new mom these days. How about you?"

She still only had two clients, income from her photos wouldn't pay her phone bill, and if she didn't have money from Trace, she'd be destitute. "Doing fine." For a woman who craved security, Haylee was in the worst possible place.

Last night her mind had worked overtime on a plan for the future because her bank-account balance had made it clear she needed a plan, and her bag-lady fear was in full bloom despite her feelings, or maybe because of her feelings, for Trace.

She had to face the fact that once her aunt's place was sold, she would have to find a job if the position in Denver didn't come through by then. No more business. No more photography. No more Delanie. No more Trace. Facts that were so much harder to face sitting with him on the porch in the calm and quiet of the evening.

"Delanie said she was going to visit her mother so did you reach an agreement on custody?" Haylee had been anxious to learn if Trace had settled the question, but over the weekend, there had never been the right time to ask.

"I've agreed to visitation once a month. Some paperwork and then my lawyer says it will be over." He let out a long breath. "I was trying to keep Delanie from knowing the reality of what her mother is or was." He looked out into the darkening sky, as if he expected to find sage advice somewhere in the shadows. "But after my experience with Melissa Leonard, I realized I can't hide it from her. Better she knows so I can help her handle it when her friends find out. She's going to go through hell probably. Best I can do is be there for her."

Haylee listened as Trace recounted what happened at the Leonard house. Hearing it made Haylee want to wrap Delanie in her arms and never let her go out into a world that seemed crueler by the day. A world Haylee knew a little about.

"I can relate to having a mother with a past."

"I thought your parents were upstanding citizens living the good life in Chicago."

"They've had their share of adversity, but truth is, they aren't my biological parents." Haylee felt the lump in her throat grow. She hated talking about her adopted status. Made her feel needy…and different.

Trace stared at her, and his stroking on her arm ceased. "That why you and your sister don't look alike?"

Haylee nodded. "We are not blood. I was born to a sixteen-year-old who had lived the good life in the Chicago suburbs with her parents and then got pregnant. Her parents made her give me up so I wouldn't ruin her life. My biological mother signed the papers and, even though it was an open adoption, never saw me again."

Trace let out a whistle. "You look for her?"

"I know where to find her. She's buried in a graveyard about a half hour from my parents' house. After she had me, she went on to college in Florida. According to a newspaper account, when she was pledging a sorority, she was rushed to the hospital with alcohol poisoning. She never recovered. Growing up, my parents only told me she had died. It wasn't until I searched the internet myself that I learned the truth. By then I was a teenager." And no father had been listed on the birth certificate, though she always wondered if he was out there, if he knew about her.

Trace squeezed her closer, kissed the side of her head. "I'm sorry, honey."

"Nothing to be sorry about. I consider myself lucky to have found parents that chose me and loved me. My parents adopted because my mother couldn't get pregnant, despite trying everything available. Then when I was three, a miracle happened, and nine months later Livvy arrived."

"Was it hard for you, growing up with a sister that was their blood?"

"Much to my sister's chagrin, my parents never treated me any less or her any more. And Livvy certainly tested that over the years. I, on the other hand, was always the good child, I think because I never wanted to test it. Never wanted to risk being given back, like some toy that had been returned because it wasn't as fun as advertised. So I did what I knew would please them—good grades, good college, sensible degree." And a divorce. She hadn't been able to confide in her parents about what happened to cause that divorce. Better they never knew how faulty her judgment had been.

He leaned forward, clasped his hands between his legs. "Delanie said she was afraid of being bad. Afraid I'd send her away." He shook his head. "Now that the custody thing is settled, I'm trying to reassure her that she doesn't have to worry."

Haylee could relate. "Unfortunately, I don't think it is as simple as giving reassurance. You make up these myths in your mind and…well, it's hard to dispel them no matter how much evidence there is to the contrary."

"And your myth was that you had to do everything right?"

Haylee feared it was. "I think that's why I married the man my father declared as perfect for me." She nestled against Trace, felt his arms embrace her.

"But you divorced that perfect man." There was a question in that statement.

"Yeah. The perfect man with a successful business, a large bank account, and a luxury apartment wasn't so perfect." She didn't want to explain the unexplainable because she couldn't confess what wasn't perfect about Roy…to anyone. Sitting with Trace, who had shown himself to be a man of good character after overcoming a difficult past, only served to remind her of what she had escaped. She could only hope her encounter with Roy at her aunt's house would be her last, but she still worried every time she went home that he would be there again.

"Are you looking for perfection? Because, honey, I'm not it."

"And that's your myth."

"My myth?" He looked puzzled.

"That you aren't perfect for someone."

Trace shook his head. "That would have to be some messed-up someone."

Like me? she wondered.

Chapter 20

The days passed, and Haylee found herself falling deeper and deeper in love with Trace. When they made love, which they did in the bright glow of the afternoon before she had to leave to pick up Delanie, she was certain Trace returned her affection, but he'd never said the words…any words…that spoke to his feelings.

Today, he was changing it up and taking her on a horseback ride out to the summer pastures so she could see the herd again and get some more pictures. He even wore his chaps for her, though he complained they were hot. Along with a shirt and jeans, Haylee had donned her cowgirl hat and brown boots. Apparently, shorts weren't appropriate for riding among cattle with horns. Thankfully, the temperature was a comfortable seventy-four, the breeze steady, and the humidity nonexistent.

"I have a surprise for you," he called from behind her as she pulled on the saddle's cinch. Buck was a gentleman and didn't puff out his stomach, something Trace had warned her about during their now weekly riding lessons. She turned around.

Her heart did a stutter beat, and she felt her cheeks flush. He was carrying a wooden platform with steps, which was undoubtedly heavy since he held it with two hands. As he walked toward her, the fringes of his chaps waved against his legs. He wore a plaid shirt and jeans under those chaps and looked like the rugged cowboy he was.

He set the steps alongside Buck and checked the saddle, making sure it was cinched correctly, that the stirrups were the right length.

"Did I pass?" she asked

He turned around and winked at her. "Darling, you are becoming a pretty good cowgirl."

She beamed at his praise. Because she wanted to be the best cowgirl ever. She wanted to help him with the ranch. She wanted to understand the concerns and issues he dealt with.

"This is some set of stairs. You made this for me?" He really was the sweetest guy, and why he thought he wasn't good at relationships eluded Haylee. He was far more considerate and caring than Roy had ever been.

"I did."

She stepped close to him and twirled a strand of her hair. "Am I getting too heavy for you to pick up?"

He chuckled. "Darling, lifting you is like lifting a bag of tissues. I just want to be sure that if you ever need to ride a horse by yourself, you can get on him."

She wouldn't read too much into his remark, but it did sound as if he was thinking of a future that had her in it.

She wrapped her arms around his neck, her signal to him to bend lower. He dipped his head, and his firm lips met hers. They stood by Buck, making out like teenagers in the back row of a movie theater, until Trace pulled back. "We better get going so we're back in time to fetch Delanie."

She felt guilty she hadn't been mindful of the time, but Haylee had a hard time focusing on anything but Trace when he was kissing her. None of her problems existed in that moment. Not her lack of money, her uncertain future, or the fear her ex-husband would surprise her again.

"Try it out," he urged.

Haylee climbed the three steps, placed her foot in the stirrup, and hoisted herself up and her free leg over the saddle. She was elated. "Works great."

He patted her leg, then removed the steps to the fence before getting on Archer.

Haylee reined Buck to follow Archer out of the corral gate, and then they rode side by side. Haylee had enjoyed their weekly lessons while Delanie was in camp. It was these times that she felt closest to Trace, closer than when they made love. Because she was on his turf, learning about him, what made him tick, how his mind operated, why he loved the ranch so much.

"You're okay giving up our usual…activities to show me around?" she said as they trotted out onto the trail.

He chuckled and shifted in his saddle. "Anything to please you."

"And you do."

Even in the bright sun she could see his cheeks turn a rosy shade of red.

"So how many acres do you have here?" Haylee asked as they ambled along, flat plains of grass stretching out for miles. "This ranch seems huge."

Trace shrugged. With his sunglasses on, she couldn't tell what he was thinking, not that she could when he wasn't wearing sunglasses.

"I've got a little over fourteen thousand acres, but some of it I have to put in hay."

She let out a whistle that got caught on a breeze.

"Takes a lot of acres to support one cow around here. Thankfully, most of it is Martin land. Some acres I lease. If I had to lease more, I wouldn't make any money."

"So how much can you sell a cow for?" And having seen only part of the herd last time, she had no idea how many cattle he had.

He glanced in her direction as Archer tossed his head.

"Trying to gauge my net worth or something?"

"No," she said, flustered. "I'm sorry if I'm being nosy."

"This year I expect to get a little over seven hundred a head."

She let out another whistle.

"Don't go thinking it's all gravy. Running a ranch is an expensive proposition. And I made it more expensive having to take out a mortgage on some of it. I'm trying to save on labor by hiring part-time help and doing the rest myself. That's why Camille's leaving made it so much more difficult." He smiled. "And your coming so much better."

Even that small compliment warmed her. "I'm glad I can help. Maybe I can help around the ranch now that I know how to ride."

The horses walked at a leisurely pace, the bright sun warmed the air, the breeze ruffled her hair, and the beauty of the grassy plains and distant mountains fed her soul.

"Maybe." Trace shifted his weight. "If you're interested."

"I'm interested."

"In trading in your city-girl ways for cowgirl ways?"

Haylee swallowed, not sure what he was asking but certain what she was answering. "I like it out here."

"Not too isolated for you?"

She'd have to answer truthfully. "A little."

He nodded. "Got to my mother, you know. Once my grandparents passed, seemed she just turned into herself like a turtle in its shell."

She heard the warning. "There is the internet now. Speaking of which, would you reconsider letting me post some pictures of you?" She took a deep breath. "I could use the money."

"Business not good?" He frowned.

She hadn't exactly been forthcoming about her finances either.

"Market has changed, and frankly, I'm struggling."

He pushed up the brim of his hat. "If it will make you happy, post them."

Haylee knew it was a personal sacrifice for this private man to allow his photos to be sold. "Thank you. It means a lot."

He nodded and patted Archer, as if it were no big deal.

For the first time in a long time, she felt content. Happy. Optimistic. Those were dangerous feelings. The kind of feelings that could lead to heartbreak if she had to leave.

If only things were different. If she were rich instead of poor. If her business were profitable instead of struggling. If she could be a help instead of a hindrance. If Trace could love her in spite of her being clueless about being a ranch wife.

Because she could get used to this, used to riding in open country. Used to lunchtime activities with a man she loved. Used to the sticky kisses of a little girl she adored. Used to working hard and seeing that work pay off. Used to belonging to someone who cared about her, who would sacrifice for her, and she for him.

They rode on in silence for a bit. Trace had warned that the summer pastures were a good distance and she might be sore as a result. But the chance to photograph the herd, and Trace, against the backdrop of the distant mountains was too much of a draw to worry about a few muscle aches. Besides, Buck walked with a rocking gait that could lull her to sleep if she wasn't so curious to see everything unfold around her.

The country changed as they rode. From flat prairie to rockier ground, from land with just a few trees to land dotted with copses of trees. Prairie dogs, rabbits, and birds were flushed out as the horses made their way through high waves of grass. Haylee was struck by the vastness of it all, and the solitude. There was something to be said about the peace and quiet that allowed a person to think, compared to the hubbub of modern life.

"Stop!" The sharp command from Trace was enough for her to pull on Buck's reins. Within a split second, Trace had grabbed Buck's bridle. "Don't move. She's got cubs with her."

About twenty yards away, a bear rose up on hind legs and stared at them. Haylee reached for her camera dangling around her neck.

"I said don't move. That means no pictures." Trace's tone brooked no argument. But Trace was moving, slowly twisting around, pulling out the rifle strapped to the back of his saddle.

"You can't shoot." Haylee felt panicked. "She has cubs."

"I know what she has. I'm not going to shoot unless she charges, and then I'll try to aim to scare her first. But a charging bear is a dangerous bear."

"Can't we outrun them?" Surely on a horse…

"First, you've never ridden at full gallop, and second, contrary to popular myth, bears have been clocked at sixty miles per hour."

Archer snorted. Buck shifted his weight as if both horses had just gotten a whiff of the bear's scent.

Trace reached in his pocket and pulled out a small spray canister. "Bear spray," he said, stretching out his hand. "It's like pepper spray. Won't harm them. Take it. In case."

"In case what?" The idea of coming face to face with a bear was making her pulse skitter, but she grabbed the spray and tucked it in her pocket.

"Slowly, turn Buck around and head back the way we came. But slowly. No running or trotting. Calm and slow."

It was hard to breathe with her heart pounding against her chest. "What about you? I can't leave you here."

"I'm going to keep my focus on the bear. If she follows, I'm here to make sure she doesn't get too close. Hopefully, she won't follow."

The bear came down on all fours. Haylee swallowed, her mouth dry. "What if something happens?"

He raised the gun, looked through the sight. A sick feeling contorted her stomach.

"I'm here to make sure nothing happens. Do as I say, Haylee. I have enough to contend with without arguing."

The cubs began to move toward them. Haylee didn't want to leave Trace to fend for himself.

"Haylee," he said, his voice low, his tone firm. "It's more helpful to me if you start back. One less thing to worry about. I'm serious here."

"I won't go far enough that I can't keep you in sight." She reined Buck to turn, and despite her instinct to flee, she nudged Buck into a walk. No way was she leaving Trace without knowing he was safe. She twisted around so she could keep at least part of him in her sight.

Trace backed up Archer and the horse shook his head in defiance. Archer didn't like walking backward any more than Trace did, but the horse obeyed, if reluctantly. Stumbling was a real possibility, and if a horse stumbled, it could injure its legs—and that would be the end of the horse. But Trace was the only line of defense between Haylee and a potentially ticked-off mama bear. The cubs were older, probably about eighteen months. They might survive without her, but he didn't cotton killing a sow with cubs if he could avoid it.

He hunted to protect his herd, and he had no problem pulling the trigger if threatened. Otherwise, he preferred to let nature be. That probably put him in the company of tree huggers, but so be it. He didn't judge others. Others shouldn't judge him.

He swung his gaze for a split second to check on Haylee's progress. She had Buck walking along at a leisurely gait. For a minute he'd thought she was going to balk at his instructions. When this was over, he'd give some thought to the fact she'd been thinking more about him than herself. Right now he had two curious cubs on the move, followed by a mother anxious that her cubs' curiosity didn't bring trouble.

The cubs moseyed along like they were enjoying the walk, not too anxious to reach him. The mother bear seemed to have one eye on her cubs, the other on him.

"Calm boy," he said as Archer snorted, obviously not pleased with the situation.

Trace sat up, making himself as big as he could. The trio of bears was closing in, and Archer was dancing. Now or never.

He waved his arms. "Hey, bears," he said sharp and loud.

The cubs stopped; the mother didn't.

He yelled again. The cubs turned tail, the sow kept moving toward him. Trace sighted the rifle away from the sow, aiming for a tree to the left. The sound was either going to spook Archer or the bears. No telling which one. The sow was now about ten yards away and closing faster than he'd like.

He pulled the trigger.

Archer reared up. Trace tightened his legs and hung on. By the time Archer came down on all fours, the mother bear was following her cubs heading in the opposite direction and he was still in the saddle.

He spoke softly to the horse and kept the reins tight as he juggled the rifle. Archer was still dancing when Haylee, on Buck, pulled alongside.

"You could have been thrown," she said, a frown

on her forehead, her mouth pursed, her eyes wide.

Trace scanned the area for the bears, spotted them running through the prairie grass, already a distance away. "I wasn't. But you should be back about twenty yards."

"I heard shots."

"*A* shot."

She straightened in the saddle. "I couldn't risk leaving you alone."

He'd never admit it out loud, but a warm, fuzzy feeling settled in his heart at her statement. It had been a long time since anyone had cared about him. A long time since anyone feared for his safety. "You want to head back?"

A bear encounter wasn't for the faint of heart. No telling if the sow felt threatened, and though black bears were usually more shy than aggressive, all bets were off when cubs were involved. He certainly could understand if Haylee wanted to bolt for home.

She took a deep breath. "Do you think they'll come back?"

By then the bears were mere dark dots in the distance.

"Doubt they'll stick around."

She squared her shoulders like she was prepping for an adventure. "Then I'd like to see the herd."

He admired her gumption. "Now you have truly gone to the other side, Haylee Dennis. Only a country girl would want to press on."

Her smile was broad and beautiful. "Guess I've gone full-tilt country then."

Trace wondered just how full tilt she'd have to be to hitch her wagon to a struggling rancher who wanted her in his life but could offer her nothing but hard work and a soft bed. And would he have the courage to find out?

Chapter 21

Trace watched Mandy stifled a yawn as he stood with her in the doorway of her ranch house living room while Delanie entertained baby Sophie, who sat in a little seat on the floor. Had Delanie ever been that little? She surely had been that cute.

"Not getting much sleep?"

"Not much. Tell me it gets better." Mandy's pink top had cream colored stains near the shoulder and her black capris had similar dots near the knees.

"I wouldn't be able to tell you when, but Delanie has been a good sleeper from the time she came to me. Sophie makes me realize that I missed a lot."

Delanie had begged to visit baby Sophie, and Trace had wanted to talk to Mandy, so a drive over after Doreen's Saturday call seemed in order. With Ty away at a rodeo, Trace could see Mandy alone, Haylee having gone on a shopping trip to Fort Collins with Jenna.

"At least you've been granted custody, all legal and right. But in two Saturdays you'll be going to see Delanie's mother?" Mandy asked.

"That's the plan." He'd gritted his teeth, submitted the paperwork, and set the date.

"I hope Delanie will be okay."

"They tell me she'll be fine. And she's been mighty happy since I told her. No tantrums after Doreen's calls either."

Mandy patted Trace on the back. "I admire how you've handled all of this, Trace. It's not easy under the best of circumstances, but as a single father and a rancher, I know it's got to be tough. I mean, I'm exhausted—happy, but exhausted—tending to Sophie. I can only imagine how it will be when she's an active five-year-old. So glad you've got Haylee to help you now."

Trace had something on his mind, and he needed Mandy's advice, even though it would likely open a Pandora's box of questions. Since the bear encounter, the idea of having Haylee in his life on a permanent basis had taken up residence in his mind. Likely he was jumping the gun, but the summer was coming to a close soon, and her business was struggling. If he didn't do something, she'd be leaving.

"Did Ty have a ring ready for you when he proposed at my house?"

Mandy inhaled. "You mean the second time? Yes. Shocked the stuffing out of me." Mandy turned to look at him. "Haylee seems like a wonderful girl, Trace. I'm happy for you."

"Don't go jumping to conclusions."

She smiled. "Have I jumped to the wrong conclusion?"

Trace shifted his weight. "If I were thinking about proposing to Haylee, would she want a ring or want to pick one out herself?"

"I don't know her well enough to say, but wait here."

Mandy disappeared into the kitchen, and Trace was left listening to the sound of his heartbeat in his ears. Who said getting it out felt better? Now one other person would learn of his humiliation if Haylee said no.

Delanie was playing peek-a-boo, and little Sophie was gurgling her approval. He didn't even know how Haylee felt about having kids. Maybe this was premature. Maybe he was reading the signals wrong. Maybe he shouldn't have told Mandy anything.

Mandy was back at his side, her hand on his back. Her other hand held out a card.

"Here's the jeweler in Cheyenne Ty used. He'll not only give you a good deal, but he has payment plans available. And if she doesn't like it, he lets you exchange it for something she'd like better."

Trace tucked the card into his breast pocket. "You won't mention this to Ty, will you?"

Mandy smiled. "I can keep a secret. Just make sure I'm the first call you make after she says yes, because I've got the perfect wedding present in mind."

His heartbeat drummed louder in his ears at the thought of following through. Because backing out would guarantee failure, asking risked rejection and only Haylee could give him a happily ever after.

* * *

"So do you think you'll be here after the summer?" Jenna asked as Haylee picked through a rack at a tiny boutique sandwiched in between a pizza parlor and a coffee shop on a busy street in Fort Collins. It was the kind of boutique that burned scented candles, provided a pitcher of lemon water with real glasses, and called their customers guests.

"I haven't a clue. The real estate broker said that interest picked up after the open house, so who knows."

She dreaded the day her aunt called and told her the place was sold. Because that meant asking Trace his intentions, and she wasn't sure what his answer would be or what she wanted his answer to be.

"Did I tell you we saw a bear? Trace and I were out on the trail, and there was a mother bear and her cubs." She still got goose bumps thinking about it.

"Did you run?" Jenna moved to another rack and paged through the merchandise.

"Not supposed to run. I walked the horse slowly back the way we came while Trace frightened them away. But it was a harrowing few minutes."

In her heart, she was in love with him. She couldn't stop thinking about him, waiting for the sound of his pickup in her driveway for some afternoon delight before picking up Delanie. Like everything about Trace, he was a generous lover, taking his time to make it right for her. Just seeing him had her body humming and her heart thumping. And when he'd faced down that bear to protect her, had chosen her over himself, she knew he was the one.

But Trace was the kind of guy who would have faced down a bear regardless of who was with him.

Jenna pulled out an embroidered baby-doll top and held it up. "Too young for me?"

Haylee had to be honest. "A little."

Jenna pushed it back into the rack.

If he did want her to stay, did want her to move in with him, where would she find work? She was almost ready to throw in the towel on her business, but she hadn't heard from the Denver company, and she didn't know where else to get a job. There was that little thing called financial security…she had none.

"Are they hiring by you?"

Jenna had just pulled out a ruffled skirt in a loud print, and it almost dropped from her hand. "You *are* thinking of staying." But the ends of her mouth drooped. "There's a freeze in the accounting department right now. They're waiting to see if oil and gas prices rise before hiring anyone."

"Know of anywhere else they might need help? I've been checking online for job postings, but so far, nothing in the accounting field."

She should have gone straight for a corporate job after her divorce. But then she wouldn't have met Trace and Delanie and her aunt and uncle wouldn't have been able to go to New Mexico—and she wouldn't be on the precipice of a broken heart.

"Can't you move in with your cowboy? Seems you two are getting along pretty well." Jenna's expression had changed to a smirk.

"He's just so hard to read."

"How about this?"

Jenna held up another ruffled skirt, but this one had a more subdued pattern. "I like that."

"Maybe he's hard to read because you haven't talked to him about it."

"I haven't because…" How did she explain all her fears? "I'm not sure he feels the same about me. And if he does, it doesn't change the fact I need a job to stay here."

"If you move in, you could care for Delanie in exchange for rent. Seems the perfect solution."

Haylee took a deep breath. “But I would still need a job, and that would mean I couldn’t watch Delanie. It’s complicated.”

“He owns a ranch. He must be rich.”

“I actually think he’s struggling. Seems you have to already be rich to ranch these days.” There was a distinct difference between well-tended Pleasant Valley and Trace’s tidy if forlorn buildings and small house.

Jenna headed for the dressing room, and Haylee trailed after her. She didn’t have any money to buy anything, but Jenna had asked if she wanted to go to Fort Collins, and Haylee thought it would be a good opportunity to get some much-needed advice.

Jenna found an open dressing room, and Haylee stood just outside the curtain.

“Are your security fears rising up again?” Jenna said

Haylee supposed they were. “I’ll need a job regardless. And if he’s serious, shouldn’t I know what I’m getting into?” He’d mentioned a mortgage and a loan from his brother.

Jenna popped her head out of the curtain. “Shouldn’t you know how you feel about him and how he feels about you before you start freaking out about money? If you love him and he loves you, you’ll figure out a way. After all, he’s lived off that land for how long?”

“His whole life. But it’s just been him. Now it’s him and Delanie. And then you add me to the mix… I’ll have to contribute something, but will it be enough?”

Jenna emerged from behind the curtain wearing

the skirt. It fit beautifully, and when she twirled, it lifted up to show off her long legs.

"It's perfect on you."

Jenna stood in front of the full-length mirror decorating the adjacent wall. "I think I'll get it." She turned to face Haylee. "Stop being so pragmatic. You are a hardworking woman interested in a hardworking man. Go for the romance. If you love each other, wouldn't it be easier making it together than alone?"

The key phrase was *if you love each other*. Haylee knew she loved Trace, but did he love her?

"You always go it alone, Haylee. Maybe this time you should work it out together. And, by the way, you've got friends and family that are more than willing to help. Seems, from what you've told me, he does too."

"My parents don't even know about Trace beyond what Livvy may have told them." She'd been afraid of what they would think if she declared she was in love so soon after her divorce to Roy, a divorce her parents hadn't understood. And then she wasn't sure of Trace's feelings.

"Seems like it's time you make your choice. And talk to the people in your life."

On Monday, Haylee worked with Delanie on riding the bike on the dusty paths around the barns. Delanie was still wobbly, but she stayed on now for a few turns of the pedal before veering to one side or the other.

The ride to the herd the other day had been spectacular, and the shots of Trace she'd put up were already selling. But one thing she'd learned on that ride was ranching was more difficult and dangerous than she'd thought. But she was still eager to be part of it. If he let her. With Trace, there was no use in guessing. She'd have to come right out and ask.

Haylee checked her watch and was surprised to find they'd been practicing a full hour. It was already five o'clock, and she had to get the chicken in the oven.

"Are you ready to help me get dinner on the table, Delanie?"

Delanie stood with each of her hands resting on the corresponding hip. "I'm exhausted," she said with dramatic flair. "Can I just color at the table?"

"Of course you can. I can handle snapping the beans myself."

Haylee had put the chicken in the oven and was ready to snap the beans when she went to check on Delanie, who had disappeared to get her coloring book and crayons but hadn't reappeared. The child wasn't in her bedroom. She checked the bathroom. No Delanie. She called her name and heard a response that sounded like it came from down the hall.

Haylee peeked into the spare room. Delanie was sitting at her father's desk, coloring book open, diligently working on her masterpiece. "There you are. Why didn't you come to the kitchen table?"

Delanie looked up. "Sorry. I found my coloring book in here where I colored while Daddy did his books, whatever that means."

Haylee glanced at the open ledger. At the tax forms that lay spread across the desk. Her gaze roved over the numbers, until she saw the bottom number on the page.

Was that all Trace earned from his hard labor? It was hardly above what she had made fresh out of college. He took in enough money, but expenses seemed to eat him alive. How did he manage to pay for Delanie's camp? Or for her?

"Find what you are looking for?"

Haylee whirled around at the sound of Trace's voice and felt the flush clear to her toes. "I'm so sorry. I didn't mean to snoop."

Trace's face was stoic and inscrutable. Embarrassed didn't begin to describe how she felt. More like mortified. She shouldn't have looked. And yet the reality was something she needed to know before…before things went too far.

"What did you mean to do then?" His tone held a definite scowl.

"I couldn't find Delanie, and she was in here coloring."

"And you just thought you would take a peek?"

He turned on his heel. "Well, now you know. Ranching pays next to nothing."

He was down the hall before Haylee could say anything.

"Uh-oh. I think you did something wrong," Delanie said with five-year-old wisdom.

"I believe I did, Delanie. I believe I did."

Haylee served the chicken and gravy over rice with string beans covered in a warm bacon vinaigrette, while Trace sat at the table not saying a word. About the meal or about finding her looking through his papers.

"Delanie was able to keep on the bike for a few

turns of the pedal today. We are definitely making progress." She was determined to get him talking.

Trace looked directly at Delanie, as if Haylee hadn't spoken. "You want to try again tonight?"

Delanie shook her head. "I'm exhausted," she said with another dramatic sigh. "Maybe tomorrow."

"Tomorrow then."

Haylee looked from Trace to Delanie and back to Trace. It was as if she wasn't there. She wanted to say something, but she hesitated with Delanie in the room.

There was another time when she'd been looking at papers she shouldn't have been looking at. The time she'd found Roy's second set of books. With payments from a strange LLC. That time the bottom line number had been too big, way too big.

"I am sorry, Trace, for invading your privacy. It wasn't my intention, but it was my failure."

"Failure. Nice choice of word."

"*My* failure. What you've been able to do with what you have is a definite success."

"You mean because of how little I have? Nice try."

Delanie looked from one to the other and asked for more milk. Both Haylee and Trace rose at the same time. She wanted to tell him that money didn't matter. But she wasn't sure she could truthfully say those words. And what did that say about her?

"I'll get it." He practically growled at her.

Haylee sat down. The air was thick with tension, and not the good kind. She picked at her food, her appetite gone.

She had no money of her own to bring to their relationship if it got so far as marriage. Nothing but her domestic skills, and based on what she'd seen, that wouldn't be enough. Without regular income from a decent job, she'd be a burden to him rather than a helpmate. Lord knew she wasn't capable yet of helping with the ranch part of things.

She sat in the chair, her back tight, her shoulders achy, and watched father and daughter eat their meal. When the last morsel was gone, Haylee rose, determined to clean up, as she always did, so Trace could spend more time with Delanie.

Instead, he leaned over and stayed her hand from stacking up the plates.

"Head out, Haylee. I'll clean up. No sense dragging things out."

Delanie had already scooted into the other room, leaving her chair out, having only drunk half a glass of the additional milk. Suddenly, waste like that took on new meaning.

"Trace, nothing I saw makes any difference to me." She wanted that to be true. She wanted to be the person for whom that was true. She'd try.

"Does to me."

"I've offered before to do a financial analysis. See if I could find some savings for you."

"You mean because I don't know how to run a ranch?"

"I didn't say that. But maybe you could lease out some of the land, grow some extra hay to sell." She was sure there were opportunities in an enterprise like Trace's.

"As I've said before, you ranch because you love it. Not to make big money. Sorry if you don't understand that."

"I'm an accountant. I'm sure I can help."

"I don't need yours or anyone else's help to tell me what I already know. Ranching doesn't always pay. If you need certainty in this here world, ranching ain't for you. Maybe it's better you find that out now, rather than later." He rose and the frown on his face deepened. "And maybe it's time you head home."

Chapter 22

Somehow Trace had ended up riding Archer along the back of the Johnson place, even though he should have been fixing the baler that had thrown a bolt. He'd taken the long way around for sure.

Maybe he'd been too quick to dismiss her. Maybe he really hadn't seen the shocked look, the wide eyes, the upside-down smile that let him know exactly how she felt about his finances.

The jeweler had told him he could exchange the ring if she didn't like it. But what if she didn't like him? He'd been a fool to plunk down money before he was sure of her heart. But after the encounter with the bear, after making love to her…

He wasn't destitute, just strapped. Land poor, his father used to say.

Maybe if he stopped in, saw her alone, talked it out… Hope was a tempting bauble.

He reined Archer toward the Johnsons' pasture that sat between his land and the cabin. As he closed in, something caught his eye. Something in the shadow of the old barn that had once been the birthing stalls for the ranch. Something long and large, like a truck.

Why would a large truck be parked behind the

Johnsons' barn? As if it was hiding. As if someone didn't want it seen from the road.

A moving van? Surely Haylee would have mentioned if the place had been sold. And no one in Wyoming could close that fast.

Haylee might not be a trucker, but her ex-husband was. And from what she'd said, a successful one.

Against his better judgment, Trace urged Archer into a trot.

He circled into the corral via the back gate that had been there since his father had refenced the pasture for his grandparents' horses. He slid off Archer and let the reins drop. The corral was overgrown from years of disuse. He prayed there weren't any toxic weeds among the grasses.

"Don't get lost in here," he told Archer and patted the horse's rump.

He shaded his eyes and stared at the big semi. It was definitely a freight truck and, according to the printing on the cab, belonged to Hauser Trucking, the last name of Haylee's ex-husband.

A chill went through Trace. Maybe he'd been a bigger fool than he knew. Haylee was already exploring another option. One that didn't include him. A bad feeling lodged itself in the pit of his stomach.

She'd said more than once that everyone thought her ex-husband had been perfect for her. And she'd never told him what went wrong in her marriage. Or who left whom. No doubt, owning his own trucking business, her ex-husband could offer her more financial security than Trace could.

He moved toward the house, filled with a mixture of hurt and anger at his stupidity. When would he ever learn? He certainly didn't understand the first thing about women, any women. From his mother to his daughter to Haylee, he read them wrong. Thought they liked him better than they did.

He climbed the stairs slowly, hoping he didn't make noise.

He wasn't sure what he would do. Knock on the door and demand an explanation, or stand outside like a lovesick dumbass?

As he neared the top step, he heard voices. Haylee and a man's. He wasn't above listening to a private conversation, not when the stakes for him were so high.

"I'm giving it up," a masculine voice said. "This is my last run. I gave them the business. And this run I'm just hauling tomatoes. That's all that's in the truck."

The guy sounded relieved and energized. Like he'd just won the lottery and all his wishes had been granted.

"I can't tell you, Roy, what a relief it is to hear you say that. You've made me happier than you can imagine."

Trace's stomach turned over.

"I did it for us. For you and me, Haylee. Together we can build a new business in a new place with the money we saved for a house, just like you wanted. With you by my side, I know we can do this. I know it."

Trace didn't need to hear any more. He turned heel and staggered down the steps. Fool? He'd been a goddamn jackass.

Haylee felt as if she was staring down from

above, watching two strangers acting in a movie. Only this movie was about her.

He'd finally done what she'd been asking of him for almost two years. He'd walked away. But she wasn't ready to walk with him. It was, to coin a phrase, too little too late. Whatever they'd once had together had evaporated a long time ago.

She'd spent a sleepless night sorting through her feelings for Trace, and if Roy hadn't stopped in, she'd be over there now, to tell him she wanted to stay with him if he'd have her. Like Jenna had said, it was time for her to do the choosing.

She'd have to give it to Roy straight.

"I'm not going to be part of your life again."

Roy's mouth flatlined and his eyes narrowed. "But I did what you wanted. I did what you said. I've been checking out opportunities in Rapid City, and there's a need for truckers, and the cost of living is low. You asked me to choose, and I've chosen. I've chosen you." Roy's hands morphed into clenched fists.

"That was before the divorce. I've moved on. I…we…things aren't the same."

His eyes narrowed. "There's someone else."

No sense denying it. Roy could always see right through her. "Yes. There's someone else."

"Didn't even wait for the bed to get cold."

"It's been a year since we separated, four months since the divorce." And she'd thought it was too soon too. But it didn't change what she felt for Trace.

"But I gave it up for you." He punched the air with one finger pointed at her.

"You gave it up for your freedom."

He shook his head. "I gave it up for *our* freedom.

I gave it up so you and I could be together. I did what you wanted. Do you know how much money I am walking away from for you? Because of what *you* wanted."

She wasn't going to let him guilt her into a relationship. "The business was successful before everything happened. You'll be successful again."

"But alone. That's what you're saying. I'm going to be alone. You are ducking and running. Wonder what the size is of *his* bank account?"

Not very big. "I will always care about you."

"Just not enough." His expression had transformed into an ugly sneer, and Haylee felt like a raw, cold wind had just hit her bones.

"I think you should leave now. There really is nothing more to say."

Roy snatched his hat off the counter. "You'll see," he said as he headed for the door. "You'll want to be with me when you see."

The slam of the door rattled the dishes on the counter.

Haylee sat on the couch for several long minutes after Roy left, feeling like she'd just been through a minor earthquake. This time he'd knocked on the door as if he was paying a social call and had expected her to go back with him as if it had been only the criminal activity that had driven her away and not his character for engaging in it.

She'd been happy he had done the right thing, but she couldn't go back with him. Truth was, she didn't love him anymore, and she wasn't sure she ever had.

One thing was certain, the doors would always be locked now.

Her cell phone chimed. She checked the ID and immediately answered it.

"Aunt Paula?" Haylee was always happy to hear from her aunt, but right at that moment she could have used a good cup of strong coffee. Maybe laced with whiskey.

"We've sold the place, Haylee." The excitement in her aunt's voice was palpable.

"To who?"

"I don't rightly know because they asked to keep it anonymous until we closed, but the agent said they checked out financially, and she doesn't see any problems. But they want to close in thirty days, and that means we have to pack up right away. Can you start packing us up, Haylee? We won't be able to get up there before another couple of weeks at least."

Haylee was still trying to absorb the news. "Of course, but this is so sudden."

"Sudden? I've been waiting months for this call, honey. We couldn't be happier, but you sound disappointed. Is something wrong, sweetie?"

"No, not at all, Aunt Paula. I'm happy for you."

"I'd think you'd be ready to get back to civilization. How's the business going? Will you have enough to get your own place now?"

Haylee's mind whirled faster than a windmill during a hurricane. "Everything is good. Don't worry about me. I'll pack up as much as I can for you."

Haylee heard some sound on the phone.

"That's the agent calling again," Aunt Paula said, sounding breathless. "It's been crazy around here. I'll call you in a few days and see how you're getting on." With that the phone went dead.

Haylee sat back on the couch. What was she going to do? She needed to talk to Trace and determine if he wanted her in his life. Because one way or another, she was going to need to find a job. Denver, if it didn't work out, Cheyenne if it did. And thirty days didn't give her much time to find one. Because in thirty days she could be homeless.

She went over to her computer sitting on the dining table, her work notes scattered about from when Roy had interrupted.

Could she make something of the photography business? She'd already sold quite a few photos of Trace after he'd signed the release. One by the barn, one at the corral against the backdrop of the ranch. And yet last night, he'd seemed ready to abandon their relationship. She hadn't expected his visceral reaction to her seeing his finances. Or his lack of interest in her helping him.

If he was serious about her, he'd have had to tell her sometime. Because she'd vowed never to go into a relationship again without understanding the other person's source of income.

She scrolled through her emails.

When she spotted one from the company she'd interviewed with in Denver, she rested the cursor there. Could it be job? Maybe it was a rejection. Right then she couldn't say which she hoped it would be. Her fingers tingled as she clicked on Open and skimmed the text.

It was a job offer. Two hours away.

* * *

Trace noted Haylee's car parked by his barn. Walking toward the house, he felt like a new recruit getting ready for a parachute jump. After what he'd overheard, he had to end it with Haylee. How had he gone from ready to ask her to marry him to removing her from his life?

But he couldn't yet remove her from Delanie's life. With Delanie's upcoming visit to her mother, he couldn't expose his daughter to more turmoil. He'd have to keep Haylee on as Delanie's caregiver and look at her every day knowing she thought he was too poor, knowing she was planning to be with her ex-husband.

He opened the screen door and stepped inside to the tantalizing smells of meat, onions, and spices. She was standing over the stove, frying chops. Her blond hair curled around her head, covering the curve of her neck, and for a second he imagined things hadn't gone to hell in a handbasket. He imagined what it would have been like to walk to his bedroom, get the small black box he'd shoved into his sock drawer a week ago waiting until he got enough courage to bend his knee, and propose.

But that was fantasy, and this was reality.

She turned. A small smile creased her face. She looked happy. Like she'd just gotten something she'd wanted.

He brushed by her without a word. If her smile drooped and her chin dropped, well what did she expect and what did he care? The ache that filled his gut and arrowed toward his heart was more painful than he anticipated. But he would get past it.

Delanie ran to greet him as he stepped into the

living room. She hugged his knees, her innocent face upturned. "I rode the bike today. By myself."

He swallowed and forced excitement into his tone. "You going to show me tonight, right?"

She nodded. "I'm not tired tonight."

That smiling face was all that mattered. And the fact she'd hugged him. Ever since she'd known they were going to visit her mother, Delanie had been a lot more comfortable with him.

Trace kissed his daughter on the cheek. "Let me take a shower before dinner, sweet pea. Moving hay is dusty business." And getting your heart slammed down on the pavement and then stomped on took its toll.

Delanie released him, and he ambled down the hallway, wondering how hot a shower had to be to take away the pain.

Didn't take him long to wash up and put on his work-out pants and T-shirt. Facing Haylee in his kitchen was not something he wanted to do, but for Delanie's sake, he'd play the part. The part of a man who hadn't just learned that the woman he loved was planning to leave him flat.

When he entered the kitchen, dinner was on the table, and Haylee and Delanie were waiting. He sat down and, without a word to either of them, picked up his fork and stabbed a pork chop. His stomach growled. Not even heartache could quell appetite worked up from a hard day's labor. As usual, the meal was savory, the meat tender, the vegetables seasoned, but he'd take burnt, tasteless food if it meant she could have found it in her heart to love him.

Delanie broke the silence first, asking if she could wear her flower-girl dress to see her mom.

"No reason you can't. It's been washed. I just have to press it."

"I can do that," Haylee offered.

"No need." He could barely get the words out.

The dinner continued in silence until Delanie asked to be excused. Trace would have liked her to stay just as a buffer, but that wasn't a reason he could say out loud. "Want to show me how you ride?"

"You'll be impressed."

He had to smile at her use of a big word. "I already am, sweet pea. Be out in a minute."

Delanie bounded out of the back door, Moose happily on her heels.

Haylee rose, plate in hand.

"Leave it. I'll clean up."

She stared at him. "I don't mind doing it."

"I do mind you doing it."

Haylee sat down again, surprising him. He'd expected her to high-tail it out of there.

"I have something to tell you." She bit her lip and rubbed her hands down her skirt.

"Doesn't sound as if it is anything good."

Trace clasped the edges of his chair. He was a hundred percent certain she was leaving, leaving for her ex-husband.

"My aunt has sold the place. She has thirty days to closing."

She was leaving. Trace sat back in his chair as the floor seemed to shift under his feet. He'd prepared himself…but not enough.

"Good to know a firm date." One day at a time. Thirty of them to be exact.

She took a deep breath. "And I've gotten a job

offer from Denver. They want me to start the beginning of next week."

Five days? And right after Delanie would visit her mother. He absorbed that news like a rock had just been slammed into his stomach. So she'd been looking for a job even before she'd seen his tax information. She'd never planned on staying. She'd never been serious about him. She was going back to Denver. To her ex-husband.

He'd been a fool. Wasn't the first time. Wouldn't be the last. Not with his luck.

Truth was, he didn't understand people, and certainly not her.

"Maybe we should call it quits right now." He'd cope. He had before.

"I didn't say I was going to take it."

"You didn't have to." He rose. If he stayed any longer, he'd say things he'd regret.

"What about us?"

He ambled toward the screen door and grabbed his hat from hook. "There is no us, Haylee. Never has been. We were just passing through each other's lives. It was okay while it lasted. It's over. No sense sentimentalizing something that wasn't."

It wouldn't matter much to Delanie whether it was now or five days later. Either way her world would be changed with little notice. He nodded toward Haylee's purse on the counter as he shoved his hat on his head. "I think it would be best if we ended it right now rather than wait five days. Delanie has enough going on in her young life. It will be easier if we make the break clean. Appreciate it if you say your goodbyes to her."

She looked like someone had just slapped her. "We don't need to end things between us. I've been thinking about it, and Denver isn't that far. We could still see each other on weekends. We can still be part of each other's lives. We can figure this out."

Appeared she was too much of a coward to just end it face to face. He wasn't.

"I don't have to figure anything out, Haylee. I know what will happen. First few weekends you'll be here because you feel you have to be. Then things will come up. There isn't enough between us to hold you and me. Best to move on, move out. And do what is best for Delanie."

She looked like a rabbit caught in a gun's sight. What had she expected? She'd made her choice.

"I can't just leave Delanie."

But you can leave me. "Quick break is easiest."

"For who?"

She jutted out her chin. "I'd like to see her over the weekends at least."

"If you can keep that promise, make it. Because if you make that promise and don't keep it, I won't take it lightly."

"I don't know how we got to this point, Trace. I just saw some numbers on a paper."

"Don't lie to me or yourself, Haylee, about what those numbers meant to you. Your face was as clear as just-washed glass. I've got to check on something in the barn. Say your goodbyes to Delanie. And then tell your husband hello."

"My husband?"

Trace let the screen door slam behind him, called to Delanie to let her know he'd be back in a minute, and headed up the path. No way could he witness what was sure to break his little girl's heart. As for his heart, well, what did it matter?

"Where are you going again?" Delanie asked. The child's lip was trembling, for God's sake.

Why had Trace made her do it now? Why hadn't he talked it out with her like any other person would have done? Why had he assumed she was taking the job?

Truth was she had almost convinced herself to take it. But the slightest hint of encouragement from Trace would have caused her to rethink it, income statement and all. His financial situation might have given her pause, but it hadn't caused her to run for the hills. Jenna would have been proud of her.

She was sure she'd find some efficiencies if Trace would let her analyze his expenses. And there was the photography. She was a worker. If she looked hard enough surely she'd find something that paid. But Trace didn't seem interested in exploring options that included her.

And what had he meant with his comment about saying hello to Roy?

She was so confused, but right now, she had to get Delanie through this since Trace had taken off like none of this mattered. She looked at the little girl who stood before her with watery eyes and took a deep breath.

"Denver, honey. It's about two hours from here."

"Daddy said Mommy is about two hours from here. Is that the same place?"

She would not have chosen to take her leave right before Delanie's first visit to her mother. She wouldn't have chosen to leave at all.

"No, Delanie. It's in a different place, a different direction."

"Do you have to go away to learn a lesson?"

Bending down, Haylee felt like she was going to lose her balance. "No, honey. Aunt Paula's place has sold. There will be new people moving in. And I have a job in Denver." Once she accepted. "Remember we discussed this when I first came that I'd have to leave sometime?"

"But I'm not in school yet."

"I thought I'd be able to stay at least until then, but it seems I have to leave earlier."

She crouched so she was even with Delanie on the swing. "I will be back to visit though. I promise that." Haylee didn't want the child to think it would be the same as with her mother.

"I don't want you to go."

Tears burned the back of her eyes. "I am always just a phone call away. When you want to talk to me, ask your daddy."

Delanie kicked the dust, causing a huge cloud. "Phone calls aren't the same. We were going to make cookies tomorrow."

She looked toward the barn. Trace stood at the entrance, in the shadows, watching her.

"The next time I see you, we can make cookies. I'll check with your dad, and we'll work it out."

Delanie slid off the swing and threw her thin arms around Haylee.

"Don't go, Haylee."

Chapter 23

Sitting at the dining table, Haylee wrapped each glass in newspaper and, one by one, rested them in the cardboard packing box. Light streamed in the wide back window, and a warm breeze fluttered the curtains. Only five more stuffed cabinets to go. She glanced at her watch.

Delanie and Trace would likely be at the prison by now. And she should be there. Or at least at Trace's, cooking a good meal for when they got home. Instead, she'd been banished like a bad child for having a moment of doubt.

Instead of hearing her out, he'd thrown her out. Maybe she had to accept the fact he didn't care, not enough.

The box filled, she grabbed the packing tape and sealed the top. Grabbing another carton, she assembled it, taped its bottom, and began wrapping the next shelf of patterned cups.

When Trace had ordered her away, it was as if her arms had been severed. She hadn't been able to do anything. For the next two days, she'd stayed in bed, ate nothing but broth, and wallowed in self-pity. But by the third day, anger had taken over. Anger at herself for tucking and running, anger at Trace for not loving her enough to believe in her.

Tears welled up behind her eyes, and she knew what was coming. She'd been crying almost every waking hour because of that man. She was in love with him. She'd fallen hard and fast, but like slipping down a well, the landing had been painful.

The email with the job offer remained unanswered. She didn't want to go to Denver. She didn't want to work for some corporation where she'd be a nameless cog, grinding out audit after audit looking for mistakes and overcharges.

She wanted to stay with Trace. But there was no way to stay with Trace when he didn't want her anymore. He'd been so hot for her one minute and cold the next. It may have started with her poking into his affairs, but it had escalated into much more when she'd told him that the place was sold and she'd gotten the job offer.

He hadn't given her the courtesy of a discussion, just assumed the answer. His pride seemed to matter more than she did.

Question was, should she accept Trace's verdict or fight for him, for them?

* * *

It had been an emotional day, ending an emotional week, Trace thought as he stood over the grill, turning the rib-eye steaks he'd gotten on the way home from Lusk. And he wasn't an emotional guy. This was why he'd been better off alone. He wasn't cut out for this stuff, didn't know how to handle it, didn't want to handle it.

For the first time in a long time, he'd felt the urge to take a drink. To let the yeasty taste of beer fill his mouth or dry whiskey burn a trail down the back of his throat. To bury the feelings bombarding him every time he thought of Haylee.

He glanced at Delanie, wearing her fancy dress and playing with her doll. Moose was apparently playing the part of the doll's brother, but mostly the dog lay on the ground by the swing set, watching Delanie mother her baby.

He knew he needed to be strong for his daughter, and that had kept him from stopping the car at the highway liquor store and plunking down a few dollars to blunt the pain. Rather than focusing on his own issues, he had to help Delanie deal with whatever was going on inside her. But he'd never felt more ill equipped. No doubt Haylee, with her nurturing ways, would have known what to say, what to do.

The visit had been held outside in the prison yard, which had been turned into a kids' play area. Basketballs were provided to use with the hoops that lined the yard. Plastic picnic tables had been set up with crafts or books or toys. Visitors had been given colored T-shirts to wear over their clothes, he guessed so the guards could easily identify who was who.

Nothing held a candle to the sight of Delanie running into her mother's arms as she spotted Doreen in the crowd of about two dozen anxious women. Trace had hung back, leaning against the fence, not wanting to crowd the scene. Several minutes had elapsed before Doreen had noticed him, and then she had simply nodded and mouthed the words *thank you*.

Doreen, dressed in a white T-shirt and jeans, her

brown hair pulled back in a ponytail, looked like any ordinary woman, except for the backdrop of barbed wire and people in uniform. She looked healthier than the last time he'd seen her. A few needed pounds heavier, color in her cheeks. His lawyer had said she'd gotten clean. He was relieved to see the positive effects.

He'd done everything the pamphlet from the prison had suggested to prepare Delanie for the visit. He talked to her about the people in uniform, about the other children who would be there to see their mothers. Once they arrived, beyond exchanging pleasantries with Doreen about the drive and the weather, he'd stayed out of the way of mother and daughter and merely observed from the sidelines as Delanie and her mom glued and pasted some sort of furry yarn on a sheet of paper.

From what he could tell, all was going well, until the end.

He had to be the one to tell his child the visit was over. Visitors had to leave first, before the prisoners. Trace had been sure to tell Delanie that they would come again in a month so Delanie wouldn't create a scene. But Doreen had broken down, try as she had to fight it, and that had started Delanie crying. Doreen had finally composed herself, calmed Delanie, and talked about the next time.

As much as he had fought the visits, he understood now how necessary they were for both child and mother.

"Delanie, dinner is ready. Head on in and wash up," Trace called, sliding the steaks onto the platter. It wasn't a gourmet dinner like Haylee would have made, but steaks were the easiest and quickest things he knew how to make, and tonight he just wanted to eat and then cuddle up with Delanie as he read her a story.

He sidled into the kitchen and set the platter on the table.

His cell phone rang. He knew that ringtone.

"Hello, Mandy."

She asked him about the visit, and keeping an eye on the hallway, Trace answered. "It went as well as it could."

He told her about the prison yard, how Doreen looked, and Delanie's enthusiastic response to seeing her mother. And then she asked the question he'd been dreading.

"Did she say yes?"

"I didn't ask her."

"Well, when are you going to?" Mandy responded.

Never. "It's not the right time."

"You bought the ring, didn't you?"

"Yup."

"I don't know Haylee well, I admit. But when she looked at you in the hospital room as you held Sophie, well, I knew that something very special was going on. But you have to have the courage to ask."

"Yup." But if you already knew the answer, asking wasn't courageous—it was foolish.

"The worst is a no, the best a yes, but there is a lot in between. Your brother risked everything to ask me, and when no one, least of all me, would have given him favorable odds. Don't assume you know her answer just because you're afraid of rejection. Tell her what is in your heart. If you don't, you'll always regret it."

He had nothing to say to that.

"Trace, are you listening?"

"Yup."

Mandy's sigh whooshed in his ear. "You Martin boys are a tough crowd. Let me know when you do. We've got a surprise for both of you."

He heard Delanie's footsteps in the hall. "Got to go. Talk to you soon. Love to Sophie." He hit the End button.

At the kitchen table, he cut up Delanie's meat and lathered butter on her potato, before settling into his chair. He glanced over at Haylee's chair, now empty. Just like he felt.

Trace had pushed Haylee out of his life, but he couldn't push her out of his heart, despite trying. He thought he would feel relieved, vindicated, but he felt lower than a prairie dog down a tunnel with no way out.

"I wish Haylee was here," Delanie said.

His child picked up her milk glass as if she hadn't just thrown a verbal grenade at him.

"Haylee has to do other work now."

"She wanted to stay, but you made her go." Delanie's tone was accusing.

"Did she say that to you?"

Delanie pushed out her chin and pouted her lips. "She wanted to bake cookies with me. She said you'd have to let her."

"We'll see. Maybe at her house." Because having her back in his kitchen and not in his life was not an option. "So what did you like most about your visit with your mom?" he asked, hoping to change the topic from the one that was shredding his heart. The pamphlet had suggested asking questions about the visit to understand how a child had experienced it.

"Seeing her." Delanie stabbed a piece of her cut-up steak.

"How'd she look to you?"

"She said she's not sick anymore and that place helped her get better." Delanie sounded hopeful.

"What didn't you like about the visit?"

"Waiting to see her."

There had been a ton of paperwork to fill out despite everything that had been filed beforehand. "I think that's just because it was our first time there. It will be better next time."

"I wish she could come home with us." Delanie shoveled a forkful of potato into her mouth.

Now they were getting in water a little too high for Trace.

"She's got to stay there awhile, Delanie. But we can visit."

"If Mommy can't stay here, can Haylee?"

Now the water was over his head and breathing felt way too difficult. "Staying here with just me isn't so bad, is it?"

She shook her head. "I never want to leave."

His heart must have expanded, because his chest got tight. "You never have to, baby girl."

It should be enough.

The sound of pottery shattering caused Trace to rush into the living room, where Delanie had been playing while he cleaned up. The sight that greeted him was a pile of pottery shards that had once been the pretty china platter that had sat on the shelf above the television. His mother's favorite piece, the one thing that served as a reminder of happier times, was gone. Well, maybe that was fitting.

The front door was open, and the ball that had undoubtedly been instrumental in the catastrophe had rolled toward the couch. Moose sat at the door as if he was an innocent party.

Trace called Delanie's name.

No answer.

Clean up the mess or look for Delanie?

Didn't take a heartbeat for him to start out the front door, Moose following.

Trace looked everywhere. The barn, the hay pile, the near pastures. He checked the pickup, the shed that housed the tractors and equipment, and the birthing barn. Moose sniffed along, but the dog wasn't a hunting breed and likely was sniffing for his own reasons.

He'd called his child for a good twenty minutes with no response. He circled back to the house to check inside. A thorough search turned up nothing and no one.

Light was fading, and Trace felt a heavy pressure in his chest as he looked out on the land that was turning a deeper shade of gray as the day slipped into shadows.

He looked at his phone. If Delanie had gone to Haylee's, surely Haylee would have called him. But maybe his daughter was somewhere else on the Johnson place.

He hesitated. He hadn't heard Haylee's voice in days. Hadn't seen her. Didn't know if she was even around. She could be in Denver, hanging with her ex.

Hell.

He dialed her cell number. His heart beat faster with each ring.

"Hello. Trace?"

Her melodic voice caused a twinge of regret in his already jumbled insides.

"Delanie is missing."

"Missing? How? Wasn't today the visit with her mother?"

"Yeah, but I don't think it has to do with that. She was playing, something broke, and she ran out of the house. I've looked everywhere and can't find her." He wondered if he sounded as scared as he felt. "Light is failing and…I've got to find her. Did she walk down by you?"

"I haven't seen her, but I've been packing up my aunt's kitchen all day. I'll check if she's around here and let you know."

"Thanks."

"Trace, I…we have to find her."

"Yeah." He hung up the phone. He couldn't think about Haylee and the way he felt, how much he missed her, how angry he was at himself for not fighting for her.

Instead, he retraced his steps and checked the hayloft, the bushes behind the birthing pastures, and another scan of the tack room. Nothing. Wasn't the definition of insanity doing the same thing over and over and expecting a different outcome?

He checked his phone. Nothing from Haylee either. If she had found Delanie, she would have called. Which meant that had been a dead end too.

He stepped inside the kitchen, calling Delanie's

name as he grabbed a flashlight. The gray light of dusk was deepening, and he only had about another fifteen minutes before dark won out. When he stepped back outside, the headlights of Haylee's car cast bright circles on the weathered barn.

He tightened his grip around the flashlight and steeled himself against the emotion of seeing her again, but if Delanie was with her, that was all that mattered.

As Haylee stepped out of her car, the wind caught her hair, blowing tendrils about her face. She knew she looked a mess from days of feeling sorry for herself. Her sweatpants had a hole in the knee, and her sweatshirt was faded. The only thing decent she had on were the boots Trace had bought her.

She looked around for Trace in the deepening shadows and saw a beam of light moving toward her from the house, a tall shadow behind it. Moose reached her first, his tail wagging in greeting.

She patted the dog and then trained her sights on the man. He didn't have a hat on, and a lock of hair curled over his furrowed brow. He was dressed in a white long-sleeved shirt and pressed black pants, and the sight of him took her breath away.

"Is she with you?" The anxiety in his voice was palpable.

Haylee shook her head. "And there was no sign of her along the road in either direction. I went all the way to the highway. Could she have gone out on the range?"

He stopped a few yards from her, as if afraid to get too close. "It's flat plains until you get out a ways.

On her little legs, she wouldn't have gotten that far. She has to be here, but where? I've checked every shed, the old outhouse, the equipment shed, every stall, the hayloft."

With every place he ticked off, her blood pressure rose like an elevator zooming to the top floor. She stepped closer, near enough she could see the concern in his eyes, close enough to see the worried lines marring his handsome face.

She wanted to run and comfort him, throw her arms around him and hold on tight. She didn't.

"I checked everywhere at my aunt's place." She clasped and unclasped her hands. "We just can't leave her out here." Tears burned the back of her eyes as she thought about how scared Delanie would be out in the dark by herself.

"I'm going to keep looking. At some point I'll find her because I'm not giving up until I do."

"I'll help." Whether he wanted her help or not, she was staying until Delanie was found.

"Thanks, but I can handle this. You've got packing to do."

"I'm not going home, Trace. I'm staying until she's found." She fought the tear that escaped and ran down her cheek. "I love that child." Just as she loved him.

Trace turned his back on her and started walking toward the house, Moose by his side. "This is one humdinger of a hide-and-seek game she is playing."

Haylee raced to catch up to Trace, who wasn't slowing down one bit. Delanie had been good at hide-and-seek. And one time too good. Haylee ran up behind Trace and grabbed the firm bicep of his arm, stopping him in his tracks. "I think I know where she is."

The beam from the flashlight almost blinded her. "Where?"

"Did you check that old root cellar?"

"Haven't been down there in years." The light from the flashlight lowered, and Trace shed her grasp as he headed toward the house at a jog.

She had to run to match his strides and called after him. "Delanie hid there when we were playing one day. Took me forever to find her."

"Hell." Trace sprinted faster toward the backyard, Moose barking and Haylee struggling to keep up. She prayed she was right even as she shuddered at the thought of Delanie down in the dark dank space with who-knew-what vermin.

Trace reached the cellar doors at almost the same time as Moose. He flung open the wooden door as if it was made of cardboard and trained the flashlight on the bottom. Haylee peered around him, her gaze following the light, and gasped. There in the harsh glow of the beam sat Delanie, balled up at the foot of the steps, tears streaming down her dirt-smudged face. Next to her something dark and the size of a half-dollar scurried away from the light, and Haylee stifled the scream climbing up her throat.

"Delanie, it's okay," Trace said in a low, soothing voice as he scrambled down the stairs as if his shoes were on fire. He scooped up Delanie and took the steps back up two at a time.

"Don't send me away, Daddy. Please don't. I'll be good," Delanie said as she buried her face in her father's shoulder. "I don't need to learn my lesson."

"No one is sending you away, Delanie. Least of all me."

Trace reached the top, and Moose looked like he wanted to go down and explore. Trace kicked the door closed. "I'm putting a lock on that tomorrow."

Delanie raised her head and stared at Haylee. "You came." She sniffled. "You didn't leave."

Haylee stepped close. The child was covered in dirt, her pretty pink dress stained with streaks of brown soil. She didn't care if Trace didn't want her there. If he didn't want her in his life, she wanted to be in Delanie's, at least. She leaned over and kissed the child's grimy cheek. "I'm here, honey. Are you okay?" That spider might have bit the child.

Delanie looked up at her father. "I'm sorry. I won't bounce the ball in the house ever again. I hate the ball."

Trace stroked his daughter's hair, as if he needed to reassure himself as much as reassure Delanie. "It's okay, sweet pea. That dish wasn't anything important."

"You said it was Grandma Martin's and the only nice thing you have of hers. You said she loved that plate."

"You are the only thing I want that has anything to do with Grandma, honey. The only thing."

"But they sent Mommy away to learn her lesson because she was bad. I don't want to go away unless I can be with Mommy."

There was a pinch near Haylee's heart at the child's tender pleas. Delanie had so much loss in her life already. And Haylee was adding to it.

Trace cradled his daughter in his arms. "No one is going away for breaking a dish, or anything else for that matter, so no more talk about being sent away. I'd never do that. Never. You are staying here, with me."

Haylee brushed Delanie's tear-stained cheek. "You must have been frightened down there."

Delanie nodded. "I didn't think it would be so dark. And then the door closed, and I couldn't get it open, and I slipped down the steps."

"You are going to need a bath, sweet pea." Trace walked toward the back door. Haylee followed. "Thanks for your help, Haylee, but I've got it from here."

"I want Haylee to give me a bath," Delanie said.

"My pleasure." Haylee slipped past him and took the lead. It would give her a reason to stay, because Haylee was going to have it out with Trace.

Chapter 24

Trace tucked Delanie into bed. Gave her an extra kiss good night and stood at the door a minute watching her drift off to sleep. Haylee was sitting in his kitchen, and he didn't know what to say to her. He knew what he wanted to say…if he had enough courage. Because if she rejected him, he couldn't say he hadn't asked. He couldn't save his pride. He'd have to live with the fact she'd said no. That one more person in his life had left him.

He had a lot in common with his daughter, he realized. And he didn't want Delanie to grow up like he had, wondering if anyone could love her. He wanted to give her security, a stable, loving home. And he wanted that with the woman sitting in the kitchen, if she'd have him. If she didn't want an ex-husband who could give her a lot more. Big ifs.

But he had a lot of regrets in life about things he'd done. He didn't need regrets about things he hadn't done.

Trace took a steadying breath and headed down the hall to his bedroom and flicked on the overhead light. The large king-sized bed with an oak headboard, which he'd splurged on when beef prices had been high, was a pile of crumpled sheets and rumpled blankets. He stepped to the large oak dresser he'd picked up at a secondhand store and pulled open the creaky top drawer. Rummaging his hands among a bunch of socks, he extracted the small square box.

He opened it and stared at the half-carat oval-shaped diamond. It sparkled under the light, small as it was. Maybe she was getting back with her ex. Maybe she wanted to move to Denver. But right now she was sitting in his kitchen, waiting for him. He tucked the box into his breast pocket.

If he never asked, he'd never know.

When Trace entered the kitchen, Haylee's head was on the table, resting on her crossed arms. She lifted her head. Sleepy blue eyes and tangled curls reminded him of just how beautiful she was and how right she looked sitting in his kitchen again.

But he was far from the finish line, and winning the race wasn't a sure thing.

"She asleep?" Haylee asked.

He nodded, his heart racing. "I thought you'd have headed out by now."

She straightened in her seat. "You thought wrong."

"I'm glad you didn't."

Haylee smoothed back her hair. If she was going to make her case, she wished she looked a little more attractive rather than like a woman who'd just climbed out of a sleeping bag.

"I don't know if you saw, but it looked like there was a black widow spider down that cellar." The thought made her shiver. "I checked her over during her bath and didn't see any bites."

"I noticed. I checked her too." He pulled out his chair and sat down. "Thanks for not screaming when you saw it."

Haylee folded her arms under her breasts. "Despite what you may think, I care about Delanie."

"I know you do."

"I didn't want to leave."

"I don't want you to leave."

She swallowed, and the back of her mouth went dry as she lifted her gaze to meet his. Gone was the anger, replaced by something she recognized. Hope. "You don't?"

He shook his head. "I want you to stay. I want you to marry me."

Haylee couldn't believe her ears—and yet he had said the *M* word. Just not those three all-important words. "Why?" Her chest felt tight, and her hands were sweaty. If he wanted to marry her just because it was convenient, just to have a mother for Delanie, she would be devastated.

"Why?" He rubbed a hand over his chin.

The pounding of Haylee's heart resounded in her ears like a bass drum in a marching parade.

"Isn't it obvious? I'm head over butt in love with you. I'm a poor rancher, and I can't offer you anything but honest hard work, a ranch out in the middle of nowhere, and a daughter who adores you. I'm crazy about you…even if you make me crazy."

A tear slipped out of her eye and down her cheek. She brushed it away. "I make you crazy?"

"Yes."

"But you fired me." The beats of her heart weren't so loud now.

"I made you leave before you left me. I'm a poor prospect in more ways than one. I don't have much money. I've a ton of baggage, and I'm not very good at relationships..."

She placed a finger against his lips, stopping him. "You are everything I could want."

"And the job in Denver, your ex-husband?"

"I haven't accepted the job in Denver, and what does my ex-husband have to do with anything?"

He raked a hand through his hair, a shaky hand, and sat back.

"I overheard you the other day when I came by to... Well, I saw his rig behind the barn, got curious, and went up to the front door, intending to knock. Then I overhead you talking about him making you happy. I put two and two together."

She bit her lip and straightened in her chair. "You got the wrong answer. My ex-husband..." She hesitated, wondering if she should tell him. If she should trust him. But he'd come clean with her. If they were going to start a new life together, she needed to be honest with him. "My ex-husband has been running drugs for a drug cartel."

"He's been what?"

Haylee took a deep breath. "He got into it by mistake. It's a long story, but the short version is someone used his truck to transport drugs without his knowledge. Once they used his truck, they blackmailed him into letting them use it again. And then they wouldn't let him stop. That's what broke up our marriage. I found out by chance one day. I tried to convince him to walk away from the business, but he said he couldn't. I gave him an ultimatum. He chose the business. That's when I knew the marriage was over. I divorced him and refused to take any money from him. The other day he came to tell me he was making one last run because he'd agreed to hand over the business to them. I was happy because if he had gotten caught, he would have ended up in jail. He wanted me to start over with him in Rapid City. I told him no. I still care about him, but I don't love him. I'm not sure I ever did."

It was a hard confession to make.

He rose, leaned his hands on the table, and stared at her like he was a prosecuting attorney ready to cross-examine his witness. "Are you sure about us, Haylee? Because for me, there's no walking away if you've gotten it wrong. I can't do that to Delanie. And I don't think I'm strong enough to survive another person in my life cutting out."

Trace fought to breathe as he waited for her answer. When she rose and wrapped her arms around his neck, she pressed her head against his chest, where his heart seemed to beat in double time.

"Say something."

"You'll let me herd cows?"

"You want to herd cows?" His lungs reinflated.

She leaned back and looked up at him. Her cheeks were tear streaked, and her hair was a mess, and she never looked more beautiful.

"And do an analysis of the ranching operation. Which means you have to trust me to show me everything."

"You want me to swallow my pride?" He would even though it left a squalid taste in his mouth.

She cupped his cheek in her hand. "I am proud of you. And if I've learned one thing, it is that a man's bank account is no measure of the man."

She smiled and a calm settled over him like prairie dust after a storm.

"Good thing because mine's going to be pretty pitiful until October when we send the beeves to market."

"No matter. I can find work in Cheyenne or at Delanie's preschool or wherever. As long as we are in this together, we can work it out. Just promise me nothing illegal."

He snorted. "Seems we already know enough criminals between us."

"Too true." She rested her hand on his arm as if she needed something to hold onto. "And would you want more children? A brother or sister for Delanie?"

"That would make me very happy." He squeezed her tight against him. He needed to know one more thing, one more important thing. He'd never asked it of anyone because he'd always feared the answer. Now was no different but he had to ask. "Can you love me, Haylee Dennis?"

"Love you? I love you, am so in love with you, I haven't been able to sleep or eat for days, my life is in a tailspin, and I have never been happier in my whole life than right now."

He kissed her on her nose. "That's all I need to hear." He set her away from him and reached into his pocket. Trace held the small black box out to her. "Haylee Dennis, I love that you can fall in the mud and laugh it off, that despite fear, you climbed on the back of a horse, that you have an amazing talent to capture the very soul of people you photograph, and that you've loved my daughter from the beginning. The thought you could possibly love me has allowed me to imagine the future without a feeling of dread. We may face tough times but if we face them together, we will be twice as strong. Say you'll marry me, Haylee, and fill my heart."

She stared up at him, a smile gracing her beautiful face. "Yes because, Trace Martin, you fill mine."

It felt like his heart had grown three sizes as she took the box from his hand and flicked open the top. The stone caught the light, and a prism of colors sprinkled across the walls.

"It's small," he said, wishing he could have given her one the size of Mandy's.

"It's beautiful. Too beautiful." She extracted the ring from the box and held up her ring finger. "Will you put it on my finger?"

He slid on the ring, relieved that it fit since he'd only had the opal ring he'd tried on his pinky to go by.

She waved it under the light, and he wrapped his arms around her and held her tight against his chest. He had no intention of letting her go anytime soon as she looked up at him with an expression that made his heart pound.

"By the way," she said, "Just so you know, I'm poorer than a proverbial church mouse."

"We'll make a fine pair."

His lips touched hers, and the spark ignited a fire in him as he slipped his tongue inside and devoured her mouth. She wasn't going home tonight.

Chapter 25

Haylee felt the blood drain from her heart as she stared at the car parked in her driveway. She knew the car. She knew the Colorado license plate. She'd spent the night in Trace's arms, but they had both felt she should leave before Delanie woke up. Trace was going to tell Delanie, and Trace and Delanie would swing by and pick her up for a celebration breakfast at the café in town later that morning.

So what was Roy doing at her place at the ungodly hour of 7:00 a.m.?

She worried her lip as she peeked in the window of his BMW. He wasn't in there. Which meant he was inside her aunt's house.

She pressed a hand to her stomach as she climbed the porch steps. She dug in her purse for keys and realized how stupid that was. She'd been so rattled by the news about Delanie being missing, it was likely she'd left a door open. She'd been in and out, trying to think of places to look. Her bad. Clearly she wasn't a very good house sitter.

She fingered her cell phone at the bottom of her purse. She thought about dialing Trace's number and having him on the line while she went in.

Overreacting a little? This was Roy. The man she'd been married to for two years. Still. She grabbed her phone and shoved it into her back pocket so she'd have it nearby. Taking a deep breath, she twisted the knob and pushed open the door a wide crack so she had a good view inside.

She scanned the room. No Roy as far as she could see.

In the distance she spied an empty liquor bottle on the counter. And an empty champagne bottle. And his jacket tossed on the couch.

Maybe he was sleeping it off in the bedroom. She stepped through the doorway. The last thing she remembered was a pair of strong arms gripping her from behind.

"Untie me, Roy. I mean it." Haylee took a calming breath, the kind she'd learned from her yoga-loving sister, but all she felt was the rope pressing against her chest and wrists as her heart drummed in double time, like it was the backbeat to a rap song.

"Not until you hear me out."

"This is absurd." She sat on the chair at her aunt's table, bound by a rope tied around her torso, pinning her arms against her body and cutting into her wrists so that her skin burned from the friction. She didn't want to panic. She didn't want to show fear. But panic and fear were at the tip of her tongue.

"If you could just see what I've got set up in Rapid City, Haylee." He slurred her name. And his eyes looked bleary. But he stood with his arms crossed over his chest in his T-shirt and jeans, logo cap on his head, as if this was all perfectly normal. "I just need you to help me. If you saw it, you'd want to be part of it. With me."

"I don't want to be part of it. I don't want to go to Rapid City. Tying me up isn't going to change that."

Roy shook his head like a wet dog shaking off water. "You'll change your mind when you see it."

"If I agree to come with you to see it, will you untie me?" It was worth a shot.

A slash of a smile formed on his lips. Haylee knew the answer before he said it.

"No. You'll just try to run."

Her arms were growing numb. She could feel the telltale pins and needles kneading her limbs. She wiggled her fingers.

"What's this?" Roy swayed a little as he bent over her right hand. "A ring? An engagement ring?"

His mouth flatlined, and his eyes narrowed. The pulsing in her temple intensified.

He grabbed her wrist. Haylee bent her knuckle, but his strong fingers flattened her hand and pried the ring off. It slid into his grubby grasp. A second later she heard it ping against a baseboard.

He'd thrown away Trace's ring.

This man wasn't Roy. Not the Roy she'd married.

But then the Roy she married wouldn't have been running drugs. Or hiding out in her house waiting to tie her up.

Her backside vibrated. She prayed he wouldn't notice. She'd put it on mute when she was with Trace last night.

"That him?" Roy's hand grabbed her butt, shoved his fingers into her back pocket, and retrieved her cell phone. His beady eyes focused on the screen. "Trace somebody. That him?"

Her mind was racing in a thousand directions and failed to land on a response.

The crack of his hand against her cheek stung, burned. Fear raced through her body like fire scorching dry leaves. Tears welled in her eyes.

Roy had never hit her before. But then he'd never been so drunk he could barely stand before either.

"Didn't mean to do that, but you answer me," he shouted as the phone vibrations stopped.

She nodded, not sure she could speak without betraying her panic. She couldn't let him think she was scared of him.

Roy fingered her phone. "He sent you a thumbs-up. Wants to pick you up in an hour for breakfast." Roy shoved the cell phone into his front pocket. "Not happening. We're going to Rapid City."

"He'll come looking for me." Because she was certain he would, as certain as she was that she loved him. And he loved her.

Roy sauntered over to the counter where the printer was and pulled a piece of paper from its tray. "Then this is what he'll find." Roy snagged a nearby pen. When he finished writing, he held it up. Roy had written, *Goodbye. It's over. I'm going back with Roy.*

She prayed Trace wouldn't believe that note. That he'd come for her, wherever Roy was taking her.

Trace pulled his car next to Haylee's. No more questions. No more doubts. For the first time in his life, he believed he could have what others had. He was marrying the woman he loved. His daughter was excited about it. Life was damn good. He felt as high as a hot-air balloon on double tanks of propane.

"You wait here, sweet pea." He lowered the truck's windows before cutting the engine. "I'm just going to knock on her door. She should be ready." No sense getting Delanie out of the car seat for what would be a thirty-second stop.

The breeze brought some coolness to the morning air. It would be a great day, he thought as he ambled up the wooden steps. Looking at the log cabin, he hated to think of the house in a stranger's hands. But then the Johnsons had been strangers, and it had worked out okay. More than okay.

He knocked and waited for the response. He stood ready to sweep her in his arms and plant one on her.

When silence greeted him, Trace knocked again on the weathered wood door, this time with more force.

Silence.

He glanced back at Haylee's car. Why wouldn't she be ready? He'd given her the time in his text.

She hadn't texted back. Which he'd thought odd at the time, but if she had been busy or in the shower by then…

He tried the doorknob. Locked.

He called her name. No answer.

Concern shot through his body like an exploding dart gun. She could be in there, hurt.

He scrambled down the steps. "I'm going to try the back door," he called to Delanie as he rounded the corner of the house at almost a full run.

His heart hammered in his chest, his breath coming in swift puffs. He took the back stairs two at a time. Tried the handle. The door opened. Relief gushed through him as he stepped inside, calling her name to avoid scaring her.

Still no response.

Closing the door, he glanced around. Several packed and taped boxes were on the dining table. Flat sheets of cardboard ready to be made into boxes leaned against the wall. Cupboard doors were open, and several shelves were empty. A half-packed box sat on the counter, along with a whiskey bottle, a champagne bottle, and one empty glass that glistened in the morning light. He'd never known her to take hard liquor, but then he'd only ever been out with her at the wedding. Strange she started celebrating so early in the morning. Only drunks did that…and Haylee was not a drunk.

He strode through the living room and into her bedroom.

The bed was rumpled.

He checked the closet.

Clothes were hung up neatly on hangers.

The hairs on the back of his neck were at attention, and his pulse square danced at his temple as he pounded down the hall, peeked into the bathroom, and checked the other bedroom. Nothing amiss, except that Haylee had vanished. Without a word.

He needed to do a more thorough check, but Delanie was still in the car.

Trace hated involving Delanie when he wasn't certain what was what, but she'd come willingly, anxious to see the house.

"Haylee isn't here?" Delanie clasped her small hands together as they walked through the front door. She had wanted to dress up for the celebratory breakfast and had put on one of her few cotton dresses. Eating breakfast out was a treat they rarely indulged in.

"I think she must have gone out and lost track of time." He hoped that was the explanation. Not that it made any sense. Haylee was too responsible to do that.

"Her car is out there."

Yeah, he knew. His mind scrambled to find a reason that wouldn't alarm his daughter. Because he was certainly alarmed. "Maybe her friend came by, they went out to celebrate, and she lost track of time." He pulled out his phone.

No messages.

"I've never been in here." Delanie stood unusually still as she scanned the room.

"Don't touch anything. I'm looking for a note." He glanced around, praying he would find something that would give him a clue as to what had happened to her. On the dining table was nothing but boxes. He strode over to check the counter. A piece of paper was under the whiskey bottle. In slanted scrawl were the words *Goodbye. It's over. I'm going back with Roy*.

He read the words again. She'd gone off with her ex-husband? After last night? After telling Trace she loved him? Had things turned around so fast? Could she be cruel enough to give him hope, happiness, and then throw him away without another thought? Doubts flooded through him like a gulley washer sweeping through open fields. He felt light-headed and nausea cramped his stomach.

"Can I keep this?" Delanie's voice pierced his painful thoughts.

"What?" He turned around and peered into her open hand.

The ring sparkled under the sunlight streaming in through the side window. His ring. The ring he'd chosen for her in hopes she'd accept it…and she had.

His throat felt like he'd swallowed sand. "Where did you find that?" he managed to say as he picked up the ring from his child's hand.

"Over there." Delanie pointed to the baseboard on the back wall.

Someone had flung it there. Someone who was angry.

He tucked the ring into his front pocket. He'd put on dress pants and a white shirt so they could go to a nice place and celebrate. And now there was nothing to celebrate. "That's Haylee's, honey. I'll give it back to her when we find her." Or not.

Even if Haylee had decided to go with Roy, throwing away a diamond ring wouldn't be something Haylee would do. She knew…knew what that ring had cost him, in emotion and cash. And she had no reason to be angry with him.

But her ex-husband, if he found it on her, could have had reason to be angry. Could have prevented her from texting him back. He examined the note again. That wasn't the neat rounded letters that Haylee used when making out the grocery list. That wasn't her writing.

He took a deep breath. He could either assume she'd abandoned him and gone willingly with her ex-husband…or that he'd taken her against her will. Neither made sense. But one made slightly more sense than the other.

He pulled out his phone and texted her. It showed delivered. Nothing came back.

He hit the call button, aware Delanie was watching his every move.

He waited, each ring causing the pressure in his chest to escalate another level. It flipped to voice mail. Trace kept his focus on Delanie as he spoke into the phone. "Call me, honey, when you get this. Let me know where you are."

"What happened, Daddy? Has Haylee left us?" Delanie's voice quivered with uncertainty.

"Nothing bad, sweet pea. But I think Haylee might have forgotten about our plans, is all." He prayed his voice was steadier than he felt.

"Or maybe she's playing hide-and-seek."

"Could be." He tried to sound unconcerned. "But I'm going to leave you with Aunt Mandy so I can find her."

"She's not in our cellar, is she?" Delanie visibly shivered.

"No, but you just gave me an idea, sweet pea." Trace hit the screen buttons on his phone and prayed she hadn't stopped sharing her location with him.

* * *

"I have to use the bathroom," Haylee said as Roy drove the car down a flat road with large lots and fifties-era houses set well back from the road, with staggered mailboxes. Her arms kept going numb, the pressure in her chest from the tight ropes made breathing difficult, and her skin was raw where the bindings rubbed against her flesh. And now her bladder felt ready to burst.

She'd looked for a road name among the signs. Took note of the street numbers on the mailboxes. If she could somehow get her phone back, she could call Trace and tell him where she was.

Or phone the police? Was she ready to do that?

She could still feel the sting of Roy's slap. She still feared what he would do next. And she had no idea how this would end. Yeah, she could do that.

"Here it is." Roy turned the car into a wide paved drive flanked by rail fencing and flat lawn before disappearing up ahead into a copse of trees. Wherever this was, it was on the outskirts of Rapid City, not in the middle of it.

As the car moved down the drive and through the trees, a clearing opened up and a ranch house sprawled before them. One of those 1950s models with angles and windows and stone facing. A huge four-bay garage was to the right, and parked in front of the building was a semitruck. She tried to read the name on the cab, because it wasn't Hauser. She was too far away, though, to make it out.

"What do you think?" Roy put the car in park and shut off the motor.

What could she think? "I'm not living here with you, Roy." Better to get that out than let him fantasize about something that wasn't going to happen. He was delusional if he thought she would stay out in no-man's-land with him after what he done.

He frowned. The alcohol seemed to have worn off somewhere along Highway 18 when they were no longer doing twenty miles over the speed limit, and he'd stopped changing lanes every two seconds. She would have thought his erratic driving might have snagged someone's attention, and they'd have called it in, but this was live-and-let-live country.

"You haven't seen the inside yet. We could have a nice little business out here. Just the two of us."

She was too exhausted and emotionally spent to fight with him. He wasn't listening to her anyway. "I need a bathroom."

"Right." He jumped out of the car, and with exaggerated courtesy because there was nothing the least bit mannerly about her situation, he opened her car door. Getting out without using her arms was more of a chore than she would have imagined, but she managed.

He shut the car door and rushed ahead, key in hand. She felt like a penguin as she walked to the front door.

"Did you buy this and the truck?" Where had he gotten the money?

"We're renting the house for now. And I leased the truck. Rapid City is a transport hub, and there will be plenty of business here. I'm not worried." He held the door open for her.

Haylee stepped into a large bright foyer. From that position she could see clear to the back of the house, where sunlight streamed in from floor-to-ceiling windows. Though a bit sterile for her taste, anyone who favored midcentury modern would like the clean lines, high ceilings, off-white walls, and angles of the interior.

"Wait until you see this kitchen. It's all been updated. We can cook up a storm here." He nudged her forward, and Haylee stumbled toward the great room.

She recognized the large taupe sectional from their Denver apartment, the round ottoman that had served as a cocktail table, and the arching metal floor lamp. All looked out of scale in the large, high-ceilinged room. But the sight of the furniture brought a lump to her throat. They had picked out those pieces together, she and Roy, and she remembered the excitement she had felt when those pieces had been delivered to their apartment. How could she reconcile this craziness with her past life with Roy? Nothing made sense.

She turned away from the memories and stared into the beautiful open kitchen. Shiny stainless-steel appliances, beautiful granite countertops, light wood cabinets. All of good quality. It was a chef's kitchen with a five-burner stove and stainless-steel hood with a large rack of familiar pots hanging next to it from the ceiling. It was so stunning she almost forgot the most urgent issue.

"I have to use bathroom." She was exhausted, hungry, and emotionally spent. A bathroom wasn't too much to ask.

"Right this way." Roy acted like he was the real estate broker giving a house tour instead of a kidnapper escorting his prisoner.

He led her down a hallway to a large guest bathroom. Painted in a pastel blue with plush brown towels hanging from the towel bar, it looked neat and clean, and unused. She wondered if Roy had actually lived in the place yet or just moved in their stuff in anticipation of this moment. The latter thought sent a shiver down her spine.

"Aren't you going to take off the rope? I can't exactly use the facilities like this."

Roy shook his head. "Can't chance it."

"Chance what? Where would I go? We are out in the middle of nowhere. You took my phone. I assume there isn't a landline in the house. What is it you think I'm going to do?" She should sound convincing because she really didn't know what she could do. She hadn't had time to think. But the rope was pressing against her chest, cutting into her wrists, and she wanted it off.

Roy stared at her, as if he was thinking.

She seized on the opportunity to plead her case. "Look—stand by the door. Won't be the first time you've seen me use the bathroom. But please take the rope off."

"You do like the place though, right?"

"Yes." She could answer that honestly. He'd actually chosen well. If he had done this a year ago, maybe things would have worked out differently.

But then she wouldn't have met Trace. Wouldn't understand what love really felt like. Wouldn't know that sacrificing for someone else that you loved wasn't sacrificing at all. Wouldn't understand true character. Character that had been tested…and passed. And would have never known the dark depths that lurked inside Roy Hauser.

Roy stepped forward and tugged at the back of the rope that bound her. "Okay, but I'm standing right here, and I'm stronger than you are, Haylee. And I won't hesitate to use my strength. We need to work this out, and I'm going to see that we do."

"Do you have any food in here?" Haylee asked as Roy's fingers dug into her arm as he walked her back to the kitchen, just like a guard would do with an inmate. Her wrists still throbbed from where the rope had bound them. She had to find some way out of the situation but, first, she needed to get some food in her stomach. She'd felt lightheaded when she'd risen from the toilet. A lack of food and water could do that.

"Sure. I've stocked the place. Wanted to have everything ready when I brought you back here."

She hoped the shiver that ran through her didn't show. "Eggs? Bacon? Water?"

He nodded as they stepped into the kitchen area.

"Where do you keep the glasses?" She was thirsty enough to drain the Rapid Creek.

Still holding her arm, Roy opened the near cabinet, grabbed a glass, and handed it to Haylee. She moved to the sink, Roy trailing, and filled the glass with cold water. She didn't say anything until she emptied it.

"Are you going to hold on to me while I make us breakfast?" Now that the rope was off, she wanted him to think everything was okay between them while she considered her possibilities.

Getting the keys to the car would be difficult enough, but then she'd have to get to the car without him noticing.

Running wouldn't be an option. She didn't know where she was or where to go. She had no money on her. Dressed as she was in raggedy sweatpants, her appearance disheveled, and, having not taken a shower before being ambushed, anyone who found her wandering around would think she was homeless and wouldn't believe her. Besides, she doubted she'd get far before Roy would overtake her.

Getting her cell phone back would allow her to call for help. They would have 911 service in a place as large as Rapid City.

Of her three options, the cell phone seemed the most viable. She just had to figure out how.

"If you make that omelet I like, I'll think about releasing you." He flashed a toothy grin.

She'd play along. "If you've got cheddar cheese, onions, and tomatoes, along with the bacon and eggs, I'm there."

His hand slipped from her arm. Free. Not totally, but one step at a time.

In a few minutes, Haylee was sautéing the tomatoes and onions in the cast iron fry pan—part of a set her aunt Paula had given her at her bridal shower. The bacon was already in the microwave. As the scent of fried onions and cooked bacon filled the air, her stomach rumbled.

Like in the old days, Roy had helped by grating the cheddar cheese and putting on the coffee. Anyone looking in the windows would think they were a happy couple. The voyeur wouldn't see the bruises on her arm from the ropes. They wouldn't be close enough to see the fear in her eyes. Or how her hand shook while she used the spatula to move the vegetables around the fry pan.

She glanced over at the man standing with his arms crossed, watching her. He'd slapped her. Tied her up. Kidnapped her. And expected a happily ever after knowing she'd accepted another man's proposal. Something in Roy must have snapped, made him delusional…and dangerous.

All during their four-hour trip, he'd talked about their future together. The benefits of Rapid City, the house, the new truck. He'd never once mentioned Trace, as if getting rid of the ring had gotten rid of the man.

Surely her confession the night before about Roy would be enough to make Trace suspicious. But if so, how would he ever find her? How would he piece together that she was somewhere in Rapid City, and if he did, how would he know where to look? Her only hope was to get her cell phone and call 911 and then call Trace. And hope both the police and Trace believed her.

As she tended to the tomatoes and onions, she focused on creating a plan to give herself some hope as well as distract from the fear climbing up her spine. First, she would have to lull Roy into complacency, and once he was comfortable enough to let his guard down, she had to capitalize on it.

"So you started a new trucking company. What's the name?" she asked as she added pepper and salt to the vegetables in the pan.

His eyebrows rose, and a smile appeared on his formerly frowning face. "Knight Trucking."

"Who is Knight?"

"No one. We thought it sounded reputable and sound."

"We? Who's we?" He hadn't said anything about partners. The only partners he'd once had were silent ones, corrupt ones.

"Did I say we?" His smiled broadened. "It was actually the loan officer at the bank who suggested the name."

Odd that a loan officer would get involved in marketing. And hadn't Roy leased the truck?

"Do you have any customers out here yet?"

"Working on it. Should be coming through in the next few days. That's why I need you with me on this.

Right now, I'm it. Can't do it all, running the business and driving the trucks."

"Trucks? I thought you only had one truck now."

He shifted his weight and leaned his elbows on the counter. "That's all. Just one. Guess I was thinking back to the old business."

Haylee's stomach growled as she transferred the tomatoes and onions to a separate dish and then poured the beaten eggs into the pan. They sizzled as they hit the cast iron. Something was off, but she couldn't think about it now. She had to concentrate on getting free.

She just worked out things with Trace, and now they were blown to bits. What must Trace think of her running out on him?

She dumped the tomatoes and onions on top of the egg, and then sprinkled in the cheese.

First, though, she had to contact 911. And then pray Trace would know she hadn't abandoned him. Hadn't betrayed him. That she loved him.

It took only a few minutes more to cook the omelet to the desired firmness. Roy had poured the coffee, and they sat down to a proper breakfast. Just like ordinary people who were married and going through their daily life on a lazy Sunday.

She dove into the omelet, savoring the egg, vegetable, and cheese mixture, though not sure it would be enough to satisfy the hunger that roared in her stomach.

"You've still got it, Haylee." Roy waved his fork in her direction, his omelet half-eaten.

"Thanks, but what is the plan, Roy?"

His bushy eyebrows rose in unison. "You come live out here with me. We run the business together. We live a nice life."

So simple. So complicated.

"I don't have anything of mine here. And my aunt still needs someone to look after the place." Not to mention he was keeping her against her will.

"Get a neighbor to do it. That rancher down the road."

So he didn't know that Trace and the rancher down the road were one and the same.

"But my things."

"You can buy new things."

"Are we going shopping then, because this is all I have?"

He shook his head. "Order them off the internet. I can run out later and get you a few things to tide you over."

That could be her chance.

"But I'll have to tie you up again."

Hope sank with the mouthful she just ate. "Why? I'm not going anywhere. I've no place to go."

"Can't trust you, Haylee." His eyes had a flinty look to them. "You left me, remember. And you didn't exactly come willingly. And you've got a boyfriend." He shook his head. "That was a bad thing to do when you already have a husband."

"We're divorced."

His body stiffened as his brow furrowed. "Let no man put asunder."

Since when had Roy gotten religious? But she didn't want to agitate him further. And she didn't want to get tied up again.

She eyed the dirty fry pan still on an unlit burner on the stove.

How hard would she have to swing the thing to knock him out? And was she strong enough? Because if she failed, he would tie her back up—maybe for good. Those news stories of men keeping women locked in basements flashed before her eyes.

The thought of hitting Roy with a fry pan horrified her. The thought of failing to knock him senseless terrified her.

Trace lifted the shotgun off the gun rack on the back of the pickup he'd parked to the side of the road by the house that had shown as a stable red dot on the phone map for the last hour. He wasn't exactly sure what he would do if Haylee was in there, how he would know if she was there willingly, but having the firearm made him feel like he could do something. He was trespassing, after all, and fair game for the owner.

He looked at the expanse of driveway that disappeared into trees. Nice of the owner to plant them, because it would give him some cover.

If Haylee was willingly in there, had abandoned Trace, he'd be the biggest fool who ever lived, and he'd know it the moment she opened up the door and saw him standing there with a gun in his hand. Hell.

From the cover of the trees, he scanned the large ranch house, noted the BMW parked in front, like someone had forgotten something and left it there while they ran inside. A semitruck with a steel-gray cab was parked by the garage. He crossed over the driveway to get a better look at the truck, still remaining in the shadows of the trees. The name on the truck wasn't Hauser, but Knight, and a knight in black armor emphasized the name. Did he have the wrong place?

Best to circle to the back of the house, see if he could get a look through a window. See if she was there.

"I have to tie you up, Haylee." Roy actually looked apologetic as they lingered over their coffee.

Think. Think.

"Let me clean up the fry pan and use the bathroom before you go." She hoped her voice sounded steadier than she felt.

Roy fingered his cup, took a sip of coffee. Haylee did the same. If she could get him to turn around, hitting him in the back of the head was easier to imagine. If he saw it coming, he was powerful enough to stop it.

Movement at the back window snagged her gaze.

Her heart hammered against her chest. Trace was there…and then he wasn't. Had she imagined it?

"I'll clean up," he said.

"I'll do it. Just take me a minute." She rose. Her legs felt like they were filled with pudding as she walked to the stove and picked up the heavy pan. Roy hadn't followed. He stood watching her from his seat at the table, sipping his coffee like there was nothing amiss.

She glanced out the window. Where had Trace gone?

Trace slunk along the side of the house, ready to disappear into the trees and go back to his pickup. He was at the right house. He'd seen Haylee. Sitting in the kitchen, sipping coffee with another man, like she hadn't just turned his world upside down and inside out.

Anger boiled up, scorching his insides like heartburn on steroids.

Women. He'd never trust one again. And she

hadn't just screwed with him—she'd let down his little girl, who didn't need to lose anyone else in her young life.

Haylee needed to know what she had done. He wasn't going to slink away. He was going to confront her. Call her out. Not for his sake. For Delanie's.

He stood at the front door, leaned his gun against the side of the house, feeling foolish for having thought he'd need it. Once he rang the bell…

"I can't find the dish detergent," Haylee said, peering into the bottom cabinet, fry pan in hand. She'd hidden the bottle behind the box with the scrub pads for some excuse to get him over to her. She had to do it now. Before Trace left. In case it didn't work.

Her stomach churned, and she could hear her heart beat in her ears as Roy rose from the table and sauntered nearer.

"This is why I said I would do it." He crouched down in front of her, peered into the cabinet, began to move the boxes. "Here it is." His hand was on the bottle, his back to her.

She swung.

The sound of cast iron hitting a skull was one she would never forget. Or the sight of Roy's body falling over.

He blinked up at her. He was stunned but not out. She couldn't hit Roy again. Not with him staring up at her.

Just then the doorbell chimed.

Trace wasn't prepared for Haylee to fling herself into his arms, but he caught her, held her, breathed her in.

"He's in there." Her words came out in short huffy breaths as if she had trouble breathing, much less talking. "I hit him. He's in there. In the kitchen on the floor."

"Roy?"

Her head moved against his chest in a nod. "He kidnapped me." A sob punctuated her words.

All he wanted to do was wrap her in his arms and carry her to the truck. Get her away from there. Keep her safe. "My truck's parked at the road."

"He'll come after me again." Her voice was high pitched, her tone anxious.

Trace set her away and stared at tear-filled blue eyes, quivering lips, a shaking body. What kind of man was Roy to kidnap his ex-wife? And make her so scared?

He grabbed the shotgun. "You have your cell?" He fished his cell out of his pocket, not waiting for the answer. "Call 911." He slapped his phone into her hand. He checked his other pocket for his keys and handed them to her. "Go for help if I don't come out in five minutes."

He kissed her wet cheek. He didn't want to leave her, but she was right—if they didn't report the creep, it could happen again. He crossed into the hallway. The kitchen wasn't hard to find, or the mass of flesh and bones moaning on the floor by the sink. Trace aimed his shotgun at the guy. "Don't move."

As Haylee rode in the passenger seat of Trace's pickup, feeling comforted by the familiar worn seats, scuffed door panels, and the man sitting next to her, she tried to digest what had happened. It had taken ten minutes for the police to arrive in a fury of flashing lights and blasting sirens. By then Haylee had gone back into the house, not willing to leave Trace alone with Roy. Though he'd scolded her for coming back inside the house, between them, they tied Roy up with the rope he'd used on Haylee, which Roy had left in the bathroom.

Haylee had spent another hour explaining to the police what had happened.

Roy had come to by that time and insisted that Trace and Haylee had executed a home invasion. But Haylee's abraded and swollen wrists, along with the fact Roy still had Haylee's cell phone in his pocket, and that Haylee had been the one to call the police had been enough to convince the officers that Haylee and Trace were telling the truth.

She'd also learned that the FBI had Knight Trucking under surveillance, out of Denver. Roy hadn't walked away from the business in Denver. He and his corrupt partners had merely changed the name of the business, and Roy was opening up a new branch in Rapid City—to run drugs along with legitimate business, no doubt.

"So Roy will get charged with kidnapping?" She wouldn't feel safe until he was behind bars. And that was an awful thing to feel for someone she'd once claimed as her husband

"Seems so, if not more." Trace wiped a sleeve across his brow. "You won't have to worry about him again, Haylee. I'll see to that, although you gave him a pretty big knock on the noggin by the looks of that bump that was popping out."

She'd surprised herself that she had been able to

do it. Having to harm someone in real life was a more sobering experience than it seemed in the movies.

"Remind me never to rile you when you have a fry pan in your hand."

For the first time in hours, Haylee smiled. "You would never threaten me like he did. He wanted to tie me up again, and I just couldn't let him do it."

She touched his arm as he drove, to reassure herself she was with him. Safe. "I was so worried that you would believe that stupid note. That you wouldn't see through it."

Trace didn't say anything.

"You didn't believe it, did you?"

He glanced her way, his hat shadowing his eyes. "For a minute. But just a minute."

"Thank God Roy didn't get rid of the cell phone."

"Doubt he ever kidnapped someone before, and it didn't exactly seem like he had a plan."

She leaned her head against his side, soaked in the comfort of his warm body. "Don't ever doubt, Trace Martin, that I love you. And after today, after coming after me, risking your life, no doubt will ever seep into my mind that you love me."

Trace didn't say anything. Just checked the rearview mirror, pulled the truck off the two-lane highway, and put it in park.

And then he undid his seat belt, leaned over, and kissed her like his life depended upon it.

Hers surely had.

Chapter 26

Haylee's heart lurched as she looked out the window of the guest bedroom in Mandy and Ty's home on the grounds of the Prescott ranch. She took in the small gathering of people who had come to see her tie the knot with the man she loved.

Trace was somewhere out there, waiting to make her his bride.

She looked down at her bridal dress, an off-the-rack number that had been on sale in her size, though the hem had to be shortened before it fit. She loved its sweetheart neckline and simple A-line style that allowed her to move. So different from her first wedding dress, an expensive, puffy number that had literally swallowed her up.

"I think they are ready for you," Livvy said, peeking into the bedroom where Haylee had asked to spend a few minutes alone. "Should I tell them to wait a bit?" Livvy bit her lip as if she was worried Haylee was having second thoughts.

"No. I'm ready." She'd been ready since Trace had asked her.

Had that only been a month ago? Fast weddings seemed to be the norm these days out in Wyoming country. Trace and Haylee could have waited, taken their time to make arrangements. Her mother had asked why the rush, as if she feared Haylee's unexpected announcement was the result of being on the rebound from a failed marriage.

The rush, Haylee had explained, was to start their lives together. A future brightened by the prospect of being with each other. Especially after the business with Roy. She was overdue in providing her family with an explanation, which she would do after the wedding, with Trace firmly by her side to lend support.

Livvy walked toward her with outstretched arms. Her sister was wearing a sunny-yellow dress that floated around her sculpted legs. "I knew it from the day I saw you two together at the rodeo. Sparks were sure flying." Livvy wrapped her arms around her sister and gave her a hug. "And thanks for asking me to be your maid of honor. It means a lot."

"I know I've been distant these last few years. I...well, after the wedding, I'll explain." She hadn't yet told her family about what had happened with Roy.

Livvy leaned back, her blue eyes watchful. "No explanations needed, sis. As long as you are in a good place now."

Haylee nodded. "A very good place. But I still want to explain."

As her sister stepped back, Haylee wiped a tear that had slipped from her eye.

"Let's just get you married. Your cowboy has been checking his watch like he's waiting for a bomb to detonate."

Haylee glanced out the window again and spotted

him beneath the arbor. He looked handsome in his rented tux, and very impatient. Her chest tightened. In a few minutes she would become Mrs. Trace Martin. It would be a fresh start. And now that she knew what love felt like, it would be the right start.

"Did Lonnie make it?" Haylee checked her makeup in the mirror, considering that errant tear and was relieved to see no damage had been done.

Livvy cocked her head and smirked. "Yes, ma'am."

"I'm glad. He seems like a nice guy." Haylee turned and tugged up the skirt of her dress.

"I sure hope so because I'm planning on marrying him. Once I get him to give up bull riding, that is."

The mischievous gleam in Livvy's eye reminded Haylee of when they were younger, and Livvy would wear Haylee's best outfit without asking.

"He just doesn't know it yet."

Haylee laughed. "Well, if you stay out in Wyoming, he's a goner."

"If you let me rent Aunt Paula's place, I will. I'll be a convenient babysitter for you."

It turned out that Ty and Mandy had been the anonymous buyers of her aunt's place and had gifted it to Trace and Haylee as a wedding present. Trace had been reluctant to accept it but Ty had successfully argued that this way the ranch would be kept intact.

"I'm sure we can work out something." She'd mentioned it to Trace, and he hadn't said no…but then he hadn't said yes.

"Hayleeeeee." Delanie scooted in. "Daddy's got ants in his pants."

Haylee chuckled as Delanie grabbed her hand. "I'm ready."

On a clear day with nary a cloud in the sky, her father proudly walked her down the dirt path covered in a red carpet outside Ty and Mandy's home. Haylee heard sniffles coming from her mother. Even her father seemed to have a case of watery eyes.

Trace's vows had been short but poignant, talking about finding love where he'd least expected. Haylee's had been longer. She talked about second chances and new beginnings as a family. Jenna, dressed in a baby-blue dress, had joined Livvy as a bridesmaid. Ty had been Trace's best man, the two brothers looking like sophisticated ranchers in their tuxes and cowboy hats, and Tucker, way too handsome to be without a date, had joined the bridal party as an usher.

When the minister had pronounced them husband and wife, Trace had swept her in his arms and kissed her long and hard, branding her as his own. And then picked up Delanie so the three of them could share a hug.

The reception had gotten underway, and after their first dance as husband and wife on the portable dance floor under the huge tent, and Haylee's dance with her father, she asked her family to meet her in the house's library. Accompanied by Trace, Haylee stood in the middle of the room while her father, mother, and Livvy took a seat on the couch and her aunt and uncle, who had driven in from New Mexico for the occasion, took seats in flanking chairs.

"Is something the matter?" Hugh Dennis asked.

"If it's that you're pregnant, Haylee, well, we couldn't be happier," said her mother, wearing a lacy mother-of-the-bride dress in a deep purple.

Haylee felt her cheeks flush as Trace shifted his weight. But he squeezed her hand in support.

"I'm not pregnant." As wonderful as that would be. "I am here to apologize for not telling you about what has been going on in my life. I realize now that I put up walls to shut out the very people that I needed, so fearful that you all would think less of me. So worried about being jobless, homeless…"

"Haylee, you would never be homeless."

Her mother's puzzled expression only made Haylee feel guiltier.

Trace squeezed her hand again.

"You have always made me feel loved, have always supported me. But somewhere along the way, security, financial security, became more important to me than anything else. As a result, I made a lot of decisions, including my career choice and my choice of a husband, with that in mind."

Haylee took a deep breath and then explained what had happened between her and Roy, the business, and his involvement with illegal drug running and Roy's, hopefully, final act of craziness. Haylee tried to ignore her father's frown and the fact that her mother wrung her hands and exclaimed "Oh" more than once. Gratefully, everyone else listened without remark.

"I can't believe Roy would do such things. And kidnap you?" Her mother held her hands to her cheeks. "Is he in jail?"

"He goes to trial in another month and I'll have to testify, but I assume, since he's guilty, he'll be convicted."

"And if he doesn't end up in prison, he'll wish he was in prison if he comes within a hundred yards of her." Trace's expression was grim.

"I am sorry I didn't tell you all of this while I was

going through it. Part of me was embarrassed, and part of me didn't understand yet why I had made the choices I had."

Her father looked over at her mother. "I'm sorry you didn't feel you could tell us, Haylee. We'd have helped you."

"I'm glad you told us now." Her mother stood up and wrapped her arms around Haylee in an encouraging hug. "You know we love you, regardless."

"I do know." Even if she hadn't always known. Even if she'd thought that as the adopted daughter, she had to be perfect. That had been her own myth. Not one she could or should put on her parents.

Her mother kissed Haylee's cheek and looked at Trace. "As long as you have found happiness now."

"I have," Haylee said with the firmness of truth. "But I want you to know everything about my new life. And it isn't all sugar and cream."

"Some of the milk is a little curdled," Trace chimed in.

Haylee told them about her business failure, about the struggles of ranching, about Trace being a recovering alcoholic, about Delanie and Delanie's mother, to which her mother had let out yet another gasp. Haylee couldn't blame her. It was a lot to take in.

"And I've given up accounting, other than the ranch books, but will be pursuing photography. I will never get rich, but my photos do sell, pictures of Trace being among the most popular." She grinned up at her husband and noted the blush in his weathered cheeks. "But as long as we have each other, I know we can handle whatever comes our way."

"Well, that's the smartest thing you've said yet." Her father rose and shook Trace's hand. "My life wasn't exactly angelic before I met Haylee's mom either. Nothing like a good woman to keep us on the straight path."

Haylee leaned over and kissed her father. Her worries all these years about whether she was good enough for her parents, good enough for her own sense of self, melted away under the hugging and kissing that ensued as her family embraced Trace.

"I'm as happy as can be that the house is going back to you both," Aunt Paula declared after she'd given Trace a bear hug. "It's all in the family now."

With that, Delanie raced into the room and stopped as she spotted the hugging crowd. Ty and Mandy followed, with baby Sophie firmly ensconced in her mother's embrace.

"Come here, dear, and give me a hug," Haylee's mother said, holding out her arms in welcome. Delanie happily complied.

Trace lowered his head so his mouth was near Haylee's ear. "Looks like we've got ourselves a family, Haylee."

"And each other. We will never have to go it alone." She wrapped her hands around his neck and kissed him long and hard to assure there were no more empty places in his heart.

Dear Readers,

I hope you enjoyed this book as much as I enjoyed writing Trace and Haylee's story. Please consider leaving a review on the book's page on Amazon's website. This helps increase visibility of the book so other readers can find it. All you need to write is a sentence or two. It means the world to authors to know what readers think of their books.

If you haven't read them yet, there are three other books in the Hearts of Wyoming series so far. **Loving a Cowboy** is Libby and Chance's story and the first book in the series. **The Maverick Meets His Match** is Mandy and Ty's story (Ty is Trace's brother) and the second book in the series. And **The Rancher's Heart** is Cat and Cody's story and the third book in the series. These books were written to stand alone, so there shouldn't be any problem reading them out of order.

Weigh in on whose story you would like to see in subsequent books by sending me an email or commenting on Facebook. Would you like to read Lonnie and Livvy's story? Will Jace from **The Rancher's Heart** find love and success on the rodeo circuit? What about that heartbreaker Tucker Prescott from **The Maverick Meets His Match**?

You can keep abreast of what is happening in the Hearts of Wyoming series by signing up for my newsletter at http://www.annecarrole.com/news.html

In the Hearts of Wyoming series, there are lots of characters who need a second chance at finding their true love!

Hugs,
Anne

About the Author

I have been creating stories since I first wondered where Sally was running to in those early-reader books. One of three sisters, I was raised on a farm where we had horses, dogs, cats, rabbits, hamsters, chickens, and anything else we could convince our parents to shelter. Besides reading and writing romances, you might find me researching Western history, at the rodeo, watching football with my hubby, in the garden, or on the tennis court. Married to my own sweet-talking hero, we are the proud parents of an awesome twentysomething cowgirl and a cat with way too much attitude.

I'm also the founder of the Western romance fan page:
http://www.facebook.com/lovewesternromances.com.

I love hearing from readers. You can friend, follow, or find me on:

Facebook: http://www.facebook.com/annecarrole
Twitter: http://twitter.com/annecarrole
Web: http://www.annecarrole.com (where you can also sign up for my newsletter)

Titles by Anne Carrole

Hearts of Wyoming series
Book 1: Loving a Cowboy
Book 2: The Maverick Meets His Match
Book3: The Rancher's Heart
Book 4: The Loner's Heart

Other titles
Falling for a Cowboy (short contemporary Western)
Saving Cole Turner (short historical Western)

Published by: Galley Press
Cover by: Rae Monet
Edited by: Dori Harrell (Breakout Editing)
Cover Copy created by: http://www.blurbcopy.com
Layout and formatting by www.formatting4U.com

Made in the USA
San Bernardino, CA
08 July 2018